GLOW

SKY CHASERS

THE FIRST HEART-STOPPING ADVENTURE

AMY KATHLEEN RYAN

MACMILLAN

First published in the US 2011 by St. Martin's Press

This edition published in the UK 2011 by Macmillan Children's Books
a division of Macmillan Publishers Limited
20 New Wharf Road, London N1 9RR
Basingstoke and Oxford
Associated companies throughout the world
www.panmacmillan.com

ISBN 978-0-330-53558-8

1 3 5 7 9 8 6 4 2

A CIP catalogue record for this book is available from
the British Library.

Printed and bound by CPI Group (UK) Ltd, Croydon CR0 4YY

GL◯W

PRAISE FOR *GLOW*

'*Glow* has it all – intrigue, action, suspense and romance set against a jaw-dropping futuristic backdrop. Amy Kathleen Ryan has woven a thought-provoking and compelling novel that readers will be hard-pressed to put down. This is a thrilling read' – Courtney Summers, author of *Fall for Anything* and *Cracked Up to Be*

'An out-of-this-world love story that takes you on a fast-paced thrill ride. I loved that the action happened less than fifty pages in and from there on in it was a completely pulse-pounding read' – *Irresistible Reads*

'Waverly's initiative and intellect ensure that even as a prisoner she is far from a damsel in distress . . . Desire to find out which of the proactive characters' bold moves end in disaster will leave readers clamouring for the next instalment' – *Kirkus*

'*Glow* captivated me from start to finish. The action-packed narrative and the characters' struggle to survive without losing their humanity make for a compelling read' – Alexandra Adornetto, *The New York Times* bestselling author of *Halo*

'Utterly engrossing. Dinner went uncooked, children were left to fend for themselves, and the dog howled all night, because I COULD NOT PUT IT DOWN' – Lauren Myracle, *The New York Times* bestselling author of *Ttyl* and *Shine*

'Leaves teens itching to find out what happens next. Readers will appreciate [this] intriguing and thought-provoking read' – *School Library Journal*'s Teen Newsletter

'*Glow* has an ingenious, twisty, heart-stopping plot, and characters that are in turns both sympathetic and sinister all the way to the last page – I don't know who I can trust, and I love it!' – Lisa McMann, *The New York Times* bestselling author of the Wake trilogy

'Waverly is a fantastic heroine, strong and fierce' – *Chicklish*

For A, B and C

For we must consider that we shall be as a city upon a hill. The eyes of all people are upon us. So that if we shall deal falsely with our God in this work we have undertaken, and so cause him to withdraw his present help from us, we shall be made a story and a by-word through the world.

– John Winthrop, founding member of the Massachusetts Bay Colony, in his work *A Model of Christian Charity*, 1630

Through all the Empyréan. Down they fell, Driven headlong from the pitch of Heaven . . .

– John Milton, *Paradise Lost*

PART ONE
TWIN SHIPS

PROPOSAL

The other ship hung in the sky like a pendant, silver in the ether light cast by the nebula. Waverly and Kieran, lying together on their mattress of hay bales, took turns peering at it through a spyglass. They knew it was a companion vessel to theirs, but out here, in the vastness of space, it could have been as tiny as a OneMan or as immense as a star – there were no points of reference.

'Our ships are so ugly,' Waverly said. 'I've seen pictures, but in person . . .'

'I know,' said Kieran, taking the spyglass from her. 'It looks like it has cancer or something.'

The other ship, the *New Horizon*, was exactly the same misshapen design as the *Empyrean*. It was egg shaped, covered with domes that housed the different ship systems, making it look like a Jerusalem artichoke, the kind Mrs Stillwell always dropped off with Kieran's family after the fall harvest. The engines released a bluish glow that illuminated the particles of the nebula, causing the occasional spark to fly when the heat of the engines ignited a pocket of hydrogen. Of course, the ships were accelerating too quickly to be harmed by these small explosions.

'Do you think they're like us?' she asked him.

Kieran tugged at one of her dark brown curls. 'Sure they are. They have the same mission as we do.'

'They must want something from us,' Waverly said, 'or they wouldn't be here.'

'What could they want?' he said to reassure her. 'Everything we have, they have.'

Inwardly, Kieran admitted that it was very strange they could see the ship at all. By all rights, the *New Horizon* should be trillions of miles ahead of them, considering it was launched a full year before the *Empyrean*, forty-three years ago. The ships had never been close enough to get a glimpse of each other. For some reason the *New Horizon* had reduced its speed to allow the *Empyrean* to catch up. In fact, given the distance and the velocity at which both ships travelled, it must have decelerated years ago – a radical deviation from the mission plan.

The other ship was a source of excitement aboard the *Empyrean*. Some people had made large welcome signs with big, exuberant lettering and hung them in the portholes pointed towards the other ship. Others were suspicious and whispered that the crew must have some disease, otherwise why wouldn't the Captain let them come aboard? Captain Jones had made an announcement soon after the ship appeared, telling the crew not to be alarmed, that he and the other Captain were in negotiations and all would be explained. But days had gone by, and nothing happened. Soon the feeling among the crew had changed from excitement to restlessness and finally to fear.

The *New Horizon* was all Kieran's parents talked about. The night before, Kieran had quietly spooned vegetable soup into his mouth, listening to them chatter about it.

'I don't understand why the Captain doesn't make another announcement,' said his mother, Lena, running nervous red fingers through her dark gold hair. 'The Central Council should at least tell us what's happening, shouldn't they?'

'I'm sure they will when they understand the situation,' Kieran's father replied irritably. 'We don't have anything to fear.'

'I never said I was *afraid*, Paul,' Lena said with a look at Kieran that communicated just how afraid she actually was. 'I just think it's strange, is all.'

'Kieran,' his father asked in his firm way, 'has Captain Jones mentioned the ship to you?'

Kieran shook his head, though he had noticed the Captain seemed more preoccupied lately, and his palsy was worse – it made his hands tremble all the time. But he hadn't said a word about the *New Horizon*'s mysterious appearance. 'Of course he wouldn't say anything to *me* about it,' Kieran said.

'Well,' his mother said as she tapped thoughtfully at her teacup, 'nothing explicit, of course, but . . .'

'There was one thing,' Kieran said slowly, enjoying the way his parents were hanging on his every word. 'I went into his office too early yesterday, and he was just shutting off the com station and talking to himself.'

'What was he saying?' Lena asked.

'I only caught one word. He said "liars".'

His parents looked at each other with real concern. The lines in Paul's face deepened, and Lena's teeth worried at her bottom lip, making Kieran sorry he'd said anything.

Now, feeling warm and safe with Waverly, he decided he would ask today before his broadcast. The Captain might not like his questions, but Kieran thought he could get something out of him. Kieran was, after all, Captain Jones's favourite.

That was for later. He'd had a reason for asking Waverly to meet him here, and there was no sense putting it off, no matter how anxious it made him. He forced his breathing to quiet.

'Waverly,' he said, wishing his voice were deeper, 'we've been dating a while now.'

'Ten months,' she said, smiling. 'Longer than that if you count kisses in grade school.'

She cupped his jaw in her hand. He loved her hands and the way they felt warm and soft. He loved her long arms, her strong bones beneath olive skin, and the silken hairs that wandered up her forearms. He lay back on the hay bale and took a deep breath. 'You know how I can't stand you,' he said.

'I can't stand you, either,' she whispered in his ear.

He pulled her closer. 'I was thinking of taking our contest of wills to the next level.'

'Hand-to-hand combat?'

'In a manner of speaking,' he said, his voice vulnerable and small.

She was unreadable in the way she looked at him, waiting, saying nothing.

He drew away from her, leaned on an elbow. 'I want to do this right. I don't want to just jump into bed with you.'

'You want to marry me?'

He held his breath. He hadn't quite asked her, not all the way, but . . .

'I'm not even sixteen,' she said.

'Yes, but you know what the doctors believe.'

That was the wrong thing to say. Her face tightened, almost imperceptibly, but he saw it.

'Who cares about doctors?'

'Don't you want children?' he asked, biting his bottom lip.

Waverly smiled slowly, deliciously. 'I know you do.'

'Of course. It's our duty!' he said earnestly.

'Our duty,' she echoed, not meeting his eyes.

'Well, I think it's time we think about the future.' Her huge eyes snapped onto his. '*Our* future *together*, I mean.'

This wasn't the way he'd meant to ask her.

She looked at him, her expression wooden, until a slow smile crept across her face. 'Wouldn't you rather marry Felicity Wiggam? She's prettier than me.'

'No, she isn't,' Kieran said automatically.

Waverly studied him. 'Why do you look so worried?'

'Because,' he said, breathless.

She drew his face to hers, stroking his cheek with the chubby ends of her fingers, and she whispered, 'Don't worry.'

'So you will?'

'Some day,' she said playfully. 'Probably.'

'When?' he asked, his voice more insistent than he meant.

'Some day,' she said before kissing him gently on the tip of his nose, on his bottom lip, on his ear. 'I thought you didn't like that I'm not religious.'

'That can change,' he teased, though he knew this wouldn't be easy. Waverly never came to the poorly attended ship's services, but she might if the ship had a pastor, he thought. The few spiritual people on board took turns delivering the sermon during their meetings, and some of them could be kind of dull. It was too bad, because otherwise Waverly might see things differently, understand the value of a contemplative life.

'Maybe when you have kids,' he said, 'you'll care more about God.'

'Maybe you're the one who'll change.' One corner of her mouth curled into a smirk. 'I'm planning on making you a heathen like the rest of us.'

He laughed and laid his head on her breastbone to listen to her heartbeat, breathing in time to it. The sound always relaxed him, made him want to sleep.

At sixteen and fifteen, they were the two oldest kids

aboard the *Empyrean*, and their relationship had felt
natural and even seemed expected by the rest of the
crew. But even without the social pressure, Waverly
would have been Kieran's first choice. She was tall and
slender, and her hair draped around her face like a
mahogany frame. She was a watchful person, and
intelligent, a trait that showed in the deliberate way her
dark eyes found their mark and held it steady. She had
a way of seeing into people and understanding their
motives that Kieran found almost unnerving, though it
was a quality he respected. She was definitely the best
girl on board. And if he was chosen to succeed Captain
Jones, as everyone assumed he would be, Waverly
would make the perfect wife.

'Oh no!' She pointed at the clock over the granary
doorway. 'Aren't you late?'

'Damn it!' Kieran said. He wriggled off the hay bale
and slipped into his shoes. 'I've got to go.'

He gave her a quick kiss, and she rolled her eyes.

Kieran ran through the humid air of the orchard,
jogging between rows of cherry and peach trees, and
took a shortcut through the fish hatchery, enjoying the
spray of salt water on his face. His feet pounded the
metal grating, but he skidded to a stop when Mrs
Druthers appeared out of nowhere, carrying a tub of
minnows. 'No running in the hatchery!' she scolded.

But he was already gone, racing now through the
dense caverns of green wheat, where harvested sheaths
hung from hooks on the walls and ceiling, trembling
with the shudder of the engines. It took five minutes to
reach the end of the wheat fields and then a quick jaunt

through the humid mushroom chamber, before a seemingly endless elevator ride up to the Captain's suite, where he was supposed to begin recording his show in four minutes.

The studio was really a small anteroom outside the Captain's office, but it was where the Captain preferred to record their webcasts. The room was lined with large windows that looked onto the nebula, which the *Empyrean* had been traversing for the past year and a half. Below the windows were short couches arranged in a row, where anyone who wanted to could sit and watch Kieran's show for Earth's children or the Captain's longer show that relayed the adult news back to Earth. In front of the couches was a small but very powerful camera and, above them, a row of bright hot lights shone on the desk where Kieran sat to deliver the news.

There were only a few people in the studio today, and Kieran hurried past them and straight to the make-up chair, where Sheryl was waiting with her powder puff.

'You're cutting it close these days,' she remarked, wiping the sweat off his face. 'You're all sweaty.'

'It never picks up on camera.'

'Your panting does.'

She ran a small fan in his face to dry him, which felt wonderful, then patted him with talcum. 'You need to be more mindful.'

'We're only recording it. We can't send it until we're out of the nebula.'

'You know how the Captain likes to keep the archives

up to date,' she said with a smirk. The Captain could be fussy.

Kieran didn't know why they bothered with the webcasts any more – there hadn't been any communication from Earth for years. The *Empyrean* was so far from the home world that any radio signal would take years to reach its destination. And, when it did, it would be so distorted that it would require extensive correction before it could be understood. He might never know if there was anyone back on Earth listening to his newscasts, which made Kieran feel like a figurehead of precisely nothing.

He examined his reflection in the mirror, still undecided about his looks. He might be kind of handsome, he thought, if his nose weren't so crooked and his chin weren't so square. But at least his amber eyes weren't bad, and he had nice rusty-coloured hair that mussed in a thick pile over his forehead. He thought it looked good that way, but Sheryl ran a damp comb through the curls, trying to get them to lie straight.

Captain Jones came to stand behind Sheryl. A tall man with a potbelly and trembling, thick fingers, he walked as if listing from side to side, which on first impression made him seem aimless. In truth, the Captain was the most purposeful man on the ship, quick with his decisions, which were almost always right, and trusted by all the men on the ship, though he was less popular with women, Kieran had noticed.

The Captain frowned disapprovingly at Kieran, who

didn't mind it. He knew the Captain was extremely fond of him.

'Kieran, you spend too much time with Waverly Marshall. I ought to intervene.'

Kieran forced a smile, though he didn't like it when the Captain talked about Waverly this way, as though he owned her and were only loaning her out.

'I trust you've practised?' the Captain asked, eyebrows smashed down in an attempt at sternness. He let out a puff of air that disturbed the grey hairs of his beard, which he smoothed with his thumb and forefinger.

'I read it all over twice last night.'

'Out loud?' he pressed with a glimmer of humour.

'Yes!'

'Good.' The Captain handed a data-dot to Sammy, the technician, who was readying the teleprompter. 'I've made a couple of small changes at the end, Kieran. I'm sorry, but you'll have to wing it. I'd planned to discuss it with you ahead of time, but you were late.'

'What are the changes?'

'Just a small mention of our new neighbours,' said the Captain with an attempt at nonchalance. When he looked out of the porthole, though, he sighed heavily.

'What's going on?' Kieran asked, trying to sound carefree. But when he met Captain Jones's eyes, all pretences sank away. 'Why did they slow down?'

The Captain blinked a few times in that strange way he had, bottom lids flitting upward. 'They have a new captain, or . . . leader, and I don't like the way she talks.'

'How does she talk?' Kieran wanted to know, but the

perpetually frantic Sammy jabbed his finger at Kieran.

'Thirty seconds,' he said.

'Later,' said Captain Jones, guiding Kieran to his seat in front of the camera. 'Have a good show.'

Uneasy, Kieran placed his palms flat on the oak desk in front of him. Then he assumed the bland smile he wore at the beginning of every webcast and watched the opening montage.

It began with the crew of the *Empyrean*, two of them Kieran's parents, young and fresh faced as they helped transplant a tobacco seedling in the occult nursery. Then came a scene of doctors in white surgical caps, leaning over a row of test tubes, carefully dropping samples into them with a long syringe. Finally there was a picture of all 252 kids on board standing in the family gardens, surrounded by apple and pear trees, grapevines growing up the walls, and baskets of fresh carrots and celery and potatoes. The image was meant to communicate plenty and prosperity so that the hungry people back on Earth could believe in the mission.

The light over the camera winked on, and Kieran began.

'Welcome to the *Empyrean*. I'm Kieran Alden,' he said. 'Today we're going to give you a special look at our fertility labs. As you might remember, long-term space travel can make it difficult for women to get pregnant with healthy babies. For six years, women aboard the *Empyrean* tried to get pregnant, and failed. This was a tense time, because if they couldn't have children to replace the original crew, there would be no surviving colonists to terraform New Earth. So creating the next generation was more important than anything else. We've prepared a video for you that looks back at how our team of scientists solved the problem.'

The studio faded to black, and the screen behind Kieran showed the video segment about the fertility labs. Kieran had a few minutes to catch his breath while the video ran.

At the back of the studio there was a sudden flurry of activity. Winona, Captain Jones's beautiful secretary, came running in and whispered something in his ear. The old man darted up and hurried out of the room.

Kieran watched the video, which showed clips of his own birth. Kieran was naturally shy, so it was uncomfortable to have the entire human species know what he looked like, slimy and screaming after emerging from his mother's womb. But he was used to it. Kieran was the first successful deep space birth. When he was born there was a great celebration, not only on the *Empyrean*, but probably back on Earth as well, which was why Kieran had been chosen to host the webvision broadcasts. He never got to decide what was said on his show; he only read the news. His job was very simple: give the people of Earth a reason to believe that Earth-origin life would not go extinct. Give them hope that even if they themselves could not emigrate to the new home world, maybe their grandchildren could.

The video was drawing to a close, and Kieran straightened in his chair.

'Five, four, three . . .' Sammy whispered.

'Unfortunately, things didn't go as well on our sister

ship, the *New Horizon*. Though their scientists worked very hard, the women aboard the *New Horizon* never got pregnant.'

Kieran's heart pounded. He had never heard this before. As far as he and everyone else knew, there were lots of children aboard the *New Horizon*, just as there were on the *Empyrean*. Now he realized that communication between the two ships had been minimal for a long time. Had that been intentional?

Sammy, whose face had turned ashen behind his round spectacles, made an urgent gesture for Kieran to keep reading.

'No one knows why the *New Horizon* kept their fertility problems a secret,' he went on, 'but recently they've slowed their progress in order to rendezvous with the *Empyrean*, so we expect to find out soon.'

The theme music began, an upbeat melody with piano and strings, and Kieran tried to match the cheerful tone with his own voice. 'This has been webvision broadcast number two hundred forty-seven from the *Empyrean*. I'm Kieran Alden, signing off.'

When the music faded away, Kieran heard shouting. The Captain, normally calm and self-possessed, was yelling so loudly that Kieran could hear him through the metal walls of his office.

'I don't care what you *think* you're going to do! You're not boarding this ship until I review the situation with my Central Council!'

He was silent for a moment but soon began shouting again, even louder. 'I'm not refusing a meeting. Come aboard in a OneMan and we'll have one.'

Silence.

'I don't understand why you need to bring an entire crew, ma'am, if all you want is a conversation.'

Silence, an angry one. When the Captain spoke again, it was with intimidating calm: 'I've given you no reason whatever to distrust *me*. I have never *lied* to you, or deviated from the mission plan without an explanation . . . Oh, that's just paranoid trash! There was no sabotage! I keep telling you!'

Kieran heard the Captain pacing. He felt guilty eavesdropping, but he couldn't stop himself. Judging from the hush in the room, neither could anybody else.

'If our two vessels cannot work together . . .'

Suddenly Sammy was in motion again, flicking switches on the studio console until the screen behind Kieran's desk glowed with a video image from the starboard side of the *Empyrean*.

Someone in the room gasped.

The *New Horizon* loomed on the screen, huge and shadowy, close enough for individual portholes to be seen with the naked eye. At first Kieran thought the image must be magnified, but with a tightening in his gut he knew this wasn't the case. In the short time it had taken him to do the show, the *New Horizon* had closed the three hundred kilometres between the two ships and was now cruising alongside the *Empyrean* at extremely close range.

Why?

A subtle movement caught Kieran's eye, a tiny dot moving like an insect away from the *New Horizon*, towards the *Empyrean*. From its bulletlike shape, he guessed it must be a shuttle craft, the kind of vessel designed to carry the colonists and their equipment from the larger ships on short missions to the surface of New Earth. These shuttles were never intended for deep space travel or for docking from one ship to the other, but that was what this one was doing now. Whoever was aboard was clearly planning to land on the *Empyrean*.

'Oh, my God.' Sheryl sat in the make-up chair, hands clamped over her pink mouth.

'How many people do those things carry?' asked Sammy, sounding bewildered and frightened.

The Captain burst out of his office and pointed at Sammy. 'This is an attack,' he announced. 'Sammy, tell the Central Council to meet me in the starboard shuttle bay.'

As an afterthought he added, 'Call a security squad, too. Hell, call *all* of them.'

Kieran's heartbeat tripped crazily. His mother was on a volunteer security squad, working every now and then to settle a dispute between crew members or help out during a community event. The squads never carried weapons.

'What's happening, Captain?' Kieran asked, his voice cracking.

The Captain put a hand on the boy's shoulder. 'Honestly, Kieran,' he confessed, 'I just don't know.'

IN THE GARDEN

'Everything we have, they have,' Waverly repeated under her breath as she marched down the corridor towards the living quarters she shared with her mother. Sometimes it seemed the more serious Kieran got about her, the more patronizing his tone. If he thought that she was going to be a passive little wifey with no thoughts of her own, he was in for a nasty surprise.

Still, of all the boys near her age on the ship, he seemed to be the best, and not just because he was tallish and well made. He was kind, and intelligent, and she liked how energetic he was, how lithe his body was, and how well he controlled it. She liked looking at his face, at his long jawline, his pale tawny eyes, the red hairs that grew on his upper lip. And when she talked to him, he bent down and trained his ear on her as though he couldn't bear to miss a single word. He would make a good husband. She should consider herself lucky.

But there was doubt inside her. Everyone expected them to marry, including the Captain and their parents, and she wondered if that pressure had made Kieran propose. Did they love each other enough to be happy together? If there weren't concerns about fertility, would she marry Kieran, or anyone, right now? She wasn't sure. Few people would have sympathy for her hesitation. There were larger concerns at play than her mere happiness.

She opened the door to her quarters and walked into the living room. Remnants of hemp and cotton covered the dining table, the leavings of a dress Waverly had been trying to sew with little success. She'd had to rip out every seam she'd put in and was considering throwing the whole mess away. Her mother's loom stood in the corner, strung with wool yarns in a blue stripe – probably a blanket for someone. The walls were covered with family photos: of Waverly as a chubby toddler; of her mother and father rosy-cheeked, holding hands in the cold conifer bay; of her grandparents with their melancholy eyes, left behind so long ago on Earth. There were pictures of Earth's oceans, and mountains, and white clouds in a pale sky. 'I wish you could have seen the sky,' her mother often said, which Waverly always thought so strange. She was *in* the sky, wasn't she? She was surrounded by it.

But no, her mother insisted, she had never *seen* it. She wouldn't see the sky until they landed on New Earth in forty-five years.

Waverly heard pounding in the kitchen. 'Mom!' she called.

'In here!' her mother answered.

Regina Marshall was tall and brunette, just like Waverly, though she wasn't as slim. She was kneading dough for rough peasant's bread and kept her back to her daughter as she worked. When it was bread-baking day, Waverly had trouble getting her mother's attention, but she knew today would be different.

'Kieran proposed,' Waverly announced.

Regina whirled around, nuggets of dough flying from her hands, and with two eager steps she had Waverly in her arms. 'I knew it! I'm so happy!'

'You are?' Waverly asked, wriggling in her mother's tight hug. 'Really?'

'Waverly, he's the best boy on this ship. Everyone thinks so.' Regina's eyes shone. 'Did you set a date?'

'No. It seems strange to plan for anything right now.'

'You mean because of the other ship? Life goes on, honey.'

'But don't you think it's strange—'

'Oh, let's not spoil the occasion with that talk,' Regina said lightly, but Waverly saw the anxiety in her eyes. 'The corn harvest is in a few weeks. Why not have the ceremony right after, when people are ready to relax?'

'So soon?'

'There'll be some lovely flowers. The lilies will be blooming.'

Waverly sat down at the table, set for two. 'I think Kieran's going to want a religious service.'

'Yuck.' Regina wrinkled her nose. 'That's one thing about the Aldens no one can understand. Why they weren't chosen for the other ship . . .'

'The other ship?'

'Oh, you know this.' Regina returned to her bread, kneading the dough with floury hands. 'The people who designed the mission chose the crews for each ship on the basis of values, for group cohesion. So we ended up with one secular ship, one religious.'

'Is that why the other ship came back? To convert us or something?'

Regina shaped the loaf and set it on the counter. 'I don't know.'

'Well, I think something strange is going on. They've been here for days, but no one has come aboard.'

'That we know of.'

'And the Captain must be talking to them. Why doesn't he tell us what they want?'

'Don't worry about that,' Regina said sharply. She never liked it when Waverly speculated about the Captain, as though keeping Waverly quiet would keep her safe. From what, Waverly never knew. When Regina turned around, though, she had a twinkle in her eye. 'You've got a wedding to plan.'

Waverly sighed. 'You were twenty-five when you married Dad, right? And you dated him for two years.'

'Yes, sweetie. But things have changed. You're at your most fertile now. We can't take any chances with the next generation.'

Waverly had heard this a million times. 'It's just so soon.'

'It's never too soon when you're talking about the survival of the species. You know that.'

The mission was the most important thing in everyone's life. It had to be. The survival of the human race depended on it. Strong young crews from both ships were needed to settle on their new planet and get it ready to support human life, and that meant that all the girls on the voyage had to have at least four babies each. Everyone expected Waverly to marry and be a mother as soon as possible. End of discussion.

Waverly didn't know how to ask for time to let her heart catch up to her duty.

'I wish your father were here,' Regina said. 'I get so angry when I think about—'

'It was an accident, Mom. It wasn't anyone's fault.'

Regina seemed to retreat inside herself at the memory of her husband's death. For a moment, Waverly thought she noticed a vague fear pass over her mother's features, and a possibility came into her mind that she'd never allowed herself to entertain before.

'Mom. It *was* an accident, right?'

'Of course it was, honey,' she said with a tight smile.

'Is there something you're not telling me?'

Regina took her daughter in her arms. 'I just meant I'm angry it happened at all. You're right, there's no one to blame.'

'OK,' Waverly said slowly. Ever since the other ship had arrived, her mother had been acting strangely conflicted, and her expression was always brooding when she didn't know Waverly was watching. But whenever Waverly asked her about it, she'd smile brightly and say nothing was wrong, she was just getting old.

'I just miss your father so much at times like this,' Regina said wistfully.

'Would he like Kieran?' Waverly had been so young when her father died that he was practically a stranger.

'I think he would. I like Kieran. He'll be good to you.'

'He'll have to be,' Waverly said. 'I know just how to punish him if he isn't.'

'Hey now,' Regina said reprovingly. 'Just because you can make Kieran walk out an air lock for you doesn't mean that you should.'

'Don't worry. He's not as spineless as he seems. He just needs . . .' Waverly trailed off. She wasn't sure what Kieran needed. He might not have the same stubborn core inside of him that she had, but she suspected there was something strong in him, deep down. He was a thoughtful, quiet person, and he considered things deeply before he would speak about them. With time he could learn to be a good leader, she thought. But this was one of the things she wanted to find out *before* they married. 'He'll toughen himself up,' she said, hoping it was true.

'I suspect marriage to you will be more than enough to toughen that poor boy,' Regina said with a playful swat. 'Have you checked the garden today?'

'I'll go now.' She wanted to be alone anyway, and working in the loose soil always calmed her mind.

Down the corridor and two flights of stairs, the family

gardens were in the centre of the ship in a bay so large that it was difficult to see from one end to the other. The lamps over the plants were set to a noontime glow, and the heat felt good on her shoulders as she walked between the rows of squash, tomatoes, lettuce and broccoli. Every family aboard the *Empyrean* had their own plot where they cultivated an array of heirloom vegetables. Because there was no way of knowing which crops would flourish on New Earth, everyone grew different strains. Waverly had chosen a pretty yellow tomato to grow, a plant that produced a delicate, tart fruit. They didn't taste as good as true red tomatoes, but they were so beautiful. She knelt before the largest plant, near the main walkway. One fruit hung fat and golden, almost ready to be picked, and she fingered the smooth skin. She was tempted to take it now for dinner but decided to give it one more day to ripen. Instead, she pulled a weed.

'You sure have grown up.'

Startled, Waverly looked up to see Mason Ardvale, the ship's head pilot, leaning on the fence that bordered her plot. He was almost as old as Captain Jones, who was his good friend. Waverly had never really liked him, and she'd grown to like him even less in the last two years when he started looking at her in a new, slithery way.

'I didn't see you there,' she said uneasily.

He smoothed a strand of fine blond hair out of his eyes. 'I saw *you*.'

She shrugged and went back to pulling weeds, but when she looked up he was still there.

'Everyone's in a tizzy these days. People think I'll tell them things because I'm the head pilot.' His chest swelled as he said this, and Waverly wondered if he was trying to impress her. 'I get tired of getting asked questions I'm not allowed to answer.'

He looked at her as though tempting her to ask, but she didn't want to play his game. Instead she said, 'Can you blame them for being curious? After forty-two years alone out here, suddenly we have neighbours.'

'Don't be too worried about that,' Mason said with a crooked grin. 'If anything happens, I'll protect you.'

'I'm not worried,' she said, ignoring his innuendo. 'I just think everyone would be more at ease if the Captain would explain what they're doing here.'

'You're not on this ship to worry about things like that.'

'Oh no?' she challenged.

'You're for other things,' he said slowly.

Waverly sat back on her heels and gave him a cool stare. When his smile faded, she said, 'What is that supposed to mean?'

'You can't expect a grown man not to notice you. Not unless he's blind.'

Waverly picked up her trowel. 'It's none of your business what I expect.'

'Is that so?' With a gleeful smile, he started over the fence that separated them.

Waverly sprang to her feet and threw her trowel at him, missing his face by centimetres. 'Stay where you are.'

He ducked, then glared at her. 'You could have taken out my eye!'

'Everyone on this ship knows what a creep you are, Mason Ardvale. All the girls laugh at you.'

'Dad?' Mason's son, Seth, came down the walkway towards them, carrying a bale of straw. 'What's going on?'

'Go to the plot,' Mason barked. 'I'll be there in a second.'

'I can wait.' Seth dropped the bale and sat on it, his sullen eyes on his father.

Is he trying to protect me? Waverly wondered.

'You shouldn't throw things at people,' Mason said to Waverly. 'That's not the way for a young lady to behave.'

'That's right. I'm *young*, Mason,' Waverly said. She picked up a hand rake, tossed it in the air, and caught it in her fist. 'I'm not for you.'

A dark look passed over Mason's features, but he tilted his head towards the sound of laughter coming from the back of the room. Mrs Turnbull and her husband were digging up turnips, well within earshot. He backed away from her, oily and slow, picked up a sack of mulch, and went on his way down the furrowed path. Seth stayed behind.

'He's not how he seems,' Seth said, unable to look her in the eye. He picked up the trowel Waverly had thrown and handed it to her.

'Thanks for sticking around.'

Seth nodded, embarrassed.

Seth was unpopular aboard the ship, but Waverly had always felt an affinity for him. The same accident that took her father had also killed his mother. Seth was a few months younger than her, but already his bones were heavy, his voice deep, and his jewel blue eyes piercing. Waverly had always noticed his eyes, ever since they sat next to each other in fourth grade.

Once, when they were still little, Seth had even kissed her in the playroom. They'd been working together on a puzzle, and she'd been conscious of his steady breathing and how he moistened his lip with a quick tongue. She'd just put in the last piece and smiled at him. 'We did it!'

He paused and then with a tortured voice whispered, 'I love you.'

Her mouth popped open. She pulled her skirt down over her scabbed knees as a fiery blush ignited her cheeks. 'What do you mean?'

Suddenly he leaned in and kissed her, very softly. But it wasn't the kiss she remembered so well; it was the way he'd let his mouth linger, the way his breath had caressed her cheek, once, twice, until he suddenly ran out of the room. She watched him go, thinking the word *Stay*. But she didn't say it.

The next day when Seth sat next to her in class, he looked at her, hopeful. She turned away. It was too much feeling, and she didn't know what to do with it. And later that week, when Kieran Alden asked her to the Harvest Cotillion, she accepted. As she danced with Kieran, she pretended not to see Seth standing by the punch bowl, hands in his pockets, looking at the floor.

Now she wondered what would have happened if she hadn't chosen Kieran. On impulse, she said, 'Do you remember that day we did the puzzle?'

He seemed surprised by the question. 'Of course I

do. Why do you bring that up?'

He looked at her, waiting. Suddenly she realized how tall he was. Taller than Kieran. He stood leaning towards her, arms loose at his sides. She felt a force pulling her into him, like gravity.

'It's just . . .' She cast around. What could she say? How could she keep from betraying Kieran? Had she already? 'It's a sweet memory.'

A smile opened Seth's face, but then he spoiled it. 'I thought you and Kieran were still . . .'

'Yes.' Her breath caught in her throat.

His smile folded up again. 'Makes sense, you two getting together. Him being the golden boy and all.'

'He's not a golden boy.'

'Oh yes, he is.'

They looked at each other for a beat.

'I guess you don't like him much,' she said.

'Let's just say I have an instinctive distrust of perfection.'

Waverly tried to sound disinterested. 'You have your eye on anyone?'

Seth lifted his gaze to hers and held it. She knew she should do something to break up this moment, so she said the first thing that came to her. 'Do you ever wonder about the accident?'

He didn't have to ask what she was talking about. 'You do?'

'Something Mom said today made me wonder.'

Seth glanced towards his father, who was bent over a melon patch. 'Yeah. I wonder about it.'

'Because I always thought it was an accident, but . . .'

Seth took a step towards her. 'That's what you need to go on thinking.'

'What do you mean? Have you heard something?'

Seth dug his toe into the roots of a pepper plant. 'Let's just say I have reason to doubt your boyfriend's benefactor.'

'Captain Jones?'

'He's not the kindly old man people think he is.'

'What are you talking about?'

Seth's chin dropped and he looked at her shoes. 'You know what? I'm paranoid. Always have been.'

'You tell me this instant what you know.'

Seth's eyes lingered on her face, but finally he shrugged. 'Waverly, to be honest, it's just a feeling I have. I don't know anything more than you do.'

Waverly narrowed her eyes at him. He was holding something back. 'I don't believe you.'

'Just be careful with Kieran, OK? Captain Jones's friends tend to lead . . . complicated lives.'

'Are you talking about your dad?'

'*We're* not talking about anything.'

'Who are you trying to protect? Your dad or me?'

Again the boy looked at her, and there was such sad longing in his face that she had to look away. She dropped to her knees and started digging at a weed.

Seth turned to follow his father, back bent under the hay bale. Waverly watched him go, waiting for him to look back at her, but he didn't.

Suddenly the ship's alarm blared. The Captain's voice came through the intercom, so shrill and loud that she didn't understand the words. She looked around her to see Mr Turnbull dropping his spade and racing down the corridor towards the starboard side.

'Waverly!'

Mrs Mbewe, her neighbour, was running towards her. 'I need you to get Serafina.'

'Why? Where is she?'

'She's in my quarters for her nap. Actually, gather all the children and take them to the auditorium!'

'Why?' she asked, dumbfounded. She dropped her trowel, which fell painfully against her anklebone. 'What's happening?'

'All hands have been called to the starboard shuttle bay. I have to go,' Mrs Mbewe called over her brown shoulder. 'Just go to the nursery to make sure all the children are on their way to the auditorium, and then find Serafina!'

Serafina was Mrs Mbewe's daughter of four years whom Waverly sometimes babysat. She was a sweet little girl whose curly black hair hovered in two round puffs of pigtails at the top of her head. Serafina was deaf, so she wouldn't hear announcements and would need help getting to the auditorium.

Waverly ran to the nearest com station and keyed in the emergency code to make a shipwide announcement. 'This is Waverly Marshall! All children report to the auditorium immediately!'

Then she ran to the central stairwell that led to the nursery room. It was slow going, because streams of adults were running downstairs at top speed, and she had to shoulder her way through the crowd. She wanted to ask what was happening, but the terror on their faces made her afraid to interfere. Once on the level for the nursery, she burst into the corridor and ran into Mr Nightly, who was holding a bloody rag to his face. She stopped him. 'Do you need help?'

'There's no time!' he yelled.

'What's happening?' she tried to ask, but he was already running away from her. Nothing was making sense.

Her limbs felt cold and floppy with fear, but she made herself run even faster. She saw Felicity Wiggam walking, dazed, in the opposite direction, and she stopped. Felicity's blond hair was mussed, her porcelain cheeks flushed, her tunic hanging askew on her long, lithe frame. 'Help me with the nursery!' Waverly shrieked at her.

At first Felicity only stared, but Waverly grabbed her wrist and dragged her down the corridor.

When they finally reached the nursery, it was empty. Building blocks and colouring books lay haphazardly in the middle of the floor. A box full of flash cards had been knocked down, splayed over the central table. 'They must have already evacuated,' she said, breathless. 'Thank God.'

'They'd have heard your announcement,' Felicity said through the curtain of pale hair hanging in her face.

'Felicity, what's happening?'

'I don't know. Where were you when it started?'

'The garden. You?'

'In my quarters.' She held her bony hands over her stomach. 'I'm scared.'

'Me, too.' Waverly took hold of her friend's hand and squeezed her cold fingers. 'I've got to go get Serafina. Can you check the kindergarten on your way to the auditorium?'

Felicity only stared at Waverly, impassive. She seemed in shock.

'Go!' Waverly shouted at her over her shoulder as she sped back down the corridor.

Just then the floor under Waverly's feet seemed to shake, and she heard a rumbling that she'd never heard before. Something had gone very wrong.

Another river of adults ran past Waverly. She looked desperately at the passing faces, hoping to see her mother, but everyone was moving too fast.

She trotted along with the adults, but when she got to the central corridor, she turned towards the Mbewes' quarters. She found their door, which was covered with a mural Serafina's mother had painted of the African savanna. Waverly pushed the button for ingress, but the door didn't open. Serafina must have locked it from the inside. There was a keypad for a numeric code. Once upon a time Waverly knew the code, and she tried several combinations of numbers, but the door remained locked.

'Serafina!' she screamed, pounding on the door. But of course Serafina couldn't hear. Waverly would have to break in.

She pulled from her pocket the folding knife she'd received as a gift when she'd turned fifteen. She opened the blade and slid it behind the faceplate that housed the door lock. She worked the metal plate off, then prised away the numbered keypad to reveal a mess of wires underneath.

She could cut the wires, but she was pretty sure that would leave the door locked permanently. No. She had to enable the mechanism that would open the door.

'There's only on, and off.' She recited the lesson about circuits she'd learned last year in electronics class and looked for the mechanism to slide the door open. It was encased in yellow plastic, but the copper ends of it were exposed and fastened under a hinged copper plate. Right now, the plate hung open. Could it be so simple? Waverly pressed on the copper plate, holding it to the wire.

A shock of vicious electricity punched through her arm and into her chest. For long moments, she was frozen in an altered state, aware only of her frantic heartbeat and her burning hand.

Emergency. There was an emergency. She couldn't go into shock. She forced her breathing into an even cadence. When she could think again, she saw the door had clicked open.

'Serafina,' she whispered as she limped through the small apartment. The electric shock had bunched up the muscles on her right side, especially in her arm. She limped as quickly as she could to the girl's room, which looked empty, but the door to the closet was ajar.

Waverly opened it to find Serafina huddled in a ball on the middle shelf, hugging her knees to her chest, eyes screwed shut. She must have felt that strange tremor that went through the ship. Waverly placed a gentle hand on Serafina's hip. The little girl opened her eyes, terrified at first, but she seemed relieved when she saw who had come for her.

'We have to go,' Waverly said, and held out her good hand.

Serafina took Waverly's hand and followed her through the apartment and down the corridor towards the auditorium. Just as they entered the stairwell, the lights blinked out. Serafina's fingernails dug into Waverly's thumb. Waverly's heart galloped from the shock she'd gotten. She thought she might be having a heart attack.

The emergency lights came on, casting a dull orange glow over the metal staircase, and the girls started towards the auditorium.

Waverly felt another shudder go through the ship – an aching groan in the metal itself. The air in the corridor started to move as though an invisible fan had been turned on.

They turned the corner to see the auditorium, dimly lit. At first Waverly thought the other children must not have made it because there wasn't a sound, a seeming impossibility if all 250 children were really gathered into a single room.

Slowly, Serafina and Waverly made their way towards the open doorway until they could see in.

'Oh, thank God, they made it,' Waverly murmured.

She saw Felicity huddled on the floor, surrounded by a dozen kindergartners, all of them focusing on a single point in front of them.

When Waverly was about three metres from the door, Felicity caught her eye. She shook her head, barely perceptibly, and held up one hand, telling Waverly and Serafina to stay where they were. Serafina stopped, but Waverly wanted to get a little closer so she could discern what Felicity was trying to say. She limped nearer to the open doorway and waved at Felicity to get her attention, but Felicity stubbornly would not look at her.

Neither did Seth, whom Waverly could now see, looking angry – no, homicidal – in the corner of the room. He had his hand wrapped around one big-boned wrist, and he twisted the skin of his arm as though trying to unsheathe a sword.

Waverly was about to back away from the doorway, ready to run away, when a man she'd never seen before appeared in front of her.

'Well, hello,' the man said.

Waverly blinked. She had never seen a stranger before.

He wasn't a tall man, and he had an ugly scar along the left side of his face that made a deep fissure when he smiled. He was holding an emergency landing weapon. Waverly recognized it from the training videos she'd watched in class. The weapons, guns they were called, were meant for use only in the unlikely event that there were hostile animals on New Earth. They lay locked in a vault in the deepest holds of the *Empyrean*. No one was permitted access to them.

The man pointed the end of the weapon at Waverly's face and shook it. 'You know what this does, right?'

Waverly nodded. If he pulled the trigger, a projectile from the gun would rip into her flesh and shatter her bones. It would kill her.

Waverly looked again into the room and saw several strange men, about five of them, looking at her. She felt disorientated to see such unfamiliar features: brown almond eyes, chunky noses, white lips, chipped teeth. The men seemed about her mother's age, maybe a little older, and they stood panting, waiting to see what she would do.

The children crouched on the floor along the base of the stage, hugging themselves, hands gripping ankles, elbows on knees. They cowered away from the men.

She tried to make sense of it: men holding guns in a room full of children. A part of her considered that she ought to feel afraid.

'Don't worry,' the man with the scar said. 'This is a rescue mission.'

'Then why do you need that?' Waverly pointed at the gun.

'In case something goes wrong,' he said in a lilting way, as though he were talking to a girl much younger than Waverly.

'What would go wrong?' she asked.

His smile was thin. 'I'm glad we understand each other.'

He jerked his gun at her, gesturing for her to enter the room. The way he turned his back on her showed that he did not expect, would not tolerate, disobedience.

Her breath labouring, she looked down at Serafina, took hold of her small sweaty hand, and obeyed.

BREACH

Kieran followed the Captain at a frantic clip towards the starboard shuttle bay. They were joined by a security detail, about twenty of them altogether, armed only with cricket bats. Kieran hoped it would be enough. He looked for his mother, but she had not arrived.

Kieran had expected chaos, but they found dim quiet. The group huddled around the porthole that looked into the shuttle bay, and they saw only the ghostly frames of the shuttles and the OneMan vessels, which reminded Kieran of pictures he'd seen of metal deep-sea diving suits back on Earth. Kieran looked at the Captain, who was stroking his beard thoughtfully. Captain Jones went to the com station near the doorway and pressed the code for his office. 'Sammy, what are they doing?' he said into the microphone. 'Can you see them on the vid?'

Sammy's voice crackled through the speaker. 'They're hovering just outside the shuttle bay, sir.'

'Have you magnified the image?'

'One moment.' In the tense silence, the security crew looked at one another. Kieran realized he'd never seen fear before. Kieran didn't like what it did to faces. It stretched them sideways, reddened eyes, widened mouths, dampened skin.

'Captain . . .' Sammy's voice was hesitant. 'I think I see a OneMan next to the outer air-lock doors.'

Kieran looked at the Captain. 'What's he doing?'

'Forcing entry.' The Captain slammed his fist into the com console and yelled, 'Security breach! All available hands to the starboard shuttle bay!'

He slapped the lock to the shuttle bay, and the security crew raced through the doorway, Kieran on the Captain's heels.

The Captain pushed him away. 'Get out of here, Kieran!'

'I want to help!' Kieran said, though he was so frightened his limbs felt wobbly.

Streams of crew members pelted across the immense bay. Alak Bhuvanath, the Central Council president, ran to the manual air-lock controls and tried several times to lock them. 'They've disabled the lock from the outside!'

The intercom buzzed, and Waverly's voice shrieked through the speaker. Something about taking all the kids to the auditorium.

Good. She'd be safer there.

Kieran watched as a team of technicians worked on the lock while the rest of the adults looked on. Barbara Coolidge's small hands were riveted to the shovel she held. Councilman Ganan Kumar's jaw worked as he stared at the door with hot black eyes. Tadeo Silva balanced his hoe over his shoulder like a spear. Everyone seemed to be holding their breath.

Already about half the crew had come. Kieran hoped that would be enough for the fight.

Unless . . .

'This might be what they want us to do,' Kieran said to himself. 'What if they *want* us all here? . . . Captain?'

But the Captain pushed him away. 'Go! Make sure all the kids made it to the auditorium, then take them through the pressurized conduits to the central bunker.'

'But—'

'You want to help? Go!' the Captain roared.

It was useless to talk to him now. Kieran ran back across the huge bay, dodging the dozens of people who were rushing in the opposite direction.

But all of Kieran's instincts told him that loading the shuttle bay full of every last crew member was a horrible mistake.

In the corridor, Harvard Stapleton, Kieran's physics teacher, was running for the shuttle bay, but Kieran grabbed his sleeve. 'Harvard, what if this is what they want us to do?'

'Not now, Kieran!'

But Kieran wouldn't let him go. 'What if . . .' The

idea formed in his mind as he said it. 'What if they're planning to blow out the shuttle bay?'

Harvard stopped, thinking, as another bunch of people ran in.

'We've got to stop people going in,' Kieran said to Harvard, whose face was pale under his thick greying hair. 'We can't have the whole crew in there! They're sitting ducks!'

'Are you asking me to defy the Captain's orders?'

'Yes!' Kieran shrieked as another group ran past. It now looked as if almost the entire crew surrounded the air-lock doors.

'Harvard, you have to tell them!' Kieran pleaded. 'They won't listen to me.'

'Maybe you're right.' The man's eyes scanned the crowd, looking for the Captain.

Another dozen people filed past them, Kieran's parents among them. He could see his father's strong back, his mother's golden hair. 'Mom! Dad!'

His mother waved him away. 'Kieran, get out of here!'

'Don't go in there!' Kieran pleaded. 'It's a trap!'

But she was already running for the air lock. How many were there now, crowded around the doors, waiting? Three hundred? Four? They seemed so stupid standing there holding their rakes and shovels, farmers who didn't know how to fight. 'Why aren't they listening to me?!'

'Go,' Harvard told him as he stepped through the doorway. 'I'll tell the Captain.'

A sudden, deafening wind ripped through Kieran's

ears. He tried to stay on his feet, but he felt the soles of his shoes sliding along the floor. He was being sucked towards what looked like an enormous hole in the side of the ship.

No. It wasn't a hole.

The air-lock doors were opening to the emptiness of the nebula.

Kieran grabbed on to the doorway. 'Oh God!' he screamed, but he couldn't hear his own voice.

Kieran looked for the other crew members.

Hundreds of pinwheel shapes were twirling out the open doorway. The shapes were people.

'Mom! Dad!' he cried into the wind, searching for his parents.

'Kieran!' someone screamed.

Harvard Stapleton was three metres away, on his hands and knees, struggling towards Kieran. The wind sucked at him, pulled on his clothes, flattened his hair, kneaded at the skin on his face.

Kieran flattened himself on the floor and stretched his feet towards Harvard. 'Grab on to me!'

'Close the door!' Harvard screamed, even as he struggled towards Kieran.

'Just another metre! You can make it!' Kieran bellowed.

Harvard lunged for Kieran's foot and held on with both hands, pulling himself up Kieran's legs until they could fight their way into the corridor.

He felt Harvard's hold on him loosen for just a moment, and then suddenly the metal door to the shuttle bay closed.

The wind stopped.

It was so quiet.

'What are you *doing*?!' Kieran screamed. 'They've got no air!'

'We can't depressurize the entire ship, Kieran,' Harvard said. But he was crying.

Kieran pressed his face against the glass and watched as a cluster of survivors opened the ramp to the nearest shuttle. A few crew members straggled towards it, but they were losing consciousness in the vacuum. Kieran studied them, looking for his parents. He was near despair when he saw his mother emerge from behind a OneMan, crawling weakly towards the open shuttle.

'She needs air!' Kieran screamed, and punched at the lock. The doors opened and the wind began again, earsplitting and deadly.

Kieran watched as his mother, revived by the air, got up and ran weakly towards the shuttle ramp. She dove onto the ramp, and someone on the inside pulled her all the way in.

Harvard closed the doors again, and the gale disappeared.

'Your mom's safe. OK?' Harvard said. 'Now go to the auditorium.'

'What about everyone else?' Kieran cried. 'We have to go get them!'

'We can't, Kieran,' Harvard said. The man seemed remote, robotic.

'We can't just leave them!'

'Kieran, they're already gone.' Harvard gripped Kieran's shoulders. 'We can't think about that now.'

Kieran stared at Harvard. Everything inside of him had been pulled out the air lock and was spinning in the thin gas of the nebula with all those dear people, men and women he'd known all his life. Was his father with them, too, already suffocated, already frozen?

'Kieran . . .' Someone shook him. The blackness in Kieran's mind cleared. Harvard put an arm around him. 'Come on. I'll take you to the auditorium. OK?'

Kieran hated himself for the tears that flowed down his face. Harvard was brave and calm, but Kieran wanted to scream, collapse, kill someone. Kill the people who did this.

'Why did they attack us?' Kieran said fiercely.

'I don't know,' Harvard said, bewildered. He took hold of Kieran's shoulders and drew him into the stairwell that led to the auditorium.

Kieran's shocked mind wanted to run backwards, back to this morning when everything was safe and normal, starting with his conversation with Waverly and ending with his newscast.

His newscast, which he'd finished only minutes before.

The newscast.

The announcement at the end.

'They have no children,' Kieran said vacantly. When he heard himself, terror jolted him out of his shock. 'Harvard, they have no children!'

The man's face went slack.

'Samantha,' Harvard whispered. The name of his daughter.

They broke into a dead run, pounding down the

metal stairs two at a time. Kieran reached the door first
and flung it open. They sprinted down the metal grating
to the auditorium door, where they could already hear
the sound of mournful crying.

'Oh God,' Harvard muttered.

They turned the corner to find the auditorium door
closed and the lock engaged from the outside. Harvard
jabbed at the keypad and the doors slid open to reveal
dozens of children huddled together at the base of the
stage, trembling and sobbing. Kieran's pounding heart
slowed. 'Thank God.'

'Samantha! Where are you?' Harvard yelled into the
din.

Kieran looked around for Waverly, but she wasn't
there, either. He ran down the aisle, looking between
the rows of seats. In his panic, he nearly tripped over
Seth Ardvale, who was splayed on the floor, barely
conscious. He had a bad cut on his forehead and a
busted lip. 'What happened to him?'

'We tried to stop them,' said Sealy Arndt. He sat on
the floor next to Seth, holding his hand over a nasty cut
on his ear as blood trickled from between his fingers.
'They took all the girls.'

'Where?' Harvard yelled at Sealy. 'Where did they
go?'

'I don't know,' the boy said in a daze.

'The shuttle bay,' Harvard said. 'The port shuttle
bay.'

Of course. After blowing out the starboard bay, they'd
have to use the port shuttle bay to get the girls off the
Empyrean.

Harvard ran to the com console and yelled into it, 'They're kidnapping our kids! All hands to the port shuttle bay!' He pushed a button, and the message cycled through in a loop, Harvard's voice endlessly screaming, 'They're kidnapping our kids . . . port shuttle bay . . . kidnapping our kids . . . port shuttle bay . . .'

Harvard started to run towards the stairwell, but Kieran cried, 'No! We have to get the guns first!'

'There's no time!' Harvard screamed and ran off, with Kieran close behind.

As he ran, Kieran heard dozens of feet pounding on the levels overhead. He skidded into the stairwell and flew down the stairs to the shuttle bay level.

Strange, piercing sounds echoed through the ship, sounding like pebbles hitting metal.

'What's that?' Kieran yelled at Harvard's back.

Harvard didn't answer, but Kieran knew. He could guess.

More than anything, Kieran wished he had a gun.

RESCUE MISSION

'We just want to move you girls to a safe place,' the man with the scar told Waverly as he and six others ushered all the girls down the corridor towards the port side. The girls, the youngest two years old and the oldest fifteen, sounded like a small army as they ran. Waverly wondered what the men would do if all the girls ran away at the same time. Would they shoot? After what they had done to Seth, she didn't want to find out.

They'd been rounded up like goats, the girls pulled from their brothers, cajoled, the men saying brightly, 'Ladies first!' The men lined up the girls by the door while the man with the scar casually pointed his gun at the boys, who had shrunk away, too scared to protest.

All except Seth, who stood up, fists at his sides. 'You can't do this,' he'd said. His eyes had skirted over to Waverly, who looked on, crazily hoping that Seth could do something.

Seth lunged for the man with the scar, but with one fluid motion he whacked Seth on the head with the butt of his gun. Sealy Arndt had run to Seth's side, and the man swung his gun again, tearing Sealy's ear and sending the boy sprawling. 'That's what happens when people panic,' he said to the rest of the boys, and turned towards the girls. 'Quick time, march!'

Now the men were walking cautiously down the corridors, but they were horribly out of breath, and sweat streamed from their foreheads. The man with the scar on his face was clearly in charge, and though he was slightly built, with weak, bony arms, he was obviously capable of anything.

Were they afraid, or sick? Waverly could hardly breathe herself. Her muscles were still horribly cramped, and her heart seemed to have lost its rhythm. She needed to catch her breath, but her terror only made everything worse.

'There's been an accident,' the man with the scar announced in response to a question that Waverly hadn't heard. 'The port side is the safest area.'

'Then why not bring the boys too?' Waverly asked.

'We *are* bringing the boys,' he said cheerily, as though she'd asked a silly question. 'They're right behind us.'

She wanted to believe him, but a nagging unease

spread through her when she looked at the gun he held so tightly. If he was trying to help, why did he need a gun?

But what could she do? She tried to think how to get away from these strange people, but her mind felt charred. She couldn't think. So she went where the men told her to go, and she kept quiet.

The corridors were empty, probably because the entire crew had been pulled away to deal with the accident. The emergency lights cast a dull pallor over everyone. Serafina clung to Waverly's shirt, letting herself be pulled along as they jogged through the hallways. Each time they crossed a junction between corridors, she looked desperately for a crew member from the *Empyrean*. But there was no one.

Finally the man with the scar stopped walking, holding up a hand for the others to stop.

Waverly looked back over the long line behind her and saw Samantha Stapleton, a tall girl of fourteen, carrying Hortense Muller, who was crying, her knees bloody from a fall. Samantha and Waverly had always had a strained relationship, ever since a fistfight they'd got into in the seventh grade. Samantha had been jealous that Waverly had been tapped for pilot's training when she herself had been assigned to farming. 'You cheated,' Samantha spat through the gap between her teeth.

Waverly didn't see the first punch coming, but she didn't let a second one land on her. Both girls walked away from the fight with black eyes and learned to avoid each other ever since. But now, Waverly could see that Samantha was the only girl here who wasn't paralysed with terror. She was fully alert, watching the guards, noticing things.

Samantha looked at Waverly with wide eyes. In that one look, their old rivalry melted away. Waverly wished she could signal something that would get them out of this somehow, but all she could do was shake her head. Samantha shook her head, too, as if to say, *I can't believe this is happening.*

That was just it. Waverly couldn't believe this was happening.

The man with the scar motioned to the girls to get moving again. Waverly followed behind him, frightened now because he was moving towards a door. At first she didn't recognize where he was taking them, but when he opened the door to reveal a cavernous room, Waverly stopped in her tracks.

The shuttle bay. He'd taken them to the port shuttle bay.

The man saw Waverly staring, and he smiled. 'Didn't you hear there's an air-lock malfunction in the other shuttle bay? We need to get you into a pressurized chamber.'

'The auditorium can be pressurized,' Waverly said. Dimly she realized that must be why Mrs Mbewe had told her to take the children there. 'We were already safe there.'

'But if the ship is lost, you'd have been trapped,' the man said.

He was lying. Waverly knew there were pressurized conduits from the auditorium to the central bunker, where they could have survived for months if need be.

'Where are you taking us?' Waverly's voice was floating in the air above her.

'If the ship depressurizes, we'll have to take you to the *New Horizon*,' the man said. 'You'll be safe there.'

'Safe?' said Waverly's voice, testing the word.

'Come along,' the man said, waving the gun in her face. The motion seemed to take all his strength, and he had to use both hands to hold up the gun.

Something was wrong with him. Had he been electrocuted, too?

Her feet came unstuck from the floor and she stepped through the doorway. The bay was cold, stark, the metal walls like a cage, the ceiling so high that it disappeared into a dark gloom. The hulking forms of the shuttle craft, arranged in a circle around the room, perched on their landing gear like watchful vultures. OneMen hung along the walls, their thick gloves extended towards the girls as though waiting for a goodbye hug. The room was so large that Waverly told herself it would take five minutes to cross it. Five minutes for Kieran to come find her, or Seth, or her mother. Anyone. Because someone would come. They had to come.

She could hear the shuffling of hundreds of little feet behind her, sounds that seemed to multiply in the room's echo. She no longer felt Serafina clinging to her shirt, but she felt too much pain to turn her head to look. She saw a shuttle that was out of place, its nose cone pointed towards the air lock, its rear pointed to Waverly, the thrusters glowing with heat. The shuttle ramp extended down to the floor, and as she approached Waverly could see into the cargo hold and the stairway inside that led up to the passenger area. A few people stood around the shuttle, holding guns. Some of them were women.

Suddenly the intercom system crackled to life, and a frantic voice shouted through the speakers, the same message over and over. But the shuttle bay was so large that the message echoed, and Waverly couldn't understand all the words. Something about kids. *Maybe it's about us,* she thought. *They're coming.*

As they got closer to the shuttle, which was surrounded by people, Waverly noticed that there was one woman who wasn't holding a gun.

It was Mrs Alvarez, the nursery-school teacher, and she was standing next to the shuttle ramp in front of an angry-looking woman. The woman's eyes scanned the girls mechanically as several of the youngest ran to Mrs Alvarez, who opened her arms wide. 'Hello, everyone,' she said. 'Captain Jones sent me to tell you that everything is all right, and that you need to board this shuttle just in case the *Empyrean* depressurizes.'

Waverly heaved a sigh of relief. Everything was OK after all. She started to go up the ramp, but she felt a hand on her arm. Mrs Alvarez was studying her.

'You don't look well. Did they . . .' she began, but with a nervous look at the woman with the gun, she seemed to rethink what she wanted to ask. 'What happened?'

'Electrocuted.'

Mrs Alvarez placed a hand on Waverly's cheek and

looked at the reddening burn on her hand, which had begun to weep clear fluid. 'This child needs a doctor,' she said to the woman.

'There are doctors on the *New Horizon*,' the woman said curtly. She had a fleshy, pinkish face that didn't match the rest of her body, which was lean and narrow.

'She can't wait that long,' Mrs Alvarez said. 'She's been electrocuted!'

'We'll see to her right away,' the woman said, and then in a low voice muttered, 'Remember what we talked about.'

Mrs Alvarez nudged Waverly's shoulder. 'Go in, honey. They'll help you as soon as they can.' But her anxious face didn't match her soothing voice.

Waverly started up the ramp but stopped. Something the strange woman said hit her: *There are doctors aboard the* New Horizon.

'We're going to the *New Horizon* only if the *Empyrean* depressurizes, right?' Waverly asked the woman holding the gun.

'Yeah,' the woman said curtly. 'Just go up and sit down.'

Waverly was about to go up when she heard shouting. She turned to see streams of people running across the bay, shrieking and waving their arms. The woman shoved Waverly up the shuttle ramp, but she tripped and fell. Mrs Alvarez dived to help, but the woman hit her with the butt of her gun, and Mrs Alvarez rolled off the shuttle ramp and onto the floor.

Piercing noises echoed through the bay, and Waverly watched as some of the people who were running towards them fell down. Mrs Slotsky, Mr Pratt and Mr and Mrs Anguli all collapsed onto the floor and lay still. Mrs Anders, little Justin's mother, fell with her eyes open, staring at Waverly, who watched, waiting for the woman to blink, move, get up. But she didn't. She just went right on staring.

Waverly felt faint and had trouble understanding what she was seeing. She wanted to scream, but her throat felt like it was filled with gel.

These strangers were shooting guns at people. These strangers were killing her friends.

More and more people poured into the shuttle bay. Some rushed to their fallen friends, others took cover behind shuttles. Mrs Oxwell ran through the doorway and stopped, searched the chaos, pointed at Waverly and shouted, 'They have them on that shuttle!'

Everyone seemed to forget about the guns, and they started running towards the assailants again. Waverly's breath came in great gulps as she watched her friends crossing the room. One of the strangers screamed, 'They're going to mob us!'

More piercing sounds echoed through the shuttle bay, hurting Waverly's ears. People kept falling down: Mr Abdul, Jaffar's dad. Mrs Ashton, Trevor and Howard's mother. They fell and lay still.

'Don't, please don't,' Waverly said to the woman who had hit Mrs Alvarez on the head. But the woman looked too terrified to hear her. She kept pumping the trigger of her gun, and people kept falling.

Waverly felt hands on her back, and Felicity crouched beside her. 'You've got to come up.'

'They want to take us away!'

'Look around you. They'll keep shooting as long as we're here. You've got to come up!'

'Waverly!' It was Kieran, running towards her with Harvard Stapleton. 'Get off the shuttle!' he screamed. His face was red, and spit flew from his mouth. 'Get off now!'

'The longer you stay here, the more people will get shot.' The voice was right above her, and she looked up to see the man with the scar standing over her. To prove his point, he fired his gun into the onrushing crowd.

'He means it, Waverly,' Felicity said.

'Let's get out of here!' the man with the scar yelled ferociously, then he knelt at the bottom of the ramp while his comrades boarded the shuttle. When he saw Waverly's eyes on him, he aimed his gun at Kieran. 'Do I shoot him or not?'

There was no decision to make. She had one choice only.

Waverly leaned on Felicity as she limped up the ramp.

'No, Waverly!' she heard someone bellow, not Kieran, someone else. She turned for one last look at her home and saw Seth. He stood next to a OneMan, all elbows and knees, his hands in his hair, head bleeding, yelling at the top of his lungs, 'Don't do this, Waverly!'

She shook her head, tried to yell, 'I'm sorry,' but she could only make herself whisper.

She dragged herself up the ramp with Felicity, and it closed behind her with a hollow report.

LEFT
BEHIND

One moment Kieran had been staring at Waverly's slender back, imploring silently, *Don't go. Get off the shuttle*. She'd turned, she'd looked at Seth Ardvale, she'd shaken her head at him, and then she'd limped up the ramp, and the ramp closed, and she was gone.

A woman wailed as the shuttle engines hummed to life. They coughed orange fire, then burned blue, their photon exhaust casting a sickly glow over the bodies of those who had been shot. People backed away from the craft, staring. Kieran looked at the faces nearest him, desperate for someone to do something, but everyone seemed paralysed. Mrs Anderson's mouth hung open. Mr Bernstein dropped to his knees as the shuttle rose from the floor and made the slow turn towards the air-lock doors.

'Override the air lock!' Seth yelled. He started for the controls himself, but his hands went up to his head and he fell to his knees.

Suddenly the room was full of action again. A dozen people ran for the control panel near the huge doors. Harvard got there first and punched at the keypad, but the panel lights were dead. He slammed it with his fists and cried, 'They fixed the doors to respond only to commands from inside the shuttle!'

'Go through Central Command,' Kieran shouted at Harvard. 'They can lock the doors from there.'

Harvard yelled into the intercom, 'Sammy! Do you hear me?'

Nothing but silence.

Harvard clicked the transmission button several times. 'Central? . . . Hello?' He looked at Kieran in horror. 'No one's there.'

They'd all run to save their kids. Everyone had abandoned their posts. Forty-two years of peaceful isolation had made them totally incompetent in the face of attack.

'I'll go,' Kieran said, and ran back the way he'd come, past Seth, who was on his hands and knees, dazed, staring at a pool of vomit.

'Everyone into a shuttle!' he heard Harvard scream.

When Kieran made it to the corridor, he closed the shuttle bay doors as a precaution, and then he turned and sped down the abandoned gangway. The ship felt empty. Corridors that had once been crowded with farmers and engineers, teachers and trainees, families and friends, were now deserted.

How many had died already? How many more?

Where was his dad?

Kieran shut out those thoughts and ran at top speed up four flights of stairs until he burst into the administrative level of the ship, where he hooked a left and pelted down the corridor into the Captain's office. He was hoping that Captain Jones would somehow be there, sitting at his desk like always, calmly in control. But of course the Captain wasn't there. He probably wasn't even alive.

Kieran ran to Central Command, where the officers controlled the various systems aboard ship. Usually this room was full of people, all of them talking through intercoms, communicating with various parts of the ship, dealing with maintenance issues. But now no one was here. The room seemed very small.

Kieran jogged around the semicircle of computer displays, looking for the one that controlled the shuttle bay doors. But none of the workstations were labelled. Kieran groaned in despair. He caught his reflection in the porthole and stared at it as though it could tell him what to do.

'The Captain's computer ought to be able to do anything,' Kieran said to his reflection. He sat down at the Captain's chair. A computer display attached to a flexible arm slid in front of him. Along the right-hand edge of the screen was a row of buttons, and Kieran tapped the one marked 'Port Shuttle Bay' from a scrolling list. A video image of the bay blinked to life, and Kieran saw a shuttle in launch sequence moving towards the air lock doors, which were still closed. He tapped the button for the door controls that said, 'Lock.' There was no way the enemy shuttle would be able to leave now.

He leaned back in his chair and sighed in relief. He'd done it.

But the video flashed to Harvard's panicked face. 'Unlock the door!' he screamed. 'They're already gone!'

'But they're still in launch sequence!'

'That's *us*!' Harvard screamed. 'Open the air-lock doors!'

Kieran fumbled to enter the unlock command, and a video display popped up showing the air-lock doors creeping open. They were so slow.

How much time had he cost them?

Harvard was back on-screen. 'Where are they, Kieran? Can you see them on the outer vid displays?'

Kieran's fingers had never felt so clumsy as he scrolled through the video images outside the ship from cameras that monitored the engines, the communication antennae, telescopes and radar. Each display showed only the static cold of the outer hull, until Kieran found the aft view, where a tiny speck caught his eye.

He magnified and saw a shuttle craft edging past the engines, heading towards the starboard side. It looked like a tiny ant crawling past the enormous exhaust tunnels.

Kieran patched the display through to Harvard's shuttle. 'They're back near the engines,' he said.

'Why back *there*?' Harvard asked.

Kieran magnified further and saw a second, smaller speck hovering next to the rogue shuttle. He could barely make out the humanoid shape of a OneMan.

'Is that OneMan ours?' Kieran asked.

'That OneMan is moving towards the coolant system!' Harvard cried. 'Kieran, get all the boys to the central bunker!'

Could they really intend to sabotage the reactors?

Kieran clicked onto the vid display in the auditorium and saw that the boys were still there, huddled in groups on the floor. He saw Sealy Arndt in the crowd, still nursing his torn ear. Kieran didn't like Sealy, but the boy would be able to motivate the rest of them to move. Kieran turned on the intercom to the auditorium and spoke into the Captain's mouthpiece. 'Sealy, gather up all those boys and bring them to the central bunker *right now*! The reactors could blow any second!' Sealy looked into the camera, confused, until Kieran added, 'Move your *ass*!'

Sealy grabbed a couple of boys by the shoulder and shoved them forward. He was rough with the stragglers, but it was what they needed to wake up. Soon all the boys were marching out of the auditorium.

Now that he had a moment, Kieran wanted to check on his mother.

Kieran looked at the video display of the starboard shuttle bay, ghostly and empty, the air-lock doors closed. No one was there. He magnified the image to look for some sign, any sign, of his mother. What he saw startled him. The shuttle she'd entered was gone. It wasn't in the bay any more. They must have left during the skirmish.

Where had they gone?

Kieran flipped to a view of the port-side bay, hoping to find his mother's shuttle there. Instead he saw dozens of sprawled bodies lying in awkward positions, looking broken and wrong. He could see only a few faces, but he recognized them all. Anthony Shaw, who had taught Kieran how to shuck corn; Meryl Braun, who made popcorn for the kids on movie nights; Mira Khoury, who had a beautiful singing voice; Dominic Fellini, who welded metal sculptures out of worn spare parts. All of them gone. Snuffed out. Finished.

The people who did this had Waverly.

Kieran flipped back to the aft display and saw that the enemy OneMan was hovering over the starboard coolant system. He wished he could see what he was doing, but he could guess. They were trying to disable the engines, the only source of power on board. If they succeeded, every plant aboard the *Empyrean* would be dead in a few days. Every person would be dead in a week, of cold or asphyxiation.

Maxwell Lester's voice came over the intercom. 'Kieran, we're suiting up right now to go after that OneMan. Go to the maintenance screen and find the reactor management system. Tell us the readings.'

By the time Kieran found the right screen, several of the boys had come into Central Command and were watching over Kieran's shoulder. Kieran could hear the rest of the boys across the hallway in the central bunker, many of them crying or talking in hushed voices. Unlike the adults who were panicked, the boys seemed shocked into solemn quiet.

'Any of you know how to find the coolant readings?' Kieran asked the room at large.

'I'll look,' said a weary voice. It was Seth, who limped to a vid display and flipped through the screens, cradling his head in his hand.

'You probably have a concussion,' Kieran told him.

'No kidding,' Seth muttered as he squinted at the schematics in front of him. Kieran wondered how he could be so familiar with the computing system, but he knew Seth spent a lot of time in Central Command with his father, the ship's head pilot.

'The coolant looks normal,' Seth said to Kieran, who relayed the message over the com system.

'That's good,' Maxwell said over the intercom. 'Now I want you to do a head count of the boys. Once you know they're all there, I want you to seal off the central bunker.'

'I can't do that!' Kieran protested. 'What about everyone else on the ship?'

'Once we get the reactor sealed off, you can let us in. It's just a precaution.'

Kieran saw that he was right. 'Seth, will you do the head count?' he asked.

Seth made an announcement for all the boys to report to him in the corridor outside Central Command, then struggled to his feet to do the count. Kieran flicked to the vid display outside the ship.

The enemy OneMan was still over the coolant tanks, its thrusters glowing as it kept its acceleration even with the *Empyrean*'s. The shuttle from the *New Horizon* was nearby. The *Empyrean*'s shuttle was speeding towards the enemy craft and, from the other end, three

OneMen were travelling along the length of the ship, towards the enemy. He had no idea what they intended to do. There wasn't much they *could* do. There were no weapons on board the shuttles or on OneMen.

'All the boys are here,' Seth said. He'd come back without Kieran noticing. 'Arthur Dietrich is sealing off the central bunker right now.'

'See if we can pick up the transmission between those two shuttles,' Kieran barked.

'Don't yell—' Seth's voice broke, but he mastered himself and sat in front of his father's monitor. His fingers flew over the display in front of him, and Kieran could hear Harvard's quietly enraged voice.

'. . . we could have shared our knowledge. You didn't have to—'

'We had all the knowledge you had.' It was a man's voice, someone Kieran didn't recognize. He sounded as though he was pleading. 'It was too late for us.'

'We would have helped you, if you'd been honest.'

'What're they talking about?' Seth whispered, but Kieran shushed him.

'We *tried*!' the man insisted. 'We begged your Captain to rendezvous with us, but he refused!'

'I'm sure Captain Jones was only trying to protect our ship,' Harvard said.

'That's what *we're* doing! We can't let ourselves go extinct!'

Kieran watched as the enemy OneMan detached from the hull of the *Empyrean* and sped towards the rogue shuttle craft.

'What did he do?' Seth asked ominously.

Suddenly the *Empyrean* rocked with an explosion. Kieran's vid screen flashed a brilliant light, and he shielded his eyes. A deep rumble moved through the ship.

'Oh God,' Seth cried as he flipped through screens to assess damage.

The enemy sped off towards the *New Horizon*. Harvard's shuttle joined in pursuit, along with the three OneMen from the *Empyrean*.

'Where are they going?' Seth asked, his usual guarded manner completely unravelled.

'I don't know,' Kieran said.

Kieran watched his com console, unable to breathe until a text message flashed to life on the Central Command computer: 'On blkout. Stay on crse. Will rndzvous.'

'They're going to try to catch up to the *New Horizon*. They're trying to rescue the girls,' Kieran said.

'On blackout?' Seth read pensively.

'Their only chance is to surprise the other crew,' Kieran explained. 'To do that, they have to cease all communication with us.'

Seth nodded, sullen. He didn't like having things explained to him, Kieran could see. Usually Seth was the one who did the explaining.

An alarm suddenly screamed through the ship. Kieran jumped in his seat.

Huge red letters showed up on Kieran's monitor, flashing urgently: 'MELTDOWN.'

Radiation was flooding the engine room. And there was nothing Kieran could do about it.

PART TWO
CAPTIVES

The devil can cite Scripture for his purpose.

– William Shakespeare

ON THE SHUTTLE

The shuttle lurched as it left the *Empyrean*, then settled into a smooth flight. To Waverly, used to the immense farming bays of her home, the shuttle felt asphyxiating and small. Passenger seats lined the walls, and the one hundred and thirty girls sat facing the centre of the room, staring out of the portholes and looking fearfully at one another.

Waverly felt sick to her stomach from the zero gravity. She was strapped in, but she couldn't feel the weight of her body, and with her palm she kept touching the seat underneath her, making sure it was still there. She had a strange feeling of non-existence, as if she'd left her body behind and were floating above these frightening people.

She should have listened to Seth. She should have run away.

'I'm still alive,' Waverly told herself. She knew it because she could feel Felicity's leg next to her own. She wanted to reach out and touch her friend, hold her hand the way they'd done as little girls. That wasn't so long ago, but Felicity seemed very far from her now, so Waverly kept to herself. She didn't want to *be* this scared, so she didn't want to *act* scared.

The red-faced woman who had started the shooting floated at the head of the cabin, strapped into a harness that hooked to the wall, holding her weapon to her chest. She kept her smallish eyes trained on the girls, but something about her was unsteady, and every so often she sniffed. Waverly thought she might be crying, but such a monster should not be capable of tears.

Waverly nudged Felicity. Even that small motion sent an ache radiating through her core. She was very weak.

'What?' Felicity whispered, barely audibly.

'We outnumber them,' Waverly said softly. The single sentence used up all her breath, and she was panting before she could finish. 'Maybe we can take over the shuttle.'

'They have guns.'

'If they get us aboard the *New Horizon*, we'll never get away.'

'But we'll be alive.'

Waverly tried to think of a response, but spasms seized the muscles between her ribs, and she bent over, wincing. She felt Felicity's hand on her back, and the girl whispered through her hair, 'Shut up and be still. You're too sick to do anything.'

Waverly's entire being cried out against this. There had to be something they could do, *something* to stop this terrible thing from happening. But the more upset she felt, the weaker her limbs, the more frantic her heartbeat, the less clear her head. She slumped against Felicity, who put an arm around her, and she concentrated on the other girl's heartbeat, listening to its steadiness, willing her own heart to slow its wild pace.

The door to the cockpit slid open. The girls shrank from it.

Into the room stepped a plump woman of middle years, her grey hair swept into a bun on top of her head. The woman had kind grey eyes and a serene smile. She held out her hands as if to embrace all the girls in the room. For a moment, Waverly wondered how the woman was able to stand on the floor in zero gravity, but then she saw she was wearing magnetic grav boots. Everyone else aboard the shuttle seemed discomfited by the zero gravity, but this woman's feet were planted firmly on the ground.

'Girls, I'm Anne Mather, and I'm here to help you. You've been through a great deal, and I'm so sorry for what happened.'

'You're *sorry*?' Samantha Stapleton yelled. 'You *killed* people!'

'*Killed?* Oh, my my my!' cried the woman. She lifted Samantha's chin until the girl glared up at her. 'No, dear. I'm so sorry you misunderstood! No one was killed in our rescue mission! Some people were stunned with our tranquillizers, but I assure you they'll wake up safe and sound.'

Many of the girls straightened in their seats, hopeful eyes fastened on this comforting, motherly woman. 'My mom's going to be OK?' Melissa Dickinson asked from beneath frayed mousy hair.

'I assure you, she is fine, dear.'

Melissa collapsed against the girl next to her, crying with relief.

Laura Martin raised her skinny arm and cleared her throat. Waverly thought how absurd it was that already the girls were acting as though this were a normal class and this woman a normal teacher. They were badly shaken and willing to cling to any bit of normalcy. 'This was a rescue mission? Rescue from what?'

'You didn't know?' the woman said, her voice full of love. 'Sweethearts, there was an air-lock malfunction that caused an explosive decompression. We tried to fix it from the outside, but when that failed we knew we had to get you girls off the ship as fast as we could!'

Waverly saw that some of the girls were eating this up. Finally, here was a trustworthy adult who would put everything to rights. But it didn't work on everyone. Samantha seethed at the woman, looking capable of choking her to death. Sarah Hodges, a short, athletic girl whose favourite sport was tormenting teachers, shook her head in open defiance.

'As soon as we know that the *Empyrean* is safe for you,' the woman said, 'we'll return you to your parents.'

'I saw the whole thing,' Waverly said as loudly as she could, but only the girls nearby heard. 'They fell down so fast. Like they were dead.'

The woman put a clammy palm to Waverly's cheek. Her eyes were dove-wing blue, her smile gentle and loving, her skin milky despite her age, her grey hair thick and silky looking. Waverly *wanted* to like her. She wanted to believe her. She almost did, except for the slow, determined way the woman spoke. 'Dear, we injected them with a powerful drug that acted very quickly. It must have frightened you to see them fall down that way, but I assure you they'll be fine, as long as they can repair the *Empyrean*.'

'But *why* did you shoot them?' It was Sarah who had spoken. Stubborn Sarah, who always had to challenge teachers, slowing down lessons and making things difficult. But here, in this terrifying setting, Waverly liked Sarah's defiance. '*Why* did you drug them?'

'There was a panic,' the woman explained. 'The people were trying to board the shuttle, but we had to keep them off. This shuttle has a specific capacity, girls. Too many aboard this ship would have meant death for us all.'

'Why did you take only the girls?' Waverly asked, barely able to make herself heard. She was getting weaker by the minute.

'We wanted to get the boys aboard a second shuttle,' the woman said regretfully. 'But after the riot in the shuttle bay, we can't risk more of our crew. It seems safer for everyone to avoid a mob, don't you think?'

Only the youngest girls seemed satisfied by this. The

older ones seemed merely shocked into silence. Sarah and Samantha stared angrily at the floor. Sarah looked pale beneath her many brown freckles, and her reddish hair hung in her eyes. Samantha's expression was murderous. Felicity's gaze had gone blank. She sat ramrod straight, as though she were being evaluated for poise, her eyes on her graceful fingers, which were woven in her lap. She'd retreated to a haven inside herself. But many of the girls looked relieved. The woman had come in with a comforting story, and they were clinging to it, hoping, willing it to be true.

'Girls, I'm needed in the cockpit,' the woman said. 'If you need anything, you just ask for Auntie Anne, and I'll come right away, all right? As soon as we get you aboard the *New Horizon*, we'll get you some nice food and something soothing to drink. You'll be safe and sound.'

The woman gave them such a warm, inviting smile that some of the girls actually smiled back. Then she turned and walked back to the cockpit, and the door slipped closed behind her.

Waverly saw that any hope of defiance, of overcoming the shuttle crew, was over. Anne Mather's story had worked beautifully. There would be no revolt. There *could* be no revolt. The other girls would not cooperate with one because most of them wanted to believe the story even more than Waverly did.

Waverly felt her breathing slow. She leaned her aching body against Felicity, finally giving in to her pain and exhaustion. She closed her eyes and, in spite of her fear, slept.

THE NEW HORIZON

'Wake up.'

At first, the voice seemed to form out of the air around Waverly. As she came to herself, she heard with great relief the profound humming she'd heard her entire life – the familiar drone of the *Empyrean*'s engines. She was safe back home. She felt a hand at the back of her neck and edged her eyes open. In the dim light, she made out the rounded features of a woman in her fifties. She had raw, pink skin, light brown hair touched with grey, and solemn hazel eyes. A stranger.

Waverly released a strangled whimper. She wasn't aboard the *Empyrean* at all. They'd taken her and all the girls to the *New Horizon*.

'Try a sip of this, honey,' the woman said. Waverly opened her mouth to receive an aromatic broth of chicken and parsley. 'You've had quite a time,' the woman said. Waverly heard a spoon slide against an earthenware bowl, and it was held to her lips. The broth was warm and delicious. As she swallowed, Waverly realized that she was ravenously hungry. 'That good?' the woman asked gently.

Something in the way the woman touched her, cared for her, spoke to her so gently, made Waverly feel precious. She nodded, disturbed by this weird intimacy.

The way the ship vibrated, the sound of the engines, the smell of the pollen from the corn crop, the oval shape of the portholes, and the view of the nebula that glowed outside like an eerie shroud: everything was identical to the *Empyrean*. It was home, and not home.

'What happened to me?' she croaked.

The woman put the spoon in Waverly's hand, then collapsed into a chair near the bed. She seemed very tired, and she moved as if each of her limbs weighed a hundred pounds. It was the same exhaustion Waverly had noticed in the men who'd taken them from the auditorium. Was everyone on the *New Horizon* sick?

'I'm your nurse,' the woman said. 'My name's Magda.'

'Where are the girls?' Waverly asked between spoonfuls.

'They're safe.'

Waverly hated how the woman didn't *quite* answer her questions.

'We're aboard the *New Horizon*?'

'The *Empyrean* was further compromised after our rescue operation.' The controlled way she spoke made Waverly think that she was reciting from memory. 'We had to bring you aboard.'

'Where are we?' Waverly craned her neck to look out of the porthole. 'Where's the *Empyrean*?'

'It can't be seen from here. We had to put some distance between us and your ship, honey. Just to be safe.'

'*Why?*'

'It wasn't safe any more.'

'Why did you take only the girls?'

'A little at a time, OK?' the woman said, indicating the spoon Waverly held, though it seemed the woman was talking about information: not too much at once.

The broth felt like a healing elixir, and Waverly swallowed it eagerly in spite of herself. If she were stronger, she'd go on a hunger strike, demand to be taken back to her mother. But Waverly wasn't strong. Her fingers were shaking, her legs ached and her throat was agonizingly dry, no matter how much broth she swallowed.

'I was electrocuted,' she said, not so much questioning as remembering.

'Yes. Your heart and nervous system were affected, and you were burned. You needed immediate attention. That's partly why we hurried you away.'

'You shot at people,' Waverly said, her brown eyes fixed on the woman's angular jaw. 'My friends.'

The nurse dropped her eyes to Waverly's knees, and she fidgeted calloused fingers. 'There was a panic. They had to control the crowd, but the casualties were few.'

'Why should I believe you?'

She thought she saw fear in the woman's eyes. The room felt menacingly quiet, as if the walls possessed an alien will.

'You have no choice but to trust us,' the nurse said slowly and carefully. There was a message in the way her eyes fixed on Waverly's, willing her to understand: *You have no choice.*

Waverly felt very fragile.

'Have you had your fill of broth?'

Waverly nodded. Her stomach had shrunk as she began to realize what was happening. She might never see her mother again, or Kieran, or Seth, or any of the other people she'd grown up with all her life. She nearly vomited.

'I know what might cheer you up.' With a knowing smile, the nurse left the room but was soon back with Felicity trailing behind her. 'This girl must be a friend of yours. She kept asking how you were. Now you two can have a lovely chat.'

Felicity looked haggard, though her pale hair was pulled away from her face in a neat bow. She wore a plain blue dress that brought out the blue of her eyes, and formal slippers on her feet. She sighed when she saw Waverly and sat on the bed.

'We've been so worried about you,' she said.

'Are you all right? Are the girls safe?' Waverly asked.

Felicity said with measured voice, 'They haven't hurt any of us.'

Waverly looked over Felicity's shoulder. The nurse

was sitting in a chair by the door, her legs crossed, her trouser legs too short so that the tops of her cotton socks showed. She pretended to peruse Waverly's chart, but she was clearly listening to the girls.

'How long have we been here?' Waverly asked.

'They keep us away from clocks. All I know is I've slept twice.'

'Where is the *Empyrean*?'

Felicity's bottom lip quivered. 'They say they haven't had any communication since we left. They're looking for wreckage.'

The bed tilted, and for a moment Waverly felt as though she might fall off. Destroyed. Her home. Everyone she'd ever known. Her mother. And Kieran.

No. It was impossible. If she gave in to this, she didn't know how she could go on living. Waverly gripped Felicity's hands and waited until their eyes met, then she whispered, 'That's what they *said*, right?'

Felicity sucked in air through her red lips. 'Right.'

'Don't shut down.'

'What do you mean?' Felicity asked distantly.

Waverly knew her friend too well. When Waverly's father died in the air-lock accident, Felicity had pulled away from her in the faintest way. Whenever Waverly talked about her father and how she missed him, she felt that Felicity was trying to listen, trying to say the right thing, but she always managed to change the subject and redirect Waverly's attention to something cheerier. 'I don't want to cheer up! I *want* be sad!' she'd yelled once, but Felicity didn't seem to hear. Their friendship changed after that. They were still best friends in name, but they were never really close again. Waverly knew that it wasn't her fault, that Felicity just wasn't very strong. But it still hurt.

In this situation, though, the girls had no choice but to be strong.

Waverly reached for Felicity's hand, held on so firmly that she could feel the girl's fingers squirm. 'I need you to stay brave with me, Felicity. Can you do that?'

'Of course,' Felicity said, but she pulled her fingers out of Waverly's grasp.

A knock sounded at the door. The grey-haired woman, Anne Mather, leaned into the room with a smile. 'How's our patient doing?'

Waverly did not answer.

The woman sat in a chair near the head of the bed. She moved the same weary way the nurse moved, and Waverly could see her face was moist with sweat. 'You're a resilient girl,' Anne Mather observed.

Waverly looked at her own knees. She didn't like looking at the woman because she found herself being pulled in, persuaded.

'You've been through so much, child,' the woman said softly.

Waverly lifted her eyes. 'I'm not a child.'

'Oh, dear, that's right. You're probably all the way through puberty, is that right?'

This was such a strange question, Waverly could only stare.

'Oh, I'm sorry. We're very frank about these things aboard the *New Horizon*. Forty-three years alone in space makes people . . . comfortable with each other, doesn't it?'

The nurse snickered but stopped after a cold glance from Anne Mather.

'Waverly,' Mather said, 'we're doing everything we can to search for survivors from the *Empyrean*. Don't give up on them yet, all right?'

'Really? You're trying to help them?'

'That's right. We're doing all we can.' Anne Mather put a friendly hand on Waverly's knee. 'Dear, we're going to count on you to help us with the other girls. Felicity has been wonderful . . .'

Felicity's eyes snapped onto the woman. Anne Mather took no notice, though the girl was standing right next to her.

'We think the girls need reassurance from you, Waverly. Since you're the oldest.'

Something wasn't right in the way Anne Mather watched for the tiniest whisper of expression on Waverly's face.

'What do you mean?' Waverly asked. 'Reassurance about what?'

'That they're in good hands here. That we'll take care of them. Good care.'

Waverly narrowed her eyes, tried to make out what this woman was really saying.

'They've been through so much. And the rescue mission must have been confusing. They'll trust you to know what's best, won't they?' She leaned away primly and waited for Waverly to say something.

She could wait forever if she wanted to. Waverly was

too angry to offer cooperation. She needed to think.

Anne Mather spoke again, her voice firmer now. 'I know you've been through an ordeal, but all the girls have. This is no time for self-pity.'

Rage swept through Waverly. She wished she were strong enough to take this woman's throat in her hands and squeeze her to death. But what if what she said was true, that the girls had been rescued rather than kidnapped? *Could* it be true?

'There can be no great journey without tribulations,' Anne Mather said, her grey eyes skirting the boundaries of the room. 'It will be so much easier if we can work together.'

'And if we can't?' Waverly asked grimly. 'What happens then?'

'Let's hope we don't have to find out,' Anne Mather said. The warmth was gone from her voice. She returned Waverly's stare and waited until the girl blinked before she spoke again. 'We're just so glad to have you girls aboard,' she said, the honey back in her voice. 'It's such a pleasure to see young faces again, isn't it, Magda?'

'It's a good thing we came when we did, that's all,' the nurse said cheerily. She'd come back to stand behind Felicity, who had shrunk to the foot of Waverly's bed and was holding on to the railing with white knuckles. The nurse laughed and put her hand on Felicity's shoulder. The girl seemed to wilt under her touch.

'It's time you got some sleep, Waverly.' Anne Mather nodded at the nurse, who went to a cabinet. From a drawer she pulled a vial and pierced its membrane with a needle.

'What's that? What are you doing?' Panic rose like acid in Waverly's throat. She started to get up, but the nurse pushed the needle into a tube that ran into her arm. She hadn't noticed it there, all this time.

Were they keeping her drugged? Was that why Waverly felt so weak?

'Sleep now, child,' Anne Mather murmured in her ear. 'And when you're well enough to help us with the other girls, we'll take you off these medicines and you can join the group. Do you understand?'

'So if I don't help, you'll keep me like this?' Waverly asked, her voice already muffled.

No answer came, but she felt dry fingers stroking her cheek. Then they moved down her neck, cupping her larynx for one brief, terror-stricken moment.

Waverly wanted to lift her arms to Felicity, beg the girl to stay with her, but her arms were so heavy. She saw the shadow of Anne Mather next to the nurse, and the two women spoke in whispers. What were they going to do to her once she was asleep and helpless, alone in the dark? She struggled to keep her eyes open, but they felt as though they were filling with sand, and soon they were too full, too heavy not to close. The smallest part of her wandered away into a corner deep inside herself.

All sound and light disappeared, and finally she felt safe.

DORMITORY

When Waverly opened her eyes, she saw the nurse, Magda, standing over her with a syringe. 'What time is it?' Waverly said, her voice sluggish.

'OK, then,' Magda said brightly. 'Do you want to join your friends, or do you want to sleep?'

'I want to see my friends,' Waverly said. Her mouth was so dry, her lips stuck together.

Magda put down the syringe and sat on the edge of Waverly's bed. 'Pastor Mather will be glad to hear that.'

Waverly looked with longing at the water jug on the table next to her bed. Magda seemed to understand, and she heaved the jug up, wincing with the weight of it, and poured a glass of water for Waverly. The girl sat

up and drank, then poured herself another glass, and
another, before finally leaning back against her pillows.
The water revived her incredibly. She even felt strong
enough to make a demand. 'I want to see the other girls
right now.'

'Pastor Mather will want to speak with you first.'
Magda pressed a button on the table next to Waverly's
bed. 'In the meantime, let's get you bathed and dressed.'

The woman drew a bath for Waverly, gave her a
fluffy sponge and some soap that smelled of jasmine,
and left the room. The warm water felt soothing against
her stiff joints. Her entire right side was still very sore
from the shock she'd got, but it was starting to feel like
a healing soreness. Waverly had to keep her burned
hand dry, so washing herself took extra time. She lost
herself in the fragrance of the soap, pretending she was
home, that her mother might knock on the door any
second to nag, 'Waverly! Hurry up!' She wanted to hide
in the bathroom forever, but she could sense someone
on the other side of the door, waiting. So she got out
and dried herself with a cotton towel, then slipped into
the pink dress that was hanging on a hook in the corner.
It was a little girl's dress, quite unlike the hemp trousers
Waverly was used to wearing. It was comfortable, even
pretty, but it felt like a costume. It must have been
borrowed from a girl aboard the *New Horizon*, though
it looked newly sewn. Waverly combed her heavy wet
hair away from her forehead, took a few deep breaths,
and opened the bathroom door.

Anne Mather was waiting for her, sitting on the chair
next to the hospital bed, writing on a notepad. She

smiled when Waverly came in.

'You're looking much better. How are you feeling?'

Waverly flexed her hand. The edges of her burn pulled and stung a little, but the pain was bearable. 'I'm fine.'

'I'm so glad. I wanted to have a chat with you before you rejoin the rest of the girls.' The pastor patted the bed, meaning for Waverly to sit next to her. Waverly sat, but much further away than the woman had indicated, at the foot of the bed.

'Come closer, dear, I won't bite.'

Waverly did not move; she looked at the woman, who was staring over the wire rims of her spectacles, eyes locked on hers.

Pastor Mather's brow hardened, but her voice remained soft and lilting. 'Dear, I'm afraid I have terrible news. Our sensors have been unable to find any survivors from the *Empyrean*.'

Waverly imploded, entered negative space. A grey film moved over her eyes.

But no. This woman was a liar, and Waverly wouldn't accept anything she said. Kieran and her mother were alive.

Pastor Mather studied Waverly's blank face. Something clicked behind her gaze, and she said, 'You must be in terrible shock.'

'I must be,' Waverly said, her voice breathy.

'Dear, I know this is a blow to you, but we need you to help with the younger girls. They need a familiar authority figure, someone they can trust. Felicity has helped as much as she can, but, well . . .' Mather smiled warmly. 'I fear she doesn't possess your strength of character.'

Waverly made herself smile humbly at Pastor Mather's compliment. 'Well, I am the oldest,' she said.

'That's right. And with that comes some responsibilities, right?'

'I'll try,' Waverly said.

Anne Mather studied her until she seemed satisfied. 'Then I'll let you announce that we're still sweeping the area, looking for your parents. They'll like knowing we haven't given up.' She stood up and took hold of Waverly's hand. 'They'll be having their breakfast, I suspect. You can make the announcement there.'

Anne Mather led Waverly down a hallway into a large mess hall filled with oblong tables. Mather seemed exhausted and out of breath simply walking down the corridor. *There must have been a sickness here,* Waverly thought.

All 130 girls from the *Empyrean* were sitting at the tables, eating. They were wearing variations on the same frilly pink dress that Waverly wore, and their hair was pulled into pigtails. There was hardly any chatter. Only the clink of silverware against metal trays broke the silence in the room.

Little Briany Beckett looked up from her full plate, saw Waverly and let out a squeak. The other girls noticed, and there was a general cry as they rushed at Waverly, who was suddenly crushed by the crowd, all reaching, touching and grabbing, patting her back, yelling questions. She held up her hands. 'I'm fine, I'm fine!'

Anne Mather had moved away, but she was sitting to the side where she could watch Waverly's face. When she caught Waverly's eye, she raised her eyebrows expectantly.

Waverly forced her voice to sound calm, and she said, 'Everyone, I have an announcement to make!' She waited until they quieted, watching her with wide, hopeful eyes. They all looked the same, in their ribbons and dresses, as they stared at Waverly, waiting for her to speak. Serafina Mbewe approached Waverly in her quiet way and wrapped her chubby fist around Waverly's pointer finger, looking up at her face to read her lips. 'Pastor Mather gave me some information . . .'

'Auntie Anne?' asked Ramona Masters, waving her tiny fat hand over her head. She looked around the room, saw where Mather was seated, and toddled over to the woman's lap. Other young girls followed, leaning against the woman or simply sitting next to her on the bench. Surrounded by children, Mather looked like a kindly old grandmother. She seemed aware of the effect and chuckled, eyes sparkling.

This woman was a master manipulator. In the few days Waverly had been unconscious, she had managed to make most of the girls think she was their friend. The thought chilled Waverly.

'The crew here is trying very hard to find our parents.' She nearly choked on the sorrow that rose in her throat. 'They haven't given up, and neither should you.'

She heard a scoff and saw Samantha Stapleton staring at her with open contempt. Sarah Hodges stood next to her, shaking her head. Waverly would talk to them later.

'When will we see our mommies?' asked Winnie Rafiki. She was one of the youngest children. Her black curls hovered over her head like a chocolate cloud. 'I miss my mommy.'

'I do, too,' Waverly said. An image of her own mother's smile flashed before her, and suddenly she needed to scream.

Pretend. Pretend. Pretend, she told herself. *Be strong.*

The room was so quiet that all the girls were able to hear her whisper, 'I don't know when we'll see our families again. We just have to hope.'

'And pray,' Anne Mather said. She held her hands as if cupping something precious and invisible in the air. Her voice rose in a singsong: 'Dear Lord, please protect the crew of the *Empyrean*. Wrap Your love around them, hold them close, keep them safe. And if it is Your will, Lord, please show us the way to them. Help us find our lost brethren, and bring them into our fold. Until then, help these dear children know that they are precious beyond measure. Each of these girls will be cared for as our own daughters. We will love them and keep them safe until the day they can be reunited with their families, either in this life or the next. Amen.'

In this life or the next. Waverly heard the words, wanted to spit on them. But she swallowed her sickening grief and smiled at Anne Mather. Samantha and Sarah stared angrily at her, and she let her gaze linger on theirs until Samantha's eyes softened. Then she said, 'Now where do I get some breakfast? I'm starved.'

Serafina led her by the hand to the kitchen area, where trays of bread and fruit and cold chicken were laid out. Waverly fixed herself a plate and went back to the cafeteria, where she found Anne Mather making conversation with Samantha and Sarah, who were staring quietly at their own hands. Waverly sat so that she could see Samantha and waited until the other girl looked at her. Waverly made no gesture, she only stared, very seriously, showing that she hadn't given in. When Samantha's eyes shifted back onto Pastor Mather's face, they glinted with steel.

Waverly felt less alone knowing that she wasn't the only one who didn't trust Mather. If the woman was lying, she was doing it well, and her story was almost plausible. But Waverly couldn't forget that her 'rescuers' had shot people. Felicity had seen the shooting with her own eyes and could help her talk to the other girls, make them understand that Mather was a fraud.

She had to find a way to talk to Felicity alone.

ALLIES

Anne Mather's prayer rang in Waverly's ears as she tried to sleep that first night in the dormitory. Something the woman said had chilled her. *Each of these girls will be cared for as our own daughters.* There was something sinister beneath these words, turning like a gear, edging Waverly nearer to some frightening truth. It was on the borders of her mind the entire night, and it seeped into her dreams.

As our own daughters.

Waverly sat up in her cot with a start. She knew what Mather's next move would be.

She had to talk to Felicity immediately.

Waverly looked towards the doorway, where she

could see a smallish, pudgy woman sitting in a chair. Anne Mather had called her a 'matron', but Waverly knew the woman was really a guard. Though Waverly couldn't see her face, she thought the woman might be sleeping. As quietly as she could, Waverly slid out from under her covers and edged along the length of the cots, towards the outer wall where she'd seen Felicity.

Crawling, the whisper of her nightgown against her legs sounding unbearably loud, she finally reached Felicity and shook her shoulder. When Felicity's eyes flew open, Waverly put a hand over her mouth and whispered, 'Quiet.'

'What are you doing?' Felicity hissed.

'I think they're going to split us up. They're going to put us with families.'

'What?'

'They're going to separate us, so we can't talk to each other.'

Felicity's jaw clenched as she took this in. 'How can you be so sure?'

Waverly tried to think why she felt certain, but in the end all she could say was, 'Because it's what *I* would do if I wanted to control a bunch of kids.'

Felicity nodded pensively, but when she looked at Waverly her eyes were hard. 'Well, so what?'

Waverly shook her head. 'What do you mean?'

'What can we do about it?'

Waverly sat back on her heels.

'Waverly, they have all the power,' Felicity said. 'I don't care if you think I'm a coward. I mean to survive.

I'm not going to start anything with you, do you understand?'

'But what they've done—'

'What have they done? Really? They took us away from a ship that was about to explode.'

'I don't believe that.' Waverly glanced at the guard, but the woman hadn't moved. 'You saw what happened in the shuttle bay.'

'I saw a panic. That's all I know.'

'How can you—'

'Stop! Stop it!' Felicity balled her fists against her eyes.

'Felicity—' Waverly's voice broke, and she pushed her fingers into her lips to keep from crying. When she felt calm, she whispered, 'I need you. I can't do this alone.'

'Do what? There's nothing to do.'

'We can't stay here,' Waverly said tearfully. 'You see that, don't you?'

Felicity wrapped her arms around Waverly and pulled her into a hug. Waverly rested her head on Felicity's shoulder, inhaled her friend's sweet milky scent.

'There has to be a way,' she said.

Felicity pulled back and spoke through her teeth. 'I'm not going to let you get me killed.'

'If you believe their story about what happened, why are you afraid they'll kill you?'

Felicity's mouth straightened like a steel pin. 'If you *don't* believe their story, why aren't you afraid?'

I am afraid! thought Waverly. A cot creaked, and she

saw Samantha Stapleton leaning up on her elbow, listening to the conversation. Their eyes met, and Samantha nodded.

The woman by the door cleared her throat. She hadn't moved, but she sounded awake. Waverly pointed her finger at Felicity. 'Fine. Give up. But stay out of my way.'

She didn't wait for a response. As quickly as she could, she crawled over to Samantha's bunk. Waverly whispered, 'You don't believe their story either?'

'No. When do you think they'll split us up?' Samantha asked, her face stern.

'Soon. We'll need a way to communicate after we're separated—'

The lights blinked on. Waverly ducked to the floor. When she looked up at Samantha, the girl seemed to have lost her mind. She was rubbing her eyes, her mouth stretched across her face in apparent agony. 'What are you—' Waverly started to ask, but a sharp voice interrupted.

'What do you think you're doing?'

The matron stood over her, short arms folded over her puffy chest, eyes on Waverly.

'It's my fault for crying. She was trying to comfort me!' Samantha cried out. Somehow she had produced actual tears. 'She heard me crying and she came over to see if I was OK.'

The woman sat on the cot and wrapped her arms around Samantha, who dissolved into the most convincing crocodile tears Waverly had ever seen.

'There's a love,' the woman crooned, rocking Samantha back and forth. 'There's a dear heart.'

The woman nodded reassuringly at Waverly, so she went back to her own cot, watching as Samantha sobbed into the old woman's shoulder. The sight almost made her smile, and she buried her face into her pillow. By the time Samantha's tears had stopped and the woman turned off the lights, Waverly's fear had subsided into something else. Something hard and wily.

Soon, it was time to wake up and get dressed. The girls were all seated at the breakfast tables, eating quietly, when Anne Mather came into the room, a mournful expression on her face. She leaned heavily on the first man Waverly had seen since coming aboard the *New Horizon*. It was the man with the scar who had taken the girls to the shuttle bay. He smiled at Waverly with oily lips. Waverly shrank away with her plate of food.

Anne Mather held up a hand. 'Girls, I have some news about the *Empyrean*.'

The room faded into silence, and all the girls looked at her, waiting. Waverly thought everyone must be holding their breath, for the only sound in the room came from the man with the scar as he brushed his fingertips back and forth along the thigh of his trousers.

'We've located some wreckage, dears,' Anne Mather said. 'I'm afraid it's not looking good.'

Several girls melted into mournful cries.

'What do you mean, wreckage?' Sarah asked, her face perfectly neutral.

'I think it's best if we simply show you. Please follow me,' Anne Mather said. She held up her hands until a few of the youngest girls came up to her, and she shepherded them out of the room.

Waverly picked up Serafina Mbewe, who was crying. Other girls ran to catch up with Mather, pulling on her tunic, asking desperate questions. The procession felt like a dream. The girls followed Mather and her companion through the corridor, which looked identical to the corridors of the *Empyrean*. It was the first time Waverly had been let out of the converted cafeteria, and it hurt her to be walking hallways that looked so much like home. They took a left towards the port side of the ship. Double doors slipped open before them, and once again they were in a shuttle bay.

Waverly gasped. This place was identical to the shuttle bay on the *Empyrean*, down to the placement of the shuttles and OneMen. Memories of the shooting flooded through her as she walked towards the air-lock doors. She looked at the shuttle nearest the air lock, which was where she'd stood when she last saw Kieran, when he and Seth begged her not to go aboard. If only she had run the way they'd told her.

Suddenly she missed Kieran so much she could hardly breathe.

Anne Mather gestured for the girls to stand in a circle surrounding what at first looked to be a rock, but which, Waverly realized, was a hunk of melted metal. Serafina kicked her legs to be let down and Waverly lowered her to the floor.

'Before I tell you what this is, girls,' Mather said, 'I want to say that we're still looking for your families.'

The girls formed a circle around the lump on the

floor and were all staring at it. The man pulled a stool towards the centre of the circle, and Anne Mather sat down, hands on knees, a regretful expression on her face.

'This is the first bit of debris we've been able to locate. We've run some tests, and it's quite clear to us that this is from the hull of the *Empyrean*. I'm so sorry, but this is confirmation that the *Empyrean* has been destroyed.'

Someone cried out. Waverly thought it sounded like Felicity, but she didn't want to look. She felt so sickened that she had to concentrate on standing up and breathing. The metal sucked at her mind, forced her to consider that perhaps her home really was gone.

Anne Mather clapped her hands to get everyone's attention. 'We haven't given up on the hope that there may be survivors aboard shuttles, and we're still searching, but I think we all must be prepared for the worst. The way this metal was denatured suggests a thermonuclear explosion. They may not have had enough warning for a shipwide evacuation.'

The walls echoed with cries from the girls. Waverly's mother, Kieran, Seth, everyone she'd ever known, vaporized into ash. Did they suffer? She couldn't hold it back any more. Days of fear and sorrow crowded in on her, and she covered her face with her hands and wept.

'Girls, you must have faith,' Anne Mather said. 'It can be hard to search this nebula. Our radar has a limited range, but we're still looking for shuttle craft. They might still be out there. In fact, I believe they are.'

The girls quieted. They looked at Mather with hope

in their eyes. Even Waverly felt herself clinging to this story, wanting Mather and her crew to succeed.

A stern look from Samantha tugged at the corner of Waverly's vision. *Don't you believe it,* she seemed to be saying. Waverly nodded, wiped away her tears and willed herself to hang on to hope. Not the intoxicating hope Anne Mather was offering. Her own hope.

She felt a tug on her collar. Serafina was biting on her lip so hard that blood spread in a thin red line between her lips. Waverly mouthed, 'It's going to be OK.'

Serafina looked doubtful, but her teeth released her bloody lip.

Anne Mather held up a hand to gather the girls' attention. 'Until we find the survivors, I wonder, are you really comfortable in the cafeteria? How are those cots serving you?'

Some of the girls shook their heads. Amanda Tobbins raised her hand and said, 'My blankets are itchy.'

'Wouldn't you like to have your own beds? Your own rooms? With nicer blankets?'

Waverly raised her hand and spoke loudly. 'I like being with my friends. I don't want to be apart from them.'

As she expected, a cry rose among the girls, and Waverly could see several friends clutching each other, terrified of being separated. Anne Mather studied Waverly, detached and calculating.

'All right,' the woman said indulgently. 'That sounds fine for now. You can stay in the dormitory until a more permanent situation can be arranged. In the meantime, how would you like to see the other parts of the ship? I think a tour is long overdue.'

Waverly watched as Mather struggled to her feet with help from the scarred man. The man himself moved sluggishly, like the nurse, like Mather, like the matron last night. Every adult aboard this ship seemed weak and tired out.

An idea in the back of Waverly's mind started working. There must be some reason for their weakness, something she could use. She *knew* it. She had only to think.

'Dear . . .' Waverly felt a hand close around her elbow and turned to see Anne Mather smiling at her. 'I wonder if we could have a word?'

'About what?' Waverly asked. Her skin crawled where the woman touched it, but Waverly allowed the older woman to hook arms with her and stroll down the corridor.

'I need your advice.'

Waverly let the silence hover between her and Mather until the woman continued.

'Why don't you skip the first part of the tour and join me for some tea?' The woman smiled at Waverly, who found herself smiling back, almost naturally. 'I think you and I should get to know each other better. You're a smart girl, and I'm sure you've got lots of questions.'

'That sounds fine,' Waverly said, hoping her voice didn't betray her racing heart.

THE PAST

Anne Mather led Waverly to what would be the Captain's office on the *Empyrean*, but here the room had a feminine quality. Embroidered tapestries of scenes from the Holy Book hung on the walls, golden and shining, and a carved wooden dove hovered above her desk. Clearly this was Mather's office, and she was the ship's Captain, though Waverly noticed that no one called her Captain. They all called her Pastor.

An earthen teapot was sitting on the desk, and Mather poured a cup for Waverly, then one for herself, and leaned back in her chair. She looked towards the porthole, showing her delicate profile to Waverly as though conscious of the tableau she was creating.

'When we first entered the nebula, I thought it was beautiful, didn't you?'

Waverly glanced at the ruddy gas rushing past the window. It was dense in this pocket, and visibility was practically nonexistent. 'I miss the stars.' Waverly sighed.

'Yes, that's just how I feel.'

Waverly sipped at her tea, refusing to acknowledge that she had even this small thing in common with Mather.

'Chamomile. Good for the nerves.' Mather stared at Waverly over the rim of her teacup. When the girl looked at her, she took a sip, then tilted her head as though noticing something new about Waverly. 'I'd forgotten how beautiful young faces are. Really, you're such a delight to look at.'

'Why did you rendezvous with the *Empyrean*?' Waverly asked. It wasn't her most burning question, but she had a feeling it was the key to everything that had happened.

Mather set down her teacup resolutely. 'How well did you know Captain Jones?'

'I saw him every day.'

'Did he seem . . . honourable to you?'

Waverly let her eyes drop. 'He was a good leader.'

'Charismatic and intelligent, to be sure. But did he seem like a good man?'

'Yes,' Waverly lied, ignoring the memory of the Captain's eyes plunging down the length of her body each time she passed him in the hallway. When Waverly's figure began to mature, she found herself disliking many of the men on the *Empyrean.*

'I trained with him before we left Old Earth. I wonder if you knew that.'

Waverly didn't know, but she didn't give anything away as she looked at Mather.

'We were in one of the orbital biospheres while the climatologists were designing the ships' ecosystems. We spent four years together with a small crew.'

Waverly picked up her teacup and sipped. The tea was sweetened with honey, and she licked droplets from her lips.

'I'll spare you the details, Waverly, but the Captain and I didn't get along.'

'Why not?' Waverly said, staring at the tea leaves in the bottom of her cup.

'We had very different ideas about morality. Decency.' The last word issued from between the woman's teeth like a shard of glass. 'He believed that people should be able to do whatever they wanted to whomever they pleased. And I didn't.'

'Are you talking about sex?'

Mather smiled bitterly. 'Not exactly.'

Waverly took another sip of her tea. She felt unsettled.

'You don't believe me, do you.'

This caught Waverly off guard, but she did her best to hide it. 'About what?'

'About why we came for you girls.'

Waverly shrugged.

'I don't blame you.' The woman got up and looked out the porthole, her fingers knotted behind her back. 'I didn't tell you the whole story. There's a reason we

wanted to rescue the girls first.' Mather walked around
the desk, placed her fingertips on Waverly's trembling
hands. 'You were unsafe on the *Empyrean*. We knew
you oldest ones were getting to be young women, and
we didn't want you to live through what happened to
us.'

'Who is "we"?'

'Myself. Magda. Ruth, the matron who watched over
you girls last night. There are others. The women who
are old enough to remember what Captain Jones really
is.'

Waverly stared out of the porthole at the nothing
outside. She didn't want to hear this.

Mather sat heavily on the desk and leaned over
Waverly. 'I don't know if I can describe what it was like
on the biosphere with Captain Jones and his friends.'
She levelled her gaze onto Waverly's eyes. 'Tell me, did
the men on the *Empyrean* ever make you feel . . .
frightened?'

'No,' Waverly said, denying her memory of meeting
Mason Ardvale in the gardens and the slithery way he
spoke to her. 'Everyone was . . . *is* . . . really nice.'

'Really? Because the women on the biosphere had a
very different experience.'

Waverly said nothing.

'It began with compliments. Captain Jones . . . well,
he was only a lieutenant then. He started it. At
mealtimes, he would remark how beautiful my eyes
were. Things like that.' Mather laughed at Waverly's
expression. 'You wouldn't know it looking at me now,
Waverly, but I was once beautiful. I felt flattered at his

attentions. Soon the others followed his lead, and all the women in the biosphere were getting lots of compliments. We enjoyed it, at first.'

The woman stood up from her perch on the desk and, supporting part of her weight with one hand on the creaking wood, walked back to her own chair, where she collapsed with a sigh.

'After a while, the compliments seemed to change. How can I describe it? I would be trying to give Jones a progress report on some seedlings, and he would interrupt to tell me how nice my blouse was. Only he wasn't talking about my blouse.' She pulled on her tunic, smoothed it over her frame with fluttering hands. 'Soon it seemed as though I couldn't get any work done without someone interrupting to tell me how beautiful I was. And then . . .' Her voice faded and she looked out the window. 'The tone changed.'

A part of Waverly couldn't help hearing this. She'd got all kinds of compliments from some of the men aboard the *Empyrean*. Captain Jones always remarked on how tiny her waist was and, just like Mather, she didn't feel as though he were talking about her waist. And the men of the Central Council seemed to look at her with appraising eyes. It was as if all the men on the *Empyrean* had taken their cues from Captain Jones about permissible behaviour with the girls. Or maybe Captain Jones had chosen a crew that thought the same way he did.

'I remember one night,' Mather went on, 'the men stopped listening to us. We were in the cafeteria, eating our rations, and Ruth made some comment to

Lieutenant Jones about how we should check something in the water-treatment facility. None of the men responded. They just went on talking to each other as if they hadn't heard. She repeated herself, and I even tried to get their attention, but they laughed as if we weren't even in the room. That's when I started feeling afraid.'

Mather poured herself another cup of tea, and Waverly noticed that the stream of liquid was trembling. Mather took a few furtive sips and set down the cup again. 'It happened to Ruth first.'

'What happened?'

'They called it a "party". I can't describe to you how it changed her. She went from being a vibrant young woman to—'

'What happened?' Waverly shouted. 'What are you talking about?'

One of the guards looked into the room, but Mather waved him off. 'I think you know what I'm talking about, Waverly. I can see it in your face.'

'I have no idea . . .'

'Yes, you do. You know the men I'm talking about. Who they are and what they're like. You *know*!' Mather pounded on her desk. 'They made their way around to all the women on the crew.'

'I don't believe you.'

'It wasn't quite violent, that's the difficult thing. It was cajoling, teasing, begging, nagging. Talk about how we're building a new society, how the old rules don't matter any more, how we had to maximize our potential, make sure there would be plenty of babies.

They had the audacity to claim it was about fertility. We relented, each of us. Gave up the fight. Stopped resisting. Out of fear, I suppose. But, mostly, we desperately wanted to be chosen as crew members on one of these ships.' The woman laughed, her smile sour. 'People romanticize Old Earth, but, believe me, it was a horrible place by the time we left. Almost the entire planet had turned to desert. It was hard to live there, for women especially. We needed to seem like we could play along. Fit in. So we did what we thought we had to do. We . . .' The woman sighed, her voice distant. 'We *let* them.'

Waverly was suddenly aware of the engines vibrating through the floor underneath her. They seemed to bend the space around her, turn her mind upside down.

'That isn't even the worst of it.' Dimly, the woman smiled. 'When both ships were having problems with fertility, you may remember that the research team on the *Empyrean* had a breakthrough.'

Waverly huddled her arms around herself.

'They transmitted the formula to us. It was a drug meant to stimulate the ovaries. Well . . .' Suddenly the woman dropped her face into her hands. When she looked up, her eyes were red rimmed. 'The formula they sent killed our ovaries. They sabotaged us.'

'That's not possible. There's no way the crew would do that. My parents . . .'

'Maybe not your parents, but the Captain's inner circle? Are you sure they're not capable of such a thing?'

Waverly shook her head. Images flew through her mind of the Captain and Mason Ardvale laughing together. They'd always seemed unsavoury, but could they do *this*?

'Wait,' Waverly said as the implications dawned on her. She felt cold, suddenly, and very afraid. 'Do you mean to say that there are no children on this ship?'

'That is precisely what I'm saying. And your Captain Jones is responsible.' Waverly started to deny it, but Mather held up a hand. 'I'll show you the records if you like, Waverly.'

'But that's crazy. Why would they want to make you infertile?'

'Power. They never liked the way we did things on the *New Horizon*. We were more religious and less . . . I believe they'd call it "freethinking". I think they wanted to make New Earth into their idea of a free society.' Mather shuddered. 'Well, I couldn't let them do that. It wasn't just about our own futures, Waverly. It was about your future, too. And the future of every generation of women to follow on New Earth. Do you understand what's at stake here?'

Outrage poured into Waverly. She was furious at Mather for making her doubt herself. But she did doubt. She couldn't help it. A great deal about the woman's story made sense and even confirmed her own impressions about how so many of the older women seemed to resent some of the men. Many times Waverly's own mother had taken her by the shoulders and made her promise she would tell her if any of the men bothered her. She would never say explicitly what made her worry, but Waverly knew that her mother was trying to protect her from something. Mather's story fell in line with all of this.

'I can see you're having trouble with this, Waverly. While I hate to cause you pain, I really think it's necessary that you see this.' The woman twirled a vid screen towards Waverly and pressed a button. The screen showed a much younger Captain Jones in a communiqué, speaking to Anne Mather. He looked strange without his beard. His face was thinner, and his eyes seemed somehow bluer.

'Anne,' he said, 'I don't know what you expect us to do. We've sent our research. I don't see how further help is possible.'

'You sent us a bastardized formula,' the voice of a younger Mather spat back. 'You ruined us.'

'It must have been a lab error.'

'No. The formula you sent was purposefully designed to ruin our fertility.'

'We're talking about a misplaced phenol molecule, Anne. An easy mistake.'

There was an unsteady pause, and then Mather's voice filled the void, shaking with rage. 'How do you know about the phenol? I never told you that.'

'When we heard about your problems, we checked it ourselves.' The Captain nervously pulled on his upper lip. For a moment he looked afraid, but then his features twisted into outrage. 'Do you know what you're accusing me of?'

'Of course I know. And now I expect you to make it right. We need to rendezvous as soon as possible, and we need some of your families to come aboard the *New Horizon*, or we'll all be dead in sixty years.'

'A rendezvous is impossible. You're nearly a light-year ahead of us!'

'You can increase acceleration. If we decrease, we can meet up in a few years.'

'Do you know what that would do to our crew?'

'Don't forget, the force would still be far less than Earth's gravity. No more than our bodies are designed for.'

'After a lifetime at low gravity? I can't ask that of them.'

'You must! Or I'll report your crimes to the authorities on Earth. They'll effect a mutiny.'

'There's nothing they can do to hurt me, Anne, and you know it.'

'So you admit it. You admit you sabotaged us!'

Captain Jones's face took on a vicious expression, and he pointed his finger at the vid screen. 'Listen, you frigid bitch, I'm not going to risk the health of my crew to satisfy your paranoid delusions.'

'I ask again. How did you know about the phenol, Captain? If you didn't send a bastardized formula?'

With a sour smile, the Captain said, 'What's the matter, Anne? Disappointed you won't be the Prophet of New Earth?'

Mather pressed a button, and the image of the Captain froze. The twisted look on his face frightened Waverly.

'So you see,' Mather said, 'we had no choice. I'm so very sorry you and the girls got caught in the middle. But we're talking about our survival.'

Waverly didn't want to buy into Mather's story, but

something about the Captain in the video seemed wrong, just as wrong as Anne Mather seemed.

'So you were lying about the decompression,' Waverly said. 'That wasn't why you came for us at all.'

'No, I wasn't lying. There was a decompression, but it merely hastened our actions. We didn't have time for diplomacy any more. We had to rescue you girls immediately, in whatever way we could.' Mather closed her eyes as though pained by the memory. 'We tried to prevent loss of life. It's looking more and more like we failed.'

The two looked at each other across the desk, taking measure.

'I think maybe that's enough for today, dear. You have a lot to take in.'

The woman struggled to her feet and walked with Waverly to the door, her hand on the girl's back. Waverly felt so confused that she wanted to burst away and run to some abandoned place on the ship where no one would ever find her. But she could only follow the guards as they plodded down the corridor towards the elevators.

Everything Mather said twirled like a sickening gyroscope in Waverly's mind, mixing up her thoughts. As she followed the guards, she tried to find a hole in Mather's story, but she couldn't. In truth, she believed what the woman said about how Captain Jones behaved towards the women on the biosphere, because her own experience confirmed it. Still, she did not trust Mather. Could not.

She barely noticed when the engines kicked into a

higher drive, making the floor shimmy. The artificial gravity inched up a notch. She felt heavier as she lifted one foot, then the other, thinking about what the Pastor had said. The guards seemed to feel it, too. They walked hunched, with laboured breathing, sweat beading on the backs of their necks. The ship must have increased its rate of acceleration just now, and the artificial gravity increased as a result.

Waverly stopped in her tracks.

Gravity.

She was flooded with understanding. The hunk of metal in the shuttle bay couldn't possibly be from the *Empyrean*, and the *New Horizon* couldn't be conducting any kind of search for survivors. Above all, Waverly finally understood why the adults aboard the ship seemed so sick and weak.

'Keep up,' said one of the guards breathlessly. Waverly ran to catch up to where they were waiting for the elevator.

By the time the elevator doors opened and she boarded with the guards, she was certain the *Empyrean* was still out there and that she'd found the key to getting back home.

IN THE
BANYAN TREE

Waverly met up with the rest of the girls in the tropical produce bay.

Though the rest of the ship was identical to the *Empyrean*, the agriculture bays looked completely different. The coffee trees were twice as large as the ones Waverly was used to. In fact, all the plants on the *New Horizon* seemed to thrive especially well. The tour guide, a smallish man in his fifties with a gentle voice, spoke with pride about how the crew had experimented successfully with different fertilization techniques that increased crop production by twenty per cent. Feigning interest, Waverly wove among the girls until she stood by Samantha and Sarah at the back of the crowd.

'Where did that witch take you?' Sarah hissed, and Waverly appreciated again how spirited this girl was. Her small body reminded Waverly of a sapling: if you bend it too far, it'll snap back and whip you in the face. She had a steel-trap mind and a determination Waverly found very comforting.

'She took me to her office to talk,' Waverly whispered, her eyes on the two sweaty guards who stood next to the tour guide, smiling benignly as they caught their breath. Felicity was standing off to the side, fingering the necklace that hung around her long neck. Waverly watched the two guards and the guide, waiting for one of them to look at Felicity with desire as so many men aboard the *Empyrean* had done. But they barely glanced at her. In fact, they were smiling warmly at the littlest girls, who were sitting on the floor staring up at them.

'The men here are different,' she said under her breath. Both Sarah and Samantha looked at her, puzzled. 'Did either of you ever feel . . .' Waverly froze for a moment. The tour guide had paused in his lecture and was looking at her, waiting for her to pay attention. Once he turned to point out the morphology of a vanilla tree, Waverly continued. 'Did you ever feel weird around any of the men on the *Empyrean*? The Captain's friends? Or the Central Council?'

'Why?' Samantha asked, suspicious. 'What happened today?'

'Is there something you girls would like to share with the rest of us?' the guide shouted. All the other girls turned to look at the three of them. Waverly opened her mouth to come up with an excuse, but once again, Samantha was ready.

'We were wondering what kind of tree that is.' She pointed across the room at some enormous, twisted-looking trees that lined the bay. 'I don't think we had those on the *Empyrean*.'

The guide seemed pleased. 'Those are banyan trees, and we have some magnificent specimens! Follow me!'

The man and the guards led the girls between rows of peanut plants to the banyan trees, whose roots were plunged into a swampy section of topsoil. The trees were unlike any Waverly had ever seen. They were huge masses of wooden tentacles, emerging from a base of roots that twisted together to form a trunk and then unravelled towards the ceiling in wide-flung branches. 'These are some of Old Earth's most wonderful creations,' the ecologist said wonderingly.

'They look good for climbing!' Sarah suggested, and the rest of the girls agreed.

'That's true, they are! Why don't you? You've been listening to me long enough. Let's take a break, and you girls can explore. Just don't leave the room.' He nodded to a guard, who pressed some buttons on a remote device. To lock the doors, Waverly guessed.

Waverly pulled herself onto the lowest branch of the nearest banyan tree. Samantha followed her, and Sarah crept up a branch slightly above the others. The tour guide and the guards watched the youngest girls, who were toddling off towards a sunflower patch.

'You missed the latest,' Samantha said, her eyes trained darkly on their three escorts. 'We've all been invited to what they're calling "family time".'

'What is that?' Waverly asked.

'We're each having dinner with a different family tonight,' Sarah said bitterly.

This was the reminder that Waverly needed: Whatever Mather knew about Captain Jones and his inner circle didn't change anything. The girls had been taken away from their families. Nothing justified that.

'I've realized something important,' she said to her friends. 'Have you two noticed how weak the adults are?'

'Yeah,' Samantha said pensively. 'It's weird.'

'I think I know why,' Waverly said. 'They had to slow the ship down to let the *Empyrean* catch up.'

'So?' Samantha rubbed at her button nose, a tic she had that made her seem anxious and ferocious all at once.

'So, how long do you think it took for that to happen?'

Sarah shrugged impatiently. 'A few weeks, I guess, considering how fast the *Empyrean* was going.'

'Wrong. It would have taken years for them to slow down, years for us to catch up. Remember what they always tell us in physics class?'

Sarah stared blankly for a moment, but then said, 'Yes! Each year we're covering millions more miles than the previous year because we're constantly accelerating.'

'Right. And each year, the *Empyrean* and *New Horizon* were getting further apart because this ship took off a whole year before we did. We're almost at the middle of the journey right now, so we should have been the furthest we ever would be. So think of the distance between the two ships.'

Sarah looked at the leaves above her as she considered this. 'But what does this have to do with them being weak?'

'They had to slow down to let us catch up. And, remember, the inertia from our acceleration is why we have gravity.'

Samantha got it first. 'So for the last few years, while they were slowing down, waiting for us to catch up . . .'

'They had weaker gravity. Or maybe none at all,' Waverly finished for her.

'But why wouldn't they have just turned around and pointed the thrusters in the opposite direction?' Samantha asked. 'They'd have got to us faster.'

This stopped Waverly. Of course, that was the original mission plan. Halfway to New Earth, both ships were supposed to cease their acceleration, turn around, and point the thrusters towards New Earth to slow themselves down. With the ships pointing in the opposite direction, slowing down would create as much a feeling of gravity as accelerating. So why didn't the *New Horizon* just do that? Waverly was stumped.

'The nebula,' Sarah whispered tentatively.

'Oh, my God, you're right,' Waverly said. 'They had to time it perfectly so that the attack could happen inside the nebula so the *Empyrean* can't track us with radar and get us back. It gives them a huge head start.'

'And Captain Jones probably didn't know they were coming until they were on top of us,' Sarah said. 'So they had the element of surprise.'

'But why not attack years ago?' Samantha asked.

'Right when we entered the nebula?'

'The ship isn't designed to function in zero gravity,' Sarah said simply. 'The plants and animals couldn't have survived.'

'So they probably slowed down as soon as they were inside the nebula,' Waverly said, imagining the time and the vast distances. 'The *Empyrean* has been crossing the nebula for the last year and a half . . .'

'So they were waiting here for even longer!' Sarah said.

'That would be years of muscle atrophy,' Waverly said happily. 'They might never fully recover from it.'

Samantha nodded. 'So we *are* stronger.'

'I think we're much stronger than they are,' Waverly said. 'But there's one more thing. We've had near constant gravity since we got here, haven't we?'

'Pretty much,' Samantha said. 'I felt lighter at first, but for the most part it's been pretty normal.'

'So how could they be gathering up debris from the *Empyrean*? To have constant gravity, they can't be stopping and starting and changing directions.'

Samantha let out a groan of relief. 'I knew they were lying, but you're right. If the *Empyrean* exploded, we'd have left the debris behind long ago.'

'So that hunk of metal is a lie,' Waverly said.

Tears tumbled onto Sarah's freckled cheeks. 'Thank God.'

Samantha's narrow face hardened. 'That bitch.'

'There's one more thing.' Waverly's breath caught in her throat. 'They don't have any kids on this ship,' she said softly.

Both girls looked at her, alarmed.

'What do you mean?' Sarah said.

'I mean they never solved the fertility problem.'

All three looked around the room at the other girls wandering through the gardens. Waverly wanted to scoop up the little ones and run away with them somewhere safe. She knew Sarah and Samantha were thinking the same thing.

'That's why they only wanted girls,' Sarah said. Her voice quavered, and she was pale.

'More and more of the girls are starting to trust her,' Samantha said, visibly shaken. 'We need a plan right away.'

'How will we make a plan? They're going to separate us!' Sarah said, too loudly. Waverly saw that the men were standing near the tree now. They might be listening.

'It's going to be OK,' Waverly said loudly, then whispered, 'We need to figure out how to communicate with each other. Any ideas?'

Both girls looked at Waverly, anxious. 'How can we figure out a plan before we know what they're going to do with us?' Samantha said angrily.

Samantha was right. Waverly was overtaken by rage that she was here, on this ship, with these problems. Days before, her biggest worry was about marrying Kieran. She should have said yes to him, with no hesitation. *Yes, Kieran, I will marry you. I love you.* He needed to hear that, and she should have given it to him.

'OK, break's over!' the tour guide called, and the girls began to gather around him once again.

'We'll just have to find a way,' Waverly whispered as Sarah started to climb down.

The tour extended to the granaries and the orchards, all perfectly manicured, before finally circling back to the dormitory. Once the girls were left to themselves, the mood became much more sombre, for naturally their minds returned to that twisted heap of metal Anne Mather had shown them that morning. Several of them were huddled in lumps on their cots, crying. Sarah went to each girl, whispering in their ears until their faces brightened. Waverly knew she must be explaining why that piece of metal couldn't be from the *Empyrean*.

Soon two men carried in trays of food, red-faced and straining with the weight. After they left, Waverly lifted one of the trays that had seemed so heavy to them. It was surprisingly light.

Waverly saw Felicity sitting on her cot at the back of the room, facing the porthole. The glow from the nebula looked smothering. How far away must they be from the *Empyrean*? How could they ever find home in all that pink sludge?

Waverly walked up to Felicity, put a hand on her back, and sat next to her.

'What do you want?' the girl asked irritably.

Waverly chose not to answer. Instead she leaned against her friend.

'You know, one time,' Waverly said, 'back on the *Empyrean*, Mason Ardvale tried to kiss me.'

Felicity's ears seemed to perk up at this, but her eyes remained on the porthole.

'I had to slap him. He got a bloody lip.'

'And he let up?'

'We were in an elevator. The door opened and someone came in.'

'You were lucky,' Felicity said with a sour laugh. 'That guy . . .'

Waverly held her breath. *Tell me what happened, Felicity. Let me help you.*

Felicity seemed to think better of what she'd been about to say and turned away.

'You've been hurt, haven't you?' Waverly asked as softly as she could.

'I won't talk about it with you.'

'Why not? Maybe it would help to—'

'Forgetting helps. Pretending it didn't happen helps.'

'I don't think so.' She reached out to touch her friend's wrist, lightly, but Felicity buried her hands in her skirt. 'Tell me what happened.'

'You'd have found out for yourself,' Felicity spat, 'if your boyfriend wasn't the Captain's favourite.'

This stung deeply, but Waverly tried not to be angry with her. 'Felicity, I want to help.'

'So now that Kieran isn't around you have time for me, I suppose?'

'What?'

'Come on, Waverly. Don't pretend. As soon as Kieran showed an interest in you, you never had time for anyone else.'

'That's not true.'

'It is true. So don't pretend to be all caring now. I've been on my own for a while now, with no one to talk to—'

'What about your parents?'

'My dad can't handle this, Waverly. He'd fall apart. Or get himself killed.'

'But your mom—'

'Told me to avoid them. On a closed metal box in deep space.'

'Them? Who?'

'It doesn't matter.' Felicity leaned her head against the thick glass. The skin around her mouth was loose, and Waverly saw little droplets of spittle playing at the corners of her lips. She'd known Felicity Wiggam her entire life, but there was nothing she could say to help her.

'I guess I wouldn't blame you if you didn't want to go home,' Waverly said.

'What makes you think it will be any different here?'

'It might be different. Isn't that what you're thinking?'

'You're so naive.' Felicity laughed scornfully. 'Don't you see what people are? They're animals. Every one of them.'

'Felicity.' Waverly grabbed hold of the girl's hand and squeezed hard enough to hurt, until Felicity lifted her eyes to Waverly's. 'We're animals, too. We can fight back.'

Felicity yanked her hand away. 'You idiot. It doesn't matter how hard you fight.'

'It matters to me,' Waverly said quietly.

'So fight, then,' Felicity spat over her shoulder.

Waverly stood up, fists clenched. 'I will.'

FAMILY TIME

Waverly's hosts for family time were Amanda and Josiah Marvin, and they were more nervous than she was. Amanda's long fingers trembled, and Josiah kept popping up to check the food, passing by a very messy worktable that was covered with tools and wood shavings.

'As you can see, Josiah has a hobby.' Amanda smiled. Wrinkles splayed out from her green eyes, but she had a gentle, kind face that gave her a certain agelessness. She indicated the several carved wooden instruments hanging on the walls. They were variations on the guitar, of different shapes and sizes, and beautiful in a primitive way. 'Josiah builds them. He's quite an accomplished musician. He plays music for the services.'

'Services?' Waverly asked.

'Church services. We all go.'

'I see.'

Amanda gestured towards a wooden bench, and Waverly sat down. 'I can't tell you what a pleasure it is to see young faces! I forgot what young skin looks like.' Amanda leaned forward as though she wanted to touch Waverly's cheek, but the girl drew away from her.

Waverly looked warily at the woman's open face, her high forehead and prominent cheekbones, and tried to think how she might get something useful out of her. 'I had tea with Anne Mather today and she said the same thing.'

'Thank goodness for Pastor Mather.' Amanda brightened. 'I don't know what we would have done without her. Everyone aboard the *New Horizon* was so despondent until she rose . . . until she was elected to lead us.'

'I've noticed people call her Pastor. On the *Empyrean* we had a Captain.'

'We did, too, at first,' Amanda said, her expression troubled. 'Captain Takemara.'

'What happened to him?'

Amanda shook her head. 'He got sick. It was so sad. He wasn't very old.'

'But then wouldn't his first officer have finished his term?'

Amanda looked at the doorway of the kitchen as though hoping Josiah would come in and rescue her.

'Well, actually, Commander Riley had committed suicide a few weeks before the Captain gave up command of the ship.' She blinked, forced a smile.

'So then Anne Mather took over.'

'Was *elected*,' Amanda said. 'By the church elders.'

'Elders?'

'I believe it was called the Central Council on your ship? Is that right?'

'I thought if the first mate couldn't take over there was supposed to be a general election, and everyone got to vote. Isn't that in the bylaws?'

'Oh,' Amanda said, chuckling, 'I don't know anything about politics. Do I, Josiah?'

Josiah had come into the room and was setting a pot of steaming vegetable stew on the dining table. 'It's true, Waverly. Amanda pays no attention to that sort of thing. She's an artist, you know.'

Waverly looked at the painting over the table. It was a portrait of a little girl with rosy cheeks and curly black hair. 'Did you paint that?'

'Yes, I did. Can you guess who that is?' she asked Waverly, a twinkle in her eye.

Waverly studied the apple cheeks and pointed chin, the square hairline and plump body, and with a sinking sensation said, 'That's Anne Mather, isn't it?'

'At the age of three. Wasn't she precious?'

The toddler's gaze was wide and innocent, her pink lips a rosebud, her fat hands wrapped around a corncob. She was indeed a beautiful child.

'I love to paint children! It has been . . . therapeutic. Naturally I haven't been able to work from live models,'

Amanda said. 'The Pastor was kind enough to loan me a childhood picture.'

'It's really good,' Waverly said. She wanted to believe that the woman was ignorant of what had happened on the *Empyrean*, because she instinctively liked her. She liked Josiah, too. He was shorter than Amanda, and he had wide-set brown eyes and a floppy mop of greyish hair. He puttered around the apartment while Amanda talked, but he always seemed to have one ear trained on his wife, and he smiled privately to himself at things she said. They loved each other, Waverly could see.

Josiah tossed his head towards the table. 'Soup's on, girls.'

Josiah ladled a savoury stew into Waverly's earthenware bowl. Large chunks of broccoli, tomato, and asparagus floated in a fragrant broth. Waverly took a piece of crusty bread from the basket in front of her and dipped it in. She was ravenous, but she felt gentle fingers on her elbow. Amanda smiled indulgently. 'We have our customs,' she said, and closed her eyes. 'Dear Lord, thank You for bringing Waverly to us safely. We are so grateful that You saw fit to bring these children into our fold.'

Waverly put down her spoon and lowered her eyes. She'd never said grace before in her life. As far as she knew, no one on the *Empyrean* did, not even Kieran and his parents. She felt fidgety and uncomfortable, but she folded her hands in her lap as Josiah and Amanda were doing until they said, 'Amen.'

Waverly bit into her bread. 'This is really good,' she said with a full mouth, and immediately felt ashamed of her poor manners. This felt like a regular dinner with regular people, and once again Waverly had to remind herself that she was a captive.

'So how did you like the tour of the gardens today?' Josiah asked as he broke his bread into small pieces and dropped them into his stew.

'They're beautiful,' Waverly said, and meant it. The gardens on the *New Horizon* were much better tended than on the *Empyrean*. There were fewer weeds. The wheat rows were straighter, the corn greener, the berries bigger and juicier. She supposed, without children to care for, the crew had flung themselves to the task of farming. 'We played on the banyan trees.'

'Those were my favourite when I was young.' Amanda laughed. 'Can you imagine Josiah and me as children? I was four and he was six when we were brought aboard the *New Horizon*.'

'So you remember Earth?' Waverly asked, wistful. She loved hearing about Old Earth and its blue sky. 'Do you remember rain? How it fell out of the air?'

'It was beautiful to watch,' Amanda said, 'but full of chemicals.'

'Why? What chemicals?' Waverly asked. Few adults on the *Empyrean* had been willing to talk about their planet of origin, she'd noticed. They always changed the subject if she asked too many questions, and no one ever gave her a clear picture of what had really happened to make their home world such a hard place to live. She'd always wondered why it was a secret. Her mother's explanation, that it was too painful for people to talk about, never felt entirely true. Something was being held back. 'How did chemicals get into the rain?'

Amanda shook her head. 'I have never understood it. Josiah? Do you?'

'I'm no climate scientist,' he said as he nudged a broth-soaked piece of bread with the back of his spoon. 'The factories got out of hand, or—'

'Pastor Mather said that the reason Earth collapsed was because people didn't pay attention to the signs God sent them. They were greedy and lazy, and because of that—'

'They were punished,' Josiah interjected.

'For what? What exactly did they do?'

Amanda let out an embarrassed laugh. 'We were so young. This is our home now.'

'Do you miss it? Being on a planet?'

'Every single day,' Josiah said. 'But it wasn't always so terrific, either.'

'I remember feeling hungry most of the time,' Amanda said before taking a huge bite of broccoli. 'My bones didn't form quite right as a child. I had to wear braces.'

'And there was lots of violence,' Josiah said. 'We're much better off here.'

'Especially now that you girls have come,' Amanda added. She smiled at her husband, and he briefly covered her hand with his own. Something private passed between them, then Amanda dropped her gaze and took a small bite, letting her spoon linger in her mouth.

'How is it?' Amanda asked, indicating Waverly's soup with a flick of her eyes.

'Really good,' Waverly said again. They ate in silence, the only sound the clink and slide of their spoons against the earthenware bowls. Waverly took another piece of bread, though she wasn't so hungry any more. She wanted something to do with her hands, some excuse for not talking.

'Waverly, I wonder if you'd let me paint you?'

Waverly stopped chewing, surprised. 'Me?'

'I'd love the chance to work with a live model. And you're so pretty, dear.'

'You haven't seen Felicity Wiggam,' Waverly said. 'She's absolutely beautiful.'

'I like your face. I'd like to paint it,' Amanda said. 'Just a simple portrait.'

'Amanda doesn't do nudes,' Josiah said with a chuckle. 'If that's what you're worried about.'

'And it would give us an excuse to visit more,' Amanda added. 'If that would suit you. I could get permission from Pastor Mather.'

Waverly put down her bread. 'I suppose that would be all right.'

Amanda stood and gathered the empty plates. 'Who's ready for oatmeal cookies?'

'À la mode,' Josiah added with a chuckle. 'Have you ever had ice cream?'

'We don't carry cows on the *Empyrean*,' Waverly said, and dropped her chin. Any mention of her home sent a jarring grief through her, and she had to swallow back tears. *It's still there*, she told herself. *They're still out there.*

There was an awkward pause before Josiah said

haltingly, 'You haven't lived until you've tried ice cream.'

Waverly found a way to smile at him. She tried to enjoy her oatmeal cookie, though the ice cream made her queasy and she couldn't finish.

She helped Josiah and Amanda do their dishes, and then they walked her back to the dormitory. She extended her hand to Amanda, who folded it between both hands, smiling down at the girl. As tall as Waverly was, Amanda was much taller. 'Remember, you're going to model for me. I'll arrange it with the Pastor.'

'That sounds fine,' Waverly said, and even let the woman give her a brief hug. She smelled of oil paints and fresh-cut tomatoes.

Once she crawled into her bed and the lights turned off, her thoughts turned to Kieran. He would never accept that Captain Jones had sabotaged the *New Horizon*. As for why he'd refused to help them, Kieran would say that if he'd increased acceleration, that would have increased the artificial gravity, and there would be no way of knowing how the crew and livestock would be affected. He was only trying to protect his crew.

But the Captain hadn't protected his crew, had he?

Seth had said that friends of the Captain led complicated lives. Waverly wished she could talk to him about it. Seth was less naive than Kieran, more willing to see the dark side of things. He didn't let his loyalties confuse his idea of the truth.

Was she being disloyal to Kieran, thinking these thoughts? She loved his simple trust and the way he believed in his friends. She knew that was the way to bring out the best in people. Seth would always be suspicious of others and a little rough around the edges.

No, Kieran was better.

Waverly wrapped her arms around herself and rubbed her own back, imagining Kieran's arms, Kieran's hands. She imagined him burying his face in her hair. He might even find a way to make her laugh, even now. He could always do that – cheer her up even when she was at her lowest.

'What would you say to me now?' she whispered into the silent darkness, and listened in her mind for a response. None came.

Waverly turned her face into her pillow. She bit the pillowcase, gnashing it between her teeth as she cried.

SERVICES

The next morning, the matron turned on the lights and clapped her hands. 'Get up, girls. You're in for a treat!'

Waverly sat up in her cot, confused. She and Samantha looked at each other, and Samantha pretended to clap her hands gleefully, making Waverly smile. She wondered why she'd never been friends with Samantha before. They had more in common than she'd ever thought.

Several women brought in simple black dresses and stockings, handed them out to each of the girls, and told them to dress quickly. Once dressed, the girls were given white lace kerchiefs to tie around their heads, covering their hair. The girls looked like the pictures of

Russian peasants Waverly had seen in a book of stories by Chekhov.

If this were a normal Sunday, Waverly and her mother would make waffles or pancakes and lie around reading old novels from Earth. Regina loved mysteries that reminded her of the home world. Waverly liked Victorian novels, with their descriptions of the English countryside, birdsong and genteel manners. The descriptions were so complete she could almost imagine what it would be like to stand in a place and be able to look at a horizon with nothing over your head but sky. In the afternoon, Waverly would draw a bath and soak for an hour before running off to meet Kieran in the orchards. Now, there was no bath and no books. Just rough black fabric that irritated her skin and a lace scarf that hid her hair and made her feel ridiculous.

The matrons had the girls walk double file down several flights of the central stairwell to the granary, the largest room in the ship.

Hundreds of people were milling about between rows of young wheat, talking together, laughing. Absolutely everyone wore black, the women in shapeless dresses that hung to their ankles, the men in tunics and leggings. Waverly saw Amanda and Josiah through the rows of wheat stalks, and they waved at her. She waved back and contrived a smile.

The girls walked single file between the wheat rows to an acre that had been cleared away. A stage had been set up beneath the large porthole that looked onto the veiled sky. Waverly could see a few stars in the distance, shining through the haze, and she hoped that meant they were nearing the edge of the nebula.

The matron gestured towards the front rows of chairs, where the girls sat down. Josiah walked onto the stage carrying a small guitar. He sat on a stool and, with a wink at Waverly, he began plucking the strings. His music echoed through the cavernous room, seeming to trickle between the stalks of dried wheat that hung over the heads of the congregation. Pastor Mather was sitting in a carved wooden chair, and on either side of her were an older man and a young woman, each holding a black book. Holy Books, Waverly guessed. All three of them were wearing white robes, in stark contrast with the rest of the congregation. Anne Mather herself wore an elegantly embroidered mantle, sewn in rich purple, red and gold – the only colour in the room. A similarly embroidered kerchief covered her hair. The people began filing into the rows of seats. Soon Anne Mather stood, the music died down and she walked to an altar at the centre of the stage.

'Welcome, all of you, on this, the two thousand two hundred and fifty-third Sunday of our mission to New Earth. Peace be upon you.'

'And peace upon you,' the congregation answered in unison.

'I wish especially to welcome aboard our guests, the refugees from the *Empyrean*, whose presence is a source of great joy to us all. Girls, please stand.'

Reluctantly, Waverly got to her feet, and the rest of the girls followed. The last to stand was Samantha, who hunched her shoulders resentfully.

Mather crossed the stage to stand over the girls,

holding her hands out, palms down. 'Dear Lord of the heavens, we ask that these girls learn to make a home for themselves aboard our vessel. We do not ask why it was Your will to separate them from their families. We must simply accept, and try to do our best to fulfil our obligations to You, both for the sake of our immortal souls and for the sakes of all future generations of New Earth. We will overcome any trial to fulfil our destiny.'

Mather took her place behind the altar and, smiling down at the congregation, lifted her hands. She seemed to glow from within, and Waverly thought that some special spotlight must be shining on her – a cheap effect to make her seem holy.

'Let us thank the wisdom of God for saving these girls and bringing them to join our family. Thank You, Lord, for sparing them from the fate that has met our brothers and sisters of the *Empyrean*. In Your wisdom You have seen into these girls' hearts, and have found them worthy of Your mercy. Like Israel fleeing the bondage of Egypt, our young sisters have come to Canaan in search of a new life, and we welcome them with glad hearts.'

Mather obviously meant to imply that the crew of the *Empyrean* had died because they were wicked. Waverly glanced at Samantha and Sarah, who seemed to hate what Mather was saying as much as she did. Though a few of the younger girls seemed to feel proud that they'd been 'chosen' by God as Mather suggested, most of the girls looked at the Pastor with distrust and anger.

After the services were over, Waverly sat in her chair, listening to the voices of the people around her.

Several of the adults were talking about what a wonderful sermon Mather had delivered. These people spoke loudly. But underneath these voices were softer ones, murmuring to one another in hushed tones. Waverly strained towards these quieter voices. Something in them called to her.

Maybe not everyone on the *New Horizon* believed in Anne Mather.

Waverly noticed a woman staring at her from across the aisle. It was the lector with the auburn braid who'd read the ancient writings for services. She had very pale skin and pale eyes, but fine, strong bones in her face. The lector nodded, and Waverly nodded back. The woman walked across the aisle, held out a hand.

'Peace be upon you,' the woman said, and laughed brightly. 'I always need to use the bathroom after services. Don't you?'

'What?' Waverly asked.

Almost imperceptibly, the woman raised her eyebrows, then walked away.

Did she mean for Waverly to follow her?

The woman walked towards the port side of the granary, looking back discreetly over her shoulder. Waverly started after her, but the matron stood in her way. A full head shorter than Waverly and twice as wide, she was like a tank. 'Where are you going?'

Waverly stood tall. 'I need to use the restroom.'

'I'll take you,' the woman said irritably. She led Waverly through the crowd. Waverly saw a great many faces turning eagerly to look at her as she passed, smiling in welcome. She smiled back, nodding as she went, though she felt tense to be the centre of so much attention. How could she and the girls escape when they were under so much scrutiny?

Waverly hoped that the matron would let her enter the bathroom alone, but the woman came right in with her. There were two stalls, and the woman with the chestnut braid was just leaving one of them. She politely held the door open for Waverly and, nodding at the matron, went to the sink to wash her hands.

There was no way to talk to her. And Waverly felt sure the woman wanted to tell her something. But with the matron there all she could do was go into the stall and pretend.

Once she was inside the stall, the door safely closed, something caught her eye. Spread out on top of the water in the toilet was a note scribbled on tissue paper. The bluish ink was just beginning to fade into the water, but the words were still legible:

You must not tell anyone about this. Not even your friends. If you betray me, I could be imprisoned, or killed. Those who disagree with Anne Mather have learned to be silent.

Members of the Empyrean *crew are being held in the starboard cargo hold. I don't know how many, or how they got there. I do not know what the Pastor plans to do with them. Some of them might be your parents.*

I thought you had a right to know.

Waverly's knees turned to liquid, and she had to sit

down. Spots crowded her vision. She forced her breathing to a steady rhythm to keep from fainting.

Her mother might be on this ship! If she could find her mother, if she could get to her and the other parents . . .

A sob escaped Waverly's throat. She covered her mouth with her hand, crying and laughing at the same time. She couldn't control herself.

'You OK in there?' The matron knocked on the door.

'I'm sorry,' Waverly said. 'I'm not feeling well.' Quickly she stood and flushed the toilet. The note twirled with the water, turning it blue, and went down the pipe just as the matron forced her way into the stall.

Waverly stood chest to chest with the squat woman. 'What were you doing?'

'I . . .' She knew she was acting strangely and tried desperately to think of an explanation. 'It's embarrassing.'

'Did Jessica leave anything . . .' The woman's eyes turned to slits.

'I thought I might be getting my period,' Waverly said quickly. 'It's not something I like to talk about.'

A smile plumped up the matron's pink cheeks. 'Oh, I see.'

'False alarm,' Waverly said with a shrug.

'But you do bleed monthly,' the woman said as Waverly washed her hands in the metal sink.

'Well, I'm almost sixteen.'

'So you're fertile,' the woman said as she opened the door of the bathroom. 'Pastor Mather will be pleased.'

On shaky legs, Waverly followed the matron out of

the bathroom. The voices of the congregation flooded around her like brackish water, made the room spin. Panic forced its way into every breath she took, and she had to bite back a sob. Being around so many people brought the truth home to her. The girls were hopelessly outnumbered here. They were trapped.

And these people could do anything to them they wanted.

No.

Waverly squared her shoulders. She *had* to find her mother and the rest of the parents. She had to find a way to leave this ship, no matter what happened.

And she would kill to do it.

PART THREE
MANOEUVRES

*The opportunity to secure ourselves
against defeat lies in our own hands,
but the opportunity of defeating the
enemy is provided by the enemy himself.*
— Sun Tzu, *The Art of War*

CONTAINMENT

At first, Kieran didn't care about the alarm sounding through the ship warning of a reactor leak. He could only stare out of the porthole as the *New Horizon* rotated to change course. Its powerful engines spattered blue light, and it sped away, disappearing into the nebula's haze. Harvard's shuttle followed close behind. Their only hope would be to tether themselves to the larger ship, or they'd never catch up.

Soon the area outside the ship was as peaceful as it had ever been.

She was gone. Waverly . . . For a crazy instant, he imagined bursting through the thick glass portholes to chase her. He would breathe the nebula.

He would swim through it to find her.

'We have to do something!' Seth Ardvale stood in the doorway to Central Command. He was shirtless and blinking blood out of his eyes. 'Don't just stand there! Chase them.'

'We can't change course,' Kieran snapped. 'Harvard's shuttle will never find us again if we do. They'll die.'

'We'll use the radar!'

'The radar was designed to work in a vacuum,' Kieran said distantly. He thought some part of his consciousness must be floating outside the ship. 'We don't have enough range in this nebula.'

'The shuttles can't keep up with the *New Horizon*!'

'They can if they latch on to it. They had time. I saw the whole thing.'

'What if they didn't?'

'Then they'll be back,' Kieran said simply. 'And we can change course then.'

'God! You're so –' Seth slammed his shoulder into the metal wall, then slid down to crumple by the door. For a guy like Seth, waiting, doing nothing, was near impossible.

'Kieran!' someone shouted through clenched teeth. 'Kieran Alden!' Mason Ardvale, Seth's father, scowled into the vid screen. He was transmitting from an elevator that was speeding down to the engine room. 'You've got to seal off the lower bulkheads. Seal them off!'

Kieran ran to one of the terminals and punched through the menus in front of him, searching for the bulkhead controls. He felt Seth behind him, watching everything he did. He finally found a folder marked 'Meltdown Containment Protocol.'

Could it be so simple?

'Wait,' Seth said, and reached a hand towards the keypad, but Kieran batted him away and tapped the button. A list began scrolling through a series of automatic functions, completing each as it went.

'Kieran! Stop!' Mason Ardvale's face, twisted with anger, appeared again in his vid console. 'What are you *doing*?'

'You said to seal off the lower levels!'

'You stopped the elevators! We're stuck in level two!'

'Oh God!' Seth snarled.

A sinking feeling seized Kieran. Had he killed them all? 'How do I undo it?'

Just then the whine in the alarms changed. A piercing tone drilled into Kieran's ears. The vid screen had blanked out, and two words appeared: 'Containment Critical.'

'Oh God, it's happening!' he heard Mason wail. 'Never mind, Kieran. We'll have to force bulkhead one open. But we won't be able to seal it again.'

Kieran buried his face in his hands. He'd screwed up everything. He couldn't do even a simple thing like seal off the doors to the engine room. It would take them twice as long to get down there.

'You might have killed everyone on the ship,' Seth said, his eyes fixed on Kieran like pebbles in cement. 'You don't listen.'

'Get out of here,' Kieran told him. He thought he might beat Seth to death if he didn't go right now.

But he didn't leave. 'You shouldn't push buttons if you don't know what they do.'

'There wasn't time. The leak was going critical. You saw!'

'You panicked,' Seth said.

'Go away,' Kieran spat at him. 'Have someone look at that cut on your forehead.'

Seth's fingers went absently to the cut, and when he saw the blood coating his fingertips, he got woozy.

'Go on,' Kieran said more kindly. 'There's nothing more we can do from here.'

Seth hobbled to the door, his hand pressed against the cut.

Kieran closed his eyes. Images of everything that had happened fluttered through his mind: Waverly turning away to go into the shuttle, friends and neighbours being shot and crumpling to the floor, the decompression, his mother struggling into a shuttle.

Mom.

Clumsily, he activated the com system and searched for a signal from the second shuttle, the one that had his mother, but there was no communication at all. He enabled all frequencies and, his voice husky with the strain, shouted into the microphone, 'Any and all *Empyrean* shuttles, please make contact. Where are you?'

He paused to listen but was met only with silence.

Where had his mother's shuttle gone? And when? Kieran tried to think, going over everything that had happened. That shuttle must have left when he and Harvard were trying to rescue the girls. Whoever was in it might be trying to surprise the *New Horizon* by approaching the enemy ship unheard and unseen.

Or the shuttle could be floating in space, its crew injured by the decompression and unable to make contact, or already dead. There was no way of knowing.

His mom. His mom might be dead.

And his dad probably was.

He got up in a daze and wandered into the central bunker, where the other boys were huddled. Many of them were curled into lumps on their cots. Some of them sucked their thumbs. Arthur Dietrich was pacing in a circle in the corner of the room, muttering, his blond hair mussed, his spectacles askew on his face. He looked as though he were either trying to solve a complicated puzzle or raving.

Arthur needed time to calm down, Kieran knew. Arthur was a coolly intellectual boy of thirteen with a freckled moon face and large blue eyes. When he spoke he sounded as though he had a stuffy nose, so his extraordinarily bright observations often took people by surprise. He was slated by the Central Council to work as the ship's head engineer, a job that suited him. Arthur seemed capable of living with great responsibility, for he thought about things before he felt them. He was thinking now, so Kieran decided to leave him alone.

Seth and several of the older boys were bunched in a group in the corner of the dormitory, and Seth was whispering to them. His head was wrapped in gauze with a spot of blood seeping through, and his eyes were glazed over. He must have taken a pill for his pain.

Kieran couldn't hear what he was saying to the other boys, but he could guess. Seth was telling them how Kieran had disabled all the elevators at the crucial moment. He was turning the boys against him.

Kieran knew he should confront Seth to set the record straight, but he didn't have the strength.

Seth had always annoyed Kieran, even before his interest in Waverly became apparent. As two of the oldest boys with the highest aptitude scores, Seth and Kieran had grown into a natural rivalry. But where Kieran was easy to train and likeable, Seth was sullen, recalcitrant in his lessons, and scornful when his teachers didn't know all the answers. Though nothing had been made official by the Central Council, Kieran was the presumed successor to Captain Jones, and he knew this drove Seth crazy.

Kieran remembered walking with the Captain to the studio for one of his broadcasts, and he'd said something to make the Captain laugh and pat his shoulder fondly. Just then Seth had turned into the corridor, and as he'd passed he'd shaken his head at Kieran, contempt in his eyes. Ever since then, Kieran noticed that the closer he got to the Captain, the more Seth seemed to resent him.

But Kieran knew it was Waverly Seth really wanted. He knew it from the way Seth's eyes followed her through a room, his face long, looking away when she glanced at him. Waverly had seemed airily oblivious to Seth's feelings for her, but now Kieran wondered. That last look before she'd boarded the shuttle had been for Seth.

Seth was more handsome than he was. Kieran's

amber eyes were nice-looking, but did they compare with Seth's laser blue? Seth was taller and broader in the shoulders, and his movements were forceful. Kieran wasn't short, but he had a slight build and, though he was well coordinated and strong for his size, he knew he didn't have the same masculine fierceness that made girls watch Seth as he worked in his garden, whispering to one another and giggling.

Kieran shook his head. After everything that had happened, how could he even be thinking about this? What was wrong with him?

My mind wants something trivial, he told himself. *I don't want to think about what's happening in reality. I'd rather invent petty little love triangles.*

He wandered through the dormitory aimlessly, between cots holding trembling boys, crying boys, shocked boys. Kieran barely saw what was in front of him, and he knew there were a thousand things he needed to do, but he was unable to think of a single action that would make a difference in what was happening. Until he reached the galley kitchen.

Whenever she was upset, Kieran's mother would make cocoa.

He'd make cocoa. And then he'd be able to think.

He took a mug from the long line of cabinets, filled it with boiling water, and, after searching through the huge amounts of emergency rations stuffed into the deep cabinets in the walls, found a box filled with cocoa packs. He dropped the brown powder into the steaming mug and sat on one of the metal stools that were bolted to the floor, stirring compulsively. He sipped at the hot liquid, letting it burn his lips and tongue, until he felt someone standing behind him. Seth's bitter voice asked, 'Who's in Central Command?'

'No one,' Kieran said. When he heard himself, he realized how it sounded. 'I was just going back.'

'No, you weren't,' Seth said. Kieran heard a snicker and turned to see that four other boys had followed Seth in. 'You're just sitting there.'

'If you think it's so important, then you go,' Kieran said.

'I will,' Seth said over his shoulder as he left the kitchen. The other boys followed him out. Sealy Arndt looked at Kieran and shook his potato-shaped head in disgust. These traumatized boys needed to believe there was someone in charge taking care of things. If it wasn't Kieran, they'd settle for Seth.

Kieran picked up his mug and walked across the tomblike corridor back to Central Command, where he found Seth and several other boys watching a monitor. Kieran leaned in to see what they were looking at, hoping that it would be an image of his mother's missing shuttle. But no. They were watching Mason Ardvale's crew as they feverishly worked in the engine room. Several of them wore radiation suits, but most worked in their regular day clothes. They were running back and forth, jabbing at controls, reading dials, adjusting valves. One woman ran, carrying a box of tools. She tripped on the clumsy boots of her radiation suit and fell, sprawling across the floor, tools flying out of the box she carried. No one stopped to help her.

They were frantic.

'They're trying to fix the mess you made,' Seth said.

'I didn't cause the meltdown, Seth.'

'You slowed them down. If they'd got to the engine room sooner—'

'If I hadn't sealed off the doors, the whole ship would have flooded with radiation,' Kieran said.

'Big hero,' Seth spat. 'They had to force the doors open to get into the engine room, and now they're damaged and they can't be sealed off. All of level one is full of radiation. You should have sealed off the levels one at a time.'

'That would have taken more time,' Kieran said, but he knew that in the other boys' eyes he'd lost the debate. They all glared at him. Sealy's eyes were hard like cracked mud. Max looked Kieran up and down as though choosing where to punch him, but when Kieran met his eyes he scoffed and looked away. 'I did the best I could.'

'Not good enough,' Seth said.

Kieran knew there was nothing he could do to contain the resentment that was spreading through the central bunker like a cancer. He was too tired and too sad to care what the others thought of him. He went to the Captain's vid screen, knowing that sitting in the Captain's chair would provoke Seth, and found the feed to the engine room. He watched, helpless, as the few remaining adults aboard the *Empyrean* struggled desperately to save the ship.

ZERO GRAV

For hours, Kieran, Seth and several of the older boys watched the crew in the engine room as they worked at an increasingly feverish pace. Kieran sat at his own screen while Seth and his friends huddled at another across the room, glaring occasionally in Kieran's direction. Hours in front of the vid terminal made his eyes burn. It was futile to watch because it was the same thing over and over. The crew would be working on clamping down a coolant leak when someone would call them over to take readings on some dials, and then they'd abandon the leak to deal with something even worse. They scrambled over one another like rats, accomplishing nothing.

Discreetly, Kieran flipped the switch to the port shuttle bay where the shoot-out had occurred, and he gasped. So many dead. At least three dozen, lying on the floor of the bay, totally still. He studied each and every shape, looking for some sign of his father, knowing that he'd find none. He recognized most of the bodies; many of them were parents of the boys in the bunker. They would have to be told. Kieran shuddered.

Quickly, he cut power to the cameras in the shuttle bay, hoping none of the other boys would enable them. He had to think how to break the news.

In the meantime, he should check on the little ones. Kieran got up from his seat, stretched his stiff back and walked out of Central Command.

Little Bryan Peters was going on his third hour of screaming for his mother. Kieran walked between the rows of four hundred metal cots and took the baby from Matt Allbright. Kieran tried to sit the little tot on his lap, but the boy just went on screaming. He wished he knew where Mr or Mrs Peters was, so at least the little boy could see them on a vid screen, but either they were on one of the shuttles or they were . . . gone. They weren't on the crew trying to repair the engines, of that much he was certain.

'Try hugging him,' Timothy Arden suggested with one finger stuck up his nostril. Timothy was eight years old, but he was reverting to the habits he'd had in kindergarten. A lot of the boys were doing that, sucking thumbs or dragging around a pillow and hugging it to their chests. Some of the older boys, like Randy Ortega and Jacque Miro, were able to put aside their fears about their families and help the littler boys with rehydrating emergency rations. But as Kieran looked around the dormitory, he could see that the boys were confused, terrified and horribly worried about their parents and sisters. Kieran knew someone had to take control and bring back order to the boys' lives. That's what Captain Jones would do. But, as he looked around him at the chaos and fear, he had no idea where to begin.

'Get on com console six. Dad wants to talk to you,' Seth snapped as he came across the hallway from Central Command, rubbing at the blue circles under his eyes. Everything about Seth was sullen: the dark look in his eyes, his hunched shoulders, his abrupt stride as he crossed the room. Kieran knew it probably bothered Seth that his own father wanted to talk to Kieran instead of him.

Kieran went into the dark Central Command room and sat at the Captain's console. He saw Mason in the vid display, panting. He looked pale, his cheeks and eyes hollow, his lips dry and cracked.

'How are the boys?' Mason asked.

'Not so great. I wish we could get some of their parents to them.'

Mason shook his head. 'We'd flood the ship with radioactive particles if we opened up the bulkheads. We can't chance it.'

'I know,' Kieran snapped. He was irritable, and it was hard to keep his feelings inside. 'I'm sorry I closed all the doors. I was just—'

'It was the right thing to do.' Mason coughed into his palm.

'Put on a radiation suit, Mason!' Kieran said, knowing what the man would say.

'There were only enough for the regular engineering crew of six. We're taking turns.' The man's face dissolved, and for a frightening moment, Kieran thought he might cry. But Mason pulled himself together, biting hard on his lip. 'Listen, we need you to prepare the ship for an engine shutdown.'

'There's no other way?' Kieran knew that shutting down the engines was a measure of last resort. The engines not only moved the ship, they kept everyone and everything on the *Empyrean* alive. 'For how long?'

'We're hoping we can get them working in six hours.' Mason coughed into his palm again. 'Listen, with the engines off, we'll no longer be accelerating. That means no inertial force.'

'Which means no artificial gravity,' Kieran finished for him. He imagined one hundred and twenty-two boys floating around the bunker, and he cringed. Things were already chaotic *with* gravity, but without it, things would be truly crazy. 'Are you sure there's no other way?'

'With the engines on, everything is too hot to repair.' Mason held up his knuckles, which were blackened and blistered. 'I got these wearing two pairs of thermal gloves.'

Kieran cringed.

'Listen. You've got to get all the boys to go through every room in the central bunker and fasten down anything that's not attached to the walls. Seal the fishery tanks. Close every door on the ship, except for the ones down here. And shut down ventilation. We can't have a thousand tons of topsoil floating into the air filters in the living quarters . . .' He seemed to swoon for a moment, and a sickening terror swept through Kieran. How were the other adults doing? Were they all this sick already? The radiation must be very strong if it was already poisoning them. Mason gathered himself and said quietly, 'You better take notes.'

For twenty minutes, Kieran feverishly wrote down everything Mason told him to do, asking questions along the way. He had only three hours to get everything done before they powered down the engines. For a few minutes, Kieran stayed in Central Command to draw up categories of tasks and decide which boys to send where. Then he swallowed hard. He'd never been in charge like this before.

When Kieran went back to the dormitory, tiny Bryan Peters was still screaming his head off. Ali Jaffar was bouncing the baby on his knee, talking quietly in his ear, but the toddler didn't seem to hear. His face was purple, the tip of his nose was white, and his tears had dried into salty stains on his fat cheeks. Kieran called into the room, 'Hey! Everyone! I need your attention!' But the boys further away couldn't hear him over the baby. In frustration, Kieran cried out, 'Can someone please shut that kid up?'

Seth stomped across the floor, grabbed Bryan's fat arm and shouted in his face, *'Shut up! Just shut the hell up!'*

The baby was startled into silence.

Kieran knew that Seth was unravelling in his own

way, just like everyone else. Still, yelling at a baby like that was wrong, but Kieran was too tired to deal with anything but the task at hand. He called into the room, 'We've got some important stuff we've got to do! Gather around!'

Some of the boys approached him, but lots of them didn't even seem to hear. He yelled louder, and that seemed to get their attention, but already his voice was giving out.

'We've got orders from the repair crew, and we've got to work fast. I need all the boys over the age of ten to come to the front of the room. You'll be the crew leaders.'

It was clear the boys in the back hadn't heard a word of what he'd said.

Out of the corner of his eye, he saw Seth leaving the room, swinging his elbows behind him in that defiant, angry walk he had. Kieran thought of going after him, but maybe it was better if Seth stayed out of the way.

'We're going into zero gravity in three hours,' he said over the muttering in the crowd. His voice cracked. 'That means we've got a lot of work to do to prepare the ship.'

'Are they shutting off the engines?' asked Arthur Dietrich. The worry in his blue eyes was magnified by his thick glasses.

'Yes, Arthur,' Kieran said. 'And you're in charge of readying the central bunker, and reviewing with everyone how to operate in zero grav.' They'd been briefed about zero grav in their classes, of course, but never once in forty-two years had the ship ever powered down. Zero gravity would be a new experience for all of them, and there was a lot to know. How to eat, how to drink, how to pee, how to sleep . . . the list was endless, but Arthur could handle it.

Boys chattered in the back, and Kieran tried to yell over them, but his voice cracked again. He was too tired already, and there was so much work to be done.

He felt something being pressed into his chest and looked down to see that Seth had gone for the Captain's loudspeaker and was offering it to him with a disdainful look. 'Here,' he said, and walked away.

All the boys saw Seth offer this simple solution to Kieran, and all of them were looking at Seth, impressed. Kieran tried to ignore his own embarrassment that he hadn't thought of the loudspeaker himself, and he pressed the microphone to his lips. 'Listen up, now, we've got a lot of work to do.'

Kieran chose the best boys to head up the efforts. Mark Foster was in charge of the crew to close all the manual doors and vents in the forward bays, including the grain areas and the mills and processing plants. Hiro Mazumoto was in charge of securing the poultry farms and making sure the birds were fed and watered before the ship lost gravity. Arthur Dietrich took four boys to organize all the harnesses, suction bags and other equipment that would be needed for zero grav. Kieran was almost done giving out the orders and was about to let the crews go when he felt a tug on his shirt.

'What does Dad want me to do?' Seth asked. He stood behind Kieran, looking over his shoulder at his notes.

Kieran had been so absorbed that he hadn't noticed him there.

'Uh . . .' Kieran ruffled through his notes. 'You go with Arthur's crew.'

'What about the farming equipment?' Seth spoke so loudly, the boys stopped to listen.

'Mason didn't say anything about—'

'Someone better make sure all the harvest and planting equipment is tied down,' Seth said through the side of his mouth.

Seth was right. A loose tractor could punch through the hull if the engines reengaged unevenly. Kieran could feel himself blanching. He should have thought of this if he was really in charge.

'Actually, that's right, Seth,' he said, trying to act as though he'd already considered it. But he could hear how inept he sounded. 'Why don't you head that up? Take a few boys with you.'

'Yeah, OK.' Seth rolled his eyes and walked away.

Several boys shook their heads with disdain.

Seth tapped his crony, Sealy Arndt, a short, squat boy whose blockish head seemed to rest directly on his hunched shoulders, along with several other smaller boys, and they all went to the elevators that led to the large equipment.

As soon as Seth left the room, Bryan Peters started to scream again.

Kieran didn't have time to soothe him. Rubbing his tired eyes, he marched back to the control room, where he sat in front of his vid screen, watching each team's progress, shouting orders through the ship's intercom when he saw the boys missing details or if they weren't moving quickly enough. Only Seth's team moved with precision. Only Seth seemed to think of everything and knew how to do it all. When one of the smaller boys lagged behind, Seth grabbed his arm and barked orders into his ear. That made all the boys work faster.

Nearly three hours had passed before Mason's haggard face reappeared on Kieran's com screen. The man looked twice as exhausted as he had before. 'How's it going?'

'The boys in the poultry farm are feeding the last row of chickens, and Arthur is organizing the zero grav gear.'

'Call everyone back,' Mason said. 'What doesn't get done doesn't get done. You'll have to deal with the damage later.'

Mason's voice sounded so sorrowful, so resigned. Kieran paused. What did Mason mean, *you* will have to deal? Why not *we*?

That terrifying question led to others, equally terrifying. How were the adults going to get back to the uncontaminated areas of the ship if the bulkhead doors couldn't be opened?

'Mason,' Kieran said slowly, 'once the engines are fixed, how will you get out of there?'

Mason just stared at Kieran.

'We could . . .' Kieran desperately reached for an idea, however preposterous. 'Construct an artificial air lock outside the second bulkhead doors. Like a tent or something.'

'Kieran . . .'

'I know we're just kids, but we could do that. And then you can come out of there!'

'A tent isn't going to stop radioactive particles, Kieran, and you know it.'

'Or we could transport you out through the air lock. We could use OneMen—'

'Kieran.' Mason held up a hand. 'There's no time, son. And it wouldn't matter anyway.'

Kieran lifted his eyes to Mason's weary face. The man's eyes met his, and all the truth passed to Kieran in an instant.

The adults weren't planning on coming back.

Kieran's face relaxed into a mask of horror.

'Listen,' Mason said gently.

Kieran could only shake his head. No. This wasn't happening.

'Kieran, you've got to make an announcement. Get all the boys back to the central bunker, and get them strapped into their bunks, OK?'

Kieran opened his mouth to speak. He couldn't. Seth's father was going to die.

'You've got a half hour!' Mason yelled hoarsely. 'Do it!'

Kieran reached for the speaker to make a general announcement. He pressed the button, cleared his throat, and somehow made his voice work. 'Everyone. All boys. Report back to the central bunker immediately. We're going to zero gravity in thirty minutes.'

He set the message to loop and leaned back in his chair. He could hear the baby screaming in the other room. Until now, Kieran had been too busy to notice.

But there was something in the little boy's voice that sounded different.

Mason was still on the vid screen, looking at him. 'You're doing great, Kieran.'

'Thanks,' Kieran said, but he knew this wasn't true. The boys were falling apart. 'What's going to happen?'

'You're going to be OK. You just have to hold out until the shuttles can redock. I'm sending you a personal text with all the security codes for ship's functions.'

'I can't run this ship,' Kieran said. 'I don't know—'

'Hey.' Mason's smile was gone. He was deadly serious. 'There's no one else.'

What about your son? Kieran wanted to ask.

Distantly, Kieran heard little Bryan hiccup, and hiccup again. Someone should give the poor kid—

'Oh, my God,' Kieran cried, and stood up. 'I've got to go!' he yelled at the screen. Without waiting for Mason to say goodbye, he ran down the corridor at top speed towards the dormitory. He found Bryan lying on the floor, waving his arms at the ceiling weakly, still screaming, but mournfully. That's what had changed in the baby's cries. Before he'd been crying for help, now he was crying in despair. Kieran scooped the little boy into his arms and carried him to the galley, where he filled a grav bag with water.

The baby reached towards the tap with plump hands, nearly toppling out of Kieran's arms. Kieran held the container to the little boy's lips and watched with relief as the baby sucked down the water in great, frantic gulps.

How long since anyone had given the poor little boy something to drink?

The baby emptied first one grav bag and then another, before he finally pushed the container away and leaned against Kieran, content and sleepy, his fingers flexing in the fabric of Kieran's shirt.

Kieran carried the boy into the dormitory, slipped a grav harness around him, laid him down on a cot, and fastened him into a thin blue sleeping bag that was tethered to the bed. When he looked up, he saw that almost all the boys had returned from the rest of the ship and were standing in groups, waiting for instructions. Kieran pointed at Arthur. 'Tell them what they need to know about zero grav.'

Arthur clapped his hands to get their attention, and then he demonstrated how to put on harnesses and how to hook into their bunks. He showed them how to use a grav bag for drinking and how to use the vacuum bags for waste. Kieran wandered up to the front of the room and stood next to Arthur, slipping into his own harness.

It took a lot of cajoling, but soon all the boys were fastened to their bunks and waiting for the engines to turn off. That was when Seth and his crew returned.

Kieran handed out harnesses. 'Quick, put these on!' he said. Seth's team was struggling into their harnesses when a strange shudder went through the ship. A weird hum seemed to vibrate through his rib cage, and then, slowly, Kieran felt the soles of his feet grow lighter as the first thruster was shut down. There were only two more to go. 'Hook into your cots!' he yelled.

The second thruster shut down, and Kieran felt a strange vertigo.

The younger boys hurriedly tied themselves down, but Seth and his two friends stood next to Kieran, knowing smiles on their faces. They were laughing at him. Kieran knew it was a mean bully trick, but he still felt foolish. 'You heard me,' he tried to shout, but he sounded weak.

'Who's going to switch over to secondary power?' Seth asked loudly enough for all the boys to hear. They looked at Kieran, waiting to see what he had planned.

Kieran opened his mouth, but he didn't even know where the power switches were. In Central Command? Or were they in the engine rooms?

As if on cue, the third thruster shut down. All the lights blinked and went out.

A few of the younger boys screamed.

'Where is it?' Kieran could hear himself muttering, but he heard no response. A flashlight turned on, and Seth held it to his own face, making his features monstrous.

'I'll take care of it.' Seth pushed himself up from the floor, his flashlight wavering over the room to create long shadows, and pulled himself along the ceiling conduits towards Central Command.

Kieran stood still, fighting against the sickening feeling in his limbs, and waited. After what seemed an eternity, the lights snapped back on. They were dimmer than before, but at least now he could see.

He looked down to find that he was floating half a metre above the floor. He had a horrible, disembodied feeling and tried to wave his arms to steer himself, but he succeeded only in spinning, which made him feel like throwing up. He stopped moving his limbs and waited to drift to the ceiling, where he could get some leverage.

Seth floated back into the room, an insolent grin on his face. 'Don't worry, boss,' he said. 'You can't think of everything.'

Some of the boys laughed. As Kieran tied himself into his cot, he knew what they were thinking. That Seth would make a better leader than he would. Seth, who screamed at crying babies and pulled little boys by their arms.

Seth must not be allowed to take over.

GOODBYES

Kieran hadn't slept in more than forty hours. Six hours without engines had turned into ten, which turned into twenty. By now, the crew had stopped making estimates.

If the engines couldn't be fixed soon, the crops, forests and orchards would start to die. If the plants were lost, there'd be no point in fixing the engines, because there'd be nothing to replenish the ship's oxygen. The *Empyrean* would become a metal tomb.

Kieran was overcome with a fit of nervous energy and unhooked his harness to float over Sarek Hassan's shoulder at the com displays. Sarek seemed to tolerate his presence a little better than the other boys. As one of the few Muslims aboard the *Empyrean*, Sarek had always been reserved, associating more with his family than with kids his age. He liked to go jogging with his father through the immense granary bays, so he was taut and lean and very strong. He was also unreadable. He had deep-set eyes in a bronze face and, though he seemed always aware of what was going on, it was as an outsider, an observer. This quality reminded Kieran of Waverly, and it made him feel as though he could trust the boy.

Sarek acknowledged Kieran's presence with a brief nod.

'Don't worry,' Kieran said as he hovered over the boy. 'I won't throw up on you.'

'You better not.'

Kieran had always thought zero grav would be fun, but it was disorientating and frustrating. It upset everyone's stomach, made faces and hands swell up and gave everyone headaches. Every motion sent Kieran's body into an unpredictable spin, and the only way he could function was to strap himself to something.

'Any word from the shuttles?' he asked, knowing what the answer would be.

'Don't you think I'd tell you if I'd heard something?'

'But have you checked all bands?'

Sarek rolled his eyes. 'Are you deaf? There's no word. From anyone.'

Kieran trembled, from exhaustion mostly but also from anger. All the boys had begun speaking to Kieran this way, and now even Sarek was joining in.

'Sarek,' Kieran said, his voice pinched with anger, 'I asked you a question. Did you check all frequencies for communications in the last hour?'

Sarek stared at Kieran as though he were an idiot.

'If shuttle B42 is trying to communicate with us, don't you think we'd better be listening? They could be injured, dead, drifting, anything.' Kieran was so tired, his tongue felt clumsy in his mouth, but he made himself enunciate each word. 'Every hour, on the hour, you are to check every frequency for any kind of communication. Text. Voice. Video. And when I ask if you've done that, you are to answer . . .' Kieran waited for Sarek to finish his sentence for him.

The boy stared, mouth stubbornly closed.

'You are to answer *yes*. Because you will have done it. Do you understand what I'm telling you? Because if you don't, I will assign someone to the com console who does understand.'

Without acknowledging Kieran, Sarek extended his finger and tapped the console, rhythmically, pointedly, scrolling through each frequency. His posture, his expression, the way his eyes fixed on the screen, all indicated supreme and utter boredom. When he was finished, Kieran said, 'That's right. Every hour, Sarek. We don't know who's on that shuttle, or who they might be trying to reach.' Kieran's anger had subsided, and now he felt exhausted. 'Maybe your parents—'

'No! They're all gone. Everyone's gone.'

'We don't know—'

'You don't know *anything*!' the younger boy spat, and turned his back on Kieran.

Kieran knew that Sarek was only feeling what everyone felt, what Kieran himself felt. The only remedy would be if the missing shuttles docked and everyone's parents and sisters poured back into the *Empyrean* so things could go back to the way they were before.

They never could, though. Their peaceful way of life had been destroyed forever by people who were supposed to be their friends. To think of Waverly under their power? That was unbearable. If they laid a hand on her . . .

Kieran ached at that thought, so he pushed it away.

He decided to try lying down again. He hadn't been able to sleep in so long – maybe now he could quiet his mind.

Kieran unhooked his harness, drifted up to the ceiling and pulled himself along the conduits that housed the electrical wires. It was the best way to get around in zero gravity, and he wondered if the engineers had designed the ship this way on purpose. He drifted into the bunker dormitory, hooked his harness loosely to a cot, slipped into the blanket envelope, and closed his eyes. Dreams flickered, and he wanted to give himself up to them, but he could hear a conversation from across the quiet room.

'One of us will have to override the bulkhead doors from Central Command,' said one voice.

'We can do that before we leave.'

'No. Someone should stay behind.'

'I want to come with you guys.'

'You're the only one whose folks aren't down there.'

'I don't know *where* my dad is!'

Kieran wanted sleep so badly. But he knew what the

boys were planning. It worried him that he hadn't anticipated it. Wearily he unhooked himself from his cot, pushed up to the ceiling and pulled himself along the conduits until he was hovering over the four boys.

'You can't go down there,' he told them.

Tobin Ames glowered at Kieran. 'We weren't talking to you.'

'I don't care who you were talking to. If you try to go down there, you'll kill everyone on the ship.'

'No, we won't. We'll have to open the first bulkhead, but we'll seal the second, which will keep the radiation out of the upper levels.'

'OK. And then how will you get back? You'll have to seal off the third bulkhead, right? So we'll have lost another level.' Kieran passed his hand over his face while he considered. 'So there goes all the exotics and tropicals, the entire rain forest. The lungs of the ship. We'd run out of oxygen before we got to New Earth.'

'My mom's down there!' Austen Hand protested. 'And they won't answer the intercom any more. I can't just let her . . .'

The boy couldn't finish the sentence. He buried his face in his hands.

'We'll just open the bulkhead for a second,' Tobin pleaded.

'A second is all it would take to kill us all. Not right away, maybe, but slowly and painfully. Not to mention what it would do to our fertility. And if that goes the mission is over.'

'There are no girls anyway,' Austen pointed out sullenly.

'The girls are coming back,' Kieran said firmly.

'But how are we going to get them *out*?!' Tobin's freckled face twisted in anguish.

Kieran had no answer. The boys were starting to understand the situation on their own: the adults weren't coming back. No one had to tell them, but someone should have.

'Wait here,' he told the boys. He dragged himself across the ceiling and into Central Command. He found Seth Ardvale talking in whispers with Sarek, whose face wiped clean as soon as he saw Kieran enter the room. Kieran ignored both of them, pushed himself down to the com console, and tapped the call button for the engine room. It took a long time and, as he waited, he could feel Seth and Sarek staring at the back of his head. The vid screen flickered, and Kieran was looking at the face of Victoria Hand, Austen's mother. She was barely recognizable. Her face was badly swollen, and the veins under her skin had burst to create frightening bruises.

'Kieran, this has to be quick—'

'Mrs Hand, the kids here need to talk to their parents.'

'We can't spare the time. We want to, believe me—'

'Victoria,' Kieran said firmly, 'get all the parents to the video terminal right now. Otherwise the boys are going to try to come down there, and I don't know if I can stop them.'

Victoria's face went slack. What she said next came in a whisper, and tears spilled from her eyes. 'We don't want them to see us this way.'

'They know what's going to happen, Vicky. They've figured it out on their own. They need to see you so you can explain. But also . . .' He paused. 'Vicky, there are . . . a lot of . . . losses. In the port shuttle bay.'

She swallowed. 'I know.'

'What do we do?' Kieran whispered.

For a second she only stood there, hanging her head. When she could finally speak, she said, 'You'll have to put the bodies in the air lock and blow them out. All at once.'

Horror spread through Kieran, but he found his voice. 'OK.'

'Can you do that, Kieran?' she asked gently. 'I'm so sorry it falls to you.'

Kieran nodded. He dreaded the task with his whole being. But there was another task he dreaded even more.

'I've been able to make a list of . . . who they are. Who didn't . . . make it.' Kieran could speak only with his eyes closed. 'But their sons don't know yet, and I don't know how –' His voice caught on the words, and he couldn't go on. 'You're a nurse, right? How do you tell someone . . .'

The woman stared at the screen, her eyes brimming with tears. 'I'll tell them.'

Kieran gathered all one hundred and twenty-two boys and lined them up, floating in the corridor outside Central Command. Tobin Ames and Austen Hand came along with the others and waited their turn quietly.

Everyone agreed that whatever boy was talking on the console should be left in privacy. No one entered or left Central Command except for the boy who was speaking to his parents. Sometimes Kieran could hear them wailing through the metal walls, but for the most part, it was a silent procession.

Arthur was one of the first to come out of Central Command. He had hooked himself onto one of the electrical conduits in the corner of the ceiling, and he hovered outside, looking sullen and lost. Kieran knew that Arthur's parents were unaccounted for, so he hadn't had any terrible news today. Kieran tapped his shoulder and beckoned him down the hallway. 'I need your help.'

'What?' Arthur floated after him, keeping himself straight by hanging on to the upper conduits.

'Have you seen the vid screens from the port shuttle bay?' Kieran whispered.

'Yes.'

'Can you help me . . . deal with it?'

The boy blanched.

'You're the only one I can think of . . .' Kieran began. 'I can't go there alone. I know I'm asking a lot—'

Arthur cut him off. 'I'll do it.'

The ride down in the elevator was grim. When the doors opened onto the quiet corridor that led to the shuttle bay, Kieran felt such terror that his bones shook. He couldn't make himself leave the elevator.

'They're not going to be floating around, are they?' Arthur whispered. He hadn't moved from the elevator either.

Kieran couldn't answer.

Finally, the boys left the safety of the elevator and

propelled themselves into the bay. At first glance it looked as it always had, and for an insane instant, Kieran hoped that somehow the bodies had already been taken care of, that he wouldn't have to do this after all.

But no. This place was a crypt.

They were all around, so utterly still that they'd escaped his notice. Or maybe he hadn't wanted to see, and his mind had rejected them, wiped them away. But, when Kieran made himself look, they were there, lying where they'd fallen. Waiting.

Dozens of shapes on the floor or hovering just over it, pools of blackish, dried blood spread underneath them. Staring eyes. Twisted limbs. So many. He saw Mrs Henry, Mr Obadiah, Lieutenant Patterson, Harve Mombasa. They'd been lying down here all this time, turning to clay.

His gorge rose to his throat, but he swallowed it. His body shook, his limbs felt drained of blood, but he squeezed his fists as he floated over them towards the air-lock doors.

Arthur floated parallel to him, looking around at the inert forms, his expression dark, his skin pale.

'How do we do this?' Kieran asked.

Arthur's eyes snapped onto his. 'We'll need a rope.'

They worked for hours, tying the bodies to the end of a rope and, using a pulley attached to the inside wall of the air lock, pulling the bodies across the shuttle bay. Arthur did most of the pulling, but it was Kieran who had to loop the rope around the dead crew members, trying not to look in their eyes, trying not to notice how they smelled. When he was finished with one he'd somehow manoeuvre to the next, and the next, cursing under his breath at the awkward way he had to move, horrified by how he had to hang on to the bodies themselves to keep from drifting away from them. Still, if it weren't for the zero gravity, this task would be impossible for them.

As he lifted dead limbs, closed empty eyes, he made himself remember Waverly, the first time he'd got up the courage to take hold of her hand. It was during the Harvest Cotillion. There'd been beer and roasted vegetables with chestnuts and briny olives. The adults were dancing steps they remembered from their childhood on Earth while Waverly sat at one of the tables, eating the last of a strawberry upside-down cake she'd made for the occasion. Kieran had taken the seat next to her, pointed out Waverly's mother dancing with Kalik Hassan, twirling and giggling. Waverly had laughed when her mother tripped, and he'd taken her hand and pulled her closer. She'd turned to him, surprised, and then she'd smiled.

Kieran felt inhuman by the time the last crew member was put into the air lock, as though the part that made him a person had died and had left behind a creature that didn't think or feel. Arthur looked exhausted as he worked the controls, overriding the system that pumped the air out of the air lock. They had to leave the air inside or there would be nothing to push the bodies out and away from the ship. When Arthur had it all set up, his thumb hovering over the red button, Kieran put his hand on the boy's shoulder.

'Shouldn't we say something?' Kieran whispered.

'You mean like a prayer?'

The two boys looked at each other, blank. Kieran couldn't think of what to do. It was Arthur who finally began. He sang, his voice a true tenor that filled the shuttle bay. After a few bars, Kieran joined in. He knew this ancient melody and those words. He realized as he sang how beautiful they were: 'Blackbird singing in the dead of night. / Take these broken wings and learn to fly.'

When the song was done, Arthur pressed the button to open the outer air-lock doors. The sound was explosive. Kieran looked through the window to make sure they'd all gone.

The air lock was empty.

Kieran and Arthur were silent in the elevator on the way back to Central Command. When the elevator doors opened, Arthur drifted out wordlessly, looking wrecked.

Desperate for some comfort, Kieran drifted down the corridor to Captain Jones's office. Kieran needed some idea of how to go on, and he had no idea where else to look. At first it felt wrong to be here, as if he were intruding. The room felt small and dark without the Captain sitting in his chair looking out of the porthole. He hooked himself to the desk chair, and he ran his fingers over the smooth writing pad. He longed for the big man to come and tell him he was doing a good job, that he and Arthur had done the right thing. But there was no one to tell him that. He couldn't even tell himself. He wasn't sure he believed it.

Through the walls, he could hear the other boys crying their hearts out.

What could he do for them? They were lost and grieving. But if they fell apart they'd never survive this. They would make some stupid mistake, like forget to clean the air filters or fail to check the water-purification system. Then it would be all over. The boys needed a leader.

Kieran tapped at Captain Jones's personal com screen and scrolled down the diary entries. He racked his brain, trying to think of an occasion like this one when the crew faced such terrible losses. The only comparable time had been when that air-lock accident had sent three people spinning into space – the accident that took Seth's mother and Waverly's father. Kieran found the speech Captain Jones had given then, but it didn't measure up to what was happening. Nothing in the Captain's diary did, either.

One folder in the personal files struck Kieran. It was marked 'Sermons'. There might be something here.

He scanned the titles briefly and found one called 'When All Hope Is Lost'. He opened the file and began to read. It was a short speech, but it was beautiful, and by the time he finished reading, Kieran felt better. He thought the other boys would feel better, too.

Kieran transferred the sermon to a portable screen that he hooked to his belt, and he drifted back out to the corridor, now empty. The last of the boys had spoken with the parents or had learned about what happened to them if they were counted among the dead. It was over.

The loudspeaker was tethered next to the door of the

dormitory, and Kieran took hold of it. He didn't know how to get the boys' attention. Calling them over seemed wrong somehow. So he simply began to read:

'Sometimes in our lives we must face the great lack. The nothingness of loss rears up and we have no choice but to bear it. What else can we do? We look outside our empty portholes at the enormity of Creation, pinpoints of stars that seem eternal, and we feel so small, so alone. Insignificant. How could anything we do matter in such a cosmos?'

Kieran heard snickering from the corner of the room where Seth and his friends hovered, but he paid them no mind. Some of the boys were looking at him through their tears.

'We *do* matter. To believe that our lives are meaningful is the essence of faith. We are not as large, or as bright, or as eternal as the stars, but we carry humankind's message of love across the galaxy. We are the first. We are the world makers. Our nourishment is hope. Like the tender reed shaking in the wind, we will reach up to a new sun.'

Kieran paused before the last paragraph and looked up. All the boys were looking at him now. Many of them were crying openly, sending tears to float in the air of the central bunker like snow, but they were quiet. Even Seth was silent as he watched Kieran take command of the room.

'Humankind will not recede into the darkness. The journey is long, the mission is difficult, some say impossible, but we will prevail. There will come a time when children gather around a fire and look at stars unknown to us. They will remember our sacrifices. And our names will fill their songs.'

None of the boys spoke, but the room felt less stifling. Kieran attached the loudspeaker to the hook by the door and drifted down to his bunk. He slid into the blankets, zipped them closed and, hugging the portable screen to his chest, he finally closed his eyes.

But his mind went on working, seeing the bodies, the blood, the pain in their faces. And now the rest of the adults were dying in the engine room. Would he have to do this again? There had to be a way to get the crew out of there. He couldn't just give up on them. He wouldn't.

He couldn't sleep now, not with so much to do. He got out of his cot and began to walk to the engine room in perfect gravity. The more he walked, the longer the dormitory seemed. He looked around him, and every boy in every cot was Seth Ardvale, looking at him with those accusing blue eyes.

He was dreaming. He was still in his cot. He tried to get up again, but his limbs were paralyzed.

He must sleep. His body had shut down. He would sleep for a few hours.

The words of the sermon, *our names will fill their songs,* ran through his mind, soothed him. Before he dropped off, he wished that he could thank whoever had written it.

What had been the name?

Oh yes.

Anne Mather.

DECOMPRESSION

Kieran woke after a few hours, not quite refreshed but better able to function now that he'd rested. The other boys in the dormitory lay on their cots, still asleep, but a few had already unhooked and hovered near the ceiling. Now that the boys were accustomed to zero grav and the risk of injury was minimal, Kieran allowed them to hover as long as they wanted. He couldn't prevent them from doing it anyway, and he'd learned it was best not to give orders that were sure to be disobeyed.

Kieran unhooked from his cot and kicked himself up to the ceiling. He pulled himself past the galley, where Randy Ortega was rehydrating dozens of breakfast rations, and across the large room, nodding at the boys who were awake in their cots below him. Groggy, he crossed the corridor and floated into Central Command, where he found Seth and Sarek and a few other boys huddled around a console.

'What's going on?' Kieran asked as he rubbed sleep out of his eyes.

None of them answered, so Kieran pushed himself down towards the floor and looked at the vid screen over Seth's shoulder. They were watching a view of the engine room, but there was no movement.

'What is it?' Kieran asked again.

Grudgingly, Seth said, 'We can't see anyone.'

'*No one?*' Kieran asked.

Sarek shook his head. 'We can't get them on the intercom, either.'

'For how long?'

'Twenty minutes.'

'When was their last communication?'

'It was a text, forty minutes ago.'

'Where is it?'

Seth handed Kieran a piece of paper. All it said was: 'Engines back online at 08:30. We love you.'

'What the hell does this mean?' Kieran asked, his voice high.

'We don't *know* what it means!' Seth snapped. The bandage on his head shifted, and his hand shot up to press it back in place. A bloodstain, brown around the edges but red in the centre, marked the middle of the compress like a bullet hole. Seth's hair was greasy, and his eyes were wild in the way they darted over the screen. The stress was getting to him, Kieran could see. He wondered if Seth had slept at all.

'Look! There!' Sarek pointed at the corner of the screen, where Kieran saw a human foot moving. It floated off towards the aft side of the engine room.

'Are there any other video links to that part of the ship?' Kieran asked.

'Only the air locks,' Seth said. 'But the cameras are turned off, or covered up or something.'

'Why would they cover up the cameras to the air locks?' Kieran asked.

No one answered. They didn't have to. The truth came to Kieran in an instant. 'Oh no.'

With shaking fingers, Kieran engaged the intercom for the engine room.

'Stop what you're doing. Stop it! I know you hear me!' he screamed. 'And you think you're being heroic, but you're not!'

The other boys looked at Kieran, real fear in their eyes for once instead of anger. Even Seth was wide-eyed, and his teeth gnawed at his lips, which had gone white.

Kieran waited for a response, then, after hearing none, he punched at the intercom switch again. 'Here's what's going to happen. Whether you decompress the engine room or not, I'm bringing a shuttle around to dock with the air lock you're about to open. So you may as well hang on for five minutes. Just five minutes!'

'What are they doing?' Sarek asked. His lips pulled away from his teeth in a frightened grimace.

A dark realization clouded Seth's face. 'They want

to blow out the engine room.'

'Why?' screamed Sarek. 'The engine's all fixed!'

'To get rid of the radioactive gas,' Kieran said. *And their bodies*, he almost added before thinking better of it. He didn't know how many of the adults were still alive. Maybe a few. Maybe all. They'd received what was probably a fatal dose of radiation and had decided to end it quickly rather than linger, but he wasn't going to let them do it.

He released his harness and jabbed a finger at Sarek. 'Stay on the com. Keep talking to them. I'll contact you when I'm in the shuttle.'

Seth scowled. 'You don't know how to pilot one of those.'

'Neither do you,' Kieran said over his shoulder.

'I'm coming with you,' Seth said.

Kieran pulled himself along the ceiling to the central elevators and jabbed the button. The elevator door opened immediately. He pulled himself in and, without waiting to see if Seth had followed, pressed the button for the shuttle-bay level. Seth floated next to him, bracing himself against the ceiling. Kieran studied Seth's profile, trying to see him as Waverly might, but the exercise made him feel foolish at a time like this, and he turned away.

Seth seemed to read his mind. 'You must be worried about Waverly.'

'I can't think about anything else.'

'Me neither,' Seth said, his eyes steady on Kieran. 'I tried to stop them. I want you to know that.'

'I know. I saw,' Kieran said quietly. He could hear

the other boy breathing forcefully. Everything Seth did was forceful. 'Thanks for trying.'

'Of course.'

Kieran looked at him, opened his mouth to finally ask what he'd wondered for years. *You love her, don't you?*

But he couldn't give voice to it. He couldn't face it, didn't want to believe a guy like Seth was capable of real love.

Once the elevator reached the shuttle-bay level and the door opened, Kieran launched himself into the corridor. He had a straight shot to the shuttle-bay doors, and he floated there faster than he could have run. He sensed Seth right behind him.

Once inside the door of the shuttle bay, he braced his feet against the wall and launched himself again, aiming for the shuttle nearest the air lock. He felt dizzy flying through the bay so quickly. He saw the pools of dried blood, remembered how he and Arthur had blown the bodies out of the air lock. He hadn't thought about it since; he'd wanted to pretend it never happened.

He looked around, found Seth had already opened the shuttle ramp and was drifting into it. Kieran followed.

'The bodies,' Seth said quietly. 'Did you—'

'Yes,' Kieran said, clipped.

'I'd have helped.'

'You were hurt,' Kieran said as he strapped into the pilot seat.

Kieran had never thought about how large the shuttles actually were, how difficult to manoeuvre through those doors, and his stomach flip-flopped. Could he do this? He'd never even piloted a OneMan before.

'OK.' Kieran stared at the elaborate control panel in front of him, not sure which button to push first.

Seth jiggled a switch, and Kieran heard the engines cough to life.

'Thanks,' Kieran said, for once glad to have Seth around.

Seth pointed at the pilot seat. 'You're sixteen, right? So they've had you on simulations?'

'Yeah,' Kieran said, though he'd never been any good at them. Piloting shuttle craft was enormously difficult. The zero grav made it near impossible to remain spatially orientated, the engines were powerful, and the slightest miscalculation could be deadly. What he was attempting was extremely dangerous, not just to himself and Seth, but to everyone on the *Empyrean*. If he crashed into the hull, the ship could experience an explosive decompression that could kill everyone on board. In the simulations, Kieran had never even successfully *landed* a shuttle. He'd crashed every single time. He bit his lip to stop its trembling.

'Don't you dare go coward on me,' Seth said in a warning tone.

'Shut up.'

'Go to hell.'

'You're not helpful.'

'I'm here, aren't I?'

Kieran looked at Seth's stubborn chin, his hard blue eyes, and realized that, yes, Seth was here, he'd been here all along, present and thinking in a way none of the other boys had been. Kieran didn't like him, but, in truth, Seth was probably Kieran's single greatest resource.

Kieran took a deep breath and took hold of the joystick between his knees. He lifted it slightly, and he felt the shuttle move upward.

'Release the tethers,' he said to Seth, whose finger was already poised over the switch.

The shuttle bucked. Kieran barely kept it from crashing through the ceiling of the shuttle bay. After a few sickening dips and sways, he was able to steady the craft with a firm hold on the joystick. 'OK, contact Sarek and tell him to open the air lock.'

Seth murmured into the microphone of his headset. Both boys watched as the doors inched open to reveal the large air lock beyond it.

'Don't breach the hull,' Seth said under his breath.

Very gently, Kieran inched the joystick ahead, and the shuttle eased into the air lock. Once the rear of the craft had cleared the hatch, Seth told Sarek to close the doors. The boys jumped in their seats at the explosive sound of the decompression. Once the air lock was nearly a perfect vacuum, it would be safe to open the outer hatch.

'Holy God,' Kieran said under his breath. His stomach lurched. He'd never left the *Empyrean* for the infinity of space. He looked over at Seth, whose face was pallid and stretched.

When the boys' eyes met, Seth said, 'What the hell was I *thinking*?'

Kieran burst into laughter, and Seth busted up, too. But the moment didn't last long. Seth pushed the com button and told Sarek, 'OK. Open up.'

Kieran didn't know what he was expecting, but when the air lock doors opened in front of him his fear seeped away. The view of the nebula on the other side of the thick glass wasn't so unfamiliar after all.

'Slow,' Seth said to him.

'Yeah,' Kieran said as he moved the shuttle out of the hatch.

Once they were away from the protective envelope of the *Empyrean*, vertigo gripped Kieran, and for a moment he thought he might vomit. He took a few deep breaths until his dizziness subsided before twisting the joystick towards the port side.

The profile of the *Empyrean* loomed into Kieran's field of vision.

He had never seen the ship from the outside, and he realized what an amazing machine it really was. The shuttle moved along the outer hull, which rose in misshapen hills and valleys, comprising the domed housings of various ship systems. The housing for the atmospheric controls loomed higher than all of them.

'Watch it,' Seth warned.

Kieran pulled back on the joystick to clear it, but the bottom of the shuttle grazed the outer hull, making a horrifying sound of metal scarring metal. The shuttle seemed to get caught on something momentarily, but then it released.

'Watch it!' Seth grabbed the joystick at his knees, pulled it back, and the shuttle hovered upward.

'I've got it,' Kieran said. 'You can let go.'

'Don't do that again,' Seth said breathlessly, his hands hovering over the copilot joystick in front of him.

'What's the matter? Scared?' Kieran asked him.

'Shitless.'

Seth muttered into his microphone, asking Sarek to check atmospheric conditioning for damage.

After a few breathless minutes, Kieran saw the *Empyrean*'s aft thrusters ahead and knew that the engine-room air lock must be somewhere to the left. 'Where is it?'

'I don't see it.'

The com beeped, and Seth answered. 'What?'

'Let me talk to Kieran.'

It was the voice of Mason Ardvale. Kieran had thought the man must be dead. He hadn't spoken to him in forty hours. 'I'm here, Mason.'

'You're a crazy damn kid, you know that?'

'Says the man who wants to blow himself out an air lock.'

'We have to vent the poison.'

'Fine by me. But you're not doing it until I come get you.'

The man laughed, but it was a bitter, humourless laugh. 'What makes you think the shuttle can dock with the engine room?'

Kieran's body seemed to lurch as the blood drained from his torso. 'The air locks don't *match*?'

'The engine-room air locks are designed for venting gas.' Mason coughed weakly. 'They can't even fit a OneMan.'

'But that's crazy!' Seth cried hysterically. 'Who would design a ship that way?'

'In any normal scenario, we'd have got about twenty warnings before the engines went critical. The regular crew of six could have handled any normal kind of breakdown.'

'The designers never imagined a *meltdown*?' Kieran cried.

'They never thought of *sabotage*.' Mason spoke calmly, in a monotone. 'Otherwise, don't you think we would've tried, son?'

Kieran looked at Seth, who blanched to hear his own father call someone else 'son'.

'So there's nothing we can do?' Kieran asked.

An agonized silence filled the cockpit. A sheath of sweat slathered Kieran's skin, and he felt cold.

The man sighed. 'Look, this'll probably kill us, but you can try to position the cargo hold over the air lock, and when we decompress, we might blow inside.'

'Well, yeah! Let's do it!' Kieran said.

'You don't understand something,' Mason said grimly. 'The force of the blowout could damage the shuttle. It'll put a spin on it you might not be able to control. That's why we hoped you kids wouldn't try this.'

'God,' Seth said. He slumped in his chair, staring at the controls in front of him, blank. He lifted his eyes to Kieran's, all his wilfulness drained out of him.

Kieran stared back at the other boy. He might be stuck looking at Seth Ardvale's face for the rest of his short life as they drifted away from the *Empyrean*, spinning like a pulsar. But what choice did they have?

'OK, we'll try it,' Kieran said. He felt physically sick, and his head pounded painfully. He took his hands away from the joystick for a moment and flexed his fingers to stop his trembling.

'When my eyeballs stop bleeding, I'm going to tan your hides,' Mason said.

'If you can see to catch us, old man,' Seth said, and the two of them laughed in their sullen way.

'OK, Mason, what do I do?' Kieran readjusted his grip on the joystick.

'You've got to get the shuttle over the port-side hatch.'

'There it is!' Seth said, pointing to the right.

Kieran saw the oval shape of the air lock jutting up from the hull of the *Empyrean*, and edged the shuttle over to it until the air lock came into view on his vid screen. Seth pressed a button, and the words 'Docking Sequence' appeared at the bottom of the screen.

Kieran lowered the shuttle over the air lock.

The craft lurched to a stop, and the sound of metal on metal whined through the shuttle.

'God,' Seth said as he pushed a button that sucked the air out of the cargo hold into the reserve tanks so it would be available to repressurize.

The two boys looked at each other. Seth was biting the inside of his cheek, a nervous habit that distorted his face. Kieran licked his lips and said, 'We've docked, Mason. Whenever you're ready.'

'OK. The second you hear the decompression, close the shuttle doors, do you hear? You're going to have to be fast, or we'll bounce out.'

'I know, Dad.' Seth sat with his finger poised over the button.

'On the count of three,' Mason said.

Kieran gripped the joystick, careful not to jolt the ship. His eyes were on the shroud of the nebula that waited to swallow up the last few adult crew members of the *Empyrean*.

'One.'

Kieran took a deep breath. He imagined the vacuum of space, the way it would give them frostbite instantly, collapse their lungs, boil their blood.

'Two.'

Seth opened the shuttle air-lock doors to receive the crew. Kieran tightened his fists over the joystick.

'Three.'

A percussive sound slammed Kieran in the chest as the air from the *Empyrean* exploded out of the air lock, and suddenly the shuttle was spinning at an impossible velocity, so quickly that the universe had become a blur of grey and pink. Kieran felt his eyes crossing, and he closed them, holding the joystick, waiting for his head to clear enough so that he could open them.

When he did, he gasped.

They'd already spun so far away from the *Empyrean*, the ship had shrunk into the distance, looking no larger than a jellyfish. Oh God. It swung out of view from the shuttle portholes, back in, then out, as the shuttle spun away from it, completely out of control, hurtling into the nebula like a rock skipping endlessly across waves of rushing water.

SPIN

For a time, all Kieran could do was hold on to his seat. Spots crowded his vision. He thought he might black out.

Cautiously, he opened his eyes. It made him dizzy to look through the portholes, so instead he focused on the joystick in front of him. The pilot's terminal screen was blinking with a message: 'Enable Attitude Adjustment.' He tapped the screen, and suddenly the ship came alive as dozens of thrusters began firing at random intervals.

'Dad! . . . Dad!' Seth screamed. Kieran couldn't bear to turn his head to look at the other boy, who was pressing the intercom switch. 'Can you hear me?'

'Are they back there?' Kieran asked him.

'I don't know!'

'Did you close the hatch and repressurize?'

'Yes!'

'They probably blacked out,' Kieran said.

'I'm going down there.'

Seth reached for the buckle on his harness, but Kieran shouted, 'Not until we stop this spin. You'd get beaten to death.'

'Then get it under control!' Seth shouted.

'I'm trying!' Kieran shouted back.

Had the spinning slowed down, or had Kieran got used to it? He couldn't tell. The *Empyrean* was no longer visible through the cockpit portholes. Kieran hoped this meant that the shuttle was merely facing away from the ship, because the other possibility was too horrible: that they'd already drifted so far that the ship was invisible.

'Do you know how to run a nav system?'

Seth scoffed at this. 'In this nebula?'

Red letters flashed across Kieran's screen: 'Attitude Adjust Failure.'

'Damn it! The gyroscope was damaged!' Kieran spat. The screen flashed, 'Enable Manual Controls.' Kieran would have to stabilize the shuttle himself.

He punched the screen in front of him, and suddenly the thrusters all stopped firing.

'Can you feel which way we're spinning?' Kieran asked Seth, knowing it was a ridiculous question.

Seth didn't even bother answering.

The only way to slow down the spinning would be to

fire a thruster in the opposite direction of the spin. Kieran closed his eyes and imagined the shuttle from the outside. The cargo hold was towards the aft and on the bottom of the shuttle, so when the blowout hit, the shuttle would have been thrown end over end. The ship was probably spinning nose down, so that meant he had to fire thrusters that would push the nose of the shuttle up.

Kieran pulled back on the joystick. The shuttle lurched wildly. Kieran heard the sound of Seth retching, and an acrid odor filled the cockpit. He kept pulling back on the joystick, praying under his breath, 'Please please please please.'

'Stop! Stop!' Seth yelled as he wiped his chin on his sleeve. 'There it is!'

Kieran opened his eyes and saw the *Empyrean*, grey and tiny as a pebble, blurred in the nebula. It must have been 125 miles away or more. Acting purely on instinct, he let up on the joystick, then engaged the rear thrusters. He felt the back of his seat pushing against him. The *Empyrean* seemed to wobble as the shuttle rocked up and down, but it stayed in view as the thruster pushed the shuttle slowly towards home.

'I think you did it,' Seth said.

'It'll be a few minutes before we have to dock.' Kieran nodded. 'Let's check on the others.'

He unhooked his harness and followed Seth down to the hatch that opened the cargo hold, dreading what he would find there. His heart thumped in his chest, and the veins in his temple felt swollen and itchy, as though all the panic and fear of the last few minutes (hours?

days?) had collected there and was trying to get out. Seth pulled on the handle, heaved the hatch open, and looked inside.

Nothing but darkness.

'Hello?' Seth called. Kieran had never heard him sound so much like a little boy.

A groan struggled up through the darkness. Kieran flicked on the light just inside the hatch. What he saw would haunt him for the rest of his life.

They were huddled in a corner of the hold, bleeding, their faces swollen and puckered with frostbite, their eyes shut and oozing, encrusted with clotted blood. He barely recognized any of them. But they were alive.

'Can any of you speak?'

Weakly, one of the twisted figures held up a thumb. Kieran squinted at the face until he recognized Mason Ardvale, Seth's father, who said, 'You saved us all, Kieran.'

No word for his own son.

Seth stared at his father, his face blank. The boy seemed hollowed out.

'I better fly us home.' Kieran put his hand on Seth's shoulder. 'Good job.'

Seth shook off Kieran's hand. 'You think I need that from you?'

Kieran dropped his hand. 'I was just trying—'

'Stop trying to act like you're in charge,' Seth said. 'No one trusts you.'

'You made sure of that, didn't you?'

'Go to hell,' Seth said before pushing himself towards his father.

Kieran watched the boy take off his shirt and press it against a deep cut on his father's forehead, lovingly dabbing at the crusted blood, whispering in his father's ear. Kieran missed his own father terribly in that moment, but there was no time to dwell. The docking system in the cockpit was pulsing an urgent tone, and he had to get back.

He strapped himself into his seat and tried to guide the shuttle straight back to the *Empyrean*, but something was off. He couldn't seem to approach it dead-on, but the *Empyrean* seemed to be slipping further away the closer he got, as though the ship itself were . . .

'Sarek!' Kieran shouted into the com link. 'Have the engines come back online?'

'Yeah! They just reengaged!' Sarek's excited voice bounced through the wires. 'We have gravity, not much, but more all the time! Did you get the crew out of the engine room?'

'Yes, we did. And they're alive.'

Kieran heard a hundred and twenty boys whooping for joy.

'Listen, Sarek, is there any way you can stop the *Empyrean*'s acceleration? Just until we land?'

'Uh . . .' There was an uncomfortable pause. 'I have no idea how to do that.'

'OK, Sarek. Don't worry about it.' Sweat beaded on Kieran's upper lip, and he licked at it nervously. It probably wasn't safe to take the engines offline again. They might not be able to turn them back on. But trying to land the shuttle on a moving target would make this twice as hard. Kieran wiped his sweaty palms on his trousers, took hold of the joystick and pushed it forward, giving the shuttle enough velocity to keep pace with the *Empyrean*.

As Kieran watched the *Empyrean* get larger in the cockpit windows, he imagined the shuttle and the *Empyrean* from above, visualizing the trajectory the shuttle would have to maintain in order to enter the air lock correctly. He realized he'd have to travel much faster to catch up with the *Empyrean*.

Kieran pushed the thruster controls to their maximum capacity and was thrown backwards into his seat. He could barely lift his arm to steer the ship, and it took all the strength in his abdomen for him to lean forward enough to reach the joystick.

Instead of aiming straight for the *Empyrean*, Kieran aimed the shuttle for a point ahead of the ship, trying to guess where the shuttle and the *Empyrean* would intersect. He held steady, ignoring his trembling limbs, the fearful warnings from Sarek coming over the com system, the ache forming at the back of his neck and in his crushed chest. This was going to work.

Soon the *Empyrean* dominated Kieran's visual field. He was almost there. He searched the bubbly surface of the ship, looking for the familiar octagonal shape of the shuttle-bay air lock, until finally the orange lines emerged out of the mist of the nebula. The docking bay looked tiny as Kieran aimed the shuttle for it, forcing the ship into a diagonal trajectory. The outer air lock doors opened, and Kieran eased back on the acceleration. He could breathe again, and his limbs weren't so heavy. He bit the side of his cheek until he tasted blood. 'Come on, come on,' he muttered.

The reality of landing a physical shuttle was more intuitive than a simulation. Kieran held the joystick steady as the shuttle glided slowly through the outer air lock doors. The ship bumped the ceiling on its way in, then screeched along the walls. But they were in. The outer doors closed around the shuttle, the air lock repressurized and the inner doors opened onto the shuttle bay to a crowd of hopeful boys.

He wished he could spare them the sight of their parents swollen, cut up, in pain. But when the hatch to the cargo hold lowered, and the boys saw the adults lying on the floor of the shuttle, they rushed in, crying in relief. As Kieran came down the ramp, groups of boys were carrying out their parents, dragging them down the cargo hold ramp, pulling them towards the infirmary. None of them looked traumatized by their parents' appearance so much as relieved that they were still breathing. There was hope in their faces again, and it made Kieran feel hopeful himself for the first time since he'd watched Waverly disappear into the enemy shuttle craft.

Maybe he would see her again. Maybe there was a way to find her. And his parents – they could still be alive. He needed to hold on to that hope as long as he could.

Kieran found Seth struggling with his father out of the shuttle. He regretted that he'd ever treated this brilliant, resourceful boy as a threat. Kieran was the one who was marrying Waverly, wasn't he? He should try to reach past their old rivalry, make a kind of alliance and work together.

Seth was holding up his father single-handedly until several other boys rushed to help. Mason Ardvale's eyes rolled around in his swollen face, his lips were cracked, and the tip of his nose was shiny and black with frostbite. But he was alive. Incredibly. It looked as though all the adults had survived.

'I couldn't have done it without you,' Kieran said to Seth, hoping Mason heard. The other boys paused to hear what Seth would say.

Seth looked at Kieran coolly. 'Don't be so proud of yourself.'

Kieran shook his head, not understanding.

'You disabled the environmental control system when you crashed into the dome. We're going to have to repair it in OneMen.'

Several of the other boys looked at Kieran angrily. Why was Seth doing this?

'We can handle that,' Kieran said, confused. 'You were there. You saw how hard it was.'

'I shouldn't have let you drive,' Seth said loudly, as though performing for the other boys.

'*Let* me?'

'I think we'd all be better off if we kept you in the brig,' Seth said over his shoulder as he started off with his father, pulling the unconscious man out of the bay and towards the infirmary.

The rest of the boys turned their backs on Kieran and followed Seth out.

As Kieran trailed them down the corridors, he caught

more than one boy glaring at him. He rounded the corner to find Sarek in the corridor whispering to two other boys, twelve-year-olds. When they saw Kieran, they gave him angry looks.

'What are you guys talking about?' Kieran asked them, but they merely shook their heads and turned away.

When he entered the infirmary, he found chaos. Most of the adults were semi-conscious and groaning. Boys were rushing back and forth between the medicine cabinets and their parents, who were lying on the cots, their hands twisted in agonized knots, their faces blackened and bruised from the decompression.

Kieran walked between the cots, looking at the faces until he found Victoria Hand, who was a nurse. She was lying in the corner of the room, her head rolling back and forth on her pillow, groaning. Kieran fought through the group of boys crowded around her and yelled, 'Vicky! What do we do?'

Her eyes lazed open, but she seemed incapable of focusing.

'What do we do for decompression injuries?' he said loudly.

'Oxygen,' she muttered from between cracked and puckered lips.

Kieran clapped his hands over his head and yelled at the boys, 'Find the oxygen tanks and masks. Each of you tend to your own parents! Hurry!'

Drew Jones found the tanks in a cabinet at the end of the room, and fights broke out as boys tried to climb over one another to get to them. By the time Kieran crossed the room to break up the fights, they were already over, and the boys ran back to their parents, aunts or uncles and fitted the masks over their faces.

'How do we do this?' Bobby Martin asked Kieran, and pointed at the dials on top of the tanks. There were numbers along the outside edge. Kieran rushed back to Vicky Hand, who had lost consciousness. Her son, Austen, was leaning over her, clumsily fitting the clear plastic mask over her face as he cried, saying over and over, 'I've got you, Mom. It's going to be OK.'

'Vicky!' Kieran said, and when the woman didn't respond, he shook her by the shoulder.

'Leave her alone!' Austen screamed. Tears streamed down his fat cheeks as he cried over her.

Kieran shook her harder. 'Vicky! What setting do we put the oxygen on?'

Her eyes rolled in her head, but she was able to look at Kieran briefly. 'One hundred per cent,' she managed to say.

'Turn the oxygen all the way up, guys!' Kieran called into the room, and watched as the boys cranked the dials as high as they would go.

Kieran stood over Vicky, watching, anxious. He couldn't afford to lose her. She was the only medical person left on the ship.

Kieran looked around for Mason Ardvale and saw he wasn't in the room. 'Where's Seth's dad?' he asked the nearest boy.

The boy pointed at one of the private rooms off to the side. 'Seth took him in there.'

Kieran went to the cabinet, pulled one of the last

oxygen tanks out of it, and took it to the room, where Seth was bent over his father. The lights were off, and Kieran flicked the switch on. 'Seth, he's going to need oxygen.'

The boy kept his eyes on his father's face. 'He doesn't need anything.'

Mason Ardvale lay on the cot, as motionless as a carving.

Kieran lowered the oxygen tank to the floor. 'Oh, no, I'm so sorry.'

'You should be,' the boy spat bitterly before crumpling on top of his father, covering him with his torso as though trying to hold him down. It was one of the saddest things Kieran had ever seen.

Kieran backed out of the room and closed the door behind him. He looked at the other boys leaning over their parents, watching their faces, taking note of each and every breath. Others might be lost before the day was out.

Several boys huddled in the doorway. Their parents weren't among the injured, but they looked on anxiously. One of them was Arthur Dietrich, and Kieran beckoned the boy over. 'Arthur, there must be medical videos somewhere in the offices around here. Maybe Dr Randall kept them, or Dr Patel. Find them for me, OK?'

'Good idea.' Arthur nodded and trotted off.

Kieran raised a hand over his head and whistled. 'Guys, Arthur is looking for videos about how to treat radiation and decompression illness. When he finds them, we need to watch them so we know what to do.

The oxygen is a good first step, but there will be a lot more to do, and we're going to have to work hard.'

Several of the boys were looking at something behind Kieran. He was about to turn when a sharpness entered his neck just above the shoulder. It felt like a bee sting, and Kieran batted at it to find a hypodermic sticking out of him. It had been plunged up to the hilt, sickeningly deep. He turned to see Seth's tear-streaked face set in a furious scowl. 'What did you . . .' Kieran started to ask, but numbness crawled over his face, spread over his eyes. Arthur Dietrich ran back out of the doctor's office, his hands trailing bunches of papers that fell, cascading in fluttery sheaths, as Kieran fell – no, sank – wondering what had happened to the gravity in the room, swinging his arms weirdly, searching for a hold on something to keep him from floating out of the windows and into that sickly nebula, spinning, spinning . . .

THE BRIG

Kieran woke with the side of his face crammed against a metal floor. His head ached horribly, and his mouth tasted like the peat his mother used in her garden. He blinked his eyes open to see the underside of a metal cot, a dripping sink beyond it.

For long minutes, Kieran's mind was absent, and he could only look at the dripping sink, the silver water falling drop by drop into the basin.

Kitchen.

The word fell like an ice chip into his mind. Sinks are in kitchens. He could be in a kitchen.

No. He was lying under a cot. No cots in kitchens.

His neck itched. He tried to scratch it and touched

something hard, something that stuck out of him, pulsing back and forth with his heartbeat. A syringe.

It all rushed back. Seth had done this to him.

This wasn't a kitchen. It was the brig.

His body felt like sludge as he struggled to roll onto his back. Whatever Seth had given him was powerful and still dragged him down. He fingered the hypodermic, trying to guess where it was poking him. Was it in his jugular? His carotid? Was it safe to pull out? He certainly couldn't leave it in. He should go to the mirror that was hanging on the wall opposite him, but he couldn't move.

'Here,' someone said.

Something slid across the floor and hit him in the side. He was afraid if he moved his head to look at who was with him he might drive the needle deeper – or, worse, he might knock it sideways to rip through his jugular. So he groped for whatever they'd given him and, with real effort, lifted it to look.

A mirror. A woman's mirror.

'Thanks,' Kieran said breathlessly. The mirror, his arm, seemed impossibly heavy. 'Is this needle going to kill me if I pull it out?'

'Who knows?' the voice said. It wasn't Seth talking, but there was little concern in the words. Someone else hated Kieran as much as Seth did.

Holding the mirror in his left hand, he groped with his right, edging his fingers across his chest and up to the twitching hypo, closing around it. He took a deep breath and, a little at a time, pulled the needle out of himself. It felt like removing a bone from his body the way it came unstuck from such a deep place. Once it was out, Kieran threw it away and looked in the mirror again. Blood trickled from the puncture, but not very much. Kieran dropped his left hand, suddenly too tired to hold up the mirror, and clamped his right hand over the wound to slow the bleeding.

He stayed like that for a long time, catching his breath, before he could open his eyes again. He saw someone's shadow on the wall behind the sink. Someone was still watching him.

'Are you going to kill me?' he asked. Odd, how detached he felt from this question.

'Not me,' the voice said.

'Then can I have some water?'

'Get it yourself.'

'I can't walk.'

A pointed sigh, and then Kieran heard something sliding across the floor until it hit him in the head. A grav bag half-full of water.

Kieran opened the clamp around the straw with clumsy fingers and sucked down the lukewarm liquid. It ended far too quickly.

The water revived him enough that he could keep his eyes open without much effort, and he finally turned his head to see who was watching him. Sealy Arndt sat staring down at him, a long knife from the kitchen balanced on his knobby knees.

'Do you know how ridiculous this is?' Kieran asked the boy, who dropped his eyes to the floor. 'I just rescued all your parents.'

'That's not what Seth says,' the boy replied, his thin

lips a narrow pink line across his face. 'Seth had to take over because you crashed into the atmospheric dome.'

'Only for a second! I piloted the shuttle the entire way. Ask Sarek.'

The boy laughed.

With a twisting fear, Kieran realized that he was at war. He had been all along without realizing it, and he was losing.

He might not make it out of here.

If he could just talk to his dad for one minute so he could ask him what to do. Kieran thought of the way his father's hazel eyes seemed to glaze over in the middle of a conversation or during dinner. He was never quite all the way in the room with his son, but always somewhere else, thinking. Sometimes Kieran could pierce through that concentration and get his father's full attention. Kieran would explain a problem he was having, some trouble with a friend or a teacher who had treated him unfairly. Always the explaining was what made him feel better, because he knew what his dad would say: *The truth is powerful, Kieran. Just tell the truth the best you can and people will usually see your side.*

The truth. What was the truth?

'You know, Sealy, Seth has always been unstable. He's smart, that's for sure. But he hurts people. It's not that he's bad. He's just . . . angry.'

Kieran was met with perfect silence.

'We can't turn against each other like this – you see that, don't you?' Kieran said, trying to keep his tone calm and reasoning. He couldn't let his terror show.

'We need every single boy on this ship just to keep it going. We can't be throwing people in the brig just because they make a mistake.'

'You've made lots of mistakes.'

'Haven't we all?'

'Seth hasn't made any mistakes.'

Kieran lost his temper. 'You're letting Seth do this because you're angry at what happened to our families and you want someone to blame.'

'Shut up!' the boy exploded. 'I don't have to listen to you!'

Kieran held his tongue, but he could see how thin a veneer Sealy's calm really was. Underneath it, Kieran guessed, he was a churning bundle of misgivings. Probably many of the other boys felt the same doubts. If he could get to them, if he could talk to them . . .

'Sealy, do you really agree with this? Throwing me in the brig?'

The boy didn't answer. Kieran watched Sealy's uneasy eyes. He was just a kid, plunged into a situation that would be impossible for most adults to cope with. He was confused, and frightened, and ready to latch on to anyone or anything that would help him feel better.

'Sealy, you know, I think the shuttles are going to come back. When you think about it, they haven't even been gone that long. They're probably getting the girls right now.'

'You don't know anything.'

'Neither do you. So why should we assume the worst? Captain Jones might be on one of those shuttles right now, on his way back. Did you think of that?'

'Stop it,' Sealy snapped. 'I know what you're trying to do.'

'What is Seth planning on doing with me?'

'You'll see.'

Kieran's mind raced. Could Seth be contemplating murder?

'Getting rid of me will just make everything worse, Sealy.'

'You're being kept where you can't do further damage.'

'But how do you *know* I did damage? How does anyone know?'

'Seth saw the whole thing.'

'So it's his word against mine? Is that how we're going to do things from now on? Seth can throw anyone in the brig he wants?'

Again, Sealy was silent.

Kieran's blood pulsed fear through his system until he forced himself into a cool, detached space where he could think.

As long as he was in the brig, he was at Seth's mercy, and there was no way to get out unless someone let him out. His only hope would be to gain access to someone outside of Seth's inner circle. He had to talk to Arthur Dietrich. Or Sarek, who had witnessed the entire shuttle flight over the console. Sarek could contradict Seth's story. 'If Seth is a real leader, he shouldn't be afraid of a fair trial.'

'If you're trying to talk your way out of here, it's not going to work.'

'I'm not *just* trying to talk my way out of here. I'm

trying to save the ship. Do you really think Seth is the guy to lead us? Really?'

'Yeah. I do.'

'Oh, right. I'm sure he never bullies *you*.'

Again, Sealy was silent.

It was best to stop here. Let Sealy do some thinking on his own. Kieran had little hope that he could turn the boy's loyalties, but, even if he could make him doubt what Seth was doing, it might help. Besides, all this talking and thinking had exhausted him, and he had to close his eyes and try to sleep off the medication. Once the drug had worn off, he could think more about what to do.

He was still so frightened that it took a while, but finally he was able to sleep. He didn't know how much time had passed when he woke up again and saw a pair of boots in front of his face.

He bolted up, afraid of being kicked. He tried to stand, but lost his balance and had to catch himself on the metal cot.

Seth stood over him, his arms crossed over his chest. 'Well.'

'You must be proud of yourself.' Kieran raised himself up to sit on the cot. He considered tackling Seth and beating the boy unconscious, but he was so weak that it would be useless to try. Besides, on the other side of the steel bars were two boys, and they were holding guns like the ones the *New Horizon* crew had used. So they'd gone down to the cargo holds and found them. 'What do you want, Seth?'

'I have everything I want. You're out of the way, and

the ship will finally be run the way it should be.'

'Is that why you needed the guns?' God, how many did they have?

'Guns make it easier,' Seth said.

Dread oozed through Kieran's chest like hot sludge. Seth had gone insane.

'What are you planning on doing with me?' Kieran said, trying to hide his fear.

Seth sat on the cot next to Kieran, hands on his knees. Now that he was finally in charge, he wasn't sullen so much as arrogant. He moved with a kind of easy swagger, and humour even played at his eyes. Everything about him seemed disconnected, ill matched to the situation. 'I haven't decided,' Seth said.

'You think everyone will go along with whatever you decide?'

'Who cares what everyone goes along with?'

'You should. They outnumber you,' Kieran said.

He thought he saw a brief flicker of doubt in Seth's eyes, but it passed quickly. 'You're the one who should be worried right now.'

'Why? You're my only enemy. How many enemies have *you* made, you bully?'

Seth's fist flashed at Kieran's eye, exploding into pain through his head and down into his neck and shoulder. He fell backwards off the cot and rolled on the floor, unable to pretend that it didn't hurt.

'Don't call me that!' Seth screamed. All the pain of losing his father coursed through Seth's voice, and he seemed about to buckle under. But he bit his lip fiercely, reined in his emotions and said, 'I don't want to hit you again, but I will if you keep calling me names.'

After the pain dulled to a reddish haze behind his eyes, Kieran pulled himself onto his feet. He had to lean on the metal wall behind him. The steel was cold on his back, and it revived him. He realized he needed food. He needed water. He needed so many things.

'You know what happened aboard the shuttle, Seth. You were there. You saw the whole thing. I piloted us back to the *Empyrean.*'

'If I hadn't taken the controls, we'd have lost atmospheric control,' Seth said. He was playing to an audience of two: Sealy Arndt, who was scowling at the floor, his expression unreadable, and Max Brent, who was watching Seth with rapt attention, his eyes aglow. 'I know what I did.'

'Yeah. You held the joystick for ten seconds. You pressed a button to close the cargo hold. That's what you did.'

'We're still trying to fix the damage you did to the atmospheric system when you crashed the shuttle.'

'I barely grazed the surface. What did you really lose? An antenna? Does it even need to be repaired?'

'You disabled the control system.'

'If your father were here, he'd say you're a liar.'

Seth froze in shock, and for a moment Kieran thought he might cry. The boy squeezed his fist closed, and, moving so quickly that Kieran didn't see him coming, he punched Kieran in the stomach. Kieran went blind for a second, and when his vision cleared he was on his knees again. He struggled to breathe, but his diaphragm was in spasm. He gulped air desperately as the pain in his stomach doubled the pain in his head. He was hurt. He was so hurt.

He really might not get out of this.

He looked up at Seth standing over him. Kieran thought he saw a flicker of self-doubt pass over Seth's eyes as he kneaded his fist.

'Why are you doing this?' Kieran asked Seth, gasping.

'I won't let one of Captain Jones's thugs have this ship.'

'What are you talking about?'

'I'm talking about how things need to change.'

'I think you've gone insane.'

'Do you have any other ridiculous accusations to make?' Seth said, his voice low. 'Or are you ready to listen to what I have to say?'

Kieran merely looked at Seth, waiting for him to speak.

'You've been asleep for thirty hours, so you're probably hungry, right?' Seth asked knowingly.

Kieran held his sore stomach, waiting.

'We'll bring you something to eat, but first I want you to admit to your mistakes in front of everyone. That's all you have to do.'

Kieran needed food. He felt weak, and despite the pain in his gut from Seth's punch, he felt hungry. But he would not let Seth make an example of him. If he did, the ship would be lost. Kieran could feel the other two boys waiting for a response. He had to think of something he could say that would undermine Seth.

It was hard to think like his enemy. What was the worst thing he could say to him right now?

'You must be afraid,' he said slowly. He lifted his eyes to Seth's face and focused all his hatred into his gaze. 'That's why you're hiding me away from all the other boys. You're afraid I'll turn them against you.'

Seth grabbed Kieran's hair and rammed his head backwards against the wall. 'You think you're smart.'

'Otherwise why are you asking for a public confession? If you weren't afraid, you'd hold a real trial. If I'm the criminal you're making me out to be, you should be able to prove it. But you can't, so you're afraid.'

'No, Kieran,' Seth said as he backed out of the cell and slid the door closed. His face was a blank mask, but his voice trembled with rage. 'You're the one who's afraid.'

It was true, Kieran realized later that night, alone in the darkness, hungry and aching and missing Waverly. He was very afraid.

PART FOUR

SUBVERSIONS

All oppression creates a state of war.
　　　　　　　　 – Simone de Beauvoir

CARGO

Waverly smiled, half-hidden behind the fruit bowl, leaning her chin on her hands. It was a ridiculous pose, and it felt wholly unnatural, but it's what Amanda wanted.

'That's lovely, honey. It's going to be adorable,' Amanda said as she blocked out the composition on her canvas with a thick piece of charcoal. She was weak like the rest of the adults and could stand at her easel for only a few minutes at a time, so the process was slow. 'You're a natural!'

'Thanks,' Waverly said, trying not to move.

'So, Waverly . . .' Amanda's voice was precise. 'Tell me, do you want to be a mother some day?'

'I don't know.' Waverly slid her eyes over to examine the woman, who was peering closely at her canvas. 'Why do you ask?'

'Oh, I guess because I'm jealous.'

'Jealous? Why?'

For a long time Amanda didn't answer; she just stroked the canvas with charcoal. 'I wanted to be one of the first mothers of New Earth. I thought it was my destiny.'

Waverly said nothing.

'But you'll get to. You'll be a progenitor of thousands, maybe millions of colonists on New Earth. You'll be celebrated and remembered by an entire planet full of people. Like Eve in the Garden of Eden. Well, you and the rest of the girls.'

'I never thought about it that way,' Waverly said. A chill passed over the backs of her shoulders.

'When you think about it, it's almost your duty, if you know what I mean. To be a mother.'

Waverly watched Amanda as the woman drew, her hands nervous and quick as they marked the canvas.

'And to be safest, you should take advantage of your youth. Have children early, if you can. Women become less fertile as they age. You know that.'

'I'm not ready to be a mother,' Waverly said. A lump had formed in her throat, and she swallowed hard. What were these people *planning*?

'Oh, I don't mean that you should be raising babies at your age. Heavens, no!' Amanda laughed.

Waverly found a way to smile, but she felt uneasy. The woman was talking around something, she felt sure, edging towards some goal.

'I'm so glad you came for this visit,' Amanda said with a vibrant smile.

'It's no trouble,' Waverly told her.

In truth, this was a welcome change from the monotony of the dormitory. It had been five days since family time, and there had been no more word of moving the girls in with families. Instead they'd been left in the dormitory in utter boredom, spending day after day trying to amuse themselves, given only plain food, and hardly enough to satisfy their hunger. They were cranky and uncomfortable, and many fights had broken out. Waverly suspected that Mather was getting them ready to be separated. If the dormitory was a dull, frustrating place, the girls would be eager enough to get out.

A thousand times Waverly considered telling Samantha and Sarah about the woman who had left the note in the bathroom, but something stopped her. It was the kind of secret that might be impossible to contain, and her only chance to rescue the *Empyrean* survivors was to surprise Mather and her crew. They must not get any inkling that she knew there were *Empyrean* crew members aboard – at least, not until she was ready to rescue them and escape, and that would take time.

So when Amanda came looking for Waverly, asking her to come to her quarters to pose for a portrait, Waverly had jumped at the chance. She hoped to get away from the guards long enough to sneak to the cargo holds. Her mom might be there, and she had to know if she was OK.

She couldn't think about that now, or she'd cry.

A photograph on the wall behind Amanda caught Waverly's eye. It showed orange rolling hills under a swathe of blue, and Waverly forced her mind towards it and away from her worry. 'What is that?' she asked.

'What, that picture?' Amanda took it off the wall and set it on the table in front of Waverly. 'That's California.'

'California?'

'It's a part of North America, where I came from. I thought you were from North America, too.'

'My family came from British Columbia.'

'The mountains or the coast?'

'Mountains.' Waverly picked up the photo, studied the soft red land undulating like waves. 'Are these mountains?'

'Sand dunes.' Amanda chuckled at Waverly's puzzled expression and sat in a wooden chair beside her. 'Like in the fish hatchery? You've seen the sand that coats the bottom of the tanks?'

'Yes.'

'Well, that's what makes up those dunes, only lots and lots of it. And, just like the water moves the sand on the bottom of the tanks, the wind on Earth moves the sand dunes, and it makes those shapes.'

'So these are like waves of earth?'

'Yes. And if the wind is strong enough, when the sand strikes your face, it stings. And gets in your eyes.'

'What makes the wind?' People had tried to explain before, but Waverly always asked, because people always said different things.

'The sun, I think. When it rises at dawn, it warms up the air.'

Waverly tried to imagine standing on top of a sand dune with the wind in her face. It was so difficult, imagining air moving without any visible cause. She imagined standing somewhere you couldn't see any walls or a ceiling – nothing but the sky above you. Nothing to hold you in and keep you safe. The thought scared her.

'I miss being outside.' Amanda leaned back in her chair, hands folded in her lap, dreamy eyes on the photo. 'My father and I would take long walks along a seasonal stream that ran through an arroyo near our ranch. He'd hold my hand and show me the crawdaddies crawling along the shore, and I'd try to catch them until one pinched me.'

Waverly didn't know what a crawdaddy was, but she had learned not to interrupt stories about Earth, or the adults might stop talking about it altogether.

'I wish I could describe how it feels to have the sun on your face. I've tried to duplicate it. I even stuck my head in the oven once until I realized what I was doing.' Amanda laughed, shaking her head. Waverly squirmed. 'Nothing feels like that gentle buttery light on your skin. And as far as painting goes . . .' She scoffed at the fluorescent lights above. 'I've tried a million ways, but I can't capture the look of natural light in my work. I'm convinced that's what my paintings are missing. No matter what I do, the colors seem dank.'

'Are your parents still aboard the *New Horizon*?'

'My father passed away several years ago. My mother

died on Earth when I was a baby. She was never quite right after giving birth to me, and didn't last long. Daddy fought so hard to come on this mission. He took the aptitude tests three times.'

'I thought only once was allowed.'

'We had money,' Amanda said, shamefaced. 'He bribed the administrator.'

'Oh.' Waverly wondered if everyone on the mission to New Earth came from wealthy families. Did lots of impoverished geniuses get left behind because they couldn't pay off the selection committees?

Amanda took the photo from Waverly and hung it back in its place.

'I know it's unfair,' she finally said. 'But it's the way things were on Earth. Every year it got a little hotter, more farmland dried up, and so there was less to go around. Every year people got more desperate. Those conditions don't bring out the best in people.'

Amanda's expression darkened as she brushed at the canvas with the tip of her finger. Waverly watched her curiously. Few adults had ever been quite so honest about the corruption leading up to the mission. It was refreshing to be with someone who was frank about it.

She might tell me what really happened on Earth, Waverly thought.

'I've been wanting to ask you a question,' Amanda said tentatively.

'What?'

'Well, we're trying to find better living situations for you girls. We want to place you with families. Until we can find your parents, of course.'

'Of course,' Waverly said, wondering grimly if Amanda knew about the captives in the cargo hold. If she did know, she gave no sign. She simply looked happy to have Waverly in her home. She'd baked fresh bread for the occasion, and more of the oatmeal cookies sat in a bowl within Waverly's reach. They smelled delicious after the bland food she'd been eating for the last few days, but she resisted them. She'd learned how confusing it was to accept kindness from her captors.

'I'm wondering if maybe you would . . . Josiah and I would love . . .' The woman smiled uncomfortably. 'We want you to stay with us.'

Waverly looked at her warily. 'Why?'

'We like you,' Amanda said with a shy shrug. 'And we thought you might like us. We even . . .' Her eyes fell to the table, still messy with wood shavings and small bottles of paint. A half-finished guitar lay on top of the clutter. 'Well, we made you a room. Want to see it?'

Without waiting for a response, she took Waverly by the hand and led her down a short hallway and into a very small room, complete with a bed, a desk and a lamp. Above the bed hung a photograph of a horse, looking at the camera sloe-eyed. The room was hardly large enough for two people to stand in. It felt like a glorified jail cell.

'It's not much,' Amanda said, 'but it would be all yours. You'd have some privacy. And your own porthole.'

Waverly went to the oval porthole and looked into the murky nebula. There were no stars visible now, only that sludgy gas swirling outside the window. How much longer would they be trapped in this horrible cloud?

'Well? Would you like that?' Amanda asked eagerly. Waverly turned to face the woman, whose tall form seemed to fill the doorway. Amanda leaned on the door frame, straining towards the girl with hopeful eyes.

'I guess I could stay here,' Waverly finally said. If she had no choice but to be moved from the dormitory, she might as well be with people who seemed harmless.

'Oh, that's wonderful.' Amanda's bright smile made her green eyes shine. 'I'll ask the Pastor if she'll give her consent.'

'OK,' Waverly said.

'And please! Take a cookie! I baked them specially.'

Waverly took a cookie to be polite, but she didn't eat it. Somehow doing that would be giving in. 'I'll save it for later,' she murmured.

Amanda looked so disappointed at this that Waverly almost giggled. *See how far you can push her*, said a quiet, cold voice from inside. 'You know,' Waverly ventured, 'I've been feeling so cooped up. Maybe we could take a walk?'

'Of course! Why didn't you say something?' Amanda stepped into some flat shoes and picked up a sweater. 'Let's do some exploring, shall we?'

Waverly wrapped herself in a light shawl, the same pale brown one that had been given to all the girls, and followed Amanda out. The two guards stationed outside the apartment began to follow them, but Amanda said, 'Oh, surely we don't need you. What do you imagine will happen to us?'

'We're supposed to keep track of all the girls, ma'am,' the shorter of the two guards said. He had sharklike eyes, and when he looked at Waverly she felt like prey.

'I'll keep track of her. Honestly, they're just children. I don't know what the fuss is about.'

'The Pastor—'

'I'm one of the Pastor's closest friends, Nigel. If she questions you about this, send her to me.'

The short guard was about to protest, but the taller man pulled on his arm to quiet him. 'OK, ma'am. Have a nice walk.'

'Finally some privacy!' Amanda whispered happily, taking Waverly's hand. 'Where would you like to go? There's the arboretum. Or we could go to the observatory. I've heard people say that sometimes stars are actually visible. They think we're almost through the nebula! Isn't that exciting?'

'It is,' Waverly said, but she was deep in thought, trying to remember the layout of the ship. She had to get as close to the starboard cargo holds as possible. 'Actually, I was kind of curious about the orchards.'

'Oh, yes! I think the cherries are in bloom now!' Amanda said. 'We've managed a cross-pollination that's produced a beautiful fruit. Want to see?'

Waverly nodded. Amanda led Waverly down the corridor, smiling at the passers-by, who all glanced at Waverly curiously. Once inside the elevator, she tried to fill the silence with prattle about the cherries and how juicy they were and what a lovely colour; she'd have to add some cherries to Waverly's portrait. Finally the elevator stopped at the orchard level.

'Aren't these just beautiful little trees?' Amanda asked, opening her arms to the scene. The sweet smell of cherry blossoms filled the air, and the humidity was soothing on Waverly's face. Amanda was so enthralled with the blossoms that she didn't notice when Waverly took one backwards step, and another, until she was in the elevator again and the doors were closing.

Waverly jabbed the button for the cargo holds. 'Come on, come on, come on,' she pleaded under her breath. She probably had about a minute before Amanda called the guards, or maybe she'd come after Waverly herself. Either way, there was no time to lose.

Finally the doors opened onto an immense room. Stacks of metal storage containers as large as houses reached all the way up to the ceiling, fifteen metres above Waverly's head. The walls faded into a dim murk on either side of her, making the bay seem endless. She could spend weeks searching and still not find them.

She heard the hum of an elevator on its way down and broke into a run. She turned the first corner she came to and pelted down the metal floor. The woman's note had said the crew was on the starboard side, so she turned right, running as fast as she could. In the distance she heard the elevator bell and the frantic voice of Amanda calling her name. 'Waverly honey, this isn't funny!'

Waverly tried to think as she ran between the rows of the huge containers. She knew that keeping people down here would be logistically difficult. They'd need food and water, so the best place for them would be near some elevators. They hadn't been near the elevator bank she'd come down in, so she began running crosswise, looking down each row, hoping each time to see the lights over the starboard elevator doors. She ran until Amanda's voice faded away.

Waverly's heart hurt, and her lungs felt ready to collapse, but she kept running. She'd closed half the distance to the far wall when she saw a glimmer of light to her right. She turned the corner and picked up speed, the red and yellow containers whizzing by her until the glimmer took on a squarish shape and Waverly could see quite clearly that it was the light over the starboard elevators.

She stopped to catch her breath and to listen. She heard the familiar murmur of the engines, but woven into it was a lighter sound. She tried to breathe more quietly, then crept forward, certain she was hearing human voices.

Yes. They sounded canned, as though they were coming from behind a wall of metal.

The captives must be in one of the storage containers. She turned down a corridor and edged towards the sound, which grew stronger now, until finally she could hear them quite clearly. She picked up her pace and the voices gained nuance. When she rounded the corner she could almost hear . . .

Laughter.

Five armed guards stood in a circle, about thirty metres away.

She darted back out of sight.

They were gathered at the hatch of a livestock container with vented sides. That must be where the

Empyrean crew was being kept.

She circled behind the guards as quietly as she could, until she reached the back of the livestock container. A pungent odour assaulted her, and she grimaced – the powerful smell of human waste and stale sweat.

She crept up to the container and whispered into one of the vents, 'Hello?'

She could hear breathing, the shifting of bodies. Someone coughed.

'Hello!' she whispered again.

'Who is it?' someone said from inside.

'Waverly Marshall.'

She heard hushed cries of surprise and the shifting of bodies. She was afraid the guards would notice, but they were still talking and laughing loudly. 'Waverly?'

Her mom. Waverly almost collapsed with relief.

Her mother's slender fingers snaked out through the vent, reaching for her. Waverly took hold of them and held on tight. 'Mom,' she whispered.

'Honey, my God. I'm so glad you're OK!'

'I'm fine.' Waverly couldn't hold back her tears. Her entire body pumped them out, fuelled by the most powerful sadness she'd ever felt. 'Mom, I've been so worried!'

Waverly heard indistinct whispers inside the container. Then her mother said, 'Honey, what about the rest of the kids?'

'They're fine. They're all safe.'

Now there were whispers of relief and quiet sobs. The guards, oblivious, kept laughing.

'I can't believe they let you come!' her mother said.

'They didn't. I snuck down here.'

'You mean Anne Mather didn't give you permission for this?'

'No,' Waverly said. 'She told us the *Empyrean* was destroyed and there were no survivors.'

'But you didn't believe her.' The way her mother said it, Waverly could tell she was proud.

'Mom, I'm going to get you out of here.'

'Sweetie, they have guns.'

'I'll find a way.'

'No.' Her mother's fingers tightened around her hand. 'You concentrate on getting the girls off this ship. Don't risk yourselves to save us.'

'You want us to *abandon* you?'

'To be safe, yes.'

'No!' Waverly cried, forgetting herself. Then she froze.

The guards weren't talking any more.

'Hey!' a man's voice called. 'Who's there!'

'Go!' Waverly's mother pushed away her hands.

Waverly turned on her heels and ran as fast as she could, turning corners, zigzagging between containers, turning again, her heart throbbing in her ears. She could outrun them, she was sure, but their voices grew louder behind her. How could they be so fast?

She circled around, trying to get to the starboard elevators, but a humming sound came at her from the left, and she turned just in time to see a man flying at her on a OneMan conveyor, the small vehicles that were used to stack hay bales.

'Stop or I'll shoot!' he screamed, his face twisted into

angry strands of muscle. He pointed a gun at her, but she ducked around another corner and took off at top speed.

She could hear him coming, terrified he'd shoot her but unable to stop running. When she felt a hand clamp weakly around her elbow, she clawed at it until he let go, and she turned another corner.

So he shot her.

Her leg exploded into shards of agony, and she fell down with an enraged scream. She tried to get up, but her leg wouldn't work, and she felt cold suddenly, though she was drenched with sweat.

'Mom!' she screamed. 'Mom! Mom! Mom!' over and over as men surrounded her.

'Waverly?' A woman's thin whisper in the stale air: 'Waverly, where are you?'

'Mom? Help!' Waverly screamed, overjoyed. Mom was coming to get her. She'd be safe in a moment.

She twisted her neck until she could look in the direction where Mom was coming from, and a figure appeared. A tall figure, running, limping, but coming for her. The woman got closer until Waverly could see her face.

Amanda.

'No! I need Mom!' Waverly screamed, sobbing, pounding at her own eyes, her ears, until she felt hands, so many hands, clamping to hold her down. She was stronger than each of them, even hurt like this, but there were so many of them that she couldn't move. Reason had left her completely. She was filled with nothing but the agony of her leg and the breakdown of her spirit. It was over. She couldn't help her mom. They had her, and there was no hope.

Hands, gentle this time, cupped her face, and she knew without opening her eyes who it was. 'Waverly. What are you *doing* down here?'

A lie was what she needed, but Amanda's face grew fuzzy, and as Waverly faded out, she could hear the woman yelling at the guards, 'She's just a child! Leave her alone! She's just a *child*!'

WORSE FATES

The rattle of glass woke Waverly. A bright lamp hung over her, burning her eyes, and the smell of ethanol stung her nose. A man wearing a surgical mask stood next to her bed, plunging a curette into a row of test tubes. His eyes wrinkled into a smile when he saw Waverly watching him.

'It's wonderful,' he said to her. 'You responded to the therapy very well.'

'What therapy?' she asked, her tongue clumsy in her mouth.

'Let me get you a nurse,' he said, patting her arm. He walked out, carrying the tray.

Then she remembered. Her mom. She'd talked to

her mom, held her hand. Her mom was alive, and she had to get to her.

She threw off the covers and tried to sit up, but her head swam and she had to cling to the railings on the bed. She tried to move, but her leg was gripped by a pain that seared through her like a chemical burn.

I've been shot, she realized, not quite believing it.

She wasn't going anywhere for a while.

Waverly looked around. She wasn't in the infirmary. The lights were too bright, and there was no porthole looking out to the exterior. She must be in the interior of the ship, in an upper level. To her right was a row of white cabinets. To her left was a counter lined with beakers. A centrifuge like the one she'd used in biology class sat on one end.

She was in a lab.

There were footsteps, and another person in a surgical mask appeared over her. The hazel eyes were familiar and, when the woman said hello, Waverly recognized her voice. It was Magda, the nurse who'd cared for her when she first got to the *New Horizon*.

'Why am I in a lab?' Waverly asked.

'Thirsty?' Magda inserted a straw between her lips. Waverly sipped down ice-cold water. She felt a dull ache in her throat, as though something had been forced down her windpipe. And a tube snaked into bruised veins on the back of her hand, making it sore.

'Why am I in a lab?' Waverly demanded.

Magda sat down heavily. 'You're probably wondering what happened to your stomach.'

Waverly looked down and saw that her belly was

impossibly swollen into a hard mound that hurt when she prodded it.

Waverly's throat closed in panic and she began to cough. Magda helped her sit up and rubbed her back until she could catch her breath. 'What are you doing to me?'

'Calm down. You're perfectly safe.'

'I'm safe? I've been shot!'

'Well, honey, you weren't where you were supposed to be.'

'Why is my stomach swollen?' she asked. 'Did you make me *pregnant*?'

'No, no, no. You're not pregnant, Waverly. We've filled your abdominal wall with carbon dioxide so we can see in there for your surgery, that's all.'

'What surgery?' Waverly shouted. Hot tears coursed into the hair at her temples.

'I'll let the Pastor explain.'

A shadow moved over the doorway, and Anne Mather sat down next to her. She too wore a surgical mask, and her grey eyes smiled down at Waverly. 'How's our patient?' she asked with a fondness Waverly hated.

'What have you done to me?'

'We performed a very simple procedure on you, Waverly. You're in no danger whatsoever.'

'*What* procedure?' She was almost shouting again. *Easy*, she told herself. *Use your head.*

'I'll tell you that if you tell me why you were in the cargo hold.'

She stared at Waverly and waited.

A lie. Waverly needed a lie.

'I was looking for guns,' she finally said. 'They were kept in the holds on the *Empyrean*, and I thought you might be storing them there.'

'Because you wanted to escape?' Mather coaxed gently.

Waverly nodded.

The woman studied her. Waverly closed her eyes, pretending to be overcome by the medications they were no doubt pumping into her.

'Well, Waverly, I'm disappointed, but I'm not mad.'

Waverly played the naughty child who wanted only forgiveness. 'You're not?'

'You must be confused. The last few weeks have been a terrible strain on you and the girls. I'm not a bit surprised by this . . .' Mather waved a gloved hand around, searching for the words. 'Acting out.'

This trivial term enraged Waverly, but she forced a smile. 'Sorry.'

'That's all right, dear. All is forgiven.'

Mather placed a soft hand on Waverly's arm. It made her skin crawl, but she managed a smile. 'What are you doing to me? If I'm not pregnant, am I sick?' she asked, careful to keep the anger out of her voice.

'No, darling. You're wonderfully healthy.' Mather blinked a few times as though gathering her thoughts. 'You see, the timing was right. We had to sedate you to fix your leg, which should heal up quickly, though you may have a limp, I'm sorry to say.'

You're not sorry, Waverly thought.

'And while we had you under,' Mather continued, 'we performed an ultrasound and saw that your eggs were maturing beautifully. So we harvested them while we could. And they're so precious, Waverly. We couldn't bear to waste them.'

'Eggs?' Waverly asked, her voice quivering.

Mather leaned over her, the smile gone from her eyes. 'Everyone on this ship has a duty to ensure the survival of the crew. It's your duty, too, Waverly.'

'What is? What are you doing to me?' Waverly yelled, unable to hide her outrage any longer. She wanted to lunge at Mather, strangle her. 'Tell me!' she screamed.

'I will when you stop shouting.'

Waverly struggled to catch her breath. *I will kill this woman one day*, she vowed.

'If all goes well, in nine months you'll have given children to more than a dozen childless couples. Think of the gift you're giving! They've wanted children for so many years, and now, finally, you're making that possible!'

Waverly stared at her in shock.

'Right now your eggs are being fertilized, and soon we'll implant them in the women who are ready for motherhood. Amanda is one of them. She was supposed to get your consent. She told me she'd begun discussing it with you, remember?'

Waverly shook her head. So that's what Amanda had been getting at that day.

'You won't have to carry any of them, Waverly. You're giving the joy of children to women who will raise these babies in loving, spiritual homes. You'll be spared the pain of childbirth, at least until you fall in love. There are lots of single men on this vessel who would be thrilled to have you. They're a little long in the tooth compared to you, but that's no real obstacle.'

'I'm already engaged. I'm going to marry Kieran Alden.' She felt Kieran beside her, a ghost of him that she must have carried here.

Mather paused as though filing away this bit of information. Then she said, 'Kieran. I think Felicity mentioned him. He was to be Captain, isn't that right?'

Waverly kept her mouth closed. She'd already said too much.

'Sweetheart . . .' The woman leaned forward, took Waverly's hand, and stroked it. 'Darling, the *Empyrean* is gone. I'm so sorry, but you have a new life now. I know it's hard, but I believe that you'll be able to embrace it, given time.'

Waverly reached for Mather's throat, but straps tied her to the bed. She could only attack with words, and she screamed them: 'You're insane!'

'No, Waverly. I'm a pragmatist. People don't know that about me. They see me as a mystic. But the two aren't mutually exclusive.' She leaned over Waverly, peered into her eyes. 'We need children to ensure our survival, and you'll give us that chance. I truly believe that in time you'll come to accept your role in history. There are worse fates than being the matriarch of a generation of human beings. The first humans to set foot on New Earth, Waverly, think of it! They'll be your children! You're very privileged, and I feel sure that you'll come to understand when you see the faces of our first generation.' Mather smiled girlishly. 'They'll be so beautiful.'

'You'll regret this,' Waverly told Mather, her voice trembling. 'I'm going to make you suffer.'

Mather nodded to Magda, who had been standing at the ready with a needle and injected a clear substance into Waverly's IV. Mather leaned down to Waverly as the medication made a cloud around her head. With a sad smile that seemed to fade into darkness, she said, 'I'm fairly certain that you will.'

DESPERATION

When Waverly awoke, the swelling in her abdomen had been replaced by a terrible ache. She groaned and tried to move into a more comfortable position, but the restraints on her had been tightened. A shadow moved against the wall, and she jumped when a light flickered on. 'You're awake.'

The light was so bright that Waverly couldn't keep her eyes open. She felt a straw being held to her lips, and she tested the liquid with her tongue. It was cool water, and she drank it, letting it wash away the sand that seemed to coat the back of her throat. Her eyes adjusted, and she was able to squint at her visitor.

It was Amanda, her face drawn, worry lines carved

around her eyes. 'Can you ever forgive me?' she asked.

Waverly turned her head away. She didn't want to talk.

Amanda leaned her forehead on the bed railing by Waverly's elbow. Tears ran down the creases in her face. 'You can't know the misery we suffered, Waverly. We were a ship full of desperate, grief-ravaged people.'

'You want me to feel sorry for you?' Waverly spat.

'When I think of what happened in the cargo hold . . .' Amanda shook her head, her jaw tight. 'I couldn't believe they shot you! I want you to know I gave that son of a bitch a black eye.'

'So you want gratitude?'

'You must hate me,' the woman said, her voice fragile.

'Of course I do.'

'I don't blame you.'

'I don't care who you blame.'

Amanda dropped her chin, rubbed her belly, and fell silent for a while. Finally she said, 'I don't expect you to care, but I can feel that it worked. I know I'm pregnant.'

Waverly didn't want to hear this. To know that her children could be raised by these sick people . . . she couldn't bear to think of it.

'I can't imagine what you must be feeling. To be used this way.' Amanda waited for Waverly to speak, but Waverly wouldn't look at her. 'I agonized over whether I should accept embryos that were . . . created this way. There were only so many women on the ship whose cycles matched yours. And – you probably know – it's all in the timing. If I hadn't accepted implantation, this embryo might've died. And they're so precious.'

Every word the woman said seemed to drill into Waverly's skull. She didn't care about Amanda and her tragic little thoughts.

'I don't know if this helps,' Amanda said tentatively, 'but your friend Felicity freely agreed to act as a donor. We're harvesting her ova tomorrow. We only hope she'll respond as well as you did to the medications.' Again Amanda waited for Waverly to speak, and again she was disappointed. 'She's outside. Would you like to see her?'

Waverly said nothing.

'I'll send her in, all right? You two can talk.'

Amanda got up heavily and walked out of the room. A moment later, a hesitant hand touched Waverly's shoulder.

'How's your leg?' Felicity asked.

'Ruined.' She looked the girl in the eye. 'So you're going to let them do it to you?'

'Do you think I have a choice?' Felicity asked. 'Here I am, walking around freely, being treated like royalty. And here you are, stuck in bed with a mangled leg. Is it a mistake for me to cooperate?'

To this, Waverly said nothing. She knew she couldn't trust Felicity, but this might be her only chance to get a message to Sarah and Samantha.

'Are they listening?' Waverly whispered.

Felicity gave her a blank look.

'Are they listening to our conversation?'

'I don't know,' Felicity replied, then mouthed, 'Probably.'

Waverly beckoned Felicity closer until the girl's golden hair tickled her face. She whispered so softly that she could barely hear herself, 'I saw Mom. They're holding *Empyrean* survivors in the starboard cargo hold.'

At first, Felicity sat perfectly still. When she leaned away, her face was ashen. 'How did you find this out?' she asked.

'I can't say.'

'Were my parents there?'

'I don't know. I only had about a minute to talk to my mom. I'm sorry.'

Felicity shrugged as though indifferent about her parents. After the way they'd failed to protect her, Waverly wasn't surprised.

'But they caught you down there?' Felicity whispered thoughtfully.

Waverly nodded.

'Then they've moved them. Or they're going to.'

Of course. Waverly hadn't thought of this, but she knew Mather was cautious. She was probably already looking for the traitor who had told Waverly about the survivors.

There wasn't much time. Mather might kill the *Empyrean* captives. She might search out and kill the woman with the auburn hair who had left the note in the bathroom, and it would be Waverly's fault for not being more careful.

Waverly heard someone coming.

'Tell Sarah and Samantha, but no one else can know!' she whispered before Magda hustled in, carrying a loaf of bread and a bowl of broth on a tray. 'Tell them I said hi,' Waverly added loudly. 'That I'm OK.'

'I will,' Felicity promised.

'That's enough of a visit for one day,' Magda clucked. 'You need some food in you.' She slid the tray over Waverly's lap. 'You girls can talk more later.'

Be strong! Waverly wanted to say as Felicity dropped her eyes and left the room looking doubtful and troubled.

'Here, sweetheart,' Magda coaxed, holding a warm spoon to Waverly's lips. 'Isn't that good?'

'It's fine.'

'Oh, come now. Is our patient cranky today?'

'I'm not your patient,' Waverly said coolly. 'I'm your captive. You've basically raped me.'

Magda stiffened. Mechanically, she fed Waverly spoonful after spoonful, barely waiting for the girl to swallow before forcing the next on her.

'You're lucky Amanda Marvin has taken an interest in you,' Magda finally said. 'She's the Pastor's best friend, you know.'

'So?' Waverly managed to say before another spoonful was shoved into her mouth.

'So your attitude is not making you any friends,' Magda said sternly. 'You're so fertile, and you just take it for granted. If you were really dedicated to the mission, you'd be glad to help people have children, instead of feeling sorry for yourself.'

Waverly accepted another spoonful silently.

Magda pursed her lips. 'Were all the crew from the *Empyrean* as selfish as you?'

Waverly stopped chewing and trained her eyes on Magda, staring coldly until the woman dropped her eyes.

'Well, I'll tell you, the people on your ship didn't have a very good reputation around here. We even heard they were letting women have abortions. I've never heard of such wickedness! A mother killing her own infant!'

'That only happened once. To save the mother. The baby would have died anyway.'

'Well. If it was me, I'd risk everything to save my child.'

'But it wasn't you. So shut up.'

Magda bolted out of her chair and went straight to the cabinet, where she thrust a needle into a vial of clear liquid. Waverly didn't know what it was, but she didn't want it in her blood. While Magda's back was turned, Waverly grasped the IV tube with her teeth and pulled the needle out of the back of her hand, then hid it under her covers. When Magda turned back around and stuck the needle into the tube, Waverly could feel the liquid dripping onto the sheets next to her leg. Missing her medication was bound to hurt, but she didn't trust Magda, so she closed her eyes and pretended to nod off, lying still, breathing deeply and steadily, until finally the woman left the room.

Waverly lay like that for hours, drifting in and out of sleep, until the pain in her leg prevented any kind of rest. She lay in the dark, trying not to think about it. Instead she imagined Kieran's strong arms around her, his smile. Oh, she missed him. If he were here, he'd find a way to get her out of this horrible place.

A door slammed, bringing her back to the present. Someone had come into the lab and was walking around just outside the door to her room. Magda laughed, and a man chuckled in an intimate way.

'Is she out?' he asked.

'Yes, the little princess is finally asleep.'

'How long?'

'Ten hours, at least. I gave her enough to knock out a cow.'

'So you can get away?'

'What do you have in mind?' Magda asked coyly.

'Artie brewed some beer in the granary.'

'He better not let the Pastor catch him,' she said with a giggle.

'Come on. I'll buy you some.'

Waverly heard the door outside open and close, and the voices of Magda and the man grew softer as they walked down the corridor.

Could it be so easy?

She knew she shouldn't try it. If they caught her sneaking around again, they might kill her, especially now that they had what they wanted from her. But what if she never got another chance?

The restraints were a problem. She bent herself awkwardly to gnaw at the Velcro with her teeth. The position was agonizing to her leg, but she was finally able to get a good grip and pull the Velcro from her right hand. Once one hand was free, the other restraints were easy.

The next thing was most difficult: getting out of bed.

Already her leg felt flayed open, but she found the strength to swing herself into a sitting position, where she stayed. She felt woozy and nauseous and weakened by pain, but she could stay upright with effort.

When her dizziness subsided, she braced herself against the bed to take the pressure off her wound, and slowly slid her feet to the floor. She couldn't put any weight on her leg at all, and so she hopped, a little at a time, inching towards the door. She peeked out and saw long rows of counters and cabinets laden with centrifuges, scales, sophisticated-looking tanks, freezers and countless trays of test tubes. Waverly hopped slowly, covering the two metres from the doorway to the nearest counter, which she leaned on heavily to catch her breath.

This was insane. She'd had no idea how weak she was. Her arms and legs were trembling uncontrollably, and she thought she might collapse. She took deep breaths, trying to nourish her exhausted muscles until the trembling subsided.

But it didn't subside.

She needed to sit down, right now.

About three metres away was a black office chair. She dragged herself along the counter, leaning with one elbow while scooting forward, inch by inch. When she was near the chair, she caught her breath, paying close attention to the quivering muscles in her thigh. Could her leg support her full weight?

She gritted her teeth and pushed herself off the counter, hopping as quickly as she could to the chair, each motion stabbing deeper into the wound in her leg.

When she could touch the black fabric with her left hand, she cried out in relief, but then the chair rolled another metre away.

It looked like a mile.

Acrid tears rolled down her face, but she made it to the chair and lowered herself onto it, trying to spare her injured leg as much as possible. There was a moist red pit of agony in the centre of her thigh. Oh, it hurt. It hurt so much.

Too much. She couldn't go anywhere. All this was for nothing.

Waverly sat alone in the lab, crying, her face in her hands. What was the point of fighting any more? She wanted to give up, knew it would be easier. She tried to imagine how she could make a life here. There might be people here who could be her friends. Maybe after a while Mather would let Waverly's mother and the rest of the *Empyrean* crew free, or at least let them see their children.

But, no, there was no way Mather could ever let the *Empyrean* crew see their kids. If the other girls knew their parents were being held against their will, all hope of cooperation would be over. Mather would have to keep the families separated forever.

Waverly would not consent to this. She could not.

With her good leg, she scooted the chair across the room. She didn't know what she was looking for. Just something. Anything that could help her. Then she saw the com station in the corner.

Waverly dragged herself to the com desk and studied the display. This was an internal link only; no way to reach out to the *Empyrean* from here. She slammed her fists into the keyboard, causing a missile of fresh misery to tear through her leg. All that work to get here and she couldn't call home.

Tears threatened, but she savagely bit the inside of her cheek until they faded away.

OK, she couldn't contact the *Empyrean*, but she might be able to find something out. She scrolled through the menu, looking for active signals, and found only two terminals operating on the ship. She gasped. One was in Pastor Mather's quarters. The other was a moving signal.

Waverly lifted the headset and fitted it over her ears, covered the microphone with her hand, and clicked onto Mather's signal to listen.

Nothing but digitized garbling. Of course, Mather's com station was encrypted.

But that moving signal might be on an open radio frequency. Waverly fingered the dial, listening for voices. Near the top of the frequency range, the static resolved into a rhythmic thrumming sound. Waverly knew she was hearing pumps of some kind. A man's voice came on, and though it was muffled by static, she could make out the words.

'Most of them came peacefully, and now they're all locked up, safe and sound.'

Waverly had caught a transmission about the prisoners! It had to be. Her heart beating rapidly, her breath shallow and rasping, she leaned towards the terminal so she wouldn't miss anything.

Mather's response was unintelligible. Waverly would

get only half of this conversation.

'If you ask me,' the man said, 'we should just get rid of them. Just to be—'

An interruption. Waverly held her breath.

'Yes, yes, of course you're right, Pastor. I'm sorry.'

More from Mather. Waverly bit her lip, wishing she could hear what the woman was saying.

'Well, you never know what desperate people will do, Pastor. We're just trying to keep you safe. I don't think anyone's going to find them here.'

A brief response from Mather.

'Have a good rest,' he said, and the signal ended.

Waverly hit the com station with her fist and hit it again. She'd got nothing she could use. Nothing at all!

She wanted to dissolve into tears, but she knew Magda could return at any moment. She dragged herself along with her good foot on the floor, wincing with pain each time the wheels under her chair jiggled. She was almost at her room when she heard voices outside the lab and a giggle that nearly stopped Waverly's heart. The door to the lab opened, and Waverly doubled her speed, closing the last two metres into her room as quickly as she could.

She froze once she was inside her room and listened.

Brisk fingers tapped at a computer keyboard. Magda was on the other side of the lab, at the com station. As quietly as she could, Waverly dragged herself to her bed. She could barely manage to pull herself out of the chair, but somehow she found a way to fall onto the mattress. Her leg screamed, and she almost cried out, but she wriggled onto the bed until her cheek met the coolness of her pillow.

With her toe, she nudged the chair into the corner, hoping Magda wouldn't notice.

Magda might be able to dismiss a chair that was out of place, but would she ignore the IV that Waverly had ripped from her hand? Those two clues together would certainly be enough even for someone as stupid as Magda.

The thought of what she had to do made her weep.

Waverly picked up the IV needle from the mattress next to her and looked at it. It was plastic and flexible. Narrow enough. Waverly examined the back of her hand. The puncture left by the needle had scabbed over, looking angry and red, and it hurt.

Waverly picked the scab off her sore hand. It came away easily. Blood oozed out of the puncture, and Waverly licked it away so that she could see the small hole. She wished for more light, but the dim light coming from the lab would have to be enough.

She pressed the end of the needle against the puncture, testing. It stung all the way into the fine bones of her hand.

Magda was just outside the door.

As quickly as she could, Waverly pressed the needle into her hand. The pain was unbearable. An agonized cry escaped her, and she froze. Magda had stopped humming.

Waverly leaned back against her pillow and closed her eyes, panting. Her hand was searing with pain, and she wished Magda would come in and give her another shot. But she'd have to wait hours for that. She didn't know if she could make it.

She thought she felt someone looking at her, so she forced her breathing to slow. She cracked an eye open to see a shadow move across her doorway and away.

As quietly as she could, Waverly fixed the restraints on her legs and her arms, making it look as close as possible to the way she'd found them. She had to twist her body to do it, and her leg felt as though it were detaching from her body.

She didn't know how she could ever sleep like this, but she closed her eyes. She lay perfectly still, perfectly still, perfectly still, letting the pain invade every part of her until she passed out.

She dreamed feverishly of a rhythmic thrumming sound, some kind of pumps. She knew that sound; she'd heard it before on the *Empyrean*.

That sound was the key to everything. If she could find it, she'd find the prisoners.

And her mother.

AMANDA

The next morning, Amanda came for a visit. She took one look at Waverly, who was white-faced and gasping in agony, and pulled Magda by her nurse's smock to Waverly's bed. 'How did this happen?' she demanded.

Magda touched Waverly's forehead. 'She's running a fever.'

Amanda put a hand on Waverly's cheek. 'Sweetie, how are you feeling?'

Waverly tried to speak, but her throat burned, and she was too weak.

'She's exaggerating,' Magda said. 'She was fine yesterday.'

'Get out,' Amanda snapped at her.

Magda huffed and marched out of the room.

Amanda pulled away Waverly's bedding, discovered the restraints, and unfastened them. 'Now maybe you can find a better position, sweetie.'

Waverly couldn't even lift her arms.

Something caught Amanda's eye, and she picked up Waverly's right hand, examining the puncture Waverly had reopened the night before. 'Oh God, honey. You've got a really nasty infection.'

She yelled for Magda and ordered the woman to fetch a Dr Armstrong. Soon a small man came in, moving in a darting, birdlike way, and looked at Waverly's red, swollen hand. 'This isn't good,' he said.

Gingerly, he pulled out the IV. She didn't feel a thing. The skin had gone completely numb. He smeared a clear gel on the puncture and wrapped it in gauze.

'I'm going to start a line in your other hand, OK?' he asked with a smile.

Waverly thought this might be the man who had drugged her and taken eggs from her ovaries, so she said nothing.

He walked around her bed and, with a few deft motions, had an IV line going into her left arm. After feeding two different syringes full of medication into it, he said to Amanda, 'I think she'd be better off in your care, Mrs Marvin, don't you?'

'Definitely,' Amanda said with disgust. 'Magda should be banned from nursing.'

'I'll worry about that,' the doctor snapped, and left the room.

Hours and then days passed with Waverly drifting in

and out of consciousness. The pain in her leg faded to a dull throb, and after an interminable stretch of nightmares and cold sweats, her fever abated. Amanda never left her side. Waverly woke every morning to see her ready with a bowl of warm farina, and every evening ended with a delicious vegetable stew from Amanda's own kitchen. Sometimes Amanda would bring Josiah, and they'd both sit by her bed, holding hands, telling her stories about how there used to be animals that weren't cared for by humans, wild ones. How when the sun set on Earth, the sky glowed orange, something that Waverly had always yearned to see. There were rivers that ran downhill on their own, and in some places the wind blew so hard that trees grew crooked.

Most of the time, though, Amanda came alone.

At first Waverly didn't like Amanda hovering over her, but soon she appreciated how she kept her stomach full, gave her extra blankets if she was cold or took them off if she felt too warm. Lifting Waverly's leg to dress her wound looked as though it took all her strength. Carrying a tray with soup and water made her sweat, and after she'd set it down she'd rub at her sore back, but she wouldn't rest. Amanda was a much better nurse than Magda had ever been, and Waverly eventually felt soothed by her presence, even grateful.

Amanda never mentioned her pregnancy, but Waverly could tell that it had been confirmed by the happy way the woman hummed to herself, stroking her belly, smiling when she didn't know Waverly was looking. It made Waverly feel sick to know that her own baby was inside someone else, but being cared for by Amanda set her mind at ease somewhat. Amanda would take good care of the baby when it was born.

Once Waverly was well enough to stay awake for long stretches, she was able to think about that strange noise she'd heard in the background on the com signal that agonizing night. That thrumming sound was the key to finding her mom, but the harder she tried, the less she was able to imagine where it could have been. On the *Empyrean* she'd rarely wandered beyond the biosphere levels. She didn't like the cold, mechanized areas of the ship and stayed away from them, but the prisoners must be in a place like that.

Kieran had been the explorer on the *Empyrean*. If he'd heard that com signal, he'd be able to pinpoint the location immediately. For the thousandth time, she wished that she could talk to him, if only for a minute.

Meanwhile, Waverly healed. Before long she could sit up in bed for an hour at a time, and then came the day when, with Amanda's help, she could stand and even walk for short stretches.

'I want to see my scar,' she said. She'd felt through her bandages and knew that the back of her thigh was no longer smooth. 'Help me take this off.'

Amanda looked at her doubtfully but gently lifted her nightgown and unwrapped Waverly's leg, then helped her stand to look in the mirror hanging on the door. She had to steady herself on the woman's shoulder, an intimate gesture that would have been unthinkable a week ago. But things had changed. Amanda was the enemy, but Amanda had become a friend.

'It's not so bad.' Amanda tried to smile.

Waverly sighed. It was an ugly, jagged gash down the back of her upper thigh, about ten inches long. The flesh on either side of the cut was swollen and uneven and probably wouldn't heal straight.

'It will leave a mark, I'm afraid, honey. But after it heals, they can do things to the scar,' Amanda said as she rewrapped the girl's leg. 'They can make it look better.'

'What would be the point?'

'Because you're beautiful, dear. It's worth trying.'

Waverly shrugged.

A few months ago, she'd have been dismayed about any mark on her smooth body, but now she regarded it with detached curiosity. It was healing. Soon she'd be strong, and she could kill Anne Mather and find a way out of this place.

'We need to have a talk,' Amanda told her.

'About what?' Waverly said.

'When you're released,' she began tentatively, 'you'll come live with me and Josiah.'

'Why can't I go back to the dormitory?' Waverly asked.

'The girls have been moved out to live with families. I'm the only one Pastor Mather will trust to watch over you. We'll still be under twenty-four-hour guard. Because of . . . what happened in the cargo holds.'

Waverly accepted this silently as Amanda eased her back onto her mattress.

Amanda left the room briefly and returned with a bowl of chicken soup for Waverly. Billows of fragrant steam rose from the broth as she stirred it, eyes down. 'I just can't figure it out.'

'What?'

'What you were doing there. Of all places.'

Was Amanda trying to get information? Waverly studied her and saw that her brow was knitted in confusion. 'I was looking for guns,' she said.

Amanda looked at Waverly sharply. 'Violence is never the answer.'

'I didn't want to *shoot* anyone. I want to escape.'

'Escape to where? Your ship was destroyed. Anne showed me the wreckage.' Amanda's eyes were distant, as though she were working out some puzzle in her mind.

'Why did the *New Horizon* come to rendezvous with the *Empyrean* in the first place, Amanda?' Waverly asked.

'We *had* to rendezvous. We needed help with our fertility.'

'By taking us girls and stealing our eggs?'

'Of course not! Anne had reached an agreement with Captain Jones years ago that we'd rendezvous and get embryos that he'd frozen for us.'

This was so wildly different from the story Mather had told Waverly that she was too bewildered to speak.

'It was pure luck that we happened to meet up when you needed us the most. I don't know how much longer you girls would have lasted aboard that death trap. I only wish we could have saved all those little boys. If only there'd been time!' Amanda hugged herself. 'I just hope our ship doesn't encounter the same problems.'

'So you really don't know,' Waverly said to herself. She bit her lip when she realized she'd spoken aloud.

'Know what?'

Waverly looked at Amanda's open, trusting face. She might really be ignorant of all the killings aboard the *Empyrean*. She probably didn't even know about the *Empyrean* survivors. Waverly wanted to tell Amanda what was really going on, but she held back. Trusting her would risk everything.

'What, Waverly?' Amanda pressed. 'What don't I know?'

'Just how grateful we all are,' Waverly said quickly. 'That you saved us.'

Amanda's smile reached all the way to her green eyes, and she picked up the soup bowl. 'This ought to be cool enough by now,' she said, and handed it to Waverly.

The next morning, Amanda came with a wheelchair, helped Waverly into it, and covered her with a blanket. As she wheeled her through the busy hallway, people smiled at Waverly, especially the women. They must know that she'd been the source of the first batch of embryos, Waverly realized. So many of them were glowingly happy.

'You're a celebrity,' Amanda commented, and Waverly was glad she didn't say why.

When they got to Amanda and Josiah's quarters, Waverly saw that Josiah had moved his hobby table out of the living room and had replaced it with an overstuffed easy chair. Amanda put a com station in front of Waverly and ran one documentary after another about the *New*

Horizon. Every so often Waverly caught a glimpse of Anne Mather as a surprisingly beautiful young woman, but she was always in the background. In an engineering film, the original Captain of the *New Horizon*, Captain Takemara, was interviewed about the efficiency of the ship's engines. A tall man with wavy black hair and piercing eyes, he spoke of his ship with pride.

That evening, as Amanda was making dinner, Waverly asked, 'What happened to Captain Takemara?'

Amanda was tossing chunks of cucumber and melon with watercress and spinach. She glanced back at Waverly, who sat at the table, her leg propped on a chair.

'He had a strange disease. He lingered for a few months, but there was nothing the doctors could do.'

'Which meant Anne Mather could take over,' Waverly said, wondering if the Captain's death had really been caused by a disease.

'Well, she took over *before* he got sick, actually. When things got complicated,' Amanda said, but stopped herself, seeming to rethink her words. She put down the spoons. 'There's more to it than that.'

Amanda gingerly lifted Waverly's leg, sat in the chair where she'd been resting it, and placed Waverly's foot on her knee. 'That OK?'

Waverly nodded.

'The truth is, the Captain wasn't much of a leader. When we learned we were all infertile, well, you can imagine the state of the crew. We were in deep despair, and he just didn't have the vision to deal with it. That's why Anne had to step in.'

'Step in?'

'She was Pastor of the ship, so she was already in a leadership position. By then everyone on board had heard about her services, and we all went, every Sunday, because her sermons were the only thing that gave us hope. The Captain seemed to defer more and more to her, until finally he moved out of his office and she moved in, just like that. It was better for the ship, you know. She gave us a sense of purpose again, something the Captain had never been able to do.'

Waverly felt certain there was more to this than Amanda knew or was telling her. 'What disease did he have?'

Amanda smiled sadly. 'I don't know. There was a sickness aboard the ship that spread to many of the people closest to the Captain. It was a tragedy.'

'What kind of sickness?'

'Some kind of parasite, we think. Most of the Central Council seemed to get it after one of their meetings. But the doctors could never isolate the organism to kill it.'

Waverly forced herself to breathe evenly.

Amanda went back to her salad. In the silence, Waverly wondered for the hundredth time if she could trust Amanda or if the woman was a spy.

'You know what I wonder?' Waverly said slowly, tracing the wood grain on the table with her thumbnail. 'Is how they got that wreckage from the *Empyrean* aboard.'

Amanda barely looked up from the chicken she was

cutting up. 'They retrieved it using shuttles and OneMen.'

'But didn't they pick it up several days after we left the *Empyrean* behind?'

'Yes, I think so.'

'And haven't we had constant gravity the whole time?'

'Yes,' Amanda said, her knife slowing.

'I don't understand how they retrieved it, that's all. If we were accelerating to maintain artificial gravity, it seems like we would have left the wreckage behind ages ago.'

Amanda stopped cutting the chicken altogether and looked thoughtfully at Waverly, who added, 'But who knows?'

OVATION

Early the next morning, Amanda brought a black smock and a lace handkerchief into Waverly's room. Waverly watched her, pretending sleep. Amanda moved quietly, arranging the clothes so that they hung straight on the hanger, smoothing the kerchief between her hands with loving care.

She was trying not to wake the girl, but Waverly had been awake for hours, thinking of the thrumming sound she'd heard, trying to figure out how she could get away to search for it. The guards, she knew, were stationed outside Amanda and Josiah's quarters round the clock. Their presence didn't seem to trouble Amanda, which was another reason

Waverly didn't entirely trust her.

Amanda turned and saw Waverly looking at her. 'You're awake!'

Waverly rubbed her eyes. 'I'm not that great a sleeper.'

'Then you didn't see we're out of the nebula,' Amanda said gleefully.

Waverly turned to her porthole and saw black sky and stars. She was stunned by the realization that now the *Empyrean* might be able to find her and the girls, if only they could find a way off this ship!

'Dear, if you're up for it, you're welcome to come to services with us. It will be wonderful, with so much to celebrate!'

This could be a chance to see Sarah and Samantha. 'I'd like that.'

'I'm glad. Anne said she has something special planned for you girls, and I would hate for you to miss it.'

Wonderful, Waverly thought as she swung her legs out of bed. Her injured leg was stiff from sleeping, and still sore. As soon as Amanda left the room, Waverly pulled on the black smock and tied the kerchief over her hair. She hated how the outfit made her look. The smock gathered in an ugly bunch around her hips, and the kerchief framed her face in an unflattering, oppressive way.

She limped into the living room to find Amanda and Josiah waiting for her. They, too, wore plain black clothes that reminded Waverly of funeral garb. Josiah came forward and took Waverly's hand. 'You look nice,' he said.

'Thanks.' Waverly had never asked, and they had never told her, but he must have been the one to fertilize the egg that was growing inside Amanda. So in a strange way, he had mated with Waverly, but he was pretending to be a father to her. The contradiction made her recoil inwardly from him.

'Josiah made you a gift,' Amanda said.

Josiah reached behind the couch and pulled out a beautiful cane whittled from hickory wood. The handle was carved with grapevines and little birds and was surprisingly comfortable in Waverly's hand. There was even a strap she could loop around her wrist so that she didn't drop it. When she leaned on it, she felt much more stable on her feet. 'Wow,' she said. 'Thanks.'

'He worked on it the whole time you were laid up,' Amanda said.

'I finished it with beeswax to get that sheen,' Josiah said proudly.

Waverly ran her hand over the wood's velvety texture. The cane felt heavy in her hands, almost like a club. It could be useful when the time came. 'It's very nice.'

Josiah only blushed.

'Come on,' Amanda said, swatting at him playfully. 'Enough showing off. We should leave early so Waverly gets there in time.'

Their progress was slow. Waverly had to stop and rest every few minutes, but the granary wasn't terribly far from their quarters, and soon she was crossing the huge room, listening to the echoing voices of the congregation.

'Goodbye, girls,' Josiah said before taking his place onstage with the other musicians.

The worship area had been decorated with hay bales and dried flowers. Hay littered the floor under Waverly's feet, feeling like a crunchy carpet as she walked up the aisle towards the altar. The seats were about half full, and people were milling around.

One very short woman walked up to Waverly and took her hand, nearly knocking her over. The woman was florid and plump, and when she smiled her face shone. 'Oh, I just want to thank you for what you've done for me!' she said.

'What? I—'

'It means so much. You've given me a new life.' The woman wiped tears from her eyes. 'Thank you! I'll always honour you in my home!'

Waverly realized the woman must be carrying one of her embryos, and her throat tightened. Amanda nodded kindly but pulled Waverly away from the woman and guided her to a seat in the front row.

'Amanda,' Waverly asked, her voice shaking, 'how many are there?'

'How many what, dear?'

'You know *what*,' Waverly said through her teeth. 'How many women are carrying my babies?'

The colour vanished from Amanda's cheeks as she looked at Waverly.

'Tell me!'

'Eighteen,' Amanda finally said. 'There are eighteen pregnant.'

'What?! How can there be so many?'

'They gave you drugs. In the food,' Amanda said. 'You made lots of eggs.'

'And you think that's OK?' Waverly cried so loudly that people turned to look at her.

'They didn't exactly ask my opinion, Waverly,' Amanda said grimly.

'And if they had?'

'I would have told them to get your permission. Because any other way is just despicable.'

On the stage, Anne Mather sat between her two lectors, waiting for services to begin. The older lector looked nearly asleep, but the young woman with the braided auburn hair looked at the crowd with practised serenity. For an instant, her eyes met Waverly's, but she looked into the distance again as though she'd never seen her.

So Mather hadn't discovered her yet. She was still safe, for now.

'Who's that woman sitting next to Anne?' Waverly asked Amanda, who seemed glad to change the subject.

'Jessica Eaton. Jess. She's only recently volunteered to help with services, since Deacon Maddox lost his voice. She does some of the readings.'

'How'd she get that job?' Waverly asked carefully.

'She's Anne's assistant. Why?'

Waverly shrugged. 'Just curious.'

Hands folded prayerfully under her chin, Mather smiled at Amanda and Waverly. Her white satin robe reflected light onto her plump cheeks, giving her a saintly glow.

'You know, Waverly, I don't agree with everything

my friend does,' Amanda finally said. 'But I don't have her responsibilities. She's dealing with a lot.'

'You wanted a baby, right? So you don't disapprove *all that much*.'

Amanda blanched. Just as the lights dimmed, signalling that services were about to begin, she whispered, 'Imagine being offered the one thing you've wanted more than anything. Would you refuse to cooperate? Really?'

Too angry to reply, Waverly looked around the room. She saw Samantha, Sarah and Felicity all sitting in the front row across the aisle. Samantha was staring at Waverly, mouth set, brown eyes unwavering. She looked thinner, harder, too. Sarah turned towards Waverly and mouthed a word, but Waverly couldn't make it out. She shook her head. Anne Mather had walked to the microphone, and Sarah turned to face the stage, her hands gathered into a tight lump on her lap.

Felicity fastened her eyes on Mather, her expression bland. Maybe she was good at hiding her fear, or maybe, after life as the most beautiful girl on the *Empyrean*, she was so used to being afraid that she didn't know how to be angry any more.

Still, it had been so long since Waverly had seen anyone from the *Empyrean* that it felt wonderful to see familiar faces, however changed they might be. She longed for Kieran, or even a picture of him, just so she could look at his face.

Everyone in the congregation stood. Amanda motioned for Waverly to stay seated, but she stood anyway, leaning heavily on her new cane.

Mather smiled warmly and raised her hands in an embracing gesture. 'I want to begin this service by praising God for the glorious gift of stars!' She flung her arm towards the large porthole above, where a veil of stars twinkled. The congregation gave a prolonged ovation. Even Waverly smiled as she looked at the beautiful sky she'd missed for so long.

'Lord,' Mather said, and the applause die down. 'We thank You for the blessings You have bestowed on our people. You have shown us the way to create life by sending us Your beautiful daughters from the vessel of our fallen comrades. I wish to honour these generous girls who have shared of their flesh. I'd like to ask the young women to take the stage so that we can thank you properly. Waverly Marshall, Deborah Mombasa, Alia Khadivi, Felicity Wiggam, Samantha Stapleton, Sarah Hodges and Melissa Dickinson, please join me here.'

Shocked to hear so many names, at first Waverly couldn't move. But when Samantha offered her hand, she took it, letting the girl steady her as she shuffled onto the stage and took one of the chairs offered to her personally by Anne Mather. Waverly looked at the woman coldly, but Mather only smiled and even had the gall to stroke her cheek. The audience murmured approvingly at the gesture. Once all the girls were seated, Mather went back to her microphone.

Waverly looked into the audience and saw so many greying, middle-aged people beaming up at her that she almost wanted to smile back. *They're my captors*, she reminded herself. *Every last one of them.*

As for the other girls, Felicity, Alia and Deborah were composed, their faces solemn. Sarah looked as if she were on the verge of angry tears, and Samantha, fists clenched on her knees, scanned the crowd as though choosing whom to kill first. Waverly doubted very much that Mather had got their full cooperation.

'Now,' the Pastor said, one hand raised, 'I want these girls to see the beautiful work they've done in God's creation. All the women who have been blessed by these girls' generosity, please stand and show us who you are.'

Dozens and dozens of women stood up, many with tears streaming down their cheeks. Waverly looked at Samantha, whose dark eyes burned with fiery rage. Sarah's eyes were red, and she was biting into her bottom lip savagely, as if trying to hold back tears. Felicity's large blue eyes were wide with surprise. She glanced briefly at Waverly and away, her expression unreadable.

'Because of these brave girls,' Mather continued, 'we shall survive into the dark night of humanity's journey across the universe, and our children will see the dawn on New Earth!'

The room erupted. People stood, clapping, cheering, and waving at the girls. Many wept openly.

During the wild applause, Waverly shouted into Samantha's ear, 'What did they do to you?'

'They drugged us!' Samantha yelled over the cacophony. 'When we woke up it was done. *Then* they asked for permission, while we were barely conscious.'

'We'll get away!' Waverly said.

'We'll have to do it during services,' Samantha replied. 'It's the only time we're all together in one room!'

'We've got to meet!' said Waverly, conscious that the applause was dying down. There wasn't much time left.

'They watch me every second!'

'I'll talk to Amanda,' Waverly said. Of all the women who'd been impregnated, only her face was troubled. 'She'll help, I think.'

Samantha's hand clamped onto Waverly's knee. 'We can't trust *anyone* here!' she said as the last of the applause died out. 'Promise me you won't say anything to her! Waverly!'

Waverly chewed her lip as she regarded Amanda. She might be their only chance, but Samantha was right. It would be better to find another way, if they could. 'OK,' she said just as Anne Mather began her sermon.

'I'd like to take you back fifteen years,' Anne Mather said, her voice ringing over the congregation like a clarion call, and they listened, Waverly thought, as though her words meant eternal life. 'After years of carelessness and naive selfishness, we finally got to the task of conceiving our families, only to learn that none of us would ever bear children. Do you remember how that felt?'

Many of the women in the congregation nodded.

'We were devastated.' Anne Mather let that word hang in the air before continuing. 'God told Abraham once, "Know of a surety that thy seed shall be a stranger in a strange land." Yet Abraham's wife, Sarah, bore no children. So she said to him, "Behold now, the Lord hath restrained me from bearing: I pray thee, go in unto my maid; it may be that I may obtain children by her." And Abraham hearkened to the voice of Sarah.'

Mather held a hand towards the row of girls on the stage, and the congregation obediently shifted their gaze. Waverly felt mortified. They were looking at her as though she were some kind of saint. 'These girls are the fulfilment of God's promise to the people of the *New Horizon!*'

Once again the congregation burst into applause, and Mather soaked it up. She'd spoken with utter conviction, and her flock had responded in kind.

'These people actually believe they're doing God's will,' Samantha said into Waverly's ear.

'Maybe not *all* of them,' Waverly said thoughtfully.

Waverly looked at Anne Mather. Did that woman really believe what she said? Or was it all an act? Mather gazed at her triumphantly, as though the real purpose of this exercise was to show Waverly just how much power she had.

She's convinced them that they're favoured by God, thought Waverly, *and that their lives have special purpose. She knows how to make them love her. That's her power.*

After endless readings, trilling songs from Josiah and the rest of the choir, and another round of applause for Waverly and the girls, services finally ended. Waverly let Samantha pull her to her feet. Once upright, she was shocked by the sudden presence of Anne

Mather. 'I hope you girls enjoyed that,' she said with a smug grin. 'I wanted to show you our gratitude.'

Amanda joined them. 'Wonderful sermon today, Anne,' she said, beaming.

'Thank you.' Mather looked at Amanda with real fondness.

'Anne used to be my babysitter, Waverly. Way back when.'

'Amanda was like a daughter to me,' Mather said. The love between the two of them was palpable. Clearly Mather cared very much what Amanda thought of her.

'Waverly,' Amanda said, hooking arms with Mather, 'did you know Anne started as a schoolteacher? She taught Josiah and me how to read.'

'I wasn't very good at it,' Mather said with a shake of her head.

'Really?' Amanda sounded surprised. 'I think it's something I would have liked to try someday. If there had been children here, that is.'

'Now there are,' Waverly said. She was getting an idea for a way she and Samantha could communicate. 'Amanda, why don't you put together a school for us girls? The older ones, anyway?'

Mather's grey eyes darted at Waverly, and the girl smiled dangerously at her.

'That's a good idea!' Amanda cried.

'You'd be a great teacher,' Waverly told her.

'I don't know if the girls are ready,' Mather objected, and Waverly thought she saw sweat at the woman's temple.

'I'm so bored all day,' Waverly said, adding, 'it would

be nice to see my friends, too.'

'Please let me do it, Anne!' Amanda cried. 'I can't paint round the clock! And it would be good for the girls.'

Waverly kept her expression innocent, but the seething way Mather looked at her showed she wasn't fooled. Waverly didn't care. Obviously Mather wanted Amanda to think of her as a saintly leader, not a scheming liar. This gave Waverly power over her.

'I'll think about it,' Mather said carefully.

'What is there to think about?' Amanda asked, confused. 'They're young girls. They need to learn.'

'There are other considerations.'

Josiah called Amanda over to join a conversation with the choir, and she stepped away, leaving Mather and Waverly alone.

'These people certainly love you,' Waverly said, her voice menacing and low. 'Especially Amanda.'

'We're all a family,' Mather returned, her cheeks pink.

'Would they still love you,' Waverly asked, 'if they knew all the things you've done?'

Mather looked at her in surprise.

Waverly turned and limped off the stage.

SCHOOL

It happened strangely. Amanda woke Waverly early one morning and gave her a tan smock, brown kneesocks, and a knitted beret. The outfit reminded Waverly of pictures she'd seen of Girl Scouts from the twentieth century. 'I couldn't talk them out of uniforms,' Amanda said with an apologetic shrug.

Waverly didn't care how stupid she looked. She just wanted to see her friends.

Amanda wore a tan smock and brown stockings, too, but instead of the ridiculous beret, she had a black neckerchief. After their breakfast of brown rice, bananas and honey, she led Waverly to the living room and sat down facing the girl, her hands on her already swelling belly.

'I thought we were leaving,' Waverly said.

'Oh, we are,' she said, smiling.

A knock sounded at the door, two harsh raps.

'They're here,' Amanda said, handing Waverly her cane.

There were guards outside the door and behind them a gathering of the oldest girls from the *Empyrean*, all dressed in smocks and berets. Felicity's blue eyes were vacant. Samantha had taken off her beret and was crushing it in her fist. Sarah stared at Waverly, her eyes stony in her freckled face.

'Are we ready for school?' the guard with the scar asked Waverly, sneering.

She ignored him and hobbled past the other girls to stand next to Samantha and Sarah.

'Hi.' Samantha leaned towards Waverly, about to speak, when a shout from the guard stopped her.

'There will be no breaking away. There will be no wandering off. There will be no talking.' The guard jerked a finger at his ear. 'I have the hearing of a killer whale. You won't be able to get anything past me.'

Waverly looked away, trying to seem unimpressed.

'Hut two three four!' he shouted, as though he were leading the girls in a splendid game. The girls streamed behind him in a double line. Waverly had hoped both guards would stay up front so that she could talk to Sarah and Samantha, but one of them took up the rear. She could feel his eyes on her as she limped along, leaning on her cane.

They trooped through the corridors, coiling up the

belly of the ship until they reached a room in the administrative section. There were no portholes, it was stuffy and the lights were dim. Arranged in rows were small desks and chairs identical to the school desks on the *Empyrean*, except that these were pristine – no graffiti, no dents, no signs of use at all.

The guard handed a piece of paper to Amanda, whose shoulders caved when she saw it. She cast an angry glare at the guard but seemed resigned as she announced, 'Girls, we've created a seating chart to help me remember your names!' She directed each girl to her assigned chair, and by the time everyone was seated, Waverly was in the back corner, Samantha in the front row on the opposite side of the room, and Sarah in the middle of the group. They couldn't turn to face one another and were too far apart to whisper. Amanda handed out books of poetry and had the girls read verse by a poet from deep in North America's past called Walt Whitman, and then they discussed it. Most of the girls were silent, off in their own worlds, but a few seemed heartened to be in a classroom again and raised their hands to join the discussion. Waverly sat back and watched the guards, looking for some angle she could use.

The men paced the room, holding their guns to their chests. Waverly noticed Amanda glaring at them more than once, and she even stopped the lesson long enough to ask the guard to stop distracting her students. But he only smiled and went on pacing. Once Samantha turned around in her seat to look at Waverly, but the guard flicked her scalp with a finger, and she turned back around, her spine stiff and straight.

'Girls,' Amanda said to the class. Her voice shook with nervousness. 'Now that you've read a sample of Whitman, why don't you spend twenty minutes working on a poem of your own? I'll have you read what you write aloud, so do your best work!'

The only sound in the room was the scratching of pens on paper, but soon heads started popping up as girls finished their poems. Waverly watched the guards, trying to think of a way to get a message to Samantha undetected. But the room was small, and they were vigilant. Waverly imagined hitting the one with the scar over the head and running away with the rest of the girls to commandeer a shuttle. Her hand closed over the wooden leg of her chair, and she imagined it was a club. She gripped it so tightly that a film of sweat formed between her skin and the wood.

'All right,' Amanda said. 'It looks as though most of you are finished. Would anyone like to share what they've written?'

A hand darted up and waved in the air. It was Samantha. Waverly straightened in her seat.

Samantha stood, hunched over her poem, head bent, her thick brown bangs hanging in her face. Her gaze shifted onto Waverly, she raised her eyebrows and said, 'Don't everyone *copy* me.' Her voice seemed to catch. 'I worked hard on this. Every other word felt like torture.'

Amanda laughed. 'You sound like a true poet.'

Samantha stared at Waverly, then dropped her eyes to the pen on Waverly's desk.

What had she said? Don't *copy* me? Did she want

Waverly to write down what she read?

Waverly picked up her pen. Barely perceptibly, Samantha nodded. The guard with the scar stood behind Samantha, eyeing her suspiciously.

Waverly bent over her desk as she copied down Samantha's words. The girl paused between each line of her poem, lifting her eyes to make sure Waverly was keeping up.

I've often taken love like a knife,
Will I acquire love more through blood or will
We spill love?
Like a trap for everyone, love hides inside,
Its services thin.
Felicity only told in your stingy message.
Kept where mercies are paltry.
They wait, question cryptic marks.
No response.
No tomorrow.

Samantha went back to her seat, her head tilted over her desk.

'Well,' Amanda said, uncertain what to say. 'That was an intense poem, Samantha! It reminds me of the early-twentieth-century poets. Would someone else like to read?'

No one else volunteered, so Amanda called on Melissa Dickinson, who stood to read in a monotone about stars and time.

Waverly watched the guards, who had begun pacing again. The one with the scar was coming towards her.

She wanted to cover her notepad where she'd copied Samantha's poem, but that would look suspicious and she'd be found out. Her heart knocked like a broken piston as she felt the guard creep behind her. Did he stop to look at her notebook over her shoulder? She didn't know. Eventually he moved away. Waverly found she'd been holding her breath, and her lungs screamed for air, but she forced herself to breathe calmly until she could be sure the guard had lost interest in her.

When the guard circled to the front of the room, his eyes were on Samantha, who bent over her notebook. She erased words, rewrote them, crossed some out. For a moment he seemed about to take the poem away from her, but when he saw Amanda watching him with narrowed eyes, he backed away and stood in the corner of the room.

At the end of the day, the guards marched all the girls through the corridors, back the way they'd come, so that Amanda and Waverly were the first to be dropped off.

'That went well, don't you think?' Amanda asked Waverly, her voice purposefully cheerful. 'I don't like having those goons there, but I couldn't talk Anne out of it. I think you scared her when you went down to the cargo hold, and she says she doesn't want any of you getting hurt.'

'I suppose,' Waverly said, but she made it clear in her tone that she didn't believe this explanation. She could see that Amanda didn't believe it herself.

Waverly pretended to yawn. 'Sitting up all day tired me out. I'm going to take a nap if that's OK.'

'Be sure to read your history lesson before tomorrow!' Amanda chided.

Waverly shut herself in her room and turned on her desk lamp. She stared at Samantha's poem, trying to tease out the message, but it seemed just a jumbled mess of words. She'd worked herself to the point of frustration and was about to give up for a while when she remembered that Samantha had said something odd before she'd read the poem. What was it? Something about torture.

Every word was torture?

No.

Every *other* word was torture. Samantha must have laced a message through the poem.

Waverly crossed words out, playing with different possibilities, until the embedded message came through:

> *I've taken a knife. Will acquire more. Blood*
> *will spill. Trap everyone inside services.*
> *Felicity told your message. Where are they?*
> *Response tomorrow.*

Waverly worked for hours on her response for Samantha, writing and rewriting another poem in the hopes that there would be a similar assignment in class tomorrow. She was exhausted when morning came, and Amanda didn't want her to go to school, but Waverly insisted. When the guards came by with the girls, she was ready in her strange uniform, her message for Samantha tucked into her notebook under her arm.

When Amanda gave them time to write a short poem based on 'Ode on a Grecian Urn' by John Keats, Waverly waited until a couple of girls had read their work before she raised her hand to volunteer. She didn't want to seem too eager.

'Why don't you sit at your desk and read, Waverly?' Amanda said.

'Every other line was like chipping away at my teeth.' Waverly forced a giggle.

'I'm glad to know you're taking the assignment so seriously!' Amanda said, beaming.

Waverly glanced at Samantha, who had her pen poised discreetly on the writing pad in her lap. Waverly smoothed her poem out on her desk to read, careful to pause at the end of each line break:

I don't know where
The lovers go to hold each other.
They are being kept
Apart by their hard hearts and minds.
They are in a place where
Only the bravest may wander.
There's a rhythmic thrumming sound
Of their hearts beating in unison.
Like the water plant
That longs to hear a trickle, finding,
However, no sound of water,
I search for you, try to
Find others to help
Me catch you before you can
Escape. I'm going to search for

Our hearts in love's forest, calling
Them when I can
Spare my voice.
Once I find them,
I will keep yours safe for you until
We can run away
Together into the wind.

For weeks, the girls communicated this way, embedding messages in poems, in essays, right under the noses of the guards, who had relaxed over time and were no longer vigilant so much as bored. In one complex message woven into a sonnet, Waverly learned that Samantha had been boarded with a couple that had an elaborate kitchen with every conceivable gadget. This was how she'd been able to take knives without being noticed. She had a total of three and didn't dare take any more. Sarah embedded ideas for where there might be a rhythmic sound like the one Waverly described, suggesting the environmental control system, which was housed in the upper floors of the ship, or the water turbine that kept the water running for the fish hatcheries. But there was no way to go looking, and it tormented Waverly to know that her mother was somewhere on this ship, suffering and afraid, and she couldn't get to her.

They made progress in other ways. Back and forth they worked on a plan for escape, honing it carefully until Waverly believed it could actually work.

Everything depended on her being able to search for the *Empyrean* survivors. But the guards were outside her room constantly, and there was no way to get past them.

One afternoon the solution came to her in a flash. If Mather was keeping the *Empyrean* captives a secret, she'd have to keep the crew away from them. She might have restricted access to that area. It was so simple, she should have thought of this sooner!

'Amanda,' Waverly said when Amanda came in carrying a large gourd full of red grapes, 'what have you been up to today?'

'Not much. Just a little gardening.'

Waverly fidgeted with her pencil. 'I'm just curious. Because I heard no one is allowed to go into the sewage plant.'

'Really? I thought it was atmospheric conditioning they were worried about.'

'Oh?'

'They think the metal in the floor is stressed or something. Only trained personnel are allowed. Not that anyone cares. No one goes there anyway.'

'I guess that's true,' Waverly said, unable to hide the joy in her voice, though Amanda didn't seem to notice.

Atmospheric conditioning. Yes! That explained the sounds she'd overheard from the com station that night in the lab. That's where her mom was.

Relief flooded through her, and she had to leave the living room to be alone in her room because she might cry. After months of worry, fear and scheming, they finally had the key.

There was nothing left to plan.

It was time to kill Anne Mather.

SERVICES

On the day of services, Waverly rose, bleary and anxious. She hadn't been able to sleep at all. Instead she'd stared into the darkness all night with glassy eyes, going over everything again and again. Her life, Samantha's and Sarah's depended on getting this absolutely right.

She only hoped she could move fast enough with her injured leg and was glad to have the cane Josiah had made for her.

'Oh, you're up,' Amanda said, poking her head into the room, something she'd been doing a lot lately. When she stepped inside, Waverly realized that Amanda looked truly pregnant now, with a rounded belly and widening hips. Her own daughter or son was inside Amanda's body, Waverly thought with disbelief. 'Better hurry. We don't want to be late.'

'Yes, I know.' Waverly slipped on her church smock, tucked her hair into the kerchief and looked at herself in the mirror.

She was so changed. Her face was thinner, there were circles under her eyes, and a line was carved between her eyebrows, vertical and severe. She'd aged.

'Let's get a move on!' she heard Josiah call from the living room. He was eager to try out a new hymn he'd written. It made Waverly sad to think that he and Amanda didn't know what was about to happen.

Waverly limped out of her room. She knew she was weaker now than she'd been before the attack, but she was certain she was still stronger than Anne Mather. She had to be.

On their walk to services, a very pregnant woman stopped her and actually kissed her hand, glowing with happiness. 'God bless you,' she whispered.

Waverly barely looked at her. She was too frightened.

She wove between the chairs to take her customary place with Amanda in the front row, where they could see Josiah and the choir. Waverly scanned the crowd for Samantha, who was sitting where she was supposed to on the starboard side, and then for Sarah, who was in the other corner of the room, on the port side. She raised her right hand in a signal to Samantha and waited, holding her breath.

Samantha gave her a quick thumbs-up. The knives were in place. Samantha's task of getting here early to plant them had been the riskiest, but Waverly knew she was the best one to do the job.

Waverly's heart was knocking in her chest. Facing the stage she'd have to climb onto, and seeing Anne Mather's throat, soft and pliant, she felt suddenly that their plan was hopelessly simplistic. Was it really just a matter of some locked doors and a few knives? Could it possibly work?

She swallowed the nausea at the back of her throat. It had to work. It was their only chance.

'What's wrong?' Amanda asked. She rubbed Waverly's back. 'You OK?'

'Yes,' Waverly said, her voice trembling. 'I was just thinking how I'd like to thank you, that's all.'

'Oh?'

'For everything you've done for me.'

'Of course, Waverly. I love you – you know that.'

Waverly could only give her a furtive smile.

Josiah began strumming his guitar, and the crowd settled. Anne Mather, wearing a pumpkin-coloured robe embroidered with birds and flowers, walked to the podium and held up a plump hand. 'Peace be upon you!' she cried.

'And upon you!' responded the crowd.

Under Mather's joyous words, Waverly's ears picked up the faint pounding of two sets of feet, running towards the sides of the huge room.

There was no turning back.

Waverly stood. Already Sarah and Samantha had quietly closed the first two sets of doors. She could hear the soft pop and smell the ozone as they disabled the electric locks. A few people looked around at the sound distractedly, then turned their attention back to Mather. Terror gripped Waverly, and for a moment black spots shadowed her eyes, but she managed to move towards the stage as Mather spoke about celebrating the coming harvest. Amanda tugged on her tunic and hissed, 'Where are you going?'

'I need to pee,' Waverly whispered back. She looped her cane over her wrist and knelt at the pile of hay directly under Mather's podium. Probing underneath it, she felt the cool metal handle. The knife was right where it was supposed to be.

She slipped it between her teeth and quick as lightning pushed herself onto the stage.

Anne Mather stopped in mid-sentence and stared at her.

She grabbed a hank of Mather's hair and jerked her head back to expose her throat. Then she pressed the knife blade against her pulsing jugular.

She felt Mather shudder. Good. She was scared. The woman smelled of soap and coconut lotion, a sickening odour that repelled Waverly. It was disgusting to be so physically close to the woman she meant to kill, and for a moment, her determination flagged.

A surprised cry rose from the congregation. Women covered their mouths to stifle screams, men half stood as if to help Mather, but froze, staring at Waverly in shock.

'This is useless, Waverly,' Mather said through a constricted throat.

'I'll kill you,' Waverly responded, pressing her knife

edge a little further into Mather's skin.

The woman's plump body stiffened. 'Don't move!' Waverly warned, turning the knife so the blade pricked Mather's throat.

She heard footsteps behind her and whirled.

Josiah and the choir were two metres away, frozen, their eyes fixed on the blade. To Waverly's right, a few men had mounted the stage but were keeping their distance, at least for now.

In the front row, Amanda sat with her hands over her mouth.

Mather tried to pull away, but Waverly was too strong.

'What do you hope to accomplish?' Mather said through her teeth.

Waverly ignored her and spoke into the microphone. 'If any of you want to know how much I'd like to kill Anne Mather, come closer. I'll show you.'

Her words rang out like a spell, casting absolute silence. Emboldened, she pivoted to her left, then her right, glaring. 'Back off!' she screamed.

Josiah and the other musicians jumped back, arms upraised. The men to Waverly's right slowly backed away.

Waverly leaned towards the microphone, but before she could speak Mather called, 'Stay calm, everyone! You can see how confused this girl is—'

Waverly pressed the hilt of her knife against the woman's neck, closing off her air supply. Mather stopped talking.

It was Waverly's turn to make a speech.

'I want every girl from the *Empyrean* to listen,' she said, seeking out the faces of her shipmates in the crowd. They were like tiny stars in a dreary sky. 'The *Empyrean* has *not* been destroyed. You know that Mather has been lying about that all along. What you do not know is that there are survivors from the *Empyrean* being held prisoner on this ship.'

A murmur of denial moved through the crowd, but Waverly raised her voice. 'Girls! If you want to see your families again, run to the port side of the room where Samantha—'

Before she could even finish her sentence, the girls were all up, beating back hands that tried to hold them, biting at clinging limbs, getting away so easily. The older girls rushed to help the young ones, lifting them away from their foster families as the toddlers kicked at arms and faces until they were finally free.

Hundreds of feet pounded to the port side of the room.

It was working!

The adults started to follow, but the girls were strong and fast and got away easily.

Waverly let out a scream, a long, wolflike howl that stopped the adults in their tracks just long enough for the girls to slip out of the room. When the door closed safely behind them, Waverly spoke to the crowd, which was disordered and misshapen, confused, frightened. And, for the moment, easily controlled. But just for the moment.

The plan had been to leave right away. Take Anne Mather to the atmospheric conditioning plant and use her as leverage to make the guards release the prisoners. But, looking at all these people, Waverly knew there was no way to trap this many for long. They'd get out and stop the girls.

Unless she could convince them to let the girls go.

'You're good people,' she said into the microphone. She heard a cry off to her right and saw Samantha standing by the last open door. She mouthed, 'What are you doing?' But Waverly ignored her. 'You're good people, but you've allowed unspeakable crimes to be committed in your names. Anne Mather attacked our ship, destroyed our families, took our eggs from us without our consent, and separated all these girls from their parents. Your Pastor is a liar. She's been lying to you all along.'

Mather shook her head, but Waverly closed the woman's windpipe again, and she stopped.

How many people stared at Waverly in shock? How many in anger? How many more in guilt?

Most in disbelief.

They did not believe her.

But some of them did. Some of them must know the truth.

'Most of you don't know about the *Empyrean* survivors on board,' Waverly shouted. Mather's sweat had begun soaking through the thin fabric of Waverly's own shift, making her skin crawl. 'Some of you know about them.'

'She's right!' someone at the back screamed into the silence – a woman with sandy-coloured hair standing on a chair. 'I've been preparing meals for them, and taking them down! There are people down there. Strangers!'

Angry voices met this, but then a man cried out, 'Buckets of waste have been coming down to the sewage plant! They won't say from where!'

The woman who had kissed Waverly's hand stood on her chair. 'I believe her! Waverly wouldn't lie!'

The crowd erupted into a thousand protests and accusations. Waverly yelled into the microphone, 'You have what you wanted. You're going to have our babies. Now let us go and leave us alone.'

Waverly dragged Anne Mather off the stage. Some people from the congregation made a move towards her, so Waverly took the sharp tip of her knife and pricked at the skin just next to Mather's eye. The woman screamed, and the people backed away at the sight of her blood, hands held up in supplication.

'Waverly! Don't do this! Waverly!' Amanda screamed, but Waverly ignored her as she backed towards the port-side door.

She was almost there when she sensed someone behind her.

The guard with the scar had Samantha by the throat, and he was pointing his gun at her head.

ESCAPE

'Waverly—' Samantha started to say, but the guard tightened his arm around her neck, and she gagged.

'I can kill her,' he said to Waverly matter-of-factly. His scar, that angry red line, pinched and winked as he spoke. 'Don't think I won't.'

Now she saw that five other armed men had come into the room. One twisted Sarah's arm painfully behind her back. Her face was red, and tears flowed from her eyes. Another dozen girls were huddled in the doorway, staring.

They'd failed. She'd ruined everything, making her stupid speech! Of course security forces would be monitoring services. What had she been thinking?

She was about to drop her knife when she heard an animal sound, something between a grunt and a scream. Samantha had grabbed the guard's arm and wrenched it away from her neck. 'Run!' she screamed at Waverly, reaching for his gun.

For one long moment, the room, the crowd, the ship, the stars in their incandescent dance, all seemed to slow and stop as if waiting to see what would happen.

Then the universe was set into motion again by a sharp, popping sound.

And another.

Samantha fell into a strange, unhuman shape on the floor.

She was so still.

A strangled cry issued from Anne Mather's throat, and she sank to her knees. Waverly realized she'd let go of her.

'Oh no,' Mather whispered. 'Waverly, what have you done?'

The other guard let go of Sarah. His gun hung loose at his side until the muzzle dropped to the floor. Sarah ran to her friend, rolled Samantha onto her back, sobbing.

Samantha's eyes were two inert marbles in her skull.

'Sam!' Sarah collapsed over her body. 'Sammy, no! No! No! No!'

A plump woman knelt to pat Sarah's back. Another stroked the top of her head.

The crowd started to stir.

'What did you *do*?' a large man shouted at the guard. 'Are you *crazy*?'

The air was electrified.

Waverly felt hands on her back and heard the smallest whisper. 'Go.'

It was the woman with the auburn braid, Jessica, the lector who had warned her so long ago. Now Jessica pushed her towards the doorway where the rest of the girls waited. Serafina's face was twisted in fright. Briany Beckett was crying, and Melissa Dickinson was holding her hand, trying to comfort her. Most of the girls were looking at Waverly, pleading with their eyes.

'Go,' Jessica said.

'But Sarah . . .'

'I'll get her.'

Jessica pushed through the bodies that crowded around Samantha and Sarah. One of the guards was shouting, 'Stand back! Get back!' and brandishing his weapon, but a large man with the muscles of a farm labourer grabbed it away from him.

A shot rang out, and Waverly ran for the door, holding her knife in front of her to make people back away. Her leg was stiff, but she quickly closed the distance to the girls in the doorway. Another shot sounded behind her, and suddenly the crowd was scattering, running from the guns.

Waverly made it to the door and the terrified girls, who were huddled together against the wall. Sarah, meanwhile, was fighting off Jessica, who was trying to drag her backwards towards the door.

'Sarah! We have to go!' Waverly screamed.

Sarah looked around her as though waking up, saw Waverly in the doorway, and blinked. Jessica lifted her by the shoulders and pulled her towards Waverly.

About a dozen people had noticed the open door and were now rushing towards Waverly, threatening to crowd out Sarah, who was trying to fight her way through. Waverly stepped forward, swinging her cane in their faces, roaring, and the people backed away.

'Don't come any nearer,' Waverly said to them, holding up her knife as Sarah fought her way through the mass of shoulders, Jessica right behind her as they slipped through the door.

'Waverly!' Amanda pushed to the front of the crowd. Tears streamed from her red-rimmed eyes. 'Let me help you.'

Waverly pointed her knife at her. 'Leave me alone.'

'Anne won't let you go, Waverly,' Amanda said. 'You need me.'

Waverly scanned the room for Mather, but the woman had disappeared.

With a sinking feeling, she realized she'd ruined the plan. She needed Mather. Without a hostage, she had nothing to bargain with, no way to get the guards to open the locks on her mother's cage.

She needed Amanda after all.

Waverly nodded, and Amanda bolted forward. Josiah tried to chase after her, but she was too quick. She slipped through the doorway, Waverly on her heels, knife held aloft until the doors slid closed on Josiah's stunned face. Quickly, Sarah sliced through the wires with Waverly's knife. The smell of ozone burned Waverly's nostrils.

The door shook with the sound of a body slamming

against it, and another. The door wouldn't hold for long.

'We have to get the girls to the shuttle bay,' Waverly said to Sarah.

'I'll take them,' Sarah said.

'What about our parents?' Melissa Dickinson asked.

'I'm going to get them,' Waverly promised. 'Now go with Sarah and wait on the shuttle.' She turned to Sarah, whose freckled face was soaked with sweat. 'If we don't make it in time, you know what to do.'

Sarah nodded reluctantly. Would she have the stomach to leave Waverly and the rest of them behind, if it came to that?

'Go,' Waverly said.

Sarah gathered up the girls, and they took off, jogging down the corridor towards the elevators, the older girls carrying the toddlers. It would take them five minutes to get to the shuttle bay if they moved quickly.

Waverly, Amanda and Jessica took off towards the elevator bank that would take them to the atmospheric conditioning plant. Amanda pumped the button to the elevator. More shots rang out. 'Oh God, I hope Josiah's OK,' she moaned.

The elevator doors finally opened with a cheery bell tone that made the violence elsewhere on the ship seem like a dark daydream. Waverly pushed the button that led to atmospheric conditioning, but Jessica punched a button for the administrative levels.

'What are you doing?' Waverly asked her, suspicious.

'I know where Anne keeps the key to the container.'

'Oh, thank God!' Waverly wouldn't have to take Amanda hostage after all.

'Also,' Jessica said quietly, 'we should get some guns.'

'Why are you helping me?' Waverly asked, suddenly afraid she'd entered a trap.

Jessica's eyes were forlorn and deadly tired. 'I used to believe in Anne Mather, but . . .' Her expression darkened. 'Not any more.'

'I don't think any of us can imagine the kind of pressure she's under . . .' Amanda began.

'I can,' the woman said. 'I've been working with her for five years.'

'I've known her for forty,' Amanda said quietly.

'So you know that she murdered Captain Takemara?' the woman challenged.

Amanda opened her mouth to protest, but Jessica went on. 'She all but admitted it to me, one night when I found her drunk in her office. Commander Riley's suicide seems suspicious, too, but she won't say anything about it. And remember when the Central Council got food poisoning?'

'I can't believe—'

'Think about it, Amanda. Over the years, how many of Anne's critics have got sick, or had an accident?'

The elevator seemed to move agonizingly slowly, and when the doors opened the lector held up a hand. 'Wait here. I'll get the guns.'

She raced down the corridor towards Mather's office, leaving Amanda and Waverly alone.

'Why didn't you tell me you were so unhappy,

Waverly?' Amanda pleaded. 'I could have helped you find a better way than this.'

'Did you know my mom was here the whole time?'

Amanda's thin mouth tightened. 'No, I didn't.'

'Then how can you defend Mather? Knowing she's been holding our families prisoner for so long?'

'She could have killed them. She didn't.'

'So you approve?' Waverly challenged.

Amanda's eyes closed, and when she opened them again she was looking at the floor. Softly she said, 'No.'

Jessica ran back carrying a gun in each hand and a third strapped to her chest. She handed one gun to Waverly and the other to Amanda, who took it as though it were covered with slime. The elevator doors closed.

'You have the key to their cage?' Waverly asked Jessica.

Jessica held up a large key chain, selected a silver key in answer and handed it to Waverly.

When the elevator doors opened onto atmospheric conditioning, all three women instinctively pointed their guns ahead of them. But there was no one there. The thrum of the air pumps was so deep and loud that Waverly felt it in her chest.

'Where are they?' she asked Jessica, who pointed down a short corridor. A sign on the wall read: humidity control.

The women crept along, their eyes on every corner, watching for guards. At first Waverly strained to hear human sounds, but her ears were assailed by so many noises – the whirring of fans, the echoes of their footsteps on metal grating and the air rushing in and out of the ceiling vents – that she resigned herself to searching with only her eyes.

They reached a large chamber. Up high, on top of the huge metal housings for the air filters, sat a livestock container from the cargo hold. A ladder was propped against the housings, and Waverly vaulted up it before Amanda could hiss, 'Slowly!'

'Look out!' Jessica screamed, and waved her gun at Waverly, who ducked instinctively. A shot rang out. Amanda wailed, and Waverly heard a thud. She saw a guard lying on the floor below, writhing in pain, his gun lying well out of his reach. Jessica kicked it away from him and screamed, 'Hurry!'

Waverly pounded on the metal container with her fists. 'Mom!' she cried.

Faint sounds came from inside the container, then thin fingers reached through the vent. 'Waverly?' someone whispered.

'I'm getting you out,' Waverly said.

Tears blurred her vision as she ran to the lock at the end of the container. She fumbled with the key until it fitted into the keyhole, but the mechanism didn't budge. She turned it over and tried again.

'Stop.' The word came from behind her, but she ignored it. She was almost there.

The sound of a bell split Waverly's ears, and a dent appeared in the metal right in front of her face. She stared at it, and another dent appeared just near her shoulder.

'Stop shooting!' Amanda screamed. 'For God's sake, Anne!'

Bullets. Bullets were flying at her, hitting the metal. Anne Mather and several men were charging towards her from the other end of the room, pausing only to shoot. She ducked and tried the key again, but the lock didn't move.

The air crackled with weapons fire.

'Go!' her mother yelled from inside the container.

'No, Mom! I can get you out!'

Her mother's fingers reached out of the container, and she grabbed them. 'Where are the other girls?'

'Waiting in the shuttle bay!' Waverly screamed in frustration.

'They're *waiting* for you? You have to go, Waverly! Run to them and get off this ship. We'll find a way off.'

'I can't leave you, Mom!' Waverly sobbed. It was all too much. She needed someone to take over, take the girls home. She couldn't be the one who handled things any more. 'I need you!'

'Come down from there, Waverly!' Anne Mather shouted. She was closer now, though by the cracking of guns directly below her Waverly guessed that Amanda and Jessica were keeping Mather and her men at bay. 'You can't do this.'

Waverly lifted her gun, aimed and shot at Anne Mather, who ducked just in time. Waverly turned to work at the lock again, but the key stuck.

Blood sprayed the metal door.

Her blood.

A bullet had winged her arm.

'They'll kill you, Waverly! Run!' her mother shouted.

'Mom!' Waverly cried. Her arm hurt. Her leg hurt.

She couldn't do this any more.

'Run!' her mother screamed.

Finally Waverly gave up.

She threw the keys inside the container before sliding down the ladder. Bullets whizzed over her head as she ran down the narrow opening between filtration units, then turned towards the port-side elevators, which would take her directly to the shuttle bay.

She paused briefly to look at Amanda and Jessica, who were crouched behind a filtration unit. Amanda kept screaming, 'Stop shooting! Have you lost your minds?' She held her gun to her chest, too terrified to use it. Only Jessica was shooting, but that was enough to make Mather and her guards hesitate.

Amanda waved Waverly away. 'When you get through the door, close it and shoot the lock! Go!' Waverly stared at her, wanting to say something, if only, 'Thank you.' But she couldn't. So she turned on her heel and bolted through the door, her lungs ready to burst as she ducked into the corridor. She jabbed the button to close the doors behind her, then shot the keypad, hoping that would hold Mather and her guards at least for a little while. Then she ran as fast as she could to the elevators.

She skidded to a stop.

She was in a nightmare.

Standing at the elevator was the guard with the scar, the one who'd killed Samantha. His back was turned to Waverly and he was looking at the other end of the corridor, holding his gun loosely.

Seeming to sense her, he turned his head.

Their eyes met.

He held up a hand as if to ask her, politely, not to shoot him.

Without thinking, Waverly took aim. Just as her finger found the trigger, he opened his mouth to speak.

'Wait,' he said.

She pulled the trigger.

He groaned and fell down.

Simple. He was standing one moment and slumped against the elevator doors the next, his hand in the cave of his abdomen, which had burst into a show of red. Waverly waited as long as she dared (ten seconds? a minute? eternity?), until his eyes grew dim and the glistening tip of his tongue oozed out of his mouth.

Only then did she hear Anne Mather and her guards pounding on the door behind her. She heard the screech of metal as the doors were pulled open. They were coming to kill her.

She ran to the elevator and slapped the button above the dead guard's shoulder. He was so still. She knew she should take his gun, and she almost did, but she couldn't bear to touch him.

The elevator doors opened, and he fell backwards, his head bouncing when it hit the metal floor. His teeth clicked, air gurgled out of his throat and he lay still, his torso inside the elevator, his legs sticking out of it.

Waverly swallowed a sob. She had to get away. She had to touch him. It.

She forced herself to push against the body's shoulders. She could feel the sharp edges of his bones through the skin, and she could smell his open mouth.

He already smelled dead. With all her strength, she shoved and pushed and prised him away until she was able to edge him out of the door.

'No! God, Shelby!' Mather wailed through the crack in the door.

The man I killed was Shelby. That was his name, Waverly thought as she pushed the button for the shuttle bay.

The elevator doors closed, and she was away.

But it left a mark: touching a dead man who was dead because of her.

She threw up in the corner of the elevator, bracing herself against the wall. An acrid smell filled the air, but once she'd vomited, had picked the particles of digested food out of her hair, had straightened up to stand again on her own two feet, she discovered she felt nothing. Not sorrow at having to leave her mother behind. Not grief that Samantha, wonderful, strong Samantha, had been killed. Not pain in her arm, still bleeding. Not regret at having killed a man. Nothing. She felt nothing.

As the elevator moved through the floors, she heard the waxing and waning sound of gunfire. The violence had spread throughout the ship. She shrank against the back wall of the elevator, praying under her breath.

When the elevator doors opened, Waverly took off at a dead run, tearing down the corridor, not even pausing to look around corners, whispering, 'Please please please,' with every footstep.

She rounded the corner into the shuttle bay and skidded to a stop.

Dozens of women were gathered there. They had the girls.

Waverly held up her gun, pointed it at them, yelled, 'Let them go!'

She would kill them if she had to. She knew now that she could.

A few women straightened and stared at her blankly. Others loaded boxes of food and large jugs of water into the cargo hold. The little girls kissed hands, hugged legs, then trickled into the shuttle as people waved goodbye. Waverly crept towards the shuttle, her gun at the ready.

'You don't need that gun,' someone said.

It was the short, florid woman who had thanked her during the services. She held up a hand. 'Waverly, we wanted to say goodbye while the men hold off the guards. And we got you some food and water, enough for a couple months. You might be out there a while.'

As she said this, the women finished loading the supplies and closed the door to the cargo bay.

'We wish you would stay,' the woman added. 'It's not safe what you're doing.'

'We're leaving,' Waverly said.

'I know that,' the woman replied sadly. But she lifted her hands above her head and cried, 'Peace be upon you!'

'Peace be upon you!' echoed the others.

Waverly edged towards the shuttle and backed up the ramp, her hard eyes fixed on the crowd. They weren't afraid *of* her, they were afraid *for* her, she realized.

'Stop them!' Anne Mather screeched, advancing on her with eight armed guards. 'Waverly, you'll never survive!'

Inside the shuttle, Waverly slammed the control button to raise the ramp.

She sprinted into the cockpit, watching through the glass as chaos broke out in the bay. A large man shot at the guards, who scattered, firing back when they dared. Mather was screaming, her face purple with rage, hair hanging in her eyes, her embroidered mantle crooked on her shoulders. All her composure was gone, and now she seemed like an animal.

Waverly fired the engines and fixed her eyes on the air lock, her heart in her mouth. She pressed the button on the control panel in front of her marked 'Air Lock', but the doors didn't open. The monitor in front of her flashed a command: 'Enter code to unlock.'

Code? She didn't have a code!

Someone darted towards the air-lock controls.

It was Felicity. She had got off the shuttle and was hitting the keypad for the air lock. 'What are you doing?' Waverly shouted.

A blond woman wrapped her arms around Felicity's shoulders and whispered into her ear as Felicity pressed the keypad buttons until the air lock opened. They both turned and waved goodbye to Waverly.

Waverly nodded at her friend, knowing they might never see each other again. She mouthed, 'Thank you.'

Felicity smiled at Waverly for the first time in a very long while.

Waverly started up the engines, released the tethers

and felt the shuttle lift off the floor of the bay. With trembling hands she guided it towards the air lock doorway, which was open now. Trying to remember the simulations she'd practiced with Kieran, she eased the shuttle forward into the chamber. With a hiss of hydraulics, the air lock doors closed behind them, and the outer doors opened onto the endlessness of deep space. Waverly pushed the joystick.

They were out.

She punched the engine thrusters, and the ship kicked forward, slamming her against her seat. On the monitor, the *New Horizon* faded away into the black night sky.

'Where are the rest of them?' Sarah asked from the copilot seat.

Waverly started. Had she been there all along?

Sarah's face was white behind her freckles, and her voice sounded remote, as though it were being piped in from another room. 'Where are our parents?'

Waverly's mouth became a tight, straight line.

'Waverly?'

PART FIVE
METAMORPHOSIS

A leader is a dealer in hope.
                    – Napoléon Bonaparte

A PALE THREAD

How many hours – days – had Kieran been lying on this cot in the brig, staring at the ceiling? They kept the lights on round the clock, so he had no idea how much time had passed. Judging from his hunger, it had been a very long time.

Before this, when everything was normal and Waverly was safe and he lived with his parents, Kieran had never been hungry. He knew that now. He'd called that nagging emptiness in his gut hunger, back when he could eat whenever he wanted, whatever he wanted. Corn on the cob. That had been his favourite. He liked a little walnut oil on it, just a little, and just barely boiled, only enough to make it hot. So crunchy and sweet. Or navy beans, dripping in olive oil, with parsley and garlic. Chicken, roasted with tarragon and rosemary, the way it would smell coming from his mother's kitchen. He'd come home from classes, and the aroma of her cooking would stir his stomach, and he had called that hunger. But what he'd felt then was not hunger.

Hunger was this agony Kieran felt in his joints. It made his head ache and his ear twitch at every sound. It made his teeth soft and loose in his gums, as though they might fall out from disuse. And it made him weak. Kieran felt as though each arm weighed fifty kilograms. Lifting himself upright took every ounce of his strength. Getting up from his cot and walking two steps to the sink for water took an hour of planning, cheering himself on.

The only other thing he could feel, besides his hunger, was his rage. He'd saved their parents, risked his life for them and they were letting him die.

He hated them all.

'You don't look so good,' someone said.

He had forgotten there was someone on the other side of the bars. Either Sealy Arndt or Max Brent, Seth's cronies, had been guarding him constantly. It was Max this time.

'Yeah, I just had a nice salad.' Max grinned, showing big, crooked teeth. 'It was good and fresh. Not very filling, though. I think I'll get myself some eggs when my shift's done. My mom taught me how to scramble them. I like them with scallions.'

'Go to hell,' Kieran managed to say.

'I could make you some, too. All you have to do is tell everyone how sorry you are, and I'll bring you a great big plate of eggs. You'd like that, right?'

'I'd like you to shut up,' Kieran rasped, 'you sadistic little maggot.'

'If you confess, I'll get you some bread. Sarek figured out how to make flatbread and, honestly, it's not bad. Would you like some? All you have to do is admit to your mistakes in front of everyone. It will take one minute.'

Kieran wanted the bread more than anything, but if he confessed to his 'crimes' the way Seth wanted him to he'd lose the *Empyrean* forever. *Tomorrow I'll do it*, he told himself, as he did every day. *Tomorrow. Not today. I can hold out for one more day.*

'Tell you what, Kieran. I'll give you the eggs, and then you can confess. What do you say to that?' Max busted up laughing. 'Nah. I'm just kidding.'

'You're rotten inside,' Kieran spat.

'You better believe it.'

Kieran couldn't imagine how Max justified his behaviour to himself. In a way, he was worse than Seth because he enjoyed Kieran's pain. Every time Seth came into Kieran's cell, on the other hand, the lines on his face deepened.

'Come on, Kieran. Let's end this thing,' he'd cajoled more than once. 'All I need is for you to admit your mistakes to the crew, and we'll give you something to eat!'

Kieran always said no, but it was harder each time.

The door opened, and Sealy Arndt came in for guard

duty. 'Want to take a break?' he asked Max.

'Why not?' Max said as he sauntered out the door. 'Time for dinner! Yum yum!'

Sealy sat down across from Kieran, eyes glinting, and he pulled a loaf of bread from his jacket pocket.

'Oh God,' Kieran said before he could stop himself. It was ordinary wheat bread, nothing fancy, but he yearned for just one bite. He didn't expect one, though. For the past five days (four? six?), the guards had often eaten in front of him. It was their special way of torturing him.

Something dropped on the floor next to his cot.

Struggling onto his side, he scanned the floor until he saw it: a mouthful of bread.

He didn't even chew. His body took over and he gulped it down violently. When it reached his stomach, a horrible cramp doubled him up.

'Here,' Sealy said, tossing him a grav bag.

Kieran put his lips to the straw and released the clamp. The clear, delicious broth slid into his stomach like a healing balm. His body seemed to awaken, and though he was still horribly weak, he could feel the broth working on him, making him better. When he'd drained every last drop, Sealy dropped another bite of bread on the floor for him.

'Don't let it linger,' the boy snapped with a quick glance at the door.

Kieran made himself chew it slowly and swallow. Now, with the broth in his stomach, it didn't cause much of a cramp.

Bit by bit, Sealy fed him this way until the entire loaf was gone.

Kieran's stomach rumbled. He felt as though he might throw up, but he swallowed hard. He wouldn't let himself. He would keep this food down.

Only now did he consider that it might have been poisoned.

He sat up, trembling with effort, and asked, 'Did you just kill me?'

'No.' Sealy looked offended.

'Then why?'

The boy picked up the gun resting on his knees and put it down on the floor. He fingered the trigger, turned it, admired its profile. Finally he said, 'I felt sorry for you.'

So he was a human being after all.

'What are the other boys saying?'

'I'm not going to help you, if that's what you think.'

Kieran was still so weak that he fell onto his side and just lay there, panting.

Kieran preferred Sealy to Max because Sealy was merely hostile and sullen, whereas Max was cruel. He preferred the starboard wall to lean against, because he could see the mirror from there, and he could stare at the glass, imagining that it was actually a window to another room. Odd, how these things brought him a measure of comfort. How small his world had become.

'Sarek was asking about you,' Sealy said casually.

'What did you tell him?'

'I said you're looking thin.'

Kieran accepted this with a grim sigh. So the boy meant only to mock him.

'He said to say hi,' Sealy added with a strange tone.

This seemed so oddly social, so completely out of context, Kieran lifted his eyes to the other boy's face. Sealy's expression gave away nothing. Was he extending some kind of offer to Kieran?

'Well, then . . . Tell him . . .' Kieran's mind raced. What should he say? He tried to remember back to his first day here, before he knew what hunger was. He'd had a good idea. An idea for getting out of here. What was the idea?

Kieran made a fist and closed his eyes.

Trial. The word woke up his mind. Yes. 'Tell Sarek that he and the rest of the boys should request a trial for me.'

'That will give Seth a good laugh.'

'They should say they want to see my crimes exposed.'

'Yeah,' Sealy scoffed. 'Seth would definitely fall for that. Because he's stupid, right?' Sealy shook his head. 'Seth would murder me.'

Kieran waved away Sealy's words as if they were a cloud of flies. He didn't care what Seth might do to Sealy. He was starving to death. He had to get out of here.

TRIAL

Kieran slept. Since that conversation with Sealy and his attempt to reach the outside, the days had stretched like a desert plain to the horizon. He endured occasional taunts from Max and visits from Seth asking if he was ready to confess, but most of the time there was nothing to do but think. He thought about Waverly. He thought about his parents. Sometimes he convinced himself that they were on their way home and he would see them soon.

He spoke to them in his mind. He told them what he planned to do when he finally got out of there. He asked them for advice. And sometimes he listened. Sometimes he could believe that what he heard wasn't a fantasy.

Some message was coming to him in a voice that rang like a distant bell in his mind.

Soon the voice stopped sounding like his father, or mother, or Waverly, or anyone he knew. The voice was its own.

One night, when Kieran felt death hovering in the corner of his stinking cell, he reached out to it.

Let me out of here, he pleaded silently. *I don't want to die.*

You will be freed, the voice answered.

Kieran thought he'd heard it with his ears this time, not just his mind. Was someone here? He opened his eyes and looked at the ceiling over his cot. He heard breathing to the left and turned to see Max Brent sitting with his gun on his knees, dozing. The voice had not been Max's. Couldn't have been.

Kieran wondered if he might be hallucinating, but in truth he felt more lucid than he had in days. He closed his eyes again.

When? he asked.

When the time is right. The voice lived in the place between his ear and his mind, where sound becomes meaning.

But why do I have to wait like this?

There is a purpose to suffering.

Whose purpose? Who are you?

I am.

I'll give my life to you, if you'll help me.

I am already helping you.

Kieran thought maybe this was true, and his spirits lifted.

Sealy kept sneaking in bread and grav bags of broth. There had been twenty-four meals, and about a week of starvation before that, so Kieran knew that he had been in the brig for a month. The meals helped him stay alive, but they weren't enough; he was still starving and still very weak. His cramps seemed more violent now, his muscles tighter, his skin looser. He was thirsty, but he couldn't bring himself to walk to the sink.

He could only listen to the thrum of the engines, feel the vibration of the ship. To Kieran, the hum of the engines had always been the same thing as silence. But now he listened to it as though it were a far-off drumbeat.

He was no longer afraid. After so many others had died, what was one more? He imagined his body floating into space, spinning like a pinwheel for eternity, frozen and unchanged. Something about that comforted him.

The thrumming of the engines shifted, and Kieran wondered if they were changing course or increasing speed. Seth probably had some crazy idea about chasing after the *New Horizon* to start a war he couldn't win. Kieran hoped Seth would get himself and the rest of the boys killed; he was beyond caring that such savage thoughts were beneath him. If they were going to abandon him this way, and let him die in this agony of hunger, it would serve them right.

The engines got louder, and there was a new quality to the sound that he couldn't identify. He heard the guard get up from his chair to crack the door open. Now Kieran could hear the sound better.

It wasn't the engines; it was a chant. The boys of the

Empyrean were chanting, 'Trial, trial, trial,' over and over.

Had Sealy leaked his message after all?

Kieran tilted his head. Max Brent was standing by the door, listening. When he saw Kieran looking at him, he slammed the door and leaned against it.

'Don't think we're giving you a trial,' he told Kieran. 'They can shout themselves hoarse.'

'What are you going to do, shoot them all? You need them to run the ship.'

'We don't need anyone,' Max said, his eyes shifting nervously.

Kieran wanted to say something withering, but he couldn't think of the words, so he closed his eyes again. He hoped that the boys would get him out, but the idea of wanting something, requesting it and getting it no longer seemed like a logical progression. Time had broken down around him. There was only the *now*. *Now* he was in the brig. *Now* he was hungry. *Now* he was thirsty. *Now* he could not lift his hand off his chest. So he went to sleep.

A loud bang startled him awake, and Seth's angry face loomed over him. 'Pick him up.'

Rough hands closed around his arms, and then he was being dragged down a corridor. The motion made him sick. He tried to plant his feet, but dizziness overcame him, and he had to close his eyes.

When he came to, he was sitting in a chair, his limbs hanging, useless. In front of him were the boys of the *Empyrean*, all of them looking up at the stage he was on. The auditorium? He hadn't been there since the day of the attack. They'd held pageants and talent shows on this stage. He'd sung 'You Are My Sunshine' as a boy here. Now he was on trial.

Many of the boys sitting in the theatre seats seemed alarmed at Kieran's appearance, and he realized he must look pretty bad. Then again, so did they.

Arthur Dietrich, in the front row, had a nasty bruise on his arm, as though he'd been shackled or tied down. He also had a black eye, and a bloody tissue hung from one of his nostrils. As one of Kieran's friends, he must have caught a lot of trouble from Seth and his guards.

Sarek Hassan, also in the front row, had a split lip. He might have decided Kieran wasn't so bad after all and earned a punch in the face for it. He seemed as watchful and detached as always, until he met Kieran's eyes. Then he scowled, his fists clenched.

It wasn't just the older boys who were marked by Seth's style of leadership. All the little boys looked afraid. One four-year-old was crying and pale, his arm in a sling, and he startled when another boy sat down next to him.

'Shut up!' someone yelled. It was Seth standing behind a podium. He was smartly dressed in the uniform of a security officer. It was too big, but he'd belted it tightly. Sealy and Max stood behind him, holding their guns.

Kieran might get his trial, but he knew no one would speak for him because of those guns.

So this was it, the public humiliation and then the air lock. The end.

'Shut up and listen,' Seth said testily. 'We're starting

the trial of Kieran Alden. Max Brent, please read his list of offences.'

Max pulled out a small notebook. 'Kieran Alden prevented the *Empyrean* from chasing after the *New Horizon*, and now we might never find our families. Kieran prevented us from rescuing our parents from the radiation in the engine room, and now Mason Ardvale, Sheldon White and Mariah Pinjab are all dead, and the others are ill. He damaged the atmospheric controls in his reckless shuttle flight, and we're alive only because of Seth Ardvale's quick intervention. Kieran Alden showed countless other instances of incompetent leadership. He is a danger to this ship and everyone on board.'

The words were terrifying, galvanizing. Kieran watched the crowd. Most of the boys looked frightened. Many of the younger ones were crying. Expecting them to rise up against Seth was asking a lot.

'The court calls the first witness, Matt Allbright,' said Seth.

It was a farce. First one boy, then the next, stood right next to Kieran and told bald-faced lies as Sealy and Max pointed guns at them. Kieran tried to listen, looking for a way to defend himself, but he was so tired and in so much pain that it was hard to concentrate, even knowing his life depended on it. After a time, he stopped paying attention to what they were saying and instead tried to form an argument of his own. But his own thoughts proved too tiring, and soon the words faded away, the room faded away. And he just sat there.

It was the silence that finally brought him around

again. He looked up to see Seth coming back to the
podium, his face grim. 'With all this evidence against
him, it seems only right to sentence Kieran Alden to
death, unless, that is, he is willing to confess to his
crimes—'

'Yes!' someone shouted. Kieran looked at the crowd,
trying to see who it was. 'I want to hear what he has to
say for himself!' It was a familiar voice, but Kieran
couldn't place it. Whoever was speaking was hiding in
the crowd.

'Yeah!' said Sarek in the front row, his eyes on
Kieran. 'Let the bastard try to explain himself.'

Kieran looked at Sarek, whose face was carefully
neutral. He didn't know if he was trying to help or not,
but he could see this was his chance, because Seth
looked at Kieran for the first time, trying to measure
him.

'Kieran?' pressed Seth. 'Are you ready to confess?'

Kieran nodded. For so long he'd been telling himself
he'd confess tomorrow, but he'd run out of tomorrows.
If he didn't make his confession right now, they were
going to kill him. Commanding the *Empyrean* wasn't
worth dying for.

The podium seemed to be a mile away. He couldn't
possibly walk there, could he?

He pivoted on his chair, placed his hand on the back
of it, and pushed himself up. His body shuddered, and
his knees buckled, but he caught himself and forced his
legs to straighten under him. He was standing for the
first time in two days, leaning on the chair. He walked
around to the back of it until he could reach the podium

with his other hand, and he pulled himself over to it. He had to lean on it with almost all his weight, but it held him. He looked at the boys, who had fallen silent.

So many of their faces were cut and bruised, pinched and fearful. If Kieran gave in now, that's how their lives would be. He didn't know if he could live with that.

No. He couldn't give in and confess.

Instead, he searched his mind for something to say.

The truth. That's what his dad always said. The truth is powerful.

'You don't hold a gun to the witness's head in a fair trial,' he croaked into the microphone. His mouth was gummy, his voice a shrivelled reed.

'What are you doing?' Seth whispered. 'Come on, man. Let's end this.'

'This trial is based on lies,' Kieran rasped.

'What did he say?' a pubescent boy shouted. 'I can't hear him!'

'He said he's sorry,' Seth lied. 'Sorry for everything he did. So now we forget all this and get him something to eat.'

Kieran shook his head. 'That's not what I said,' he cried. 'I won't confess. You'll have to kill me.'

The auditorium was silent. Even the littler boys who'd been crying stopped.

Seth shoved Kieran aside and took the podium. Kieran tilted on his feet, tried to catch himself and fell to the ground.

'The court sentences Kieran Alden to public execution,' Seth announced. 'Take him to the shuttle bay,' he told Sealy.

The boy stared at Seth, frozen.

'Come on!' Seth shouted impatiently.

'But—' Sealy's eyes were on Kieran.

This is it, Kieran thought. He was afraid, but he would not close his eyes. If they were going to kill him, they should see his eyes. He stared at Sealy, waiting.

'Goddamn it,' Seth yelled. 'Max! Get him out of here!'

But Max couldn't move. 'I didn't think we were going to kill anybody,' he said finally.

'It's not your job to *think*, Max!' Seth bolted towards Max, reaching for his gun.

Kieran was closer to Max than Seth was. He couldn't fight, but he could tip himself over. He hit Max in the knees, and the boy toppled over, his gun rattling to the floor. Kieran used the last of his strength to lunge at the weapon and cover it with his body.

'Goddamn it, you bastard!' Seth cried. 'Why won't you give up?'

Seth pummelled Kieran with both fists, spit flying from his mouth. Kieran held on, enduring Seth's blows, holding Max's gun to his chest. He was either going to live or die. Live or die. He wanted to live to see Waverly again, so he filled his lungs with air and he screamed, 'Help me!'

Suddenly Seth's weight was gone. Sarek was pulling him back in a choke hold. Seth clawed at Sarek and kicked at Kieran, until a boy of about seven wrapped himself around one of Seth's legs. Another, even younger, grabbed on to Seth's other leg. Soon Seth was surrounded by a swarm of boys, all of them screaming furiously for a piece of him.

The crowd was electrified. A dozen fights broke out. Some boys tried to defend Seth and his guards, but they were overwhelmed by sheer numbers. A pile of boys mobbed Sealy, took his gun, and dragged him down. Max tried to make a break for the door, but a large boy of twelve tackled him and he fell hard.

It was over.

The round, freckled face of Arthur Dietrich appeared before Kieran. 'Are you OK?' he asked.

Kieran beckoned him closer. 'Throw them in the brig. Gather all the guns and bring them to me.'

Arthur fought his way through the crowd around Seth and yelled something at Sarek. Then Kieran saw something wonderful: Sarek, helped by eight other boys, dragged the snarling Seth out of the auditorium.

'You'll regret this!' he screamed at Kieran before they carried him away.

Meanwhile, Arthur had got the guns and brought them to Kieran.

'Take out the casings,' Kieran told him, and watched his clumsy fingers work the mechanisms. A boy brought him a grav bag full of water, and he sipped at it eagerly. Arthur held up the ammunition casings for Kieran to see. 'OK. Now hide them where no one can find them, Arthur. Hide all the guns.'

Nearly tripping over his own feet, Arthur hurried off with the weapons.

'Kieran, are you OK?' Little Matthew Chelembue touched Kieran's cheek with concern.

Kieran smiled. 'Bring me some food.'

RECOVERY

For the first few days, Kieran could only sip broth and eat bread. He lay on a cot in Central Command, trying to answer questions about how to clean the air filters or how many chickens to kill for dinner, but most of the time he dozed.

As soon as he could sit up on his own, he watched the vid console that showed the cell where Seth, Sealy and Max were locked up. Seth paced like a caged animal. Max was sullen. Sealy was quiet but watchful. If Seth ever figured out that Sealy had helped Kieran, he'd be in real danger. Maybe he could get Sealy out of there to a cell of his own where he'd be safe.

He put the thought aside. Sealy had been the one

who'd broken Matthew Perkins's arm. He claimed it
was an accident, but Kieran thought it was only right
that he serve some time in the brig, at least until Kieran
had a better take on the political situation. The three
ringleaders had caused complete havoc in their month-
long dominion over the ship, and many of the boys
resented them fiercely. But Kieran suspected there
might be an undercurrent of sympathy for Seth among
the boys. At times he felt that he was being watched by
unkind eyes. He'd have to take control of the ship with
a firm hand to make sure Seth didn't rise to power
again.

'I'm glad you're back,' Arthur Dietrich said one night.
He and Kieran were becoming good friends, and they
often talked late into the night after everyone else had
gone to bed. Arthur hugged his mug of hot chocolate to
his middle.

'Hot chocolate always reminds me of my mom,'
Kieran said softly.

Arthur looked at him sharply. The boys had adopted
an unspoken policy not to mention parents, or the girls,
or anything from their past lives. It was one way of
surviving. But tonight Kieran wanted to remember.
'She always put lots of cocoa into it, and a splash of
goat's milk. Made it creamy.'

'I like mine dark,' Arthur said.

'Where were your parents during the attack?' Kieran
asked.

'I'm not sure. Dad was probably in the granaries.
Mom might have been in her garden, or . . .' Arthur
looked into his mug. 'That's the hardest part. I don't

know what happened to them, and there's no one to ask.'

'I think my dad's dead,' Kieran said, surprised at himself. It wasn't something he'd allowed himself to think, and he just said it, as though he'd been certain all along.

'Really?' Arthur asked gently.

'Both my parents were in the starboard shuttle bay.' Kieran realized he'd never told this to anyone. 'I saw Mom get on a shuttle, but . . .'

Arthur gazed out of the porthole, and Kieran wondered if they were thinking the same thing: all those people were still out there, twirling in the cold darkness.

Kieran sank into silence, and Arthur sipped his cocoa quietly.

'You know, Kieran,' Arthur finally said, 'Seth did try to kill you.'

'You don't think that was a bluff?'

'It might have started out as a bluff, but I'm not sure it would have ended as one.'

Kieran squirmed in his seat. He didn't like talking about that day.

'All I'm saying is . . . he's still dangerous.'

'Yes, he is, and most of the boys know it.'

'Some of them want to break him out,' Arthur said, his cornflower blue eyes on Kieran. 'If that happens, Seth could do a lot of damage.'

'That's why we have to make sure he doesn't get out.'

'You should let me get the guns from where I hid them.'

'No guns,' Kieran said, so firmly that the words raised a cough in his throat.

'We don't know what will happen,' Arthur warned.

'True, but we can't act like Seth. The only thing that proves we're right is that we *don't* act like him.'

'You found a way out of the brig. He will, too.'

'Maybe.' Arthur could be right, unless Kieran could bring Seth's supporters around. 'Who do you think is against me?'

Arthur thought hard about the question and wrote down ten names. At the top of the list was Tobin Ames, the boy who had planned to go down to the engine room to get his mother.

'Why don't you send Tobin up to speak to me?' Kieran said.

'Are you sure?'

'I want to try talking to him.' He'd created this rift with Seth by ignoring him. He would try a different tactic with Tobin.

Tobin always reminded Kieran of a hedgehog, with coarse brown hair that stood on end, a rounded frame, and a shifting gaze. He looked sleepy when he approached Kieran's cot. 'Did Arthur wake you?'

'I was watching over my mom,' the boy said sullenly.

'How is she?' Kieran asked, keeping his voice low because he knew it made him seem wiser, calmer, more adult.

'She's not too good,' Tobin snapped. 'If you had let us go down—'

'We would all be dead. You know why we couldn't go down there, Tobin. The only way to rescue them was the way we did it. Ask your mom.'

'I would . . .' The boy's sentence trailed off.

So she was unconscious. She might be dying. They all might die.

'I didn't call you up here to debate the past,' Kieran said, trying to sound as patient as he could. 'I need a chief medical officer, and I hear that you've been poring over the instructional videos, learning a lot.'

'I've had to! They didn't just have radiation sickness. They had decompression sickness, and cuts, and abrasions . . .'

'I'm putting you in charge of the infirmary,' Kieran said. 'Choose three capable men to be your crew, and start training them.'

Tobin was so surprised that he lost his voice for a moment. 'To do what?'

'Assist you. Arthur has taken inventory of the granaries, and the corn is almost ripe. We're going to have to harvest soon. That means boys running equipment, working hard. There will be injuries. We need to be ready.'

Kieran didn't add that the infirmary was the area where Tobin was least likely to do him political damage. If the boy took the job seriously, he wouldn't have time to organize an uprising.

Tobin left the meeting that night looking confused, but he did assign three of his friends to help in the infirmary, and the four of them spent hours every day training themselves using instructional videos and the vast medical encyclopedia.

When Kieran felt well enough to walk, the infirmary

was the first place he went. There were medications littering the cabinets and empty oxygen tanks on the floors, but all the patients had fresh sheets, and they seemed well cared for, even if they were still horribly weak.

Eight. Only eight adults left. *Please God, don't let any more die*, Kieran prayed.

He sat next to Victoria Hand's cot and searched her swollen face for signs of consciousness. She was the only remaining medical person on board, and they needed her badly. 'Has she spoken?' he asked her son, Austen, who sat in a chair by her bed.

'Not today,' the boy said. He looked ghostly, with his light blond hair and pale, sallow skin. 'She was awake yesterday.'

'Has she been able to help you guys? Give you any advice?'

Austen shook his head.

Kieran took the woman's reddened hand and squeezed it, hoping to feel something in return, but not even her breathing changed. He stood. 'I think you're doing a really good job,' he said to Tobin, who was standing behind him, looking on. 'How's *your* mom?'

The boy smiled. 'She talked this morning. She knew me.'

Kieran sensed that Tobin had forgiven him. 'What has she been saying?'

'We talked about Dad, mostly, where he probably is. What we'll do when he comes back. She wants to make him a cake.'

Kieran smiled. 'Can I have a piece?'

The boy nodded grudgingly. 'Sure. You can have a piece.'

The next day, Kieran felt strong enough to survey the damage to the agricultural bays. He had no idea what forty hours of zero gravity might have done, and he was anxious to see for himself.

Seth had taken care of the most pressing issues, but there were still problems. The granary lights were much dustier than usual. A stand of aspens in the arboretum had fallen, and a team of boys was feeding them into the mulchers. In the tropics bay, a palm tree had toppled into a lemon grove, killing several smaller trees. The small herd of goats had sustained some injuries, but the chickens seemed healthy, though the coop was filthy. Otherwise, the damage was surprisingly minimal, and Kieran knew that if the boys worked steadily they'd be able to make the necessary repairs.

But keeping them working was a problem. The mood on the ship was sombre. More than six weeks had passed since the girls were taken, and with each passing day the boys' worry grew. They were no longer ruled by panic, but by a heavy despair. A few of them had stopped working altogether, and the rest were losing heart. Kieran knew he had to do something about it. He had to find a way to give them hope.

TRANSFORMATION

One evening, after a long day of running the combine in the cornfield, Kieran sat in the Captain's chair in Central Command, watching the com terminal. The sensors would pick up a ship long before he got visual contact, but he still liked scrolling through the different outside views, peering into the murk of the nebula as though he might just catch a glimpse of the *New Horizon* or his mother's shuttle. The only other person with him in Central Command was Sarek, eating mashed grain and beans, his face awash with the bluish light from his com screen. Kieran sipped a mug of tea from the Captain's private reserves, a deep Earl Grey made from bergamot flowers and cured tea leaves grown back on Earth. It was fragrant, sharp without sugar or goat's milk, and it focused his mind.

Sarek set his bowl down on his desk and rubbed his hands over his face. Always serious and quiet, he'd matured even more since the attack and had shouldered almost as much responsibility as Arthur.

'I never thanked you, Sarek,' Kieran said.

The boy turned. 'For what?'

'For helping me out at my trial. I think you might have saved my life.'

'I don't think so. Seth looked more scared than you did.'

'You stuck your neck out just the same. I appreciate it.'

Sarek's black eyes fixed on Kieran's. 'Morale is low, you know.'

'How could it not be?'

'Matt Allbright didn't show up to relieve me today. I found him in his mother's bed. He said it's pointless to keep trying because we'll never find them. Too much time has passed. He's not the only one saying it, either.'

'I'm not sure what I can do about that, Sarek,' Kieran said, wishing he *were* sure. He sounded like the old Kieran who never knew what to do.

'All I know is I'm doing more work with less time off,' Sarek said. 'And I see more guys shirking their duty and sulking around. The ship can't run like that.'

Kieran set his mug of tea in the cup holder next to the captain's chair and leaned back. He'd come to trust Sarek almost as much as Arthur. He was reliable in a way few other boys were. 'What makes the

GL◯W

difference, do you think?'

The boy looked at him, puzzled.

'You haven't given up. What's the difference between you and Matt Allbright?'

Sarek leaned an elbow on the arm of his chair while he thought about it. He shook his head. 'All I know is that I get up every morning, I point myself towards Mecca, and I say my prayers.'

'And that helps?'

Sarek shrugged. 'It's what my dad would want me to do.'

Kieran nodded, thinking back to that terrible night when he was nearly at the end of his strength, the night the voice came to soothe him.

'So you believe in God,' Kieran said.

'Yeah.'

'Why?'

Sarek seemed bewildered by the question. 'It just seems obvious to me, I guess. That there must be something behind all this.' He gestured out of the windows, where a star or two winked dimly through the nebula. 'I mean, all of creation? You? Me? Just because of some cosmic accident? It doesn't seem realistic.'

'I know what you mean,' Kieran said pensively. 'But do you think we're in the minority?'

'How do you mean?'

'Do you think we're the only believers on board?'

Sarek shook his head. 'Not by a long shot. Not any more, anyway. Dad always said there are no atheists in foxholes.'

'Why wasn't your family chosen to go on the other ship?' Kieran asked. It was something he'd often wondered about his own spiritual family, who had never quite fitted in on the *Empyrean*.

Sarek shrugged. 'I don't think the Muslim families would have fitted in on the other ship, either.'

Kieran nodded pensively.

That night, Kieran lay in the Captain's bed and reflected on how he'd led the boys until now. He'd been practical, logical and responsible, but he hadn't inspired them.

'Am I failing them?' he whispered into the dark.

They need a vision, said the voice.

He sat up, his sheets rustling around his legs.

'Are you really there?' he whispered. 'What do I do?'

Give them a vision.

'How?'

You'll find the way.

'I need more than that!' he yelled.

But he was alone again.

A vision, the voice had said. That's what the boys lacked. A place they could imagine as their destiny, some goal to work towards even as they grieved.

Kieran remembered the night when so many of the boys had learned they'd lost parents in the shuttle-bay massacre, and the sermon he'd found. That sermon had given the boys enough hope to keep trying, or at least not give up, because, Kieran realized, it helped them to feel that they were still connected to their lost loved ones, as Sarek said.

He had to find more sermons like that.

He got out of bed, turned on the desk lamp and scrolled through the Captain's computer. He found the folder with the sermons in it and read through titles like 'Barren of Womb, Fertile of Heart' and 'Our Crops Are Our Children'. Few of the sermons spoke to the problems he and the boys faced, but he read them all. They talked about the greater mission and the glorious day when the ships reached New Earth and the work of terraformation could begin. It was a sacred mission, a pact with God and the rest of humanity, not only those back on Earth, but their children, and their children's children, for millennia to come.

These words caught at Kieran, and he felt them to be true. The *Empyrean*'s mission *was* the greatest endeavour in all of human history. The continuation of Earth-origin life depended on it, and it must not fail. Surely this must be the work of God.

Why, then? Why had God let those people kill their families and take the girls away? Why would He put the mission in jeopardy? Unless . . . was that part of His plan?

Suffering has purpose, thought Kieran. His time of pain and starvation in the brig had purified him and made him ready to receive God's message. God allowed the attack so that all the crew of the *Empyrean* would be open to His voice.

Kieran stayed up all night long, reading the sermons, taking notes and writing down his own thoughts in the wreath of yellow light from his desk lamp. The more he wrote, the more strongly he felt that he was meeting his destiny. The voice had pointed him here, and he'd found what he was meant to do.

By morning, when the rest of the boys stirred from their beds and wandered into the central bunker for their breakfast, they found rows of chairs arranged before a podium. At the podium, wearing his black suit and tie, stood Kieran Alden, clean-shaven, reddish hair slicked back, fingernails spotlessly clean. Kieran fitted the loudspeaker to his mouth. 'Please take a seat, everyone,' he said. 'I have some thoughts I'd like to share with you.'

The boys hesitated until they saw the pieces of fresh bread with generous dollops of blackberry jam placed on each chair. Then they sat down happily enough.

Only about half the boys had come, but that was all right. It was a good start. He nodded at Arthur, who pressed a button on the intercom, and a recording of a Beethoven sonata began to play. Arthur dimmed the lights, keeping a single spot on Kieran so that he glowed. Kieran imagined himself reflecting the light in manifold, taking it into himself and releasing it as a gift to the sad, frightened little boys.

Could he really do this? Was he really this kind of man?

'Thank you for coming.' Kieran looked at his notes, which had seemed so brilliant the night before. Now that sixty pairs of eyes watched him, waiting, his words seemed thin and weak. He felt his light fade.

But thin and weak was better than nothing.

'We've been through a lot in these past months,' he began. 'We've lost loved ones, been separated from our families, our friends, and we don't know where they are or if they're safe. Until this nebula clears, there's nothing we can do but wait and hope for the best.'

Kieran heard an angry scoff from the back of the room, but he didn't pause to look up or even acknowledge it.

'Why did this happen to us? We've been sent into the vastness of creation to remake our new home in the image of God's perfect creation on Earth.' Many of the boys looked at him with puzzlement; still more looked thoughtful. 'We all believed unquestioningly in the rightness of our mission, didn't we? Let's raise our hands in a show of solidarity that our mission is God's work.'

Kieran raised his right hand, and most of the boys raised their hands, too.

'Look around you. Look at all these raised hands. The majority of us have known all along we were performing God's work, haven't we? Now, put your hands down, and let me ask you another question.'

Obediently, the hands dropped, and Kieran paused, looking at the boys, all of them watching him, waiting to hear what he would say next.

This was so much easier than he'd thought it would be.

'Now, raise your hand if you attended services once a week.'

Only about five hands went into the air, as Kieran knew would be the case. 'How many went once a month?'

Six more hands raised, but most of the boys looked at Kieran shamefaced.

'You can put your hands down.' Kieran waited for the boys to drop their hands. 'Now I'm wondering how different things might be if we had been paying attention to the spiritual side of our mission. What if we'd been more mindful? Would God have been kinder to us in the hour of our need? Would our mothers and fathers and sisters be with us here today, if we'd paid Him more attention? If we'd got down on our knees, just once a week, and thanked God for giving us the privilege of being the first generation to set foot on the planet that soon all of humankind will call home, forever after?'

He looked around the room. There were sceptical faces in the crowd, sure, and plenty of boys seemed not to be paying attention at all, but most of them seemed to be thinking about what he was saying. Some of them even looked tearful.

'I think in our day-to-day lives, we've forgotten who we are. We are the forefathers of a new civilization. We will lay the foundation for countless generations of human beings in a corner of the galaxy where nothing –' Kieran drew breath to build his voice and called out – 'I say *nothing* like us has been seen before. We *will* get the girls back, and with them we will create a new world!'

He had them. Many of them were looking at him with guarded awe. Amos Periwinkle had folded his hands under his chin and was staring at Kieran, rapt and amazed. Tobin Ames, the boy who had been plotting against him before, seemed thunderstruck by the enormity of Kieran's ideas.

'This is why I'm starting a new tradition. Every Sunday morning, we're going to come here, we're going to eat bread together and we're going to talk about these things. We'll end every service by getting on our knees and thanking God for putting us on this miraculous ship and sending us across the galaxy. We'll give our thanks to God for choosing us to be . . .' Here he paused, made them wait for it: 'The world makers.'

Kieran walked around the podium so the boys could see his full length, and with great ceremony he got on his knees, folded his hands and bowed his head in prayer.

It took a few minutes. At first they just stared at him, but then, one by one, the boys got on their knees, leaned on the chairs in front of them and bowed their heads.

A few stayed seated. Kieran expected this. But the overwhelming majority had latched on to this new idea. Kieran stayed kneeling for several minutes, feeling the pulse of the room. It was perfectly silent while the boys prayed, but, slowly, some indefinable tension in the air seemed to ebb away. When finally Kieran felt a peace settle over his congregation, he looked up, smiled and said, 'Amen.'

The next Sunday there was flatbread with garlic and olive oil, and Kieran gave thanks to God for the harvest. The Sunday after that, there was cornbread and sheep's butter, and Kieran praised God for the new batch of chicks that had hatched in the poultry bay. After a few months, he added a segment during which anyone who wanted could speak his prayers aloud. This was a good way to get a sense of how the crew was feeling. He knew the services were helping morale when one Sunday a boy named Mookie Parker stood and squeaked, 'I thank God for these services because they make me feel better.'

Kieran saw several heads nodding in agreement and many other faces looking at him with admiration. It had worked. He'd become a leader who inspired, with God's help, and he felt grateful.

One Sunday, about five months after the attack, Kieran looked up from his podium and realized that almost every single boy on the ship was attending his services. He was even more gratified when a young boy walked up to him after the services and tugged on his jacket. 'Are my parents in heaven? Can I talk to them?'

Kieran looked into his softly freckled face, and he said, 'Yes. There's a heaven. And you should talk to your parents every day.'

The answer came so automatically, so naturally, Kieran felt it must be the truth.

The boy relaxed into an apple-cheeked smile, and he walked away to tell a group of his friends what Kieran had said.

Kieran felt sure of it now. He was doing the work of God.

THE SETH PROBLEM

The ship was dark. In his new quarters, Kieran lay on the Captain's bed, a wonderfully soft, extra-wide mattress. This would be a good place to bring Waverly, if he ever saw her again. He pressed his face into his pillow, imagining it was her soft hair.

For the thousandth time, he thought of changing the ship's course to go look for her. It was almost a physical need, to take control of the *Empyrean* and begin circling towards the direction he'd seen the *New Horizon* take. He'd almost given the order yesterday, but Arthur Dietrich had urged him that the best hope was to stay on course. 'Let them come to us,' he'd said.

Even Sarek had agreed. 'You were right all along,

Kieran. There's nothing to do but wait. If they're looking for us in this damn nebula, the only way they'll find us is if we're where they expect us to be.'

'It was tactically ingenious,' Arthur had said owlishly, 'to attack inside the nebula.'

'We'll get back at them,' Kieran had said darkly. 'If we have to wait until we get to the planet, we'll get them.'

The fact was, now that the ship was under control and all the boys were working, Kieran thought about Waverly all the time. He worried for his parents, of course, but Waverly needed him, and he wasn't there for her.

It was pointless to try to sleep, so he turned on the lamp by his bed. A framed reproduction of an old Van Gogh painting, brilliant yellow haystacks, hung opposite him. It made him long for Earth in a way he hadn't before: If they'd never left Earth, there'd be an easy way to find Waverly – he could walk or run to where she was and simply bring her back. But he wasn't on Earth. He was on a ship cruising through a hideous pink nebula, and there was nowhere to go.

He startled when the com station on his bedside table blinked on. 'Captain, you've got to come down to the brig!'

Over the relay, Kieran heard crashing sounds and grunting. 'What's happening?'

'The prisoners are fighting, sir. They're killing each other!'

Kieran pulled on his loose hemp trousers and stepped into his sandals. He reached the elevator in seconds and was speeding down to the brig before he even tried to catch his breath. When the elevator doors opened, he could hear the fight echoing down the corridor. It sounded like animals wrangling over a bone.

When he reached the brig, he found Seth standing over Sealy, kicking him in the stomach while Max tried weakly to make him stop. Sealy was unconscious, and Max wasn't much better off. Seth's breathing was laboured, and his knuckles were blue with bruises, but he kept kicking at Sealy, over and over.

'Stop,' Kieran said.

Seth didn't seem to hear him.

'Stop!' Kieran shouted. He took the keys from the guard, unlocked the cell door, and fell on Seth. Then they were on the floor and Kieran was hitting him in the face, over and over again, swearing.

At first Seth clawed at Kieran's face and tried to beat him away, but he couldn't. So he went limp and allowed Kieran to pummel him. When Kieran finally stopped, Seth's eyes were swollen, and his bottom lip was split and bleeding.

Kieran's fists stung where he'd cut his knuckles on Seth's teeth. He was out of breath, exhausted. The guards, two young boys who were new to this, stared at him in terror.

'What are you looking at?' he spat.

'S-sorry,' said one of them, a thirteen-year-old named Harvey Markem. He was holding one pale hand over his belly, as though he were going to be sick.

'Separate them, one per cell,' Kieran ordered, getting to his feet and only now surprised at what he'd done.

'They should have been split up long ago.'

'Sorry,' Harvey said again.

'It's not your fault,' Kieran forced himself to say. 'It's mine.'

Without looking Kieran in the eye, Harvey and the other guard, a fifteen-year-old who called himself Junior, stepped into the cell and took hold of Seth by the arms. As they pulled him across the corridor, Kieran stood in the doorway to make sure that Max couldn't run away. But the boy was spent. He lay on the floor watching Kieran with indifferent eyes.

Sealy was motionless, and Kieran eyed him with regret. He'd known Sealy might be in danger around Seth, but he hadn't separated them. Now Sealy was half dead.

When the guards came back for Max and dragged him to another cell, Kieran turned Sealy onto his back.

His face was purple with bruises, his wrist lay across his chest at a sickly angle, and his twisted hand looked like the claw of some stricken animal. Kieran ripped open Sealy's shirt. The boy's torso was blue and yellow from old and new bruises. He should have moved him long ago.

'Contact the infirmary and tell them to bring a stretcher with restraints, and some bandages and antiseptic for the other two.'

A few minutes later, two sleepy-eyed boys from the infirmary, wearing pyjamas, bore Sealy away on a stretcher. They'd brought metal bowls full of antiseptic, ointment and bandages, which Kieran pushed through the bars, first to Max, who was lying on the cot clutching his forehead, and then to Seth, who was leaning against the wall, panting through grotesquely swollen lips.

'You'll probably want some painkillers,' he said to Seth.

'Probably.' Seth rooted through the supplies, found a tube of ointment, and dabbed at his bloodied lip. By the competent way he treated his wounds, Kieran guessed that Seth had nursed himself through many beatings, most likely from his father. That could be one reason for all his anger.

'I guess the great Pastor Kieran Alden isn't so perfect after all,' Seth said, bandaging a scrape on his arm. 'You beat the shit out of me.'

'I never said I was perfect.'

Seth laughed at that. 'You didn't have to.'

Kieran looked at his bloody fists, ashamed. 'I'm sorry I attacked you.'

'You had cause.' Seth unscrewed the cap on the bottle of aspirin, tossed a handful into his mouth, and chewed them loudly. He limped to the sink and drank from the tap.

'Why did you attack Sealy?'

'Take a guess.'

'He did something you didn't like.'

'You could say that.' Seth gave Kieran a sidelong look. 'He's the reason I'm in here.'

'How did you find out?'

'He told me.' Seth laughed, shaking his head. 'What a fool. He felt guilty.'

The two sat in silence until Seth finished treating his injuries. Then he lay back on the cot with a grunt, placing an arm over his eyes.

'I wish I could go back in time,' Kieran said.

Seth looked at him, startled.

'I'd do a lot of things differently,' Kieran admitted, wondering at his need to talk to Seth this way when the boy had almost murdered him. But with Waverly and his parents gone, Seth was the person he felt closest to. Arthur was smart, but too young; Sarek was trustworthy, but too distant. And it wasn't just because he and Seth were about the same age or able to lead the boys, thought Kieran. It was more than that.

He knew he was exceptional, and he knew Seth was, too. Under different circumstances, they might have been friends.

'I guess I'd do some things differently, too,' Seth finally said grudgingly, then added, 'Like that trial kind of backfired.'

'Would you really have killed me?' Kieran asked, hoping that Seth didn't detect the fear in his voice. Even now, with Seth safely locked away, Kieran was afraid of him.

Seth gave it some thought. 'I was just trying to break you,' he said, 'so when I let you out, you wouldn't cause any more trouble.'

Kieran shuddered inwardly. It had nearly worked. There'd been moments when he'd been ready to do almost anything for a meal.

'But then kids started asking for a trial,' Seth said. 'They tried to act like they wanted your blood, but I could tell they were trying to help you. I knew that I'd never have control unless . . .'

'So you would have?'

Seth twitched as though the question were an annoying fly. 'That's not what I did, is it?'

'But you wanted to.'

'Wanting and doing aren't the same things.'

'You starved me.'

'I didn't do any worse to you than my dad did to me when he found out I got into his liquor. One bowl of soup a day for the entire harvest. Try that sometime.' Seth's face was so swollen that it was hard to read, but Kieran knew that mentioning his father caused Seth pain. 'Of course I snuck food when my dad wasn't looking,' he added. 'But then so did you.'

'You knew about that?' Kieran asked. 'That Sealy was sneaking me bread?'

'I told him to do it,' Seth said irritably. 'I didn't want you to know it came from me. That bread was supposed to be the beginning.'

'Of what?'

'Incentives. For good behaviour.'

It would have worked, too, Kieran thought. Seth had no idea how close he'd come to giving in. *And he'll never know*, he told himself. 'If I let you out of here, you'd try again, wouldn't you?'

'Try what again?'

'To take over the ship.'

Seth was quiet for so long that Kieran assumed he wouldn't get an answer, and he stood. When he was at the door, Seth said, 'That's what you did, isn't it?'

Kieran stopped in his tracks. Then, without a trace of emotion, he said, 'I'll have fresh clothes sent down to you tomorrow,' and left the brig.

STARS

Kieran was running the combine, binding hay into bales. Two other boys stacked the bales using OneMan conveyors, lifting each one gingerly with the clawlike attachments on the fronts of the machines. The conveyors looked like fun, and if Kieran thought it would be safe to put a younger boy in charge of the combine he'd take a turn. But for now he was stuck high up on the seat, driving the huge machine down row after row of grasses, gathering them for use as mulch or as bedding for the chickens and goats.

He jumped when he felt a hand on his shoulder and turned to see Arthur leaning over him, balanced on the footboard of the combine, out of breath, his face sweating, eyes wide and alert behind filthy lenses. Arthur spoke, but Kieran could hear nothing over the engine and had to switch off the tractor, and then the baler, before Arthur could make himself heard. *This better be good*, he thought.

'I said the nebula is thinning out!' Arthur yelled up to him.

'What!' Kieran stared at the boy. 'What do you mean, thinning out?'

'I mean we can see stars.'

Kieran had to see this for himself. He waved to the two boys running the conveyors and followed Arthur out of the grassland bay and to the elevators that would take them directly to Central Command.

'How many stars?' Kieran asked, unable to wait. 'More than just a few?'

'A lot. I think we're almost to the edge of the nebula.'

Kieran's heart pounded, and he had to lean against the wall of the elevator. Over the months he'd got most of his strength back, but that period of starvation had left a mark on him. If he became very excited, the adrenaline in his system seemed to weaken him, and he'd feel dizzy and light-headed. He felt this way now as he waited for the elevator doors to open onto the corridor so that he could follow Arthur to the command room and see for himself.

There were about a dozen boys in Central Command, but there was no sound. Kieran could hear them breathing as they gazed out of the windows. Behind the thin haze still left of the nebula, there were stars. Millions upon millions of them, and more all the time as the ship sped towards the outer boundary of the pink gas. The effect reminded Kieran of the night his father tried to explain that back on Earth, during the day, you could not see the stars. 'At dusk, they seemed to come out one at a time,' he'd said.

Kieran had been incapable of visualizing this, but now it was happening before his eyes. The stars appeared one by one, as though pushing through a silk curtain.

'My God,' he said under his breath.

It really was true. They were reaching the outer limits of the horrible cloud that had swallowed them years ago.

For a time, Kieran looked at the stars, squinting his eyes, seeing the differences among them. Some of them twinkled red, some blue, some had a yellowish cast. But an idea took hold of him, and he shouted at Sarek, who was manning the com station, 'Start a radar sweep! They might have come out of it, too!'

Sarek stared at Kieran for a moment as though not comprehending, but suddenly his hands flew over his control panel as he enabled every radar dish on the ship to receive every possible frequency, and then he turned on all eight radar beams, sending their light waves into the darkness, searching for any solid object within ten million miles.

The cabin remained silent. No one seemed to expect anything to happen, so it was a bodily shock when a human voice found its way through Sarek's com link.

'Mayday, mayday, *Empyrean*, if you receive this signal, please respond. This is Waverly Marshall.

Mayday, mayday, *Empyrean*, if you—'

'What is that?' Arthur said, breathless.

Other boys cried out. One boy in the corner sank to his knees. Kieran could only stare at Sarek as a tremor worked its way from the ends of his fingers into the deepest part of him. Her voice.

The message looped end on end, many times, before Kieran could remember how to speak. 'Answer it,' he said.

Sarek picked up his microphone, matched the frequency of the message, and said, 'This is the *Empyrean*, Waverly, where are you? . . . Hello?'

They crowded around Sarek's com station as Waverly's thin voice echoed in that endlessly repeating message. Kieran strained his ears towards it, searching for some clue about her. She sounded small and shaky but calm, determined. She sounded brave.

'Sarek,' Kieran said desperately, 'loop your message back at—'

'Hello?'

It was a young girl's voice, frail and tentative.

Kieran grabbed the microphone from Sarek. 'Get Waverly.'

'Who is this?' the girl asked.

'Get Waverly!' Kieran yelled, but already another voice was coming through the microphone.

'Kieran?'

Kieran's heart felt rubbery. He was hearing her. He was hearing Waverly.

'Waverly, where are you?' Tears streamed down his face, but he didn't care what the other boys thought of

him. In that moment, all he wanted was Waverly. Right
now.

'I don't know. But we can't be too far away. There's
hardly any delay in the transmission.'

'Are you all right?'

'Yes, we're fine. Are you OK?' Kieran thought he
heard tearfulness in her voice, too.

'We're OK!'

'Can you tell Captain Jones he needs to come find
us?'

'Isn't Harvard there? Or my dad?' Kieran asked
shakily.

There was a pause, and Waverly's voice changed, a
strain of bitterness in her throat. 'No adults, Kieran.
Just us girls.'

Several of the boys cried out. Peter Stroub punched
the metal wall repeatedly.

Kieran's heart sank. But he gathered himself, muted
the microphone he held, and said to the room at large,
'Then the adults are in the shuttles, and when they
emerge from the nebula we'll make contact with them,
too.'

A few boys nodded, but most of them only stared at
the floor in despondency.

'Please, Kieran, can you get Captain Jones?' Waverly
asked. There was an edge of hysteria in her voice. 'Or a
pilot? Someone who knows how to find us?'

'The Captain . . . isn't here right now. Let's get you
guys on board and we can talk about all that stuff later,
OK?'

Arthur went to the radar display and flipped through

the screens until he found one that was flashing a red message, 'Object in Motion'. He pointed at a moving dot. 'This has to be them. They're in front of us, coming towards us.'

'Can you plot a course to intercept?' Kieran asked Arthur, who looked doubtfully at the navigation equipment.

'I can try.'

Rage flared in Kieran, and he had to fight to control it before he said quietly, 'Do your best.'

It seemed like such a difficult thing, but Arthur found that, with the stars clearly visible, the navigation program was able to plot an intercepting course automatically. Kieran felt a weird sensation in the pit of his stomach as the ship veered to the starboard side.

'How long?'

Arthur looked at the screen in front of him. 'A few hours.'

He couldn't wait that long. He wished he could clear out all the boys from Central Command so that he could talk to her privately over the link, but that seemed unfair. 'How are you, Waverly? Are you healthy?'

'Yes, I'm healthy. I think we all are.'

'Who's there!' yelled Sarek.

'All the girls except Felicity Wiggam, and . . . and . . . Samantha Stapleton.'

'How did you get away?'

She was silent for a long time before she finally said, 'I don't want to talk about it over the com, Kieran.'

Something very bad had happened. He could hear it in her voice.

'I want to talk to my sister!' Alfie Moore reached for Kieran's headset, a scowl on his face.

Kieran wanted to keep the headset and talk endlessly to Waverly, but she quickly said, 'Kieran, there are lots of girls here who want to talk to their families.'

Kieran felt hurt. Why didn't she want to talk to him?

Alfie pulled at the cord on Kieran's headset. He let the boy have it and sat down in the Captain's chair.

Waiting was agony. He could not stand to talk to anyone. He ignored questions as the boys pestered him and sat stiff as a brick, his fist crammed against his forehead, his jaw clenched, eyelids wedged shut, until they finally let him alone. He kept imagining Waverly crashing the shuttle into the hull of the *Empyrean*. She'd never flown a real craft before. What if she died just when she was almost home?

Soon the crackle of the intercom sounded, and Waverly's voice pierced through the speakers.

'I can see you! I can see the *Empyrean*!' Waverly squealed. 'Oh, my God!'

Kieran bolted upright.

'Ten minutes,' Arthur said. His fingers flew over the keyboard in front of him, and Kieran felt the *Empyrean*'s speed drop dramatically. He felt light in his seat as he watched Arthur's vid screen and the darting speck of Waverly's shuttle, circling around to aim for the port shuttle bay.

Kieran leapt from his chair and ran full speed through the corridors. He couldn't make his feet move fast enough. He punched the elevator button and kicked at the door while he waited. 'Come on, come on!' he shouted through his teeth. Once in the elevator, he thought that if he could cut the cables to make the car move faster he would.

When he finally reached the shuttle bay, he found almost all the boys had gathered there and were staring at the air-lock doors in quiet expectancy. Kieran ran to the com station and shouted, 'Sarek, patch me in to shuttle communications.'

'She turned off her headset,' Sarek said.

'What!'

'She said I was distracting her.'

'How close are they?' Kieran asked.

'I've just opened the outer doors.'

Kieran could feel veins in his face pulsing. He stared at the doors, his lips stretched tight over his teeth, and he waited, every muscle in his body tense and pulsing.

'Please,' he whispered once, under his breath.

The room was silent. Tobin Ames chewed on his upper lip, his hands tucked into his armpits as though to keep his fingers warm. Jeremy Pinto squatted, rocking back and forth, heel to toe, as he stared at the doors.

Suddenly the sickening whine of metal scraping against metal sounded through the shuttle bay, and Kieran's heart froze. But then he heard the hydraulics slamming the outer doors closed and then the rhythmic pumping of air into the air lock.

The inner air-lock doors opened. The boys scattered to make room as the shuttle drifted inside and eased its way to the floor like a giant, awkward bird.

It stood before them, silent and still, but then the

ramp lowered and dozens of little-girl feet appeared, hesitant at first, but then more quickly, as the girls saw brothers, friends, boyfriends. Suddenly the room was filled with voices, crying, laughing, shrieking, or simply talking together as the girls fell into the arms of the waiting boys.

Waverly was last. Kieran knew she would be.

She looked so thin and pale. She walked with a limp. Her hair was stringy and matted and hung flat against her head. Her cheeks were sunken and her eyes were gaunt. Kieran walked up to meet her, put his arms around her, and as she fell against him, he lifted her off her feet and carried her down the ramp.

'I can walk,' she said, the tip of her nose tucked into the cup of his ear.

'I know,' he whispered back as he carried her across the bay and to the outer corridor.

Once they were alone inside the elevator, Waverly wrapped her arms around Kieran's neck as though fearful of being ripped away, and her body shook with sobs.

She had not bathed in days, maybe weeks, but Kieran didn't care.

He wasn't ever going to let her go.

TOGETHER

He pulled off her clothes and left her sitting naked on the edge of his bed while he ran a bath. The steam made a pattern on the mirror over the sink, and he ran his fingers in the hot water, watching her as she sat staring off, blinking her eyes as though she couldn't believe where she was. Kieran dribbled essence of vanilla into her bath to make the steam fragrant, and then he went to get her.

'Won't the Captain be angry?' she asked, her voice small and vulnerable.

Kieran knelt in front of her. Muscles twitched at the corners of her mouth, and she searched his face, seeming to hesitate between the need to understand and the fear of knowing.

'No,' he finally said, as gently as he could. He waited to see if she asked another question, but she didn't. He took hold of her thin arm and lifted, gently, until she wobbled to her feet, and he led her to the bath.

As she lowered herself into the water, Kieran saw the scar on her leg. It was a jagged, angry red slash that seemed to dig at a hole in the muscle underneath. There was an ugly scab on her shoulder the size of his thumb, black and glistening. When she sat down, he saw the scars on her abdomen, one in the middle near the belly button and two lower down, just near her hip bones. They looked like surgical scars.

'What did they do to you?'

She looked at him with desolate eyes. 'Everything.'

He didn't want to know any more right now. He picked up a sponge and drizzled castile soap onto it, squeezing until it lathered into a fragrant foam.

He rubbed the sponge over her back, along the curve of her neck, down her thin arms, along the crevice of her armpits. With his thumbs he smoothed the skin between her vertebrae, he kneaded the muscles on her shoulders, he rubbed at the nape of her neck. Slowly he guided her back until she leaned into the bath, and he watched the water invade her hair, soaking it in rivulets that hovered between the curled strands on her brow. He poured soap into her hair, and he rubbed at her scalp, feeling the thick, ropy tendons of her hair between his fingers, committing this moment to memory. He never wanted to forget what she looked like in the water, lying back, trusting him.

Next he ran the sponge down her rib cage, and with his fingers he pressed at the flesh between her ribs gently until he heard her sigh. He ran the sponge along her belly, across the small scars, and then down her legs to her feet, where he worked at the spaces between her toes with his fingers and then pushed his thumbs into the arches of her feet until she sighed again.

When her eyelids drooped over her eyes, Kieran helped her stand so that he could enfold her in a cotton blanket. He guided her to the Captain's bed, where she sank gratefully. She rested her head on his pillow and fell asleep immediately.

He watched her in the dim lamplight, worrying over her, listening for each and every breath that escaped her lips. She was so lovely, so soft, still his Waverly, but changed. She seemed weary and disturbed. There was a fierceness to her sleep, and she turned over once, crying softly, 'Mom . . . Mom.' But then she was still again.

His stomach rumbled, and he realized he hadn't eaten all day, but he couldn't leave her. He was irrationally afraid that if he got up to go to the kitchen for some bread and fruit, when he came back she'd be gone, that he'd have dreamed all of this. So he waited, watching her, listening to her breathing, seated in his chair all night long.

When finally she woke, Kieran started from a shallow doze and opened his eyes to find her sitting up in bed, hugging her knees to her chest, looking around the room. He rubbed at the sleep in his eyes.

'So the Captain is gone,' she said, her voice low,

reminding him again of how he loved hearing her speak.

'That's right.'

'What about your parents? Are they here?'

Kieran shook his head.

Waverly watched him, her mind working behind her eyes, reading him, remembering. 'There were no adults in the shuttle bay when we got here.'

'That's right.' It was painful letting her work her way towards the truth. Telling her directly would be worse, so Kieran waited for her to get there.

'There are no adults aboard, are there, Kieran?' she finally said, the corners of her deep pink lips turned downward. Her hand was in her hair, holding up her head, and he longed to cross the room and touch her hair, too, stroke it.

'There were only a few left behind, but there was a reactor leak, and they're all very sick. Those that weren't killed in the attack left to go after you guys.'

She nodded slowly. She was so far away from him, and he was scared.

'What happened to you, Waverly?'

She lay back down on the bed, her eyes empty. 'Is there anything to eat?'

'I'll be right back,' Kieran said. 'Please don't go anywhere, OK?'

She nodded but turned away as he opened the door and left the room.

Kieran ran through the corridors. The ship was eerily quiet, and Kieran guessed that all the boys were talking with their sisters, girlfriends, friends, catching up, learning awful truths. In the kitchen he grabbed a loaf of yesterday's bread, a slab of goat cheese, some apricots and plums, and some cold chicken breast seasoned with sage and rosemary, Waverly's favourites. He poured a small bowl of precious olive oil because he remembered Waverly liked to dip her bread in it.

He put everything into a basket and ran back to the Captain's quarters, where he found Waverly sitting at his desk, leafing through a portable reader, a scowl on her face. She was wearing his trousers, which hung on her hips enticingly, and a thin hemp shirt of his that seemed to swallow her up. But now that she'd got out of bed, she looked more like herself. And he was heartened by the determined look on her face.

'Here,' he said, and put the food in front of her. She tore the loaf in half and handed him the larger piece.

'So I guess you're the new Captain?' she said, one eyebrow raised.

'Who else?'

'No, it's logical. It's good. You'll be good,' she said absently. She dipped a mouthful of bread into the olive oil and put it into her mouth, closed her eyes, savouring it.

He sat down across from her, studying her. She seemed utterly traumatized, and he knew that she needed to talk. Maybe she would if he talked first.

As she ate, he told her about losing contact with the shuttles, the reactor leak and rescuing the parents with Seth. He told her how Seth betrayed and imprisoned him.

'I can't believe Seth did that.' Waverly bit her lip.

'It doesn't sound like him.'

'Believe it, Waverly,' Kieran said, and he watched her face as she tried to take this in. 'His dad died. I think that sent him over the edge.'

He told her about how Seth had starved him and how he'd ultimately got a trial, which led to Seth's overthrow, and that ever since he'd been learning how to be a leader. He almost told her about the services, which were his greatest achievement, but he wanted to surprise her. Besides, he couldn't wait any more.

'Tell me what happened since you left, Waverly. Can't you tell me?' Kieran put down the bread, though he was ravenous. He couldn't eat until he understood what had happened to her and the rest of the girls. He needed to know everything.

She nodded, seeming to accept there was no avoiding it.

They talked for hours. She spoke of a woman named Amanda and the strange customs on the *New Horizon*. She told him about how she got that horrible scar on the back of her thigh and why there were puncture marks on her abdomen. He learned that she was going to be the mother of more than a dozen babies on the *New Horizon*, and he was horrified. The last thing she told him was the worst, though. She had left behind all the adults on the *New Horizon*, and now they were trapped.

'Did you see my mom or dad?' Kieran asked, frantic.

'No, Kieran. I could only see my mom. We had no time to talk at all. I have no idea who else was with her.'

'You didn't *ask* about my parents?' Kieran demanded. He felt his face grow cold.

Waverly's features seemed to wilt, but her voice was strong when she spoke. 'There's a civil war going on right now, Kieran. I think if the opposition wins they'll let them out. They'll be able to come back soon.'

'But what if they don't win? I can't believe you left them behind!'

'You have no idea what you're talking about.' Waverly's dark eyes rested on his face like heated stones. 'They were shooting at me, Kieran. They would have killed me.'

She watched him angrily, but her face seemed to dissolve before his eyes, and she dropped her head into her hands. 'I should have tried harder.'

'I'm sorry.' Kieran rushed to her side. He wrapped her in his arms. 'Waverly, you did everything anybody could have done. You had to get the girls out of there.'

She broke into sobs, leaned against him. Words escaped her like spikes. 'I didn't want to go. Mom made me. She said they'd get out. Kieran, what if they don't? It'll be my fault!'

'You're a hero,' he told her with absolute conviction. He realized again that this was the astounding woman he was meant to spend the rest of his life with.

He took her face, wet with tears, between his hands, and he looked into her eyes. 'Don't blame yourself! Do you hear me? None of it was your fault. You saved the girls.'

'Not all of them,' she whispered. She hid her face in his shirt and spoke with such a small voice, Kieran could hardly hear her. He realized that she didn't really want to be heard as she told him about Samantha. How she'd been shot by a guard, how she'd crumpled into lifelessness before Waverly's eyes.

'You know that's not your fault, right?' he said.

'I didn't imagine the services were being monitored,' she said, sounding robotic. 'I wanted the plan to work so badly that I didn't let myself think of how we could get caught.'

'Waverly . . .' He smoothed the hair out of her eyes, dabbed at the tears running down her face with his sleeve, then kissed her eyelids, her nose, her chin, her cheeks, her forehead, her lips. She leaned towards him, but he pulled away from her long enough to say, 'Your plan worked. You're here. And so are the girls. You did it.'

'I'm going to miss Sammy,' she whispered.

Kieran could say nothing to this. He took her by the arm and pulled until she got up from his desk and followed him into the bedroom. He sat her down on the mattress, he got down on one knee, and he took her hand and kissed it.

'I need you,' he told her.

She only watched him, but he could see the emotion in her eyes.

'I feel like you're already my wife,' he told her.

She tucked her chin, nodded. 'I do too.'

He rose towards her, pulled her face to his, and kissed her, kissed her, kissed her.

They lay back together on the bed, wrapped around each other, clinging, lips on skin, hands in hair, rolling over each other, silent except for the sound of their rushing breath.

EPILOGUE

*Those who are faithful know only the
trivial side of love: it is the faithless who
know love's tragedies.*

– Oscar Wilde

STRANGERS

They slept tangled together until a knock sounded on the bedroom door. Waverly lifted her head, drawing breath sharply, then remembered where she was and dropped back to her pillow. *I'm home*, she whispered in her mind, and smiled.

Kieran rose, scrubbing his hand over his face, and cracked the door open. Arthur Dietrich stood outside the bedroom door, gnawing his bottom lip. 'Kieran, everyone's waiting.'

Kieran stared at Arthur blankly. 'For what?'

'Services. You're late.'

Waverly sat up, rubbing sleep from her eyes. She was surprised to find herself overjoyed to see the moon face of Arthur Dietrich. She waved; he nodded shyly.

'Is everybody there?' Kieran asked, sounding embarrassed.

'Yes! I put out the bread. We had to make twice as much last night, for the girls, and we're out of jam until next week when the strawberries are ready, so I used honey.'

'What time is it?'

'Eight twenty! You better get a move on!'

'Stall for me,' Kieran said, and closed the door. Waverly watched as he ran to the bedroom closet and slipped into a flax shirt, kicked into his suit trousers, muttering, 'I can't believe I forgot.'

Waverly wrapped the blanket around her shoulders. She'd been sweaty-cold all night. Now she simply felt cold. 'What's going on?'

'It's a new thing,' he said distractedly. 'I started it to cheer everyone up. You should come.'

'Come to what?' she asked with the slightest pang of dread. Had Arthur said 'services'? Dazed, she looked at the objects in the room – an old saddle, a sepia photo of a nineteenth-century hunter holding his rifle – and felt almost as disorientated as she'd been aboàrd the *New Horizon*. Watching Kieran knot his silk tie, she asked warily, 'What are you getting ready for?'

He smiled. 'Services. They're in the central bunker. Hurry or you'll miss them.'

Waverly felt as wooden as the chair in the corner. She sat there motionless as Kieran ran to his desk and picked up a portable reader. He was at the door when he remembered her and dashed back to kiss her goodbye.

'Will you come? I want you to know what I've accomplished here.'

She wanted to ask him just what he'd accomplished, but he was gone before she had the chance.

She stared at the door as it closed behind him, her arms wrapped around her knees, fighting to suppress a dim panic that threatened to overtake her.

Calm down, she told herself. *This isn't the* New Horizon. *You're home.*

But she didn't believe it.

She felt the traces of Kieran on her skin, the rough feeling on her chin and lips where his whiskers had grazed her. Her muscles were sore from the needy way they'd poured into each other. She'd imagined it so many times; she'd wanted it to be perfect. And it nearly was, the way he'd looked so attentively at her eyes and body, his fingers wandering over her skin, the way he'd pulled strands of hair from her face. But when it was over, she couldn't help feeling as though there'd been something else that was possible, something more that could have blossomed between them.

But she'd told herself that would come, with time. It didn't all have to happen in one night. And she'd lost herself in the wonderful feeling of sleeping in his arms.

Now, last night seemed unreal, as though it were something she'd watched on a com screen. She barely inhabited her body as she dressed. She pulled on a pair of Kieran's hemp trousers, a tunic from his closet. She didn't bother with the mirrors or her hair. She walked barefoot down the corridors, letting the metal chill her soles. Her heart seemed to be pulling blood away from her arms, her legs, her mind. She blinked away dark spots.

The central bunker was crowded, noisy with chatter and laughter. If the girls were sad not to find their parents – or any adults – here, they were also very happy to be back on their home ship with their brothers, friends and boyfriends. And now that the boys knew that at least some of their parents were alive on the *New Horizon*, they were happy also. Waverly could feel the hope in the room, but at a remove, as if it couldn't really touch her.

She sat in the back row and watched Kieran take the podium. He was beaming.

'Thank you for coming,' he said, waiting for the crowd to settle. His eyes landed on Waverly, and he smiled at her before continuing. 'First, I want to welcome back the girls. We missed you all very, very much.'

There was a great whoop of assent from the boys, and Kieran laughed, motioning for them to quiet down.

'About five months ago,' he began, 'our community was torn apart. The boys were left behind, worried for our parents and our sisters, and afraid for ourselves. The girls were taken to live with strangers, and had to endure unforgivable violations.'

'What does he know about it?' Waverly heard the whisper from a few rows ahead. It was Sarah, shaking her head and frowning. They looked at each other, and Waverly knew they were wondering the same thing: Why was Kieran preaching a sermon? Did he know he sounded just like Anne Mather?

'When you're dealt such a horrible blow,' he went on, 'there are two choices. You either give up, or keep going. But you can't do it alone. We humans are social creatures. We boys needed each other while we waited for you girls to come back. We had to find a way to join together, to create a new, stronger community. And we did.

'The *Empyrean* has remade itself into something vibrant and healthy. We have our trials, our issues, our thwarted dreams, and our private grief, but we also know that every week we can set all those things aside and come here. We break bread together, we talk, and we remind each other of the purpose that's so much greater than our small plans and concerns.'

He looked out over the audience, and Waverly thought of an old film she'd seen about the proud, single-minded conductor of a symphony orchestra. He'd looked at his musicians the very same way.

'There is a design working behind the curtain of the stars, and we are fulfilling it, drawn towards the future on the tide of time, towards our destiny as the first settlers of a new world.'

The room was still. *He has them*, she thought. Even the older girls were listening hard.

'We don't know what's going to happen tomorrow,' said Kieran. 'We've learned that the hard way, haven't we? We had a peaceful existence for so long that we thought we'd always have it. But we were wrong. There was a threat behind the veil of the nebula that we didn't see, and it left us hurt, bleeding, near death. But now we understand who our enemies are. And we will triumph over them.

'How do I know that? How can I be so sure that we are meant to avenge our loved ones? I'll tell you what I know, deep in my heart.'

He paused. His knowing, calculated delivery reminded Waverly so much of Anne Mather that she nearly groaned. *This is his talent*, she realized. *His gift.* It had been hidden all along, this strange ability to make people believe he knew some secret truth, that only he could show them the way. *Because only he knows the mind of God.*

It was such a dangerous, terrifying lie.

And all the more terrifying because he believed it.

'What we've made here, after all our pain and hardship, is special,' Kieran said. 'It's like a glowing light in the dark universe, kindled by God and burning inside of us. The sacrifices we've made, the pain we've endured, has been for a purpose: to make us into this.'

Kieran's arms opened wide, as if embracing all the young people sitting before him.

'We are the new generation. With God's help we will make our new home into a land of plenty. We'll welcome the millions that follow us to our rich, bountiful world. But before that, I promise you this: we *will* find our parents, we *will* punish the people who took them from us, and we *will* be the victorious makers of our new world, our New Earth, our new home!'

Kieran smiled at the rapt faces before him, stepped away from the podium, and sank to his knees. Folding his hands under his chin, he prayed.

Seeing the entire congregation follow Kieran's

example, Waverly got to her feet and stumbled out of the room.

I got Samantha killed, she thought, leaning against a wall in the hallway. *I killed a man. I left my mother a prisoner. And after all that pain and misery, I finally escaped from Anne Mather and her insanity.*

Except I didn't.

KIERAN

Kieran got to his knees, thankful that his sermon had gone so well. He'd had to update it, extemporizing the parts about the girls being back, but, even so, it had flowed seamlessly. As always now, he'd felt as though something greater were speaking through him, using him to show his congregation the way.

Each sermon made his faith stronger.

When the congregation got to their knees, he glanced around quickly to find Waverly, but she wasn't in her chair. Had she gone? Though her absence startled him, he went on smoothly, calling out, 'Who has thanks to share?'

It turned out that almost everyone in the congregation

had something to be thankful for, so the service went on for a long time. Kieran listened as patiently as he could, but his attention kept drifting to Waverly's empty chair. Where *was* she? And why had she gone?

Was she sick? Did her leg hurt? Had he angered her somehow? He knew he'd said nothing offensive or wrong in his sermon, so that couldn't be it.

When the final prayers were over, Kieran wove through the crowd, looking for her in vain. A few kids shook his hand and thanked him. Little Serafina Mbewe wrapped her chubby arms around his legs adoringly, but he was so impatient to leave that he almost tripped trying to disentangle himself.

He jogged through the corridors to his quarters, but Waverly wasn't there. He sat down, stood up. Finally, after feeling stupid, confused, hurt and useless, he figured out where she'd gone: home.

He jogged down two flights of stairs to where the families had lived.

The door to her quarters was ajar, and he found her on the kitchen floor, crying. There were rotten black vegetables on the floor and an enormous mound of moldy green bread dough on the counter.

'Waverly,' he said, bewildered.

'Just go, please,' she said. She wouldn't look at him.

He knelt and put a hand on her knee. 'What's wrong?'

'Everything!' she groaned, leaning back against a cabinet.

'Tell me.'

'No, Kieran,' she said, pushing him away. He resisted,

but she was still too weak to move him, so she gave up and crumpled into a heap.

'I am not going anywhere until you tell me what's wrong,' he said. 'What is it?'

'You,' she whispered.

'What?'

'You, Kieran.' She swiped at her tears. 'What the hell *was* that back there?' she demanded.

'What do you mean? The services?'

'Yes, the services,' she retorted. 'Do you have any idea what you're becoming?'

She reached up, took hold of the counter and pulled herself to her feet. She seemed unsteady, but she wouldn't let him touch her.

'Waverly, I don't understand!' he said, following her into the living room.

Instead of speaking she started tidying, gathering cups from the coffee table, straightening a stack of papers, and lining up three pairs of shoes next to the door. She picked up a jacket that had been draped across a chair and hung it lovingly in the closet. All the while, Kieran watched her, confused and hurt.

'Talk to me,' he pleaded.

When she met his eyes, he saw she was furiously angry. 'I just can't believe it, Kieran.'

'What?'

'You're just like her.'

'Who?'

'Anne Mather!'

'*Who?*' He wasn't sure he knew the name, though it sounded familiar. Had he read it somewhere?

'She's the leader on the *New Horizon*, Kieran. The mastermind behind the attack.'

He sat down heavily on the couch. How could Waverly compare him to one of those evil people?

'She's their Captain,' Waverly went on, 'and their priestess, and their messiah. She has all the power on that ship, Kieran, and she does terrible things with it.'

'I'm not like that,' Kieran objected. 'I'm a good person.'

'So was she,' Waverly said. Softening a little, she sat next to him and put a hand on his arm. 'But now she says she knows the mind of God. Kieran, nobody knows what God wants.'

'There's nothing wrong with telling people what I believe, Waverly,' he said with a hint of resentment.

'There *is* something wrong with pretending to be a prophet,' she said, her jaw set.

The unfairness of what she was saying crashed down on him, hard. 'Do you know what I've been through?' he protested. 'I've been beaten and starved and nearly *murdered*!' He stood, pushing her hand away. 'You have no idea what it was like on this ship after you left!' he shouted, red-faced. 'No idea at all!'

He expected her to shrink away, but she stood nose to nose with him. 'I know what it was like on the *New Horizon*, Kieran. Anne Mather acted pious, but underneath it all she was violent and insane. And if you continue on this road, that's what you'll become, too!'

'I'm making us into a community! I'm making us into a family!'

'You can do that without pretending to know what

God's plan is. No one knows that, and it's wrong to act as if you do!'

'Why? That doesn't make any sense! Everything we think and do and say is His plan for us. It's obvious, isn't it?'

'Not to me,' she said, her mouth compressing into a stubborn line.

'Whatever human beings decide to do, events unfold in a way we can't control.'

'And you think God is in control.'

'Of course He is! Everything He does, everything that happens, has a reason! And talking about it has helped the boys. It's what keeps them going! Otherwise they would have given up, Waverly. Everyone was so . . . sad and useless. I had to strengthen them somehow.'

'And the only way was to preach the Sermon on the Mount?'

'I gave them something to believe in. I gave them a future!'

'*You* gave them a future?'

Kieran stared at her. How had this happened? Where had all her trust gone? She stared back at him, her face immovable. Had her eyes always been so hollow, her mouth so rigid?

'But . . . Waverly, it's me.'

Her face fell into a mass of pain. She nodded, her head flopping, fingers shaking as she pressed them against her eyelids. 'That's why it's so horrible.'

'Honey . . .' He reached for her, put his hands on her arms. 'You can trust me.'

'Can I? Then prove it, Kieran. Give up this sickness.'

'What sickness?' he cried. 'I've never felt better in my life! I know my purpose, Waverly. *Our* purpose. We have a destiny to fulfil, and I need you to help me.'

'This isn't the way. If you'd seen what I've seen . . . Please, Kieran.' She took his hand and kissed it. 'Please, please don't turn into that woman.'

'I am *not* Anne Mather!' he shouted, pushing her away so hard that she stumbled. He stormed down the hallways, burst into his quarters and threw himself onto the bed he'd shared with her only hours before.

How could she judge him like this? How could she think that the beautiful thing he'd created was bad? Everyone else loved it! Why didn't she?

He'd expected sceptics. But he'd never thought that Waverly would be one of them!

He had never, ever, felt so deeply betrayed. Yet he still yearned for her.

Maybe when she calmed down, she'd change her mind. Maybe she'd learn to trust him again.

I'll make her trust me again, he thought.

There was a knock at the door, and he sat up. 'Come in!' he called hopefully. Maybe she'd come to apologize.

But it was Arthur Dietrich, his face flushed with excitement. 'Kieran! We think we've found the *New Horizon*!'

'Where?' He bolted to his feet.

'Come on, I'll show you!'

He followed Arthur to Central Command and peered at the radar display. There was a dot on the screen ahead of them, moving parallel to their own course, towards New Earth.

'It was so easy,' Sarek said, smiling for the first time since the attack. 'With the nebula clear, the radar works perfectly!'

'That has to be *New Horizon*,' said Arthur. 'Look how fast it's going.'

It was true – the dot was practically zipping across the screen. *It's them!* thought Kieran, transfixed.

He forgot about Waverly and the heinous things she'd said about him.

He had work to do.

WAVERLY

Waverly lay on the floor of her mother's untidy bedroom, unchanged from the way her mother had left it months before as if frozen in time. Waverly held her mother's worn cardigan to her chest, and she sobbed. She wasn't missing just her mother. She was missing her old life, because now she knew that it was gone forever. She'd never go back to being Waverly Marshall again. And Kieran – she didn't know who he was.

That smile of his at the podium, the way he'd held up his hands as if to embrace the congregation, the words he'd used, everything about him reminded her of . . . If Waverly thought about it, she'd get sick to her stomach.

When she was all cried out, Waverly wandered down

to the orchards and picked a few plums and almonds. She sat at the base of an apple tree to eat. She was glad to be in the orchard, listening to buzzing bees as they flirted with the blooms above her head. It had been horrible to be in the apartment she'd shared with her mother, knowing that she might never see her again.

What would Mom say to me now? Waverly wondered. *She'd probably ask me how I feel about him. She'd ask if I could look past all this.*

'I do still love him, Mom,' she whispered, her eyes on the mossy soil of the orchard. She probably always would. But she couldn't let herself become blind the way Amanda had been. There had been something pathetic in Amanda's childish trust of Anne Mather, taken to the point where she couldn't see all the evil things happening right before her eyes. No. Waverly would not be like that.

But could she remain objective as Kieran's wife? How could she marry him now?

This thought pushed her into fresh spasms of grief, and she buried her face in the fragrant soil of the orchard. Loam worked its way between her teeth and she chewed on it, her mouth a frothy mixture of earth and saliva as she cried herself to sleep.

The next morning, when the sun lamps flickered on, Waverly sat up. Her mouth was mossy, and there was dirt in her hair and on her clothes. She found an irrigation hose and took in mouthfuls of cold water, swirled it in her mouth, and spat. Then she drank long and deep until she felt refreshed.

She picked apricots, knowing they'd do little for the

rumbling in her belly. She'd go to the central bunker for some eggs, but she wanted to do one thing first.

She limped between the trees, breathing in the beautiful scents of fruit and blossoms. She got in the elevator, selected her level, and waited. She wiped her mind clean, and forced her breathing to slow down and soften. What she was doing was logical. She needed information, that was all.

The brig was quiet. There was one guard on duty, Percy Swift, a slow-moving boy whom she caught dozing on his chair with a nightstick on his knees. He stirred when Waverly approached. 'Visitors are allowed, aren't they?' she asked.

'No. He's in solitary confinement. Kieran Alden's orders.'

'Don't worry. Kieran said it's OK,' Waverly said.

'Really?'

'I'm his girlfriend. He trusts me.'

The boy looked at her warily, but she stared him down.

'You have to sign in,' Percy said as he pushed a ledger towards her.

This isn't a betrayal, she told herself as she signed her name, then glided past Percy and down the corridor to look for Seth.

She found him lying on a cot in the furthest cell to the right. She cleared her throat, and he turned to look at her, then sat up, surprised.

'Did you know we came back?' she asked. She felt the old pull towards him. He'd grown since she'd been gone, and his hair was long and hung in his eyes. She took in the bruises on his face and the thinness of his wrists. What had Kieran been doing to him?

'I knew about it,' Seth said, then seemed to think better of his tone and muttered, 'Welcome back.'

'You got yourself into a real mess,' Waverly observed.

'I guess,' he said, guarded. His eyes shifted over her suspiciously. 'Why are you here?'

'I've got questions.'

'What questions?'

Waverly sat on the floor, one leg extended in front of her, the other bent so that she could lean her chin on her knee. 'Why did you starve Kieran?'

Seth chuckled. 'He told you about that?'

'Seems a pretty harsh thing to do.'

'He starved himself. He kept lying to the crew, and I had to stop him. So I denied him food to try to get him to admit the truth, but he wouldn't.'

'He's stubborn,' Waverly said, a deep sadness welling inside of her. 'But he didn't deserve that.'

'I didn't let him starve. I let one of my guards pretend to sneak him some food. So he'd eat.'

'Oh.' Waverly's voice was softer now. 'It was right after your dad died, right?'

'After Kieran killed him, yes.' Seth scratched at a raw patch of skin on his neck, and Waverly remembered this was a nervous habit with him. 'There were a million ways to get them out of the engine room, and he chose the most dangerous.'

'So that's why you tried to take over the ship?'

Seth nodded wearily. 'That, and he made mistakes that endangered us all. He crashed into the atmospheric control dome, did you know? We had to work around the clock repairing it, guys in OneMen who had never flown them before. And he left our parents trapped –'

Seth choked up.

'I'm sorry about your dad, Seth.'

'I am, too!' he cried, as though this amazed him. 'He was a mean son of a bitch, but I miss him now. I guess you learn to love what you're used to.'

Waverly studied Seth. He seemed changed, more humble, and only too willing to cooperate. She liked him better now, she decided.

'Do you know about the services Kieran is holding?' Waverly asked him, one eyebrow raised.

He nodded. 'He's built up quite a little cult for himself, hasn't he?'

'You don't like that?' Waverly said, trying not to give any hint in her voice of how she felt about it.

'All I know is that he hasn't held an election for himself or for a Central Council. He's ignoring all the bylaws. He makes all the decisions himself, and anyone who might question him is either locked up in the brig or sick almost to death in the infirmary.'

Hearing Seth put it this way, Waverly felt her blood run cold.

Seth was eyeing her. 'Why are you here?'

Waverly tilted her head, cautious. 'I had some questions.'

'You're Kieran Alden's girlfriend. Get your information from him.'

'I don't know who he is any more,' she said. Tears dropped from her eyes, and she wiped them away.

Seth looked at her, surprised. 'Trouble in paradise?'

'No such thing,' she said, not even certain what she meant.

'I still don't see why you're here.' His eyes travelled up to her face and he watched her reaction. 'Even if you guys are fighting, why should anyone's version matter to you but his?'

'I like to make up my own mind,' Waverly said with a dry smile.

'Well, then you and I have something in common.'

The nausea had come back, hovered at the back of her throat. She didn't know what to do. She didn't want to betray Kieran, but was he really the Kieran she'd loved? Or had he turned into something dangerous?

'So, Seth,' Waverly said, her voice careful and even, 'you don't like Kieran's politics. What do you think can be done about it?'

'Don't ask me. I tried and failed.'

'It's your own fault if you did.'

'I know.'

Her mouth popped open with surprise. This was the last thing Waverly expected to hear him say.

'I'm too rough with people. Too much like my dad,' Seth said softly. He wouldn't look at Waverly, though she stared right at him. 'Kieran is kind. That's why he won.' Seth leaned his forehead on his knee, mouth pointed to the floor so that Waverly almost missed hearing him whisper, 'I'm not a good person.'

Waverly searched for a comforting word, but everything she thought of to say would have been a lie.

'I'll tell you one thing,' Seth said, raising his eyes to

hers. 'Kieran can't become some two-bit cult leader. We can't let him destroy himself that way, or this ship.'

This was precisely what she wanted to hear, and that's what worried her.

'Just get me out of here, OK?' Seth said. He grasped one of the iron bars and pulled himself closer to her. 'We can save Kieran from himself. I'll show you I can do better.'

'I don't need you to show me anything,' she said softly.

They looked at each other through the iron bars.

Suddenly the floor under her lurched. Waverly fell to her side, feeling as though her world were sliding. She looked at Seth, who was wide-eyed and clinging to the bars of his cell.

'It's happening again,' Waverly groaned, and rested her forehead on the cold metal floor. 'They've come back.'

'No,' Seth said calmly. 'We're changing direction, and speeding up, I think.'

Waverly lifted her head and looked at Seth, who was pale. She'd never seen him look afraid before.

'Why would we—'

'We're going after them,' he said, sounding eerily calm. 'But Kieran is crazy if he thinks we can catch up to them.'

'Then what can we do?' Waverly said. 'We can't just abandon our parents.'

'We're going to have to make a deal of some kind,' Seth said.

Waverly laid her head down on the floor again,

stared at the minute scratches and nicks in the steel. She tasted the bitter word as she whispered it: 'A deal . . .'

'Yes,' Seth said quietly. 'We're going to have to be brave.'

ACKNOWLEDGEMENTS

The theories of Sacvan Bercovitch, PhD, described in his remarkable book *The Puritan Origins of the American Self,* shaped the major themes in *Glow*. I owe a debt of gratitude for many nice turns of phrase to my friend and mentor, Stephanie Spinner. Also many thanks to DJ and Jane Boushehri, Laura Resau, Todd Mitchell, Victoria Hanley, Catherine Stine and the Slow Sanders for their enthusiasm, support and wisdom. Dad, Mike and Mom, thanks for the years of encouragement. Rich, thanks for all your help with the physics, for the years of fun and for going to work with numbers every day so that I can do my work with words every day. I thank Jennifer Weis and the whole team at St Martin's Press for showing me such a warm welcome. Last but not least, I must thank Kathleen Anderson, the wizard who has made all this possible.

Get ready for the second heart-racing

SKY CHASERS adventure . . .

coming soon!

D4RK

INSIDE

JEYN ROBERTS

IN A WORLD GONE MAD 4 WILL FIGHT TO SURVIVE

'SOMETHING BAD IS ABOUT TO HAPPEN. A LOT OF PEOPLE
ARE GOING TO DIE AND IT'S ONLY THE BEGINNING.'

A murderous rage has been unleashed. Moments after
earthquakes rock the world, people start to change in the
most terrifying of ways. Friends turn on friends, girlfriends
on boyfriends, brothers on sisters. Nobody can be trusted.

For those who survive the first wave of killing, the world is a
different, deadlier place. Michael, Aries, Mason and
Clementine must battle to stay alive in a world determined to
kill them. All they have is one another . . . but can they even
be sure of that?

**AN APOCALYPTIC, HEART-STOPPING SAGA OF RAGE, HOPE
AND SURVIVAL**